PRAISE FOR
HARMONY OF FIRE

"Brian's writing is lyrical, emotional, unexpected, and explosive. Beyond extraordinary."
—Christine Feehan, #1 *New York Times* bestselling author
of *Recovery Road*

"Complex world-building, interesting characters, and lots of action blend together to make Brian Feehan's debut novel a real treat."
—Charlaine Harris, #1 *New York Times* bestselling author
of *The Serpent in Heaven*

"Fans of angels and demons, battles of good vs. evil, and dancing the gray line will want to dive in [and] read *Harmony of Fire*."
—Caffeinated Reviewer

"Very exciting and intriguing. I really loved the chemistry between Owen and Alice. I also loved most of the secondary characters, as Mara, Damon, and Cornelius had amazing powers. . . . *Harmony of Fire* is very well written by Brian Feehan, and I look forward to the next book."
—The Reading Cafe

"An amazing world built in such a descriptive way that you will be able to see it all easily. Owen and Alice are very well fleshed out and likable, as are the other secondary characters. There is very strong chemistry between them that seems very realistic."
—Fresh Fiction

"A stunning beginning. . . . This book took my breath away; it held a captivating note all throughout the story that will charm . . . its readers and have you yearning for more of this power couple! Truly an exhilarating read!"
—Addicted to Romance

"Engrossing, unique, and beautifully executed. If you enjoy contemporary paranormal romantic suspense and urban fantasy novels, then this author may be one you will enjoy as much as I do."   —*Mystery & Suspense Magazine*

Titles by Brian Feehan

HARMONY OF FIRE
HARMONY OF LIES

HARMONY OF LIES

BRIAN FEEHAN

BERKLEY ROMANCE
New York

BERKLEY ROMANCE
Published by Berkley
An imprint of Penguin Random House LLC
penguinrandomhouse.com

BERKLEY and the BERKLEY and B
colophon are registered trademarks of Penguin Random House LLC.

ISBN: 9780593440551

First Edition: February 2023

Printed in the United States of America
1 3 5 7 9 10 8 6 4 2

Book design by George Towne

I dedicate this story to Christine Feehan.
You have given me so much love, so much
strength and so much wisdom.
My writing, as with my life,
would not have happened without you.
You were right—a great imagination
should never be wasted.
Thank you for sharing so much of who
you are with me. I will always be grateful.
I love you, Mom.

HARMONY
OF LIES

Lies—be them inside or out—are the wedges we place between each other. No matter how soft, sweet or mighty, lies are and always will be a wedge between true connections. Moving, shifting two souls until their hands can't reach each other. To grasp and hold on to each other, the lies must end.

CHAPTER ONE

A+O

Owen Brown sat on a log, his legs stretched out toward the large steel-ringed fire on an old farm in Denver, Colorado. For the last couple hours, the cool wind of autumn had done battle with the heat of the tall blaze as Owen silently pressed and released the strings on the neck of his old acoustic guitar with one hand while his free hand held a warm beer he had forgotten about.

Around Owen were his people and Alice. They were all laughing and drinking and smiling up at the moon while he mostly held still but for the drifting fingers of one hand over the guitar and his mind singing with chords of music. This time, as with the last number of nights, he held a secret. A secret he wasn't prepared to share. It would be foolish to share, knowing Alice as he did, knowing what he knew.

This time, as with those other times he had created music just in his head, using his imagination, Alice was singing with him. In his mind, her voice was strong and rich and had the ability to curve around words as easily as a dancer could move around a room. In his mind, where it was safe and he was entirely in control, they rode the sound together as it poured out of him into the night, his fingers digging into the strings of his acoustic, moving and tucking and pressing as the music in his mind reshaped and charged forth. He did this all deep within while the others talked, joked and drank beer, leaving him alone with his secret.

"Hey! Hello! Why is nobody listening? I am trying to perform here," Max said from across the fire with enough force that the music was pulled back into Owen's body and away from his eyes and fingertips.

"Max," Clover said with a warning, "you don't need to be rude about it."

"I was listening. Don't bunch me in with the two of them," Daphne said, referring to Jessie and Clover.

Owen knew if he needed to, he could pull back the conversation but didn't bother to after this many hours around a fire under a night sky. It was about letting the stress out. Letting go and letting the magic of the stars above sink into your soul.

"Daphne? I'm not sure you were even in your own body, the way you have been staring into the fire for the last five minutes. Something on your mind? Something you need to get off your chest?" Jessie asked with genuine concern.

"Hey, leave her chest alone; she's only eighteen," Clover shot back with a grin. "Pervert!"

"Not cool, Clover," Jessie said quickly, pointing a finger off his beer bottle in accusation.

"No, nothing is on my mind!" Daphne called, ignoring Clover and the attention she was bringing. "Nothing I need to talk about. I just like the fire tonight. It's pretty and sort of alive as it dances in the air, and I'm not sure those veggie tacos were all veggie." Just then, a small burp slipped out of Daphne's mouth, and everyone chuckled as her face turned a little red, and she apologized.

These were his people. His people who lived outside the rules of normal humans. Clover with her sass and spice. Jessie, his best mate, smooth and handsome. Max, tall and always able to find trouble. And Daphne, new and far too skinny, but bright and intelligent. And then there was Alice. Her left hand was in his hair and on the back of his head, strong but gentle fingers moving over his scalp. A slow rhythm as her fingers moved this way and that. Her other hand held an almost empty beer. She, too, seemed to simply be basking in the night air.

Alice was something altogether different. Her soul was broken, but it didn't stop her from burning bright. Owen could feel her, sense her in the deepest fog, the blackest night. Sure, an etherealist like everyone else around the fire, with an incredible well of ethereal power, but it was the fight within that made them a match. Their love was new but genuine, a tangible force between them. She had been quiet the last half hour, the pressure of being reunited with her family three weeks ago slowly easing with each passing star.

"I am not rude," Max defended. "You are rude. I will say it again and again—musicians make the worst audience members. It's not cats, and it's not children. It's you people."

"No one says it's children. Besides, the worst are politicians. I think that's right. Politicians make the worst audience members," Daphne repeated.

"Not true. I used to think that, but it turns out politicians make for a great audience because they assume everyone is looking at them and they play the part. What about A-list actors?" Jessie continued. "But I might be wrong. Now that

I am thinking about it, a comedian once told me the worst audience she ever went onstage for was at a corporate retreat. The retreat was in Atlanta at one of those big places. Anyway, she said she would give her left eye never to have to perform for any of them ever again. So there you go."

"How drunk are you?" Clover asked.

"About the same as you. Why?" Jessie said with a grin that lit up his eyes.

"Because, first, don't screw with actors, they entertain me!" Clover clarified. "And, second, which female comedian were you quoting? Was that the short woman in Michigan who wasn't funny, who you flirted with for like four hours and got nowhere? Or the tall blonde with that lazy eye you went down on inside the coat closet at that bar in DC, who also wasn't funny?"

"Thanks for that, Clover. And neither," he said.

Both Daphne and Clover shared a smile as Jessie shook his head in frustration.

The song inside Owen's mind was calling, a relentless pull to be both finished and played aloud. He had seven songs already stored in the back of his mind with Alice at the microphone; he could hear or play them at a moment's notice. Alice and the others didn't know about any of them. There was a balance, a fine line with people, with a band. Press too hard, twist the knob too tight, and the string breaks.

You can only break a string so many times before you have to start all over, he thought. *I don't want to start over with them, and I'm about to twist the knob again*. His last thought held real regret and concern.

A chilling air swept around the six people, and the fire's flame, hot and fierce, climbed higher into the night sky. Owen understood this couldn't last. In fact, it was over. He had stretched the relaxing time around the fire out for as long as he could have without being reckless. Soon Daphne

or Jessie or one of the others would head off to bed. Or
Alice would tap him on the back of the head and say, "Let's
take a walk."

"Hey, that's enough. Everyone shut up and give me your
attention. It's time for my magic trick. Alice, you want to
kick Owen and wake him up or something?" Max said.

"I can hear you, Max," Owen said, and shifted the guitar
to the empty camping chair on his left.

"That's good, Owen, because we all thought you were
going to start drooling if you played in your head any longer," Clover said.

Owen felt the laughter as much as he heard it from the
others. But it was Alice who held the spotlight. Her skin
held the glow of the firelight, and her internal strength
never seemed to dim. His chest moved, and he drank her in.
The smooth skin, her sharp hairstyle and her deep green
eyes captivated his mind and soul.

She was a punch he couldn't defend against and didn't
want to try. A single contact from her was like water in the
desert. A natural force to worship over.

How can I walk away from you? His thoughts drove a
spike into his chest, and for a single perfect moment, he
wondered if he would feel real blood pouring out of his
chest.

"We will settle down and give you the stage. You tall,
lanky, oddly dashing man-diva," Clover said, opening up
the ice cooler and taking out a set of beers. One she took
for herself, the other she passed to Jessie, who took it and
tapped glass.

Everyone else seemed to settle for the first time in about
an hour. But Owen couldn't feel the comfort. He looked
toward the fire, the golden orange and black embers moving with an alien life that refused to be bound.

I can't hold still any longer.

Max moved from sitting forward to standing, the orange

light of the campfire shading the stubble around his jaw, and for a moment, he held everyone's attention.

Behind him, the dark night swallowed the world, so it seemed as if Max's face and body could command the unnatural space between light and dark.

"All right, now that I finally have your attention. I have been working on a magic trick, and tonight, with each of you here as witness, I would like to perform for you." The voice that spoke was different, aged perhaps.

"Max, is one of your tricks tonight removing the tattoos you placed on Owen and me? Because that's the only trick I really want to see," Alice said.

Once more they laughed, and Owen tried to smile, but his face felt two-dimensional instead of natural. Laughter wasn't inside him right then. A phone call had come earlier, and he hadn't shared it with the others or with Alice. And they all needed to know. He had pushed the clock as far he could.

"No, it is not," Max said. "I told you—I told everyone—I'm working on finding a way to remove your tattoos, but it's been difficult. I am still not sure what went wrong with that magic trick, and every time I ask for help, no one here, not one of you," Max accused, "is willing to be my volunteer."

"He has a fair point," Alice defended.

Everyone laughed again. And Owen could see the defeat on Max's face.

Owen understood completely. Max used ethereal magic to perform his tricks. It was incredibly subtle work, using the tiniest, thinnest cords of magic. No one else in his group even attempted such a thing. But Max seemed to be obsessed with his tricks. Only, every once in a while, they went wrong, and that was how Owen wound up with a king-of-diamonds tattoo on his butt cheek, Alice the queen of diamonds on hers. Of course now, with the connection between Alice and him, Owen wasn't sure he wanted the tattoo of a playing card removed, but nobody needed to know that tonight.

"Okay, again, everyone shut up. I love you all, but can you please just shut it? Tonight, to break the tension, for my first magic trick—"

"Hold it!" Owen said, raising his flat beer high into the air and climbing up onto his feet.

"Owen?" Max asked. Then he swore with a knowing grace.

"I love you, Max, but I have no idea what your next trick or tricks are going to do, and I have something to say before we all start diving into chaos or for cover."

"Why are there so many days in my life"—Max paused to wipe the frustration off his face—"that I can't understand why I put up with any of you?" He sat back down.

Jessie was there with an arm around Max's left shoulder. "It's all good, buddy. Owen's just building some anticipation for the next time you do your thing. Let's hear what our fearless leader has to say. Go ahead, boss. We're all listening. We are all ears, just like Clover."

Clover reached over and good-heartedly punched Jessie, and Owen ignored the byplay.

"Thanks, Jessie. You're too kind," Owen said. Unable to help himself, he looked back and down toward Alice, some deep part of his soul needing to hold on to her.

Owen's eyes met hers, and the world became so simple and then overwhelming. What he was about to say would change everything.

I have to go, and you have to stay.

Internally he swore as she broke the contact with a questioning look crossing her face. Not sorrow, but perhaps a sense of what was about to come.

"Boss, is this where you tell us we aren't working hard enough with our instruments?" Clover interrupted. "Or is this . . . is this where you tell us we aren't pushing ourselves as artists? Oh, I know—you're about to tell us we need to anticipate one another, to think and feel and move like one heartbeat when we are up onstage, or we will all burn to death." She and everyone else gave a small chuckle.

And this time, when Owen smiled, he thought he could feel humor on the outskirts of his emotion. And then his will for what needed to be done hardened over his heart.

The road is a brutal place to call home. Tell them the truth.

"I received a call a couple of hours ago. Mara is asking for our help." Owen was shaking his head no before Alice could ask if the call had been about her missing priest. After all, Father Patrick was being held by a secret sect of the church, and Owen's uncle Cornelius was working on getting him back.

"Does this have to do with Father Patrick and me getting him back? Cornelius said just a couple of days ago everything is on track with the negotiations," Alice said.

"No. This call had nothing to do with Father Patrick or the negotiations to get him. This was just a request to do a thing for Mara and the Golden Horn, do them a solid by hand-delivering some personal invitations in San Francisco." Owen turned to include his people. "We all know the secret ballroom under Mara's club was a special, important place for our kind and the We population before Mara shut the doors, years ago. I don't have the details, but it's been alluded to me that reopening the space is a big deal in the We world, and Mara needs the right We to sign off on it. I said yes to hand-delivering some invitations. I plan for us to be on the road by no later than eleven tomorrow morning. If we drive all night, we should arrive in San Francisco around the time the invitations show up."

Jessie said, "Do we have to be on the road that early? I have been working hard on getting a solid hangover by tomorrow. It would be nice to sleep most of it off."

"Sorry, Jess, eleven it is," Owen said with a smile for his friend. "Unless you all want to stay. I can go alone."

"I think I can pull myself out of bed, but you are on notice, Owen. No more of these early-hour-leaving ideas."

"Sure, Jessie. Clover?"

"You think I am going to let you go to San Francisco on your own? I missed the last time you went. I'm going. Do we know who the invitations are for? And how many there are?" Clover asked. "Must be some important people if Mara wants you to hand-deliver them."

"I have no idea, just that the invitations will be at the Grand Hotel around noon the day after tomorrow, and I need to make the delivery right away. Then I figure we can hit some shops, take in a club. There's an old friend I want to see too. Might have a line on some musicians."

"Sounds good to me," Clover said. "I have never been. You?" she said, directing her voice toward Jessie.

"No, never. I'm an East Coast man."

"Of course you are."

Owen didn't sit, didn't let go of the spotlight, but he waited.

"Road trip?" Max said. "It's about time. If I have to spend another week here with all of you in a barn, I am going to go join the circus. No offense, Alice."

"None taken," she said.

"San Francisco," Daphne said low under her breath to Clover. Owen thought he could actually see her spirit rise at the idea. "I have always wanted to see the Golden Gate Bridge. And Alcatraz; I hear it's haunted. Will you go with me?"

"Hold on," Owen said. "Daphne, you aren't going with us." Owen paused, letting his words sink in and over the group.

"I'm sorry, what? Did I do something wrong?"

"Not at all. Our group is just too dangerous a place for anyone not in the band."

"Wait, what? What do you mean she isn't coming with us?" Jessie said.

Ignoring Jessie and the reaction of the others, Owen pressed on. "We told you we would do our best to keep you safe and unbound until you turned eighteen. You're unbound and relatively safe now. When we head out tomorrow, we will drop you off at the Denver Airport. It's not very far from here. We'll cover a ticket back to your home in North Carolina. I am sure your parents will be happy to see you. After all, the holidays are only a few months away."

Each word broke her inside. He could see it. Read it on her too-young face and soft frame. *You want to stay. You thought you were part of the band.*

He watched as she held in the pain. Held back tears that were even now pushing against her control.

Show me the fire. Let it burn out the lie.

"Owen," Clover said with a reprimand.

"Ah, man," Max added from the side.

To his surprise, it was Alice who stayed silent. He had thought she might interfere.

Jessie stood up. "Hold on a second. You can't just make that decision and tell us how it is. Daphne has done everything we asked her to. She belongs with us. If she wants."

"Of course I can. It was the deal, Jessie. You asked if we could take her in and keep her safe until she turned eighteen. Well, we did that. Our group is in more danger than most, and now with Mara and what happened at the Golden Horn—all those hunters and who knows how many We killed—we just don't know if we are clear of that mess. Not to mention, I want to put a band together, and you know what kind of heat that will bring. We aren't normal, Jessie. She belongs at home with her family. Daphne will be safe there. She's eighteen and isn't in danger of being bonded by a high-level We. She knows what to look out for, and we can give her some names and numbers to call in her area if she gets in trouble. I won't place a person in the fire if they are not ready. I did it once before and I will not do it again."

"You didn't even ask, and you can't possibly know she will be safe there. That she's not ready. Why didn't you talk to us?" Jessie said.

"Hey, she's a nice girl, and she hasn't stepped wrong this whole time, but you know what we do, how we live. She made it clear this isn't her place. I'm not a babysitting service, but if you want to be, you go ahead. No one is stopping you."

"You're being an asshole, Owen," Jessie shot back.

"You're right, Jessie, me getting Daphne out of harm's way and sending her back to her parents is me being terrible. Grow up. Have you all forgotten the world we live in and the danger we face every time we open a door to a new bar, a new club? Not all the We out there are happy with us, and there's an unfinished payback with hunters who could show up at any moment. You know what we are about; we aren't a safe place for her now that we aren't hiding."

"You aren't just talking about her safety, and we all know it. You didn't give Daphne a chance to be in the band. You just made up your mind without talking to us, and now you are sending her off. That's not fair, Owen. Fuck you, man," Jesse said.

Owen held still as the last words vibrated inside him. His skin started to itch, and the flames dancing between Jessie and him seemed a minor inconvenience as he looked at his best friend in the world.

Is this where you leave me? Is this the place and time, old friend? Owen wondered, not for the first time.

Owen breathed, and as he did, he felt the heat of the fire mix with the cool night sky.

"Give her a chance? We are musicians; every moment is our chance. She spent three weeks inside the Golden Horn. Three weeks. Surrounded by some of the best musicians in all of Miami, and that includes you. She never took the stage. Not even when it was closed. We were in Chicago, and she didn't step up there, or at Tim's. She plays in the van with the door closed, where no one can hear her. She doesn't fight for the stage, for the moment. Did she tag any one of you to jam with? No. She listens to each of us, then goes and plays all by herself. At the same time, we took her to stage after stage after stage. And you know what, kid? There is nothing wrong with not wanting to take the stage with us. When we play and layer in ethereal energy, and we take our souls and those in the crowd on a ride designed for angels and the dead, there is always a chance we will burn to death. So we don't force people to play, and we don't ask them. Because this is a calling, but if you're not onstage with me, I cannot protect you. Shit." Owen took a beat and held Daphne's gaze. "The best thing I can do to keep you safe is to send you home. If that makes me a terrible guy, I'll own that scar over my soul. God knows I have far, far worse."

Owen felt her pain, her crushed heart as his eyes held on to her big browns. He held her pain, tucked it inside, where it flared bright and real inside his own chest, the sensation multiplying as Daphne's first tears started to fall. But his face held, unchanged.

I will not watch you burn to death because I was not strong enough to say no. If you're not ready, go home. If you are, fight.

Quick and nimble as only the young can be, Daphne got up and ran from the firelight. The sound of her muffled cries flowed behind her.

"Clover, go with her," Owen commanded.

"Why are you such a dick sometimes? She's just eighteen. Not everything is about Heaven and Hell and you," Jessie said.

"Clover, she went out into the farmer's field, and there could always be some barbed wire out there. She might not see it in the dark."

"I'll stay. Max?" Clover said, quick and cool.

"Yeah, I'll go." Max got up quickly, tapping Jessie on the shoulder and giving a nod Owen's way at the same time.

"I can't believe your hubris. You are worried about wire? You just crushed Daphne's soul. You broke her heart in front of everyone she looks up to. And you're worried she might bleed a little. You know she is one of us. She is not just an eighteen-year-old, she is an etherealist. She is a musician, and you treat her like she is less than you are," Jessie said.

"I'm aware," Owen replied.

"You and your rules. You never think. Not everyone is like you. And that's a very good thing. I get that you didn't grow up with a family, and so no one taught you how to ask permission. You weren't taught about the advantage of being nice. But you just broke her heart, and you didn't have to. She would be safe with us. We've kept her safe so far, and now she's an adult. What's wrong with that?" Jessie asked.

"I know you like her, and she's a good kid. But this isn't a safe place. Next to me isn't a safe place. And if you're being honest with yourself, you know it's true. Now, I'm not talking about this anymore. We all have to be packed and leaving by eleven. Alice, you want to take a walk with me?"

"Just like that, you're walking. Walking away."

"Yeah, Jessie, I am. Before we both do something we can't take back."

"I'm not done talking about this," said Jessie.

Owen felt his fist tighten. And one of the rules he lived by onstage crawled up his leg and bit into his spine. "There can only be one leader onstage."

To his surprise, Alice's cool hand caught his forearm and slid down, opening his fist until her fingers were locked with his own as they started to walk away.

"Jessie, let him go. You know how Owen can be."

Owen continued to walk with Alice in hand, back toward the barn as Clover finished speaking.

"I know. No, Jessie, stay here. Let's talk it out. You've been drinking. Let him go," Clover continued.

CHAPTER TWO

A+O

Alice held Owen's hand as they walked side by side, passing from firelight into the depths of starlight as they headed toward the low-lit lights of the barn Owen's people were using as a makeshift home.

"Sometimes Jessie drives me crazy. He knows the truth, I know he does, but instead, Jessie pretends he doesn't understand the rules of this screwed-up world we live in. As if he hasn't lived in it ever since joining us. It's been four years since he came on, and now he wants to pretend we live a flowered lifestyle."

"I get it. But why did you do it that way?" She struggled over her words.

"You mean, why didn't I tell you I have to leave earlier?"

She could see the heat coming off his breath, but she wasn't afraid. "No, I understand that part. You didn't want to tell me because you know I can't just walk away from my parents and go all across the country with you. So, knowing that, you wanted to stretch out the time for as long as you could."

"At least someone understands."

She felt the pull on her arm and went with the force. His lips found hers, and the kiss stole some of her resolve even as it warmed her toes. "I love your kisses, Owen. They sweep me away sometimes. But . . ."

"But I didn't answer your question?"

"You didn't," she said.

"All right," he said more slowly as he turned, and they continued to walk toward the main side door of the barn. "You want to know why I did what?"

"You were deliberate with Daphne. You raised her spirits and then broke them. You're not a cruel person, so why did you do it that way? I know you like the kid. Hell, I like her. I like her a lot. I think everyone who has met her likes her. So, why did you set her up to be crushed?"

"I like her too." His words were distant, and she felt some of the layering he often wore over his soul slide into place like scaled armor.

The feeling was uncomfortable between them.

She was missing something, something Owen didn't want to say out loud. Maybe didn't want to hear? Her mind moved over the conversation she had heard and back again.

The crunching sound of their footsteps could be heard as the barn climbed higher into sight. The orange glow of LED lights within the barn shone through the cracks in the wood and doorframe as the peak of the roof blocked out more and more stars and just a touch of a white moon.

"You don't want her to leave. You don't want Daphne to go home to her family."

And you don't want me to stay with mine, she thought.

Owen stopped and turned slowly. "Don't let anyone hear you say that. But, no, I don't want her to go. She just can't stay as she is."

"Why?"

Owen swore. His words were low and folded into the shadows of the cool night air.

"I have tried letting people join me onstage with a lie just floating in the air between us. And they normally die, or I have no choice but to kick them off my stage."

"Like what happened with your brother."

"No. Well, a little. With David, I didn't know about his secret. I was so caught up in myself I didn't see he held a secret. Then he burned onstage, and I almost died. I swore I wouldn't let it ever happen again. Not with my people."

Owen didn't say anything else, and neither did Alice as they walked forward.

"How we play up on that stage, when we infuse our song with ethereal energy . . . there are rules. Pureness, you might say, of a kind that is required to pass into the flames without being burned. Lies eat a piece of you. They hold you back, separating musicians, making them weak, too weak, and the band burns up onstage." There was an edge to his voice she didn't care for but couldn't help but hear.

"You don't talk about your brother much."

"Not much to say. But the image of him burning onstage as my skin boiled was enough to sear the lesson into me. Daphne's lying to us. She thinks it's a secret."

"You know she is? Lying?"

"Yeah, I do," Owen said, solemn.

"So, maybe her going home to her family is the best place for her," Alice said, stopping by the door to end the conversation. If this was going to be their last night together, and it could be for some time, she didn't want to spend it talking about Daphne and the dead.

"Maybe, but I don't think so."

"What? You just went toe to toe with Jessie over this." She paused as Owen pulled the large wooden door to the barn open for her. If this had been her first time in the barn, she would have been surprised. But for three weeks Owen's people had been making this barn their own. Now, glowing string lights and even a neon OPEN sign lit up the hay-baled space. Two curtains were pulled across cleaned-out stalls that had become makeshift bedrooms for Daphne and Clover.

"Jessie and I are fighting over other things. He wants to protect her, but in our world, we first have to learn to protect ourselves. Daphne doesn't need a protector anymore. She needs someone to wake her up."

"That's pretty fucking arrogant, Owen."

"No, it's not. I think she's more like me than Jessie," Owen said.

"And what does that mean?"

"Look, I love the man. And my God, he's one of the smoothest piano players I have ever heard. He can make a rock cry and a no-legged frog hop."

"But?"

"But he's all rules and guidelines. We live by our music, but he worships what was versus what is to come. Do you know what I mean? Learning how to take people's spirits on a journey on the road made for angels isn't about following the rules. It's about demanding the lines be reshaped. It's about burning them down and holding the weight of the consequences in your hand and still going forward. Still reaching for the impossible. Not reading sheet music."

"Is there some disdain you have for sheet music? I like seeing the song on paper."

"Stop it. You know what I mean—I know you do. You can feel the difference, and I believe Daphne can too."

"So, you're breaking her. To build her back up?"

"Maybe, or maybe I'm wrong, and she gets on the plane."

Alice thought about it.

"You think I'm the worst person in the world? I probably am. Alice, I don't know any other way to teach her. It has to be her choice. I can't give her the words. She already has them. She is refusing to let them out."

"What words?"

"She's not a bass player. She was born to play six strings, not four. Her soul wants to be in the front, demanding the audience see her, not someone who is too afraid to be heard."

"Have you heard her play guitar? How can you possibly know that?"

"You're a hunter at heart now, so it's the same way you know who is the toughest person in the room. Who to hit first in a fight. It's a vibe thing. She's like me—I'll bet every dollar I have I'm right. She was made for center stage. Instead, I think she has been practicing in the van where no one can hear her. So she can learn the bass. Because . . ." Owen left it open, his eyes begging her to see the end.

"Because you don't have a bass player." It all fell into place.

"Yes. Daphne is not shy. She's not scared of crowds. In fact, she looks for them. You can see it when she is working behind the bar. She's smart, and when she isn't hiding her true talent, I'm guessing she has skills with the six-string." Owen pressed his lips together. His chest was tight, and there was a pain he had to accept. "Sometimes an etherealist with the power of creation inside them is scared, terrified even, to let it out."

"Afraid?" Alice asked.

"Yeah. They are afraid because, if they do, if they stand all the way up, it will change their world and the world of everyone they are connected to. I wish there was a way for Daphne to stay here as she is, but we kept her safe by going low-key. Basically, we tried to avoid attention from the We and the world while we waited for her to turn eighteen. Now that time is up. We can't do what we do if she isn't up for it. And until she chooses to be her full self, she's not safe beside us."

Alice thought about it and had to admit she could see it Owen's way. She didn't like the idea of breaking the girl, but soft knuckles couldn't help anyone in a fight. She had learned that early. Too early.

"Okay, then. Now, are we going to talk about us? Or—" She nodded toward the hayloft that sat on the second level of the barn. An old wooden ladder led up toward the space Owen had claimed for himself. More importantly, it was private.

"We aren't going up there tonight." Owen smiled, and in that smile, it was easy to see he had been looking forward to this moment.

"We aren't going up to your bed? That's a first. Where are you taking me?"

"This way," he said, leading beneath the loft and deeper within. They moved past a trove of shovels and tools until she spotted a door she hadn't used before. Owen pressed hard, and hay and dust fell off the frame as another wave of the night air broke over them both.

"So what's out here?"

"It's a surprise. It took a little work, but Max and I finished it this morning."

Alice's eyesight adjusted to the low light as Owen shut the barn door behind them. She took a glance around. She had thought this side of the barn was just where the farmer parked his rusted tractor and broken-down truck. Toss in a couple of old oil barrels and some leftover parts, and there wasn't much to look at, particularly at night. She couldn't fathom why Owen had brought her out here.

"You know I'm not really a tractor kind of girl. If you're thinking we are getting kinky on that old thing, you're far better off taking me back up to the loft."

Owen laughed, and she felt it down deep.

It was nice spending time with the others, but every time they found a chance to be alone, she saw it was easier for Owen to be himself.

"Back here. I set this up for us," Owen said.

They weaved around an old rusted oil barrel and some

empty propane canisters until she spotted a large something covered up by a sheet of old gray plywood and blue
tarp.

"It's not jewelry or a gun. For the record, I like both
those things. What is it?" she asked.

"Patience," he said, letting go of her hand and moving
around the side. With practiced ease, Owen spread his long
arms and grabbed both the old plywood and tarp beneath.
A gentle pull and lift, and a large curved wooden hot tub
was uncovered.

"How in the world did you find this? We are in the middle of nowhere."

"We found it right off. It took some heavy lifting and
more than one hour of cleaning. But the real problem was
the pump and heater. You like it?" he asked.

"It's clean?" she asked.

"Of course." Owen used his foot to flip the metal switch
that started the pump. Already there was steam rising into
the air.

"And bubbles. Owen, I feel like you're giving me the full
treatment."

Owen didn't answer.

There was something about the night sky mixed with the
back-glow of the barn that framed Owen. He stood there
watching her but was lost under the weight of leaving . . .
leaving her. She could see it as clearly as his deep green eyes
and strong face.

Owen reached over toward an instant propane heater
and clicked it on. She heard the whoosh as gas met spark.

"Owen?"

"Yeah?"

"Are you okay?" she asked.

"I have never met someone like you."

And I don't want to say goodbye.

It was his thoughts that drifted in the air between them,
but she thought she could hear him and understood his

view. For the last couple of weeks, he had made a point of talking about the chaos of his life. How every road traveled twisted and turned, and those devoted to living as musicians changed with every trip. In short, he was saying that now that it was time to leave, this could be the end of their relationship. That he didn't know where he was going, but he was sure he couldn't come back.

She smiled. "Take your clothes off," Alice said, slipping her sweatshirt up over her head.

Owen didn't follow the command at first.

"There is a small table to the left," he said.

"I see it. Thanks," Alice said absently as she removed the small arms holster from around her shoulders and the weapons they carried.

Her hand crossed over her belt buckle, and a razor-sharp knife made of pure ethereal essence formed in her hand. With a pinch of concentration in her face, Alice placed the knife just over her left wrist. Gold light sparkled, and the knife reshaped into a gold-chained bracelet with a dangling green gemstone.

"You're staring, Owen. I told you to take your clothes off."

"You did." He didn't apologize. Alice didn't expect him to.

Slowly he took his used leather jacket off and hung it on the propane heater. His boots, she knew, had strong laces that took a practiced hand to undo. Those he set to the side.

Alice slipped her shirt over her head. Her shoes and socks came off next, and it was all Owen could do to look away as he slipped his T-shirt over his head.

"Owen, you can't stop time. And I can't go with you tomorrow. It's only been three weeks since I came home. My parents need me. Get in the hot tub," Alice said as her exposed skin shined in the starlight, covered only by her lacy black smallclothes.

Don't you know I can find you wherever you go? I

tracked Kerogen across the globe. I can find you, Alice thought to herself.

She touched the bubbling water and found it was hot. It didn't take much energy to imagine Owen scrubbing the wood and tinkering with the heater and pump.

All for our last night—or so you believe.

She moved one leg in, and with a hop and a twist, she jumped in the rest of the way.

Water splashed, and she was already turning to see him as the heat washed up her body.

Owen moved like a cat locking down his prey. Alice felt her skin prickle and her body come alive with electricity as he stalked in. The angle of his chin, the set of his shoulders—there was no question left on the table.

He wants me. He wants every part of me, Alice thought as Owen climbed in and moved with his own small wave of water. She didn't have to wait as he wrapped his cool hands around her back. His lips found hers, and light bloomed inside her mind as the world shifted to lips and skin. His thick dark hair was in her hand before she knew what she was doing. And one leg wrapped around his hip. His thick erection pressed against her body, and a shiver crawled up her spine. Without thinking, Alice drifted a hand over his chest, where she could feel his heart beating.

A question entered his eyes.

"I just wanted to feel your heartbeat." *I want to remember this.*

As if he could hear her inner thoughts, the storm inside Owen seemed to pull back. And his own hand closed over the top of her own. "You can feel my heart anytime, anywhere. But I am still taking your bra off."

Alice laughed, then shook her head. "You do push, Owen."

"I don't know how else to be." Despite his words, he hadn't moved. Not his hips to help align body parts or his

free hand toward her underwear. Instead, he simply stood
still. His hand over hers. It was close and intimate, and easy
to see Owen wanted this time to matter as much as, if not
more than, she did. "Kiss me, Alice. Kiss me slow."

Alice thought for one single moment, thought about him
and her and the crazy, screwed-up journey they'd each
taken just to find each other.

Alice kissed him, and she did it slowly.

The moon and the stars were their companions as their
minds entered another universe. Slowly, Alice and Owen
found their way. Clothing came off. Water was spilled, and
bodies aligned. If the jets of the tub didn't cover their
sounds, they simply didn't care as their bodies pushed and
pulled against and with one another. At times they paused
just for the sake of holding still and allowing their hearts to
feel what was between them.

When it was done and their bodies were spent, Alice
held her toes up to the far edge and floated with her back
against Owen, whose breath, even now, pushed her slightly
forward and then allowed her to fall back.

"Owen, can you talk?"

"I'm not completely sure."

"Tell me something I don't know. Tell me something
about you."

Something I can hold on to after you leave.

"What would you like to know?" Owen said as he held
her from behind.

"You met my parents. What happened to yours? Your
birth parents. Before Mara took you in." Nothing in Owen
moved, and it caused the subtle rhythm of his chest to
pause.

Alice slowly twisted around, and there was his strong
face, so layered with responsibility and beauty it was as if
she were looking into the eyes of a Greek god who thought
he could hold up the world. He was too beautiful in this
light. In any light.

"That's not a very fun story. Perhaps something else is better?"

"Okay," Alice said slowly. The connection between them felt raw, like he was hurting and unwilling to share it.

"Then tell me about Mara and your uncles. Damon and Cornelius. I don't need to know every secret. But I want to know what you were like as a kid."

"I was a huge pain in the ass."

"Now, that I can believe." Alice reached up with her left hand and pulled his head in close for a gentle kiss. When she pulled back, she checked his eyes for the pain and was glad to see most of the shadow was gone.

"I am not kidding. I drove Mara and the rest crazy."

Alice turned, needing him to talk, to share his life. If he was going to leave, she wanted more to remember than just what had come before. "How did you end up there? Did you find Mara, or did she find you?"

"I think it was Cornelius's people. He has this network of We all across the world. They are constantly telling him things."

"What kinds of things?" she asked.

"Anything and everything. Stories of people. Who is sleeping with who. Who is starting a business. It always seems like random information, but Cornelius loves it."

Alice didn't say anything. She wanted him to keep talking. So often, Owen wore mantles of responsibility that hid the whole of him; other times he was writing music inside his head. But right now he was open.

"So, Mara and I? How did we meet? Ah, I was living on the streets, and I was about eight or nine years old. I was used to playing on the sidewalk for the tourists and anyone else with some cash. I started when I was around six. So, by then, I knew where I could play for tips without the cops coming or someone kicking me away from their store. I had this little guitar that looked broken and a harmonica. I had this whole routine I would play while I stomped my foot for a beat. And one day, I was playing, and I drew this little crowd like normal, and there she was. Mara was just standing before me."

"She convinced you to come to the Golden Horn?" Alice asked.

"No, she scared the hell out of me. I could sense how much ethereal power she had inside and recognized her as a level four We. So I jumped up and ran for my life."

"You could see the marking at the age of eight? I thought that normally starts around the teen years?"

"Not age; it has to do with power. Most etherealists simply don't have enough ethereal energy in them until their teens to see the marking of a We. I assume you could see the We markings when you were a child?"

"I honestly don't remember. I might have been able to. But it's hard for me to remember much before Kerogen bonded my soul to his. Then I escaped to the secret sect of the church, and they kept me away from all We. What did Mara do when you ran from her?"

"I don't know because I didn't stick around to find out."

"You got away from her?" Alice said, surprised.

"I did for about an hour, maybe an hour and a half. Then I came back to where I was staying. It was this abandoned building over on School Street where I could fit between the fence and the chain. Anyway, when I came into the room I had been using, Mara was standing there. I tried to run, but this time she used her power and lifted me up off the floor. When I was calm, she set me down, and we talked. She told me she had an adopted son, David, around my age, who was like me, and that I should come take a look at her club. I would have food and shelter and music. And I wouldn't have to worry about the state system or the cops ever again."

"Did you go home with her?"

"No, not at first. She left, and I promised I would check

it out. Summer ended, and the tourists went home. Winter started up, and I found myself scoping the place out. Damon likes to say I was a stray, and all Mara had to do was feed me. It's mostly true, I guess. Every time I came around, she had sandwiches or a burger and hot fries. And then there were all the instruments on the wall. She or someone else there would show me how they worked, and then I would get paid to clean them."

Alice's foot slipped from the side of the hot tub, and for a moment she thought she might drop under the surface of the water. But Owen's chest at her back and his hands on her hips caught her. Gently he lifted her higher. Water ran across, over and down her breasts as they crested the warmth of the waterline. She could feel his eyes on her. And a heat that had nothing to do with the temperature and everything to do with the desire that pulsed within.

"Tell me something else. Tell me a story," she said gently as he lowered her skin back under.

"You want a story?"

"Yeah, rock star. Tell me one more." Her voice had found a huskiness she couldn't control.

"Okay, I have one. Cornelius is the man of chaos in that place for sure. He moves at a different speed than the rest. And he and I hit it off right away. Mara and I sort of orbited around each other. Oh, she would make sure David and I had clothes and food, and she watched over us. She was good to us both. But for all Cornelius could be unpredictable, Damon always had the biggest surprises. He was like a mountain when he decided to come into view. You couldn't help but be stunned."

Owen reached out and touched her gold bracelet that wasn't a bracelet but an item made of pure ethereal essence.

"Do you know what this is?" he asked.

"It's ethereal essence currently in the disguise of a bracelet. Just like what you wear around your own neck. It's my weapon to help kill the We and anyone else who can wield ethereal energy."

"Sure. But do you know what ethereal essence is? At its core?"

Alice shook her head.

"Watch this," Owen said.

One of his hands moved behind her. When it came back into view, it was holding his own gold necklace that wasn't a necklace at all but essence in the form of a chain. Gently, and with great precision, Owen lowered the chain so it made contact with the bracelet. At first, nothing happened. And then something did.

A pain like a small needle shot right behind her left ear, and before Alice could move her hand, tiny gold sparks like electricity danced from the contact point.

"Don't do that," she said on instinct, moving her bracelet away.

"You see. Why did they do that? They are made of the same stuff. Ethereal essence. However, to have contact with each other is a natural fight between them. A fight for competing goals. A fight of will and force. And some believe soul."

"I don't understand. I mean, I get the fight because they can be weapons. But the rest doesn't make any sense."

"I know. Damon was the first who taught me about ethereal essence. I was maybe fourteen. I was working the accounts for Mara in the back office, and it was around nine, maybe ten o'clock at night."

Owen took a breath, and Alice enjoyed the feel of the water moving across her skin.

"He just told me to come with him. I didn't know where we were going or anything. But then, Damon isn't one for talking much when it comes to music. Anyway, we went downtown, climbed up onto the roof of this building and waited. The night was sort of like this, clear and full of stars, and the moon was so full it took up most of the sky.

We waited for about a half hour. Not long, but I can remember Damon didn't say a word. Not after he told me to sit and wait."

Owen paused, and Alice just waited. It felt good to hear him share. To just stay still and listen.

"A We he knew, a friend of his, stepped out on the roof of the building beside us. He didn't look our way. And Damon used his hand to tell me to be quiet. Before I knew what was happening, Damon's friend put his horn up to his lips and started to play. I can still hear it. The man was good. Clean, crisp and knew how to dance with the notes. I mean, this guy could play, but it was more than that. I remember I started crying, and I didn't know why. Damon must have sensed I was about to talk because he leaned in close and said, 'Don't ruin it. He's not playing for us. He's playing for the moon and the sound of the horn.' So, I kept quiet and I watched and I listened. The man played all night. Not a single horn from below blew in protest, not a single complaint as the sun started to rise. And then it happened. With horn in hand, the flames came. Only they weren't the golden flames of Heaven or the blue fire of Hell. This was green fire, and it started in his chest until it covered his whole body and his instrument.

"It didn't take long—a few more bars and a bright green flash, and the man, the We, was gone. He gave everything he had, gave all his ethereal energy to the music and the force of the universe. Up until that moment I hadn't known a We or perhaps even one of us could do that.

"Damon told me to follow him, and we jumped from our building to the musician's building. There, in a small pile where the musician had been standing was gray ash, and atop the ash was a copper mouthpiece to a horn, and it was made of pure ethereal essence."

"Owen?"

"That's what we have, Alice. My guitar and the strings I hide around my neck, and your knife that you have hidden as a bracelet. Even that shroud of tears that protected you from the bond with Kerogen. Each was made out of one or more We that gave their soul and their magic for something other than Heaven and Hell. They gave it for a cause. I have been told that with enough will and power, you can reshape essence into a different cause. But it never works the way you plan. It's all pretending. My essence wants to be the strings; yours wants to be a knife."

Alice let her feet drop down to the wooden bottom of the tub, and for the first time in over an hour, she created space between them. "You think that is how the shroud of tears was made? But not your guitar? You think someone re-shaped the shroud of tears?"

"I don't know about the shroud of tears you used to wear. But I can't imagine any We demanding that price for their help. Even the evil ones. But my guitar—I know every name and soul within her. And each soul wants me to pass through the fourth gate of Heaven and come back to tell the tale."

Alice stood there, quiet, simply taking him in. "You said no one has ever done that. Passed through the fourth gate."

"If they have, no one has ever come back. It's possible a group made it through, or their souls made it through and their bodies burned here. Similar to what happened to Ker-ogen when you killed him on the Devil's bridge. But I don't think so. I don't think anyone has ever made it that high up the path made for angels."

"But that's what you want to do?"

"I honestly don't know. It's what the souls inside my guitar want. And there is a part of me. A large part of me that wants to defy the rules of this world. However . . ." Owen trailed off, and his head dipped to the side as if he could shake out his thoughts.

Tell me what is inside you.

"I want to hear it, Alice. I want to hear the song. I want to feel the notes and the vibration that would unlock the fourth gate. Sometimes it's like my whole body moves with the music, and I can fly. Like this body of mine is holding my soul back from doing the impossible. Do you know what I mean?"

"Owen." She said his name softly, a whisper over the water. His head shook ever so slightly. Alice couldn't tell if he was shaking off his thoughts or her.

"I used to understand that feeling, or something similar. Mine was a little different. I wanted to kill Kerogen so badly I would imagine what it was like. Over and over again until I thought I could feel it. Until it was in my blood and bones, in my fingers and hair." A pain in her chest had her closing her mouth.

He screwed me up so bad. I am not normal. If I ever was.

"Alice, what is it? I know it's not Kerogen. That We, that asshole, deserved his death and then some. Anyone who would bond another like that, let alone a child. He was an asshole," Owen repeated.

"I don't regret killing Kerogen. Not for a second. It's just, he shaped my whole life, right up until his body dropped with me atop him. He shaped me into this, and now he's gone, and I am supposed to be normal. What am I supposed to do now? I'm not even going after Father Patrick. I am just sitting in that house. I used to move with a purpose, with a single-minded drive, and now I just stand in place. Owen, I don't know what I am doing."

Owen crossed the water that separated them, his arms pulling her in tight. "You're not lost, Alice, you're just at a crossroads. The whole world is in front of you, and you can do anything your heart wants. Go to school, get a job, see the sights or change the world."

"You are just trying to get me to go with you. Again."

"Of course I am. I want you to come with me, to be by my side. I care about you. I care for you."

I don't want to let you go.

The words vibrated between them until she could taste them in her mouth.

I can find you, Owen, she thought, but this time, there was a weakness in her own mind. This time a touch of doubt crept in. *But what if I don't? What if I have to stay here and keep moving?*

"I know," she finally said, "but I can't go with you."

CHAPTER THREE

Owen Brown sat in his truck, looking at the simple house on a plain cul-de-sac. The taste of Alice's goodbye kiss was still fresh on his lips as he watched the front door of her parents' home. The goodbye they had shared only minutes earlier had been sweet and soft. Alice had promised to be safe, and they would see each other soon.

Metal on metal with far too little grease screeched as Clover, his number two, opened the passenger door to his truck and moved to climb in.

One quick appraising look and Clover read him like a billboard ad.

"Owen, you're like a lion with a thorn in your paw. Are you going to be moody the whole drive? Because if you are, I'm going to ride with Jessie and the others. Seriously. You are hardly fun at the best of times, and after three weeks in this place, I am looking forward to getting back on the road." Clover smiled, but her words couldn't cut through his thoughts.

"Get in the truck, Clover," he said.

"Damn, you're punchy. Can we cut the bull and just spill what's really eating you? This isn't the first time we have driven away from a girl," Clover said as she slipped onto the bench seat and shut the door with an audible bang.

Owen didn't respond. Instead, he started the engine. The familiar feel and sound of fire, air and gas pushing metal should have helped calm the pressure inside his chest as his seat rumbled beneath him. It didn't. The radio kicked on a moment later.

Owen tried to breathe in the great magic of The Who as it pounded into the cab from his speakers. Feeling like his lungs were in a vise, Owen inhaled the music as if it were a life raft for his soul. Right then, at that very moment, he felt as if he were a drowning man. Desperate to live, to breathe again, grasping for a grip so he might climb back up and out of the hell he was in.

Owen drifted with the harmony along the current of the song, as if through the music was his only way to salvation. His lips curled in over his teeth in a grimace, and he could see Alice's perfect, beautiful face just beyond reality. In his mind, he locked on to her eyes, and she stole his thoughts even there.

Clover's voice spoke from the side, but it was a low, tempered voice compared to the furnace within. "Is it Jessie you're so upset with? Or just leaving Alice? Or is this about Daphne? Give me a clue."

Owen breathed out. His chest was tight and struggling. How could he explain what he knew, what he understood the dangers to be? Even to Clover.

He wanted to shout and move with the emotion running inside him.

He lived in the dark places found across the world; the

stage wasn't for the ordinary. It called to those who refused to play by the rules. It wasn't safe, it wasn't kind, and it changed people every day. You grow or you burn, and you can't stay the same.

Next time I see Alice, I'll be different; the next she sees me, she will be different and possibly planted in a new life.

Right now, we fit. Right now, we work, and I never thought I would find someone like her. She's one of a kind, and she's just inside that stupid house with its simple wood walls, but when I leave, I drive into the chaos of my life. The twisting road of chaos, and I can't hold on to her when she is so far away.

Owen stared at Clover, and it was as if she was trying to read his thoughts.

How can I even find the words? Owen thought among the burning fog in his mind.

"Screw this," Owen said and turned off the truck.

He didn't look to Clover or the rearview mirror where he knew he would see Jessie inside the van. Owen opened his door and stepped from the truck. The door shut behind him but not before he heard Clover swear with a knowing finality.

For a moment, he thought Clover might call for him to come back as he made his way back to Alice's parents' uninviting front door. But no, Clover knew far better than to go against the fire living inside his soul. And right now it was ablaze.

His hand grasped the doorknob, and he twisted and pushed, ignoring the niceties of civil life.

The door held firm, as the top lock was already engaged, and it was everything he could do not to break the door down with one solid push. Ethereal energy sprang in his blood, power of creation, the power he was born with filling his body and igniting his soul into far too familiar heights.

With a wave of his right hand, the upper lock snapped

back, and the door opened with such force it created a *whoosh* that ended in a thud.

Three adults stared at him from inside the Davises' house.

"I don't care," Owen announced as he walked in. "Alice, I understand your mother went without you for seventeen years and has only had you back for three weeks. But I don't care. You need to get your ass in my truck. I know that she's upset because you won't tell her the whole story, and you have your reasons. But again, I don't care; you need to get your ass in my truck. What's out there moves and changes and is too big, might be far too strong for me to hold on to you, to us, and damn it, I love you. And this, what's between us, is too new. Get in my damn truck." His last words were soft, as if he might be able to find control.

Power and rage from within stormed in his heart as he looked at her. The struggle feasted on every smooth line of Alice's heart-shaped face. His warrior, a broken soul to match his own, a shelter he didn't deserve.

"Now, son," Liam said, taking a small step forward. He was a good man, and Owen knew it. "I know you care for Alice, but she needs some time. We need some time. I am sure you can understand—"

"Stop," Owen commanded with power in his voice, holding up a hand.

Liam's lips closed, sealed by Owens's will, as did Dede's, Alice's mother. Alice's eyes narrowed in a knowing accusation.

"I don't care anymore. I know it's not right, but something is coming, and I won't let you go. Time and distance can do unbelievable things, and I won't just let you go. Get in the truck, Alice." The space in the living room was far too constrictive despite the high ceiling. A cathedral right then would have been too constricting. "I need you, Alice. I can't protect you if you're not with me." He struggled to find the words to hold the bond. She was slipping through his hand, and he couldn't hold on.

From the moment he had come through the door, Alice had set her feet for a fight. Muscle and skill developed over a lifetime of fighting for survival meant she knew what she was doing. *Warrior-like*, *unbreakable* and *unrelenting* were the terms people used to describe her. Yet as he watched, Alice studied his face, examined his heart, and a hardness in the center of her chest melted.

Alice moved to Owen, not as a scared, frightened thing but as a woman coming home.

Owen rejoiced as his Alice slid her arms around him, squeezed once and then reached up and, right there in her childhood home, kissed him.

This kiss was warm and tender, soft, and yet she lingered, and the chemistry between them built and arced, twisting his toes and centering his soul.

Owen didn't care about decency. Right then, he didn't care about anything but the fact that Alice was in his arms.

Too soon, she slipped back, and her eyes met his. "No, Owen. I'm staying here."

Alice let her words linger. *I'm staying here.*

She could see his struggle. See the fight inside his body as Owen grasped for control. It took effort not to kiss him again. This was the true him—a fighter both inside and out as he struggled to protect everyone he cared for. Struggled to do right while everything within his soul demanded he dive into the open air and be as free as a burning flame.

The struggle was real, and she watched it play out.

"Alice?"

"No, Owen. It's too soon for my mother. It's too soon for me." *And I know you. I also know you won't fail no matter what comes your way.*

His voice shifted, soft, quiet even. "You don't have all the information. I know what is out there, and it's a type of chaos I can't control. The road, no matter how simple it looks, is always moving."

I can find you anywhere. You're a lighthouse, Owen. You can't hide from me, and the dark places only make you easier to find.

"I know that's what you believe," Alice said.

You're not sure if there is a way back to me.

She placed her hand on his chest. The muscle beneath his black T-shirt was hard and solid as his lungs pumped with air. "Mom, Dad, can you give us a minute? I need to say goodbye to Owen." She turned her head to reassure both parents.

And noticed neither could open their mouths to answer.

Without a thought, she squeezed Owen's nipple in a reprimand. His body twitched under her hand, and then both Mom and Dad let out an open-mouthed breath.

"What in the world was that?" her mother said angrily, and Alice closed her eyes in shame.

She had hoped to keep her parents free of the chaos that had surrounded her last seventeen years. Owen and the others had played along for three uncomfortable weeks, hiding the truth that they weren't normal humans. That magic was real.

"Mom, Dad, can I say goodbye to Owen? Then we can talk."

"This is my house," her mother started, but it was Liam, her father, who cut her off.

His voice was comforting but firm. "Come on, De. Let's give them some space. Alice isn't going with him." Liam wrapped an arm around his wife in comfort and waited for her to make up her mind.

"I don't like this," Dede said while eyeing Owen with primal aggression.

Alice felt shame tighten over her skin.

"It's okay, De, just let them say goodbye. Alice is home," Liam said.

Alice watched her dad walk her mother down the hall before turning for the study and out of sight.

"I want you to come with me. What do I need to say?"

"Owen." Her heart turned over.

He was a living contradiction—so strong, so unrelenting and good, and yet had such fire as to burn like the sun. She leaned into him, pulling his head down to kiss him again. This time, when the electricity arced and snapped between them, she gave in, fed the flame. Heat and sizzle pulled the kiss, pressing her body against his. His tongue pushed and explored, meeting her own, and the chemistry doubled. His hands, so skilled and knowing, found skin between the seams of her shirt and pants.

It took strength and resolve to pull back, pull away. Even so, her hand touched his cheek.

"I can't go with you right now, and you know why. My mom, my parents, have been through hell. And if I go, they will be right back there. She needs a little more time. But listen to me. If you need me, just call." Alice swallowed. She wasn't good at this stuff, damn it, but she had to try.

Owen held up his hand. Before she could go on, she felt the ethereal energy settle out of his system, and she understood the fight was over.

"I don't want you to go. I don't want to be away from you either," Alice said.

"I owe Mara. She never asks anything of me. I have to go."

And the need to go forward is calling you. I've watched it build for weeks.

"I know, even if I don't understand all of it." She gave a sad half smile, knowing perhaps she might never fully know all of it. Owen was like that, layer over layer, but with each new layer, there was more of him.

Alice let herself be pulled in and felt warm and safe and

sad as Owen's lips brushed a kiss to her forehead. He was the wrong guy, and she was the wrong girl, and Owen was right—they were too new. The bond was still fragile. Easily broken.

But I won't be broken. Not by anything. Not now, not ever.

Owen turned and headed back to the open door. He was taller than he appeared, stronger than anyone knew.

Father Patrick's voice came into her mind. *You are stronger than anyone can ever understand. I believe in you.*

"Owen!" He stopped but didn't turn around. "Believe in me, even if you can't believe in us."

Owen slowly turned to face her, and as he moved, she moved.

With a practiced hand and muscle, Alice shifted in a blur. Her favorite throwing knife left her fingertips, crossing the fourteen feet and driving hilt-deep into his left shoulder just as he turned to face her. She stood tall.

Well, at least he didn't stagger, she thought absently.

"Don't take that out until you get to the car. I don't want to explain to my mother why there is blood on the carpet or her walkway."

His breath was heavy as he looked from the hilt to her. She could see the pain in his face, but Owen wasn't a normal guy, and being an etherealist, the knife was little more than an inconvenience.

"This isn't goodbye," Owen announced as they held eye contact.

"No, it's not," Alice said.

"Okay, then." Owen turned and walked out of the house. The door he didn't shut behind him was left open to the wider world, and yet her world felt smaller with every step he took.

Her own ethereal power followed her call, and with a gentle focus of will, the door to her parents' house shut once more. With a dry humor she didn't feel, she used a trickle of ethereal energy to push the top lock back into place.

"Mom. Dad," Alice called in a low voice, knowing both were listening.

Her mother was the first to come back into the hall, her father a few steps behind. Seeing them, spending time with them over the last couple of weeks, had been perfect despite the story she had kept to herself. The story of where she had gone and how she had been able to come home.

How can I tell them I am a killer? I kill—I have and will. Because that's who I really am.

Two lives. The child she had been and the hunter she had become. Easy to understand why she was pretending to be the innocent child who had disappeared instead of the hunter who had killed Kerogen the asshole and then come home. For three weeks, Alice had done her best to remind her parents and herself that once, long ago, she had belonged here. In a house like this, with people like them.

"You're staying, right, Alice? Your friend Owen left?"

"He's gone, Mom, but I need to tell you something."

And when I am done, you will want me to leave too.

She watched both her parents as she gestured toward the couch.

It's time. I can't be their little girl anymore.

It hurt to think it, but it was true. She had been taken at the age of nine, and her parents deserved answers. But those answers would come with the pain of who she had become.

Her father stopped, and she urged him to take a seat as her mother had, but he shook his head in refusal. "Alice, not yet." He didn't look up. Instead, he kept his head down as if he were ashamed, which was crazy. He had no reason to feel that way, but then all the emotion within her parents and herself, she could admit, was crazy and didn't make straight-line sense.

"Dad, it's time I tell you the whole story of what happened at the church and after, and, well, about me."

"No, wait. Alice, we want to know. Your mother can hardly sleep because she doesn't know. But part of the reason you haven't told us is because it was bad, very bad. I can see it. And, well, I want us to have one more night. One more night to hold up against the bad. A movie night." He said it as if the idea had jumped up at him. "We can eat ice cream and popcorn and laugh at a bad movie and, for one last simple night, just be a normal family and safe. Then, tomorrow after breakfast, when your little sister goes to her preschool, you can tell us the whole story."

"Dad?" Alice watched as he lifted his face, and for the second time since coming home, she saw the tears on her father's cheeks.

"You are home, Alice. Everything else, I mean everything else, comes second."

Alice looked to her mother, not with the eyes of a child but with the knowledge that everything was on the point of changing. The slight accepting nod was enough.

"I like movies and ice cream and popcorn. And then tomorrow I will tell you everything."

O wen walked back to the truck, ignoring the way the sun caught the black shine of the hilt in his shoulder and reflected its rays back toward his eyes. Only Alice would drive a knife into him as a goodbye kiss. A memento to remember her by. And, well, fear her by. Despite the pain, it felt good.

He opened his truck door, groaning a little as he did.

"She stabbed you? I knew I liked that girl. Have to say she has style," Clover said as she watched him get into the truck.

Owen settled into the seat, turned the engine over and

clicked off the radio before it could start up. The movement caused more discomfort, and so he pulled the blade out, his body tightening with the pain. In reaction, he pulled on his ethereal source, the well that contained his God-given gift.

Warmth instantly flooded his senses as the energy started to heal his wound.

"Owen, I always thought you had a way with women that wasn't healthy, but I'm afraid it's getting out of hand. Maybe we should find you a therapist to talk to."

"Funny, Clover," he said as he examined the now blood-covered blade. From hilt to tip, it was six inches, blade black as the paved road but now covered in his own blood. However, it was the grooves carved into each side that held his attention. They were designed to rip and tear both on the way in and on the way out, like violent ribs neatly carved into its slick surface. By his estimation, they had done their job.

"I am funny. Very funny, in fact. And all that without anyone stabbing me or shooting me." The last wasn't as loud as Clover reached back over the seat in search of the first aid kit.

The truck pulled forward at Owen's command. Clover found the kit—in this case, an old gym bag that contained all sorts of supplies, from sterile and sealed surgical scalpels to gray tape and superglue.

"So what's really been eating you? Is it because you're not coming back here? You know it's okay, right?" Clover's voice was soft and gentle. It didn't really fit her.

"What do you mean?" Owen said as the truck lifted up and dropped down as it cleared the small speed bump.

"Owen?" The way she said his name, it was as if it was caught between regret and accusation.

He spared Clover a look, taking his eye off the road.

Clover had clean skin with healthy earth tones and wide, clear eyes. Her haircut was bold and it fit her well. Their eyes met, and a conversation passed between them in seconds.

Don't make me ask out loud. Don't make me be all soft and personable, but I'll do it if you need me to, Clover's eyes said.

You don't understand, and I didn't give you all the facts, his eyes said in response, but it was too cryptic even for them.

"I'll see her again. I'm not running away from Alice," Owen said to clear the air. He turned the wheel, following the street out toward the highway. Jessie and the others in the van followed right behind, confirmed by a glance in the side mirror.

"You don't have to see her again. It's okay to walk away from her, Owen." Clover's voice was soft, too soft for the woman who repeatedly stepped into the ring of fire with him, beside him, without fear or complaint.

"Why are you saying that? And why are you saying it now?" Owen looked at her again.

Clover took her time before their eyes met. "Because I know you, both sides. The side that fought for me to be free and the side that needs the flame, the same side that needs to be protected from other people. The musician who needs to leap." Clover didn't say the words very loud. Hell, she didn't even speak them with her eyes. But they were there in the cab, across her body and soul, from fingertips to toes. "It's okay to leave her behind. You're not a bad person, Owen."

"Yes, I am, Clover. And I'm getting worse because I can't say goodbye to her. I should. I should run from Alice and let her live a new life. A safe, perfect little life with her perfect little family. But I can't. And it's worse than you know." The truck came to a stop at the red light before the entrance to the freeway, and Owen pulled his body to the side as his right boot was placed upon the dashboard. The angle was awkward with the steering wheel pressing against his leg, but he didn't care.

In a moment, his sock was down, laces untied enough, and with a single strong pull, the tongue of the boot and side folded back to reveal the skin of his ankle.

"What am I looking at—" Clover's voice cut off as she spotted the mark.

A perfect circle, no more than a large coin, and a faded shape in the center that could just be seen.

"What is that?" she asked.

"You know what it is," he accused.

"No, I don't," Clover said in defense, but this time there was fear, and to Owen's way of thinking, the fear was well-founded.

"Yes, you do. It happened after Alice killed Kerogen as we were leaving the Devil's bridge. I jumped over his dead body, and in the middle of my jump, something I didn't see and that shouldn't have been there reached out and touched me, causing me to trip midair. A couple of days later, this mark showed up."

He dropped the boot back to the floor as the light turned green.

Clover didn't move, didn't speak as the truck gathered speed. Owen double-checked to make sure Jessie and the van were right behind him.

More than a few blocks but less than a mile later, Clover spoke again, and this time her words were crisp and to the point. "Do you want me to cut off your leg? I'll do it. I'll do it, Owen. Max and the others shouldn't watch."

His body tightened, and he gripped the steering wheel with more force than he needed. He looked to his right. Clover sat staring his way with the old gym bag of medical supplies in her lap, and he knew without a single doubt she would do it. His number two would cut off his leg if he said yes.

"Not yet. We need to know more about the mark. I need to know more about the rules that surround it and if there is some other way to get it off me. Mostly we need to know what it means, and soon."

"Okay," Clover said as she double-checked the bandage she'd wrapped around his shoulder.

Owen turned the radio back on. Clover settled in as cars passed behind them, and they all shifted along the highway.

"The Devil's coin?" Clover said after a time.

"It looks that way to me."

"You're screwed, Owen."

"Yes, Clover. I am."

Clover didn't respond, and Owen took this opportunity to ask a question that had been nagging at him. "Were you going to use an axe?"

"Chainsaw," Clover said instantly.

"Right."

"I figure it's faster."

Owen couldn't help but picture blood and bone being shot against the glass of his windshield. His blood, his bone in neat little chunks. "And you really would have been able to . . ." Owen didn't finish the question. Instead, he let the words fade as he held the uncomfortable feeling of chained steel chewing its way through his body.

Clover spared him a glance that said, *Don't question me.*

"That's rock-star status," Owen said, impressed.

"You bet your ass it is."

"Okay," Owen said, slowly closing the conversation.

"Okay."

The music played, and the truck ate up miles as they both thought and listened. Some time passed, but it was Clover who asked the question that had been haunting his thoughts for weeks.

"Who do we ask to help us? Not Mara, Damon or Cornelius."

"Nope, I can't ask them. They made it clear they do

things their way. And, well, Cornelius is helping Alice find her priest." Mara and the rest had kept too many secrets. "This is my burden, and I'll solve it my way this time."

"So, we are going to do something foolish. After all, that's your way."

Owen smiled. "Absolutely."

Chapter Four

Liam Davis stood tall and comfortable in the low-lit glow coming off the ice machine of his kitchen's fridge. The world was not so simple, not easy. He filled the kettle with tap water from the sink, and as quietly as he could, he set the half-filled kettle over the stove. *Tick, tick, tick*, a repeating spark in the silence of his home. The gas burner caught and lit orange and blue with a glowing heat that didn't penetrate the anxiety he was feeling.

"Alice?" Dede called out with fear from the comfort of his own soft recliner.

Pain and worry both ran thick in his wife's voice, twisting his heart as he turned and hurried toward her. Liam moved as fast and as silently as he could from the kitchen to the living room. To his wife, his first love. He was by her side within in a few heartbeats.

Strong, kind and beautiful, both in the soul and of the

body, with eyes of green, his wife held his full attention as she fought to come out of the sleep she had been in.

"She is safe, dear. Alice is in her room. I was only making myself a cup of tea." His voice was calm, reassuring. With each syllable, he pushed for his wife to relax, needing her to stay settled.

Liam moved beside the old recliner so as to whisper and soothe as he looked his wife over.

Dede sat with her favorite throw covering her legs and lap. The chair was rotated ever so slightly from its normal position so Dede could watch. Not the television in the corner, where they had watched movies while eating popcorn, but instead the long hall that held the doors to both children's rooms.

"Alice? And Kendra?" Dede asked. Her voice was still full of sleep but low in the quiet house.

"Both girls are fine, safe and sleeping soundly. I just checked on them." Dede's eyes were wide and blinking the fog away. She hadn't been getting much sleep, and with the news that Alice was going to finally tell them both what happened all those years ago and where she had been, he was afraid Dede wouldn't get any rest this night.

"Are you sure? I thought I heard something."

From under the blanket, she pulled out a small screen that was designed to spy on babies. Using the night vision built into the camera that still overlooked Kendra's bed, Dede double-checked to make sure their youngest was safe and secure in her room.

In all honesty, the camera and monitor were past their date of use, as Kendra was now almost four years old. But trying to convince Dede of such a thing was far beyond the capacity of his own heart. Not after Alice had been taken away from them at the age of nine and only come back three weeks ago. They had barely survived the seventeen years, and only by the grace of God had she come back to them.

Too much pain and loss lived inside his wife, inside his home.

The light of the little screen shined brightly in the darkness of the living room. And he couldn't help but check for himself. There, its small three-inch black-and-white screen showed his youngest daughter sleeping soundly—her favorite stuffed bear in hand. A small red light beside the screen continued to blink, indicating that once again, his youngest daughter was snoring as Kendra was prone to do.

Dede breathed out, and after twenty-seven years of marriage, Liam could hear her voice in the exhale: *Kendra is where she is supposed to be.*

"I just checked on Alice. She is sleeping too. Why don't you go to bed, my love, and I'll keep an eye out tonight?" Liam repeated.

"No, I am fine. What time is it?" Dede said as her hand pulled the blanket to the side and she stretched out her back.

"It's about three forty-five in the morning. Really, I have some reading I want to catch up on, and you need to get some real rest. The girls aren't going anywhere. Go on, honey. I will keep watch and drink my tea."

"Are you sure?" There was weight in the question, a hard, rotating weight that could mean the difference between his wife getting much-needed sleep or watching her push her body and heart to the breaking point once more.

"Very sure. Go to bed, dear. They are safe. I'll keep an eye out." Liam held out his hand for the monitor, doing his best not to overstep or underpush.

Gently, she handed the monitor over, but he watched as her eyes tracked once more to the screen.

"She is safe. They are both home and sleeping," Liam lied.

"Okay, I'll be up at five," she said, rising to her feet. She caught the small throw blanket and slipped it back over the chair before it could fully fall to the carpeted floor.

"How about six o clock?"

"Maybe," she said, distracted as she looked again to the long hall that held both doors to either bedroom.

A muscle in the back of his throat tightened as, there in the dark room of his home, he watched the woman he adored stare with a will that was too pure, too soft and filled with too much love. A love that held too much pain.

"I think I will just check on Alice before I go."

"De, I just peeked in, and she is sleeping. We don't want her to know we are spying on her." Liam's voice was soft and pleading.

Their worlds were upside down since Alice had come home. Alice wasn't a little girl, not the nine-year-old who had disappeared, but instead a full-grown woman at twenty-six.

Back then, she and her mother had gone to practice a solo at the church. Hours later, there had been an explosion, and Dede had barely made it out alive. She had cuts and bruises, but Father Jacob hadn't been so lucky. Father Patrick and Alice had never been found. This was seventeen years ago. Seventeen years she was gone without a trace. And now she was here. Prayers were answered, even if they had taken a very long time.

"We are not spying," Dede said. "I just like knowing where she is."

"You heard her today; she's not going anywhere." He didn't shove. Instead, Liam let his wife make the right decision.

It took a moment, an internal struggle, then Dede turned back away from the hall, toward their room on the other side of the house. Instinctively Liam reached out a hand, and Dede did the same. The contact was light and quick, with a small loving squeeze as their fingers touched one another—a gesture they had done a thousand times and, God willing, they would do ten thousand more.

Liam stood in the dark with the glow of the monitor

shining up from his hand as Dede finally went to bed. A victory, not always found. So many times she had refused to leave his chair. She refused to stop watching the hall and the two simple white-painted doors that held her heart.

Bubbling from the kettle had him moving back to the kitchen in a hurry. A soft click of his forefinger and the light of the monitor went out.

Kendra is safe.

Quietly and slowly, he made himself a cup of tea. His eyes once more looked out into the blacked-out backyard of his home. The square window over the sink granted a view of shadows and obscure shapes—outlines of trees and kids' toys.

His mind drifted as he waited for the water to steal caffeine from the leaves of the tea. All the while, he stared into the depths of darkness his backyard was covered in.

This was a good home. A solid home. It'd made sense to buy the month before they got married. Back then, Alice had already been on her way, and they had borrowed money from both Dede's parents and his own. Of course, he had paid both back the money he had borrowed. Money made sense, he always said. Even back then. After all, money was simply numbers. And numbers and columns were akin to his way of thinking. They didn't lie, and if one was quiet and listened, the numbers said a lot more than people liked to admit. He could be quiet, and he enjoyed listening.

Numbers were simple, always adding up when you had all the information. But now, his home didn't add up. Alice was home, but where had she been all that time, and why hadn't she come home? This was the mystery that had been eating at both him and his wife. An accounting untold.

His eyes tracked from left to right and back again as he stared out into the shadows. He felt the tears slide down his face and didn't mind. Seventeen years. Alice had been only nine when she disappeared in the terrible explosion. Five years ago, he had planned a fake funeral. A last-ditch effort to save Dede. Kendra had followed not long after, thank the Lord. And now Alice was home.

But is she? Will she stay? His own thoughts chased his mind as his eyes searched and tracked the darkness for answers.

Liam let his mind be free as he stared out into the backyard where Alice had once played as a little girl. Where she had called out, "Daddy, push me higher. Daddy, look at this." Over and over again, she had called out until one day she wasn't there. Nine years old.

More tears fell as he remembered and watched.

He left his cup of tea on the counter. He hadn't really wanted it anyway. Coffee was more his style, only he hadn't wanted to open the fridge where he kept his grounds, as every time he opened the door, the light inside would brighten the kitchen, and anyone looking in from his backyard would be able to see the house wasn't asleep.

Liam walked down to the small door beside the pantry and quietly entered his two-car garage. One bay held an old van Alice had bought with cash, a thick lock securing the sliding door. The van, too, held secrets—his daughter made a point of keeping the door securely shut.

With a pajama sleeve, he wiped away the tears and took a water bottle out of a half-open case on the floor. He set the bottle up on a ledge before grabbing the small ladder and opening it up in front of a high, dusty shelf.

A few moments later, Liam took the small plastic item he had retrieved from storage, along with the water bottle, and, clad only in his pj's and slippers, stepped out of the garage and into the night air. He was out of time. Alice would break her silence tomorrow, and there were things that needed to be said before she did. His family's future depended upon it.

Shadows crawled across his skin as he moved as silently as he could, not wanting to wake his wife.

I wish I was greater than I am, he thought.

Liam walked from the side of the house, past two motion-detecting lights that didn't turn on—even though they should have—past the fenced-in pool, heading toward the barbecue that overlooked the small playhouse and still swing set. He covered the length of his home until he reached Alice's closed window.

There were secrets in his house. Not nefarious secrets but secrets based on love. Secrets based on protection. He had never checked on Alice, as he had told Dede he had. For he had known his oldest daughter had not been in her room asleep but in the backyard. She had been cloaked in shadows as she ran and moved, attacking the night air as she had done every night for the last three weeks. Liam had been watching his daughter for a number of nights, and he waited until she was done and headed back to her room.

A slight double tap on the cold glass of Alice's window, and he waited. And waited.

The window rose up, and he inwardly exhaled.

His security system had been a premium purchase, and yet there were no alarms going off. It meant Alice had bypassed the security somehow, just as he had suspected.

"Dad?" Alice asked.

His title, his name, didn't sit right in his ears. Not that they didn't have a connection, but it was offbeat even though they were both trying.

Seventeen years stolen. She's a twenty-six-year-old woman now. With a lifetime of history I don't know. I wasn't there for her.

"Hey, my daughter. I thought we could have a chat. Why don't you grab a sweater or something and come on out."

"Is everything okay?" Alice asked with a voice that said she wouldn't need him to handle a problem if there was one.

"Everything is fine. I just wanted to talk with you." Another lie, and they both knew it. If that were true, he would have knocked on her door, not the window that was supposed to be closed and locked at night.

Liam stepped away, giving Alice room to come out. She moved like pouring water, sliding so gracefully and controlled, it was difficult to see the child she had been.

This time he did fight a tear from falling.

"Come on, let's just take a walk." His voice was staccato, as if he couldn't find a rhythm. He hadn't missed the evidence of sweat around her hairline. Proof enough of her working out in the night.

"What is that in your hand?" Alice asked.

"It's your fishing box. I'll explain," he said as he handed over the water bottle. "I thought you could use a drink."

Liam wanted to be gentle, wanted more than anything for Alice to know she was loved and that this home was her home, now and forever. But a look passed between him and his daughter as he handed over the water bottle.

I know, he said with his eyes.

"Thank you," Alice said, accepting the water bottle.

Slowly she unscrewed the cap and took a deep drink as they walked in the soft starlight. Each step took them farther away from the house and closer to the fence line.

"Dad?" Alice asked. If there was a plea in her voice, one had to search deep to hear it.

The woman before him never seemed to be afraid.

"I was supposed to have more time with you. Years and years, Alice. It was supposed to be me and you and your mom. We were doing really well before it happened. Before the explosion at the church."

Liam took his time, searching the shadows for his next words as he searched his heart and the past.

"As a father, as a dad, you want your little girl to be safe and healthy and good. And after that, all I wanted was to be a better man so I could do everything you needed me to do."

A small tree branch in the grass broke and poked up into his foot, and Liam simply closed his eyes and continued forward. "God help me, I was supposed to have more time with you." He pushed on. "More time for trust and love and faith. More time to teach you that above all, you can trust me. You can believe in me to have your back no matter what happens." Liam couldn't keep his voice from breaking.

"Dad, it's okay. It wasn't your fault or anyone else's. I can tell you that for sure," Alice said.

"No, look." He held up the tiny pink tackle box made for a little girl long ago.

In the soft starlight, he watched her face shift into confusion. "I am sorry, I don't remember that."

"I never gave it to you." Liam let out his breath, knowing he had to do the impossible. His home had too many lies.

His hand rested on her shoulder as they came to a stop. He squeezed once and looked into his daughter's eyes. In a soft whisper of love, he spoke.

"I was supposed to have more time to tell you I'm your dad. Over and over. Again and again, I was to tell you we are family, you and I. And then I was to give you this. This little pink tackle box. And then I was going to take you fishing, away from your mom. Just you and I." He let out his breath and pulled in the cold night air. "But it didn't happen, and now you're a grown woman, and we don't have the time." He let his hand fall away.

Taking a step forward along the path they were traveling, Liam was thankful when Alice followed.

"Dad," she said behind him, "I will go fishing with you. I can't say you will want me to after I tell you and Mom the whole story. But we can go fishing. It's not a big deal. I already know a little about it. We are fine."

"I don't fish, Alice. Never have and have never wanted to. But thank you for the offer." Liam knew his voice was cold, but he couldn't help the loss inside his chest from frosting his words as he searched for an impossible key to relate what he wanted to relate.

"I don't understand. Is this because I snuck out of the house? I just wanted some fresh air, and I stayed in the backyard. That can't be that big of a deal?"

"You're twenty-six years old, and your mother and I feel you can do anything you want. Anything. But, Alice, when it is just you and I, please don't lie to me."

Alice started to talk. And Liam cut her off.

"I know you're doing it for us, Alice. Why you waited to tell us what happened to you. It's because you are protecting us. It's for your mom. It's for me. Even your little sister, Kendra. But not telling is its own form of a lie. Isn't it? Just like you did now. Alice, you weren't out here for fresh air."

"You saw me?" Alice said with conviction.

"I have very good eyesight. Once I knew there was something to look for, it didn't take long." Liam gave a small smile, but there was no joy within it. "Between you and me, I thought it was your boyfriend, Owen. A couple of nights back, I watched for him, thinking to give him a piece of my mind."

"It wasn't Owen."

"No, it wasn't. Your boyfriend is far more straightforward, or so I found out today."

"Dad, I . . ." She trailed off. Unable to talk about the secrets she held deep inside.

Liam decided to change tactics. "Did your mom ever talk to you about the day we met?" Talking about his past had him relaxing a little.

"You were high school sweethearts?" Alice said.

"We were. At fourteen, I was besotted, completely taken away by her at first sight. I was young and didn't know anything. And she has this sparkle. I see it in you too. Like God gave you a little piece of the sun that can't help but shine through." Liam swallowed. "Never forget, this is your home, and we love you," he said quickly, then continued on before Alice could turn away. "Well, it was the first day of school when I came across your mom. We said hello. And I asked her what her first class was, and she said it was music class, of all things, and I said, 'Great, that is my first class too.' And I asked to walk with her."

Liam gave a weak smile, remembering the audacity of his youth.

"Now, what I am about to tell you, your mother doesn't know. So we go to class, and I sit next to her. And one by one, the teacher asks people what instrument they play, followed by a request to give a small demonstration of their skill. Now, I'm in the class sitting beside her, and I don't have an instrument, and he isn't calling my name because I don't belong in the class. One by one, people are saying, 'Here,' and then playing a little something. With each call, there are fewer and fewer students to go. I am getting more and more worried.

"I had a choice, so I had decided I would play the piano because that was what your mom played, and I wanted to spend more time with her, and it made sense to show up without an instrument if you played the piano. Simple, right?

"So, your mom's name is called, and De goes down the steps to take her seat at the piano." Liam's voice drifted back, remembering. "She played like an angel. No joke, it was as if her music captured me and my heart, and I was just stolen. I am not kidding—hook, line and sinker." Liam tapped the tackle box. "De finished playing, and I told her how well she had done. I remember the red cheeks and other kids looking at me funny, and I simply didn't care. More kids were called and played, and I just sat there staring at her. Finally, the teacher asked if there was anyone he had missed. Your mom, always so helpful, spoke up on my behalf.

"So, I gave the teacher my name, and I walked down toward an instrument that in my lifetime, I had never touched. I mean ever. I was sunk. I sat at the keys, and I thought to myself, 'Well, Liam, the jig is up, might as well go out with a bang so the girl of your dreams never forgets you.' And I dropped all ten of my fingers on the keys. The sound that traveled up through the air was dreadful.

"But something in me shifted, and my smile faded. And I remember stroking a single key once, and then twice. It was like a bird calling through my touch. I know now it was simple C. But there in that moment, in my mind, the sound shifted. Took on a shape. Before I knew what I was doing, my fingers were stroking other keys, both exploring and building something . . . something special.

"Every once in a while, your mom still calls me a wild man for the way I banged around, then created something soft and touching. She still doesn't know I had never played an instrument until that day. So, you see, daughter, I know you have secrets because I have secrets. Long ago, I planned to take you on fishing trips where we didn't fish, but instead I told you all about my secrets. Secrets I have never shared with your mother or anyone else. Secrets that can harm people who weren't born into them and can't understand."

"Father?"

In answer, power came to Liam's call. He used all his will and strength to call it forth until a small black tentacle shaped up out of his hand like sprouting oil. Carefully he adjusted until a ray of starlight caught the ethereal energy. "This is your home, no matter what or who you are. Never are you going to be alone again. But if someone is coming for you, then I need to know. I need to be ready."

Alice took in a breath as she watched the small tentacle of ethereal power sprout out of her father's hand. A cold shock shifted into something warm.

"You're an etherealist?" she asked her father in shock. Questions swirled in her mind far too fast for her to grab on to.

I never considered, not really.

"Is that the name for it? Etherealist? I never learned. Long ago, I decided to just keep it to myself. I had to find ways of dealing with what was inside me, and it was difficult, but in time it started to fade. Then you were born. I had hoped, but then you were so talented at singing and music."

"I can't believe it. You are an etherealist. You have ethereal magic," Alice said.

"I am right, aren't I? Alice, you're like me? And you disappeared because you are like I am? You have this power, and that is why you were taken away?" Liam asked.

"There is a long story. A long story, and it ends with me no longer being a little girl. Or a good one." Her words caught in her throat now.

"Hey, look at me."

Alice raised her eyes from her father's hand and the proof of his gift, but it was the overwhelming shame and pain within him that struck her.

"You will always be my little girl. I don't care what you did. I don't. Are you in danger? Are we in danger? What am I supposed to be doing?"

"No, nothing. Not anymore, I don't think." Alice couldn't help but pull with her eyes, demanding he understand. "There was nothing you could have done, and it's over."

"It's over." Liam rolled the words over. "So, you were in danger, but not anymore?"

"Yes," she said.

"Okay, okay. Whatever you decide to tell your mother and me tomorrow, I want you to know this is your home. And, Alice? For me, the world I live in, this world is your mother, your sister and you. Everything is that simple. I have seen the other things out there, and if you're in danger . . . How do I say this? I have a shovel, and I know how to use it. Do you understand me?"

Confusion shifted within Alice. She wasn't sure what her father was saying.

A shovel was used to dig holes or fill them in. Then it hit her like ice water down the back. Her father, Liam Davis, a man who by all accounts lived simply, who had never hurt a single person in his adult life, was offering to help her bury whoever needed to be buried.

Alice tossed her arms around his neck.

"He's dead, Dad, and never, ever coming back. The monster who took me. He's dead and gone. I am so sorry it took me so long. I couldn't come back until I killed him. But he's dead."

Alice felt the tears coming, and she couldn't hold them back any longer. Her body shook and her father squeezed tighter.

"It's okay. It's okay. You are safe now. You are safe now, and this is your home."

CHAPTER FIVE

DAYS UNTIL A+O

"Owen?" Max said as he unfurled himself from the blanket around his legs and the jacket pressed into a ball against the glass of the passenger seat door.

"Yeah, Max."

"This doesn't look like the Golden Gate Bridge. Where are we? And do you have any coffee left?"

"This is the Bay Bridge. And that," he said, pointing across the water toward the tall towers, "is San Francisco."

Max shifted, his socked feet touching down as he straightened himself up. About halfway across Nevada, Clover had changed seats with Max at one of the stops for fuel and food.

"I thought we were going to take the Golden Gate Bridge? I'm confused."

"Look, it's simple. You place your left hand up like you're going to give a high five, then make a fist." Owen stuck his left hand in the air and closed his five fingers. "Now stick out your thumb. Your hand is San Francisco, and your thumb is the Bay Bridge, connecting Oakland to San Francisco."

"And where is the Golden Gate Bridge?" Max asked.

Owen uncurled his left pinky and pointed it up. "The Golden Gate Bridge connects north and south."

"Okay, how long have you been up again? And where did we land on that coffee?"

"I've been up for maybe twenty-six hours. As far as coffee, I'm empty. There's a warm, flat soda in the bag. I don't recommend it, but . . ." Owen trailed off as Max reached into the bag. "It's clear you don't care about that."

"Anything happen while I was asleep?" Max asked as the truck bounced over a small bump.

"Hit a little traffic, but it cleared up. We made solid time. See, over there are the piers. You can get almost anything you want there. The food is fantastic. And before you ask, yes, they have coffee. Max, I think you're going to like this city. I spent only a couple of weeks here last time, but it's got this up-and-down vibe to it."

"I can't wait," Max said as he looked up at the support for the bridge passing overhead.

Owen picked up the phone and checked it for incoming messages. Seeing it blank, he set the device back down.

"No word yet?"

"I was told the invitations would be by the Grand Hotel no later than noon today. It's only just after ten. I'm thinking we go park the cars and grab a bite to eat." Owen slipped on his blinker and moved lanes to the right.

"Hey, there is no reason we all need to come with you, right? To deliver the invitations? It seemed like a 'Mara's adoptive son' thing and that it doesn't require a lot of heavy lifting?"

"You're ditching me already? We just got to the city."

"Jessie is pretty pissed at you. Clover and I were talking, and we thought maybe it would be better to take him around the sights rather than trail after you all day."

"Really," Owen said.

"Yeah, well, Clover and I do talk sometimes, and we just thought it would be best."

"No, not that. I mean Jessie is that pissed at me."

"Clover and I think Jessie might have had a crush on Daphne."

"What? No, he didn't. He was treating her like a kid sister. And she's only eighteen."

"Yeah," Max said, backing his single word with a face that said, *Put the pieces together.*

Owen swore, then tapped the steering wheel. "Wait, so you think he is into Daphne and—what?—Jessie has been secretly waiting until she was a little older before he took a shot at dating her?"

"No. I don't think he was aware of how deep his attachment to her was until the other night. No, that's not even true. I still don't think he knows. Jessie is like most of us. A little lost, and there was a connection between the two of them. And now, with the connection separated, he's a little more lost. Add in the pressure that has been building between you and him over music stuff and, yes, I think a little time where he's not following you around all day could help."

Owen checked his rearview mirror, and there, right behind him, was his best friend driving the beat-up van. "Sure. Take him anywhere you want. Get him a shave or a haircut, or just take him shopping. There are some crazy cool shops here. Get him a jacket that doesn't say, 'East Coast prep school.'"

Max let out a laugh. But Owen couldn't feel it.

"We have extra cash. Let Clover know it's cool to spend some. When I'm done hand-delivering these invitations, I'll meet up with you at a place called Whiskey Jack's. You ever heard of it, Max?"

"What?" Max said, but his words were soft and distant. Owen looked over and noticed Max was leaning forward in his seat, just staring up at the city as it came closer and closer.

"Max, are you listening? Whiskey Jack's. It's an old blues spot that was revamped a couple of years ago. Have you heard of it?"

Max didn't answer. Instead he sat at the edge of his seat, and his eyes seemed to glaze over. Owen could feel his friend was starting to breathe hard.

Owen reached out a hand, grabbing Max by the shoulder. "Max. What is going on?"

"Owen, it's beautiful." His voice was slow and strange, like he had to work hard in order to speak.

"Max, what's—what are you talking about?" Owen took his eyes off the road and noticed Max wasn't sitting anymore, instead he was leaning forward and was perched just above the seat.

"The city. It's covered with streams of magic, like rainbows or diving fish. I have never seen anything like it. Do you see it?"

"No, Max. I don't know what you are talking about," Owen said with concern.

"It's amazing. Such small strands shoot up like fireworks then curve back down toward the ground. Oh, I can feel them. It's like a big magic trick, and they want to talk."

Owen put on his blinker early for their exit, allowing Jessie enough time to see he was taking the upcoming off-ramp. "I don't know what you are talking about. I can't see anything out of the ordinary."

"I wish you could see this. Oh, the buildings are starting to get in the way. We need to go somewhere higher." Max turned his body and leaned forward so his head was almost touching the glass of the windshield.

"Max, back up, I can't see. You're blocking my right side." But Max didn't back up. Instead, he struggled to see higher as Owen took the off-ramp that would swing them in the direction of the piers.

Owen thought he heard a whine like a small animal come out of Max, but he couldn't be sure. Then his friend shook his head and sat back in his seat.

"Are you okay?"

"No. That was the craziest thing I have ever seen. Owen, the whole city seems to have tiny rainbows of ethereal magic running through the air, and it's unbelievable. I don't know what it does."

"What do you mean?"

"Based on what I just saw and felt, this city is amazing."

"Amazing? Are we in danger?"

"I don't think so. The strands of magic are skinny. I'm not even sure the magic is strong enough to shift dice. But I need to see more of it before I can fully understand what is going on. It's like someone painted the air with it. Like a giant rainbow spider."

"It just spouts up out of the ground, or is it coming from a person?"

"I think it's the ground, but it could be people, I guess? Not one person. It would have to be hundreds. You didn't see it?" Max shifted in his seat, and this time he looked out the passenger window.

"I have never seen anything like what you're describing. And I sure didn't see it the last time I was here."

"Maybe it's too small for you. Too subtle," Max said, giving a shrug. "Like when I do the magic tricks, the ethereal energy is just woven too small."

Owen followed the way until the street sign said EMBARCADERO and the water of the bay was on their right as they headed north toward the Ferry Building. The light ahead turned green, and Owen eased his truck down the road.

"Owen, the giant art installation right over there. Pull the truck over. I can see them again."

"You mean the two-story sculpture of an arrow and bow sticking out of the ground? Max, you're not acting like yourself, and your eyes are starting to glaze over again."

"Just pull the truck over. I want to see the magic up close. It's going into the arrow."

"Max, I'm about to turn the truck around and get you the hell out of this city until we understand this better."

"Owen, I'm fine. I just want to see what's going on. Come on, man. How often do I ever really ask you for something? Pull the truck over."

Reluctantly, Owen slipped into a parking spot that read PERMIT ONLY. Before Owen could shift into park, Max's door was open and he started to run. Jessie had to hit the brakes hard to avoid Max and the passenger door as he eased into the tight parking spot beside the truck.

"Max, damn it, get back here!" Owen said, moving as fast as he could to remove the keys and slam his door shut in pursuit.

"What is going on?" Jessie called out the window.

Owen was already running and could just hear Jessie swearing and Clover running behind him as they chased Max over the cement and grass, until everyone came to a stop. They stood below the giant fifty-foot bow in the ground with a notched arrow tip buried down in the dirt.

Max had one palm up to the arrow shaft, with a small space between his hand and the art piece.

"Max, don't move. I don't know what's going on, but this is getting real. Just don't move, and don't touch that arrow shaft," Owen said, slowly moving closer.

"Owen, there's a hundred little lines of power all wrapping around this shaft. How can you not see it? It's amazing and alive. There is power in the little strands. Tiny little threads, but when they all come together, I can almost see a pattern."

Owen couldn't see Max's face, but with each word Max spoke, his voice seemed to change, slowing down and becoming less Max-like.

"What the hell is going on, Owen?" Clover said beside him.

"Something is up with Max. He says the whole city has magic arcing over the buildings, and some of the lines connect to this thing."

"To the arrow?" Clover asked.

"Yeah," he finished, then raised his voice. "Come on, Max, I told you not to touch that. Take a step back because you're scaring the hell out of me. Come on, Max. Back up!"

"Scared? I'm not scared. See?" Max said.

Fear, raw and real, drove deep into Owen's heart as Max looked back, and Owen could see a drastic difference in him. Max's face was glazed gray, and his eyes wore a gray-white film over them that seemed inhuman.

Clover moved at the same time Owen did, but neither was faster than Max as he leaned forward and pressed his palm against the twenty-four-foot arrow sticking out of the ground.

Max flung his head up to the sky and his mouth opened wide, but no sound rang out as he screamed in silence.

Owen had already pulled ethereal magic into his arms and legs. And he closed the distance that had separated him and Max in just a few heartbeats. Without a second thought, Owen shoved Max with enough strength that the kid should have landed ten feet away. But he didn't. Owen's breath exploded out of his lungs with the unexpected force that drove back his way.

"What do we do?" Clover asked in a panic.

"I'm not sure. It's anchored him in place. Try pulling his arm away."

"Max, let go!" Clover called as she pulled with enough force that her shoes slipped over the cement.

Owen swore as he noticed more and more color fade from Max's face. "This isn't working. I can't get his arm to budge. Why aren't we being affected?"

The question shifted the pieces of the puzzle around in his mind as he stared at his friend.

"It's his connection to magic. We all know Max works differently than us. Subtle tricks, and he said this was done with tiny hairs of magic. It's connected to him now. Connecting his magic to this thing," Owen said in a rush. Then, without pause, Owen screamed in his friend's ear, hoping to penetrate whatever was truly going on. "Max! Close the lid on your magic. Break the connection. You have to close the lid. Shut it off as I taught you. Max, break the connection!"

Clover stopped pulling, and vaguely Owen was aware of Jessie just running up the small mount behind them, but his focus was on Max and looking for any change.

"Come on, Max! Shut the lid! Break the connection, damn you," Owen repeated.

"It's not working. Owen, what do we do?" Clover asked.

Owen looked from Max's open mouth to his arm to the shaft of the arrow in the ground and considered everything from ripping his friend's arm off to ripping out the art piece altogether. Though he wasn't sure he could do either with magic flowing through the two of them.

"I have to disconnect him. Sorry, Max."

"Owen, he's starting to shake. What's the plan?" Jessie called out as he came forward.

"I got it, stay back." Owen slipped around Max, coming up from behind and wrapping his arm under Max's chin in a classic chokehold.

"Owen?" Jessie asked, but Owen ignored the question.

And like a python with its next meal, Owen squeezed, placing pressure over the veins that allowed blood to flow freely to Max's brain. "Go to sleep, Max. I need you to go to sleep and disconnect."

As Owen whispered, nothing happened. Max didn't move, didn't blink or shift. And real, paralyzing fear drove deep into Owen's gut.

"Come on, buddy, go out," Owen said.

It happened in a blink. Max's tall frame just dropped.

And Owen dropped down with him, careful not to do more damage.

"Max!" Clover called. "Is he dead?" Owen could hear her panic.

"Check his neck," Jessie said, coming in, but Owen was already reaching out.

His fingers felt the pulse and his world narrowed to his fingertips. "He's alive. Son of a bitch!" Owen said, then swore some more as he stood up.

"Let me see him," Clover said while getting down low with Jessie to inspect Max.

"He looks like trash. His skin is pale, and his eyes look bruised, to say nothing of his neck, which is already turning purple. How hard did you have to squeeze?"

"You could have killed him. How hard were you squeezing, Owen?" Jessie said as he took note of Max's neck.

"As hard as I needed to. There was ethereal magic reinforcing his body. It was the only way I knew to disconnect him, and we're damn lucky it worked."

"Well, at least when he wakes up he can heal himself from all this. What the hell is that thing, and what happened? This can't be normal. We would have heard about it. Right?" Clover asked.

"Can anyone else see the thin strands of ethereal magic Max talked about?" Owen asked.

"I can't see anything like that," Jessie said with concern in his voice. "What happened exactly?"

"It started as we came over the Bay Bridge. All of a sudden Max was transfixed and said he could see tiny lines of magic dancing up over the buildings then arcing back down. He said there were a lot of them, and that they were pretty. But the closer we got, the less control he seemed to have. Then the building blocked his view of them until we came around it, and he became really focused on this." Owen pointed toward the art installation. "It happened fast."

"I can't see anything out of the ordinary with it, Owen. If it's ethereal magic, we should be able to see it too, right? Or at least feel it?" Clover asked.

"Not necessarily. Max isn't like us, and we all know it. His connection to ethereal magic is different. It's why he does magic tricks more and more, and less shaping music." Owen looked at his sleeping friend, then back at the art installation. "What if it's a trap or a giant trick? Do either of you feel different?"

"No. A little pissed, but that's not different," Clover said.

"So how do we beat this thing if it's only after Max, or connected to Max? Should we get him out of the city?" Jessie asked.

"We don't have time to get him out of the city. Look, Max was sort of in a trance before he touched that thing. If he wakes and wants to get back to it, and we stand in his way—say by forcing him into the truck—he might fight us with his ethereal energy."

Owen could feel the reaction from both Jessie and Clover.

"We can't fight him. Jessie said. What do we do?" Clover said.

"I don't know, but we have to do something; he's going to wake any second," Jessie said.

"I was trying to have Max close the lid on his well of magic."

"Yeah, I understood. So whatever this is," Clover said, pointing toward the giant art piece and the strands of magic she couldn't see, "won't be able to connect if his lid is shut."

"Right," Owen said.

"But, Owen, that's not easy to do. Most likely it will take Max time when he wakes up, so what if this thing grabs his control again before he can shut the lid over his well? We are back to Max being cooked alive right in front of us," Clover said.

Owen considered for a long moment.

"He's only going to be asleep for a few more seconds," Jessie said, looking from Max to Owen.

"When he wakes, he'll go for it again," Clover said. "What do we do?"

"I'm not taking any chances. This whole thing just scared the hell out of me. Move, Clover," Owen said as he made his way back over toward Max. "I won't lose Max."

Despite his words, Clover didn't move away. Instead, she sort of scooted over while keeping Max's head from the ground.

"I got him," Owen said, once more coming up behind Max as he sat down. "Help me adjust him," Owen added as he scooted closer.

Jessie swore before saying, "You're not going to do what I think you're going to do. Owen, that's messed up and dangerous, even for you."

"Shut up, Jessie. And grab Max's arm. He's going to wake up, and when he does, he's going to struggle," Owen said. "And I have to get this right," he said low under his breath.

"Wait, what are you about to do? Oh!" Clover said, nodding with understanding as she grabbed Max's free right arm and pinned it down with her whole weight. "This is not cool, but I don't see another way."

Owen wrapped his left arm around Max's chest. He was like a barnacle on Max's back. "Sorry, Max, but I won't lose you because I'm too scared to do the right thing." He couldn't help himself as he glanced toward Jessie.

Owen closed his eyes just as Max was starting to come to. Carefully he placed his right hand over Max's spine and followed it down toward his lower back until his hand settled over Max's well of ethereal magic.

Everybody, be it a We or an etherealist, had a well or a storage center inside their body. It was located low, around the spine and kidneys. Owen filled his mind and body with ethereal magic, coated his right hand and dug his fingers deep into Max's flesh, and then sent his will in with the magic to attack and overtake Max's well of energy.

Max let out a scream and his body convulsed, and still there was a clash of wills as every cell between Owen's claw and the well of magic called out in protest. But Owen and his magic were ruthless as they took command, forcing the ethereal magic inside Max's body to go a different way. To form a different path.

Time slowed for a moment, and Owen thought Max might have a chance to stop what was happening. Then Max's magic flooded out of his body and into Owen.

A pure, euphoric joy rushed into every nerve ending Owen held as he greedily took from his friend. It was a shock on an intellectual level—how much magic Max was storing. But also a sheer high as his body buzzed and tingled with Max's magic mixing with his own.

"Owen?" Clover called.

"You're draining him dry." Jessie shook Max, who had stopped struggling and lay limp like a rag doll. A man entirely under the control of Owen.

"I'm taking it all," Owen said. He had hoped to use a controlled voice, but his words rang in his ears with pleasure. Ethereal magic was the magic of the hereafter, and right now, his own well was flowing over with all of Max's magic. "As long as I stop right at the moment he's all out of ethereal energy, and I don't pull out the well itself, I won't kill him."

"That's enough. Owen, I think you are there."

"Just a bit more. I need him empty."

Jessie swore.

Owen could feel the anger and worry rolling off his friend.

Owen pushed aside every emotion of euphoria created by the ethereal energy rushing into his system and focused fully on the small sensation of Max's well of energy. Jessie was right: Too much and Max would die. Not enough and Max might be caught again.

I can do this. I will not lose another person I love.

It was a small shift in sensation, but Owen recognized it. "There," he said as he drew his hand away.

Jessie let go of Max's arm, and it dropped weakly to the ground. Clover slowly backed her weight off the other arm and Owen reached around to give his friend a combination hug and to help hold his body upright. It wasn't just magic he had taken, it was strength—the will to fight him. Max was beaten, but knowing his friend as he did, Owen knew it was a wound Max could climb back from.

"Owen?" Max asked with a low, scratchy voice.

"Yeah, buddy?" Owen asked, while looking for signs he had made a mistake and drawn too much.

"You took all my magic."

"I did. Can you see the lights anymore?"

No one spoke or moved as Max slowly—too slowly—raised his head to look from the ground up toward the giant art installation.

Max started to speak, and Owen felt as much as heard the cough come out of his friend. "No, I can't see them anymore. What happened?"

"We will figure it out. You're safe now. Just rest a second."

Owen sat with Max in his arms. He could feel the tall man's short breaths. All the while, his own skin itched with live ethereal energy running through it. And something else. Fear.

Owen felt the rise and fall with every breath Max took. As he replayed the moment he had cut off the withdrawal of ethereal energy, he asked himself, *Did I get it right? Will Max pay for another one of my sins?*

But Max's body did not start to shake or give any other sign of going into organ failure. Instead, the opposite was true: with each moment that passed, Max came back.

I almost lost another one.

Owen's body shook as his brother's death from long ago played out in his mind.

The last memory of his brother crystalized. The flames of angels had burned bright as they roared over the drum set and body.

Never again.

As the memory faded, he couldn't help but think of Alice and her absolute, unbending strength. His heart felt too big in his chest, and it was all he could do to hold still and take his next breath as he held Max while the others stood and watched.

CHAPTER SIX

DAYS UNTIL A+O

Alice sat at the kitchen table drinking coffee. Her father's newspaper decorated one corner of the table, and to her left, her mother folded a pile of freshly dried laundry from a wicker basket in the living room. Liam had taken her sister to preschool. He would be back soon, and rather than fill the room with idle chitchat, both she and her mother had settled for silence.

My dad is an etherealist, and he knows some of what happened. But how do I tell them both the whole story without giving up his secret? she asked herself. *How about, "Mom, Dad, I'm not an average human." Or, "Hey, guess what? I have superpowers. You want to watch me bend light around my body with a power called ethereal energy? It's basically magic. You know, the same magic as creation."*

Yeah, that's not going to work. She took another sip of coffee and looked at her mom.

Okay, I can do this. She started again. *"Mom, Dad, I love you, and what I am about to say is shocking, but I need you to trust that everything is just fine now. The church that I disappeared from did not blow up from a gas main. There was this guy—well, a creature called a level six We who had just tied my soul to his, forming a connection so strong only the greatest relics of another age could conceal it."*

No. This isn't working. Alice took another sip.

How about, "I'm not your little girl anymore. I can take a clean headshot from over three football fields while the target is in motion. However, I am far better at hand-to-hand. And right now, there is nothing more I want than to set up against someone who outweighs me by over two hundred pounds and watch his face turn into red paste."

Alice took a deep breath. *No, I shouldn't tell them that one.*

"Everything okay, Alice? You're breathing hard."

"Coffee is hot." *That, and I can't tell you that I'm a walking machine for violence. And I won't be taking your advice to become a chef. Even if I do have skill with a knife, because those are not the knife skills I like to practice. Only, I can't tell you that.*

Focus, Alice. Keep it simple.

"Oh, okay. Do you need some ice or something?"

"No, Mom, I'm okay. Thank you." *You don't have a neighbor who is bothering you, do you? I could break down their door and give them a good shake so that they know to leave you alone. Damn it. I'm losing it.*

"Of course, but try to be careful. I was also thinking we need to buy you some more pants and tops, and how are you doing with underwear? You didn't bring a lot of things in from your van." Her mother didn't care for her van and had made it known on more than one occasion.

"I'm good on clothes. Really, I'm fine."

I don't know where to start. The truth is, I was gone

from you for seventeen years, and I had to survive in a different world than you know or could ever understand.

Alice looked at the living room and thought about her past.

"Mom, what happened to the piano?"

"What, dear?" her mother said, looking up from folding clothes.

"You taught me to play the piano, and I remember you would give lessons right over there." Alice pointed toward the wall beside the fireplace. In the piano's place sat a tall green plant, and behind the plant, a framed picture of a red barn.

"We moved it into the garage a long time ago." Alice didn't miss the pauses her mother spoke with.

"It's in the garage? I didn't see it in there."

"Your father refused to sell it or give it away. It's in the far back, covered by some old blue moving blankets. There are some boxes stacked on top of it now. Why do you ask?"

If for no other reason than to distract her mother, Alice answered gently and honestly. "I don't remember a lot of my childhood, but I do remember playing music with you. I remember Dad laughing and you smiling when he would sing off-key on purpose. And I just wanted to know what happened to it."

"Well, like I said, it's in the garage."

"You mind if I go see it?"

"Alice, not all the memories with that piano are good ones. If you never learned to sing, you wouldn't have been in that church on that day that gas main exploded."

"Oh, Mom, the gas main never exploded. And you teaching me to play the piano and sing is not why I went away for all that time. There was one man—well, let's call him the asshole. None of what he did has anything to do with you teaching me to play the piano." Alice paused, unsure whether it was from the look in her mother's eyes or the stiffness in her own body. "Owen and his people believe music is God's greatest gift for us. That everyone has a song in their heart, and we are meant to share it. Not to trap the song and keep it in. But then, they are all just a bunch of crazy musicians." Alice looked across the room, her eyes meeting her mother's. "But it would be nice to hear you play. I used to dream about it, you sitting at the piano, and the fire warming me as it rained outside."

Dede took a deep breath, closed her eyes tight and then slowly stood up. "Well, come on. I'll need help with the boxes, and I don't think the two of us can manage to move the thing until your father gets back. But you can at least take a look."

"Okay. Thanks, Mom."

I love you so much.

They walked in a line down the hall and into the garage. The lights were turned on, and they started to file past the front of her van toward the more cluttered side of the garage. And suddenly some of the weight over her shoulders lifted. Perhaps it was the sight of her van or the fact that she had started the conversation with her mother. Or simply the knowledge that today was the day she would come clean. But, be it any of those reasons or all of them, the weight lifted, and she found herself standing taller and stronger with every step.

"It's right over here. Oh, your father's tools are in the way. I don't think one of the wheels works. He's complained about it. We will have to wait until he gets back."

Alice could see what her mother was talking about. The double-stacked stainless-steel toolbox was as tall as she was and was undoubtedly loaded down with heavy tools inside. "It's okay. We don't have to wait for Dad. I can move it."

"No, Alice, that's way too heavy. One of the wheels isn't working," she repeated. "I don't want you to get hurt."

Alice continued forward. "Mom, it's okay," she said, gripping the sizable stainless-steel box. Using ethereal magic to support her actions, Alice dragged the box out of the way and to the side.

"Alice, are you okay? That was too much! Are you hurt?"

This time Alice took the question slowly. Even her mother's voice felt different in her mind. She could see the piano of her childhood beneath two old blue packing blankets with boxes stacked neatly atop it. More, she could see the real concern in her mother's eyes—for her safety and good health.

Without thought, she reached out and gave her mother a deep hug. Her mother's arms were slow as she embraced her back, then squeezed even tighter. For a long-overdue moment, they held each other. Then, slowly, Alice pulled back. And looking her mother right in the eyes, she told the truth.

"Mom, you don't have to worry so much about me. The reason I was taken away, the reason this whole thing happened, was because I am different from a normal human. I am stronger, faster and have what we call ethereal magic running through my body. So I can do things like this."

She reached back and took a long, thick adjustable wrench from her father's tools. Alice placed it in both hands. Using her thumbs, she moved fast, and a loud snap raced through the air as the steel wrench broke in two.

Alice held up both pieces for her mother to see. "I'm telling you this because you deserve to know the truth. The truth of who I am, and that I am a woman who forged myself into a force that could come back to you. Though I am very sorry it took so long."

"Alice?" Dede asked, taking the two pieces of the wrench in her hand. "What are you telling me? I don't understand."

"I'm trying to tell you I'm different and strong, and that you don't have to worry quite so much about me. I am not a fragile thing that can be broken easily. In fact, if I am being honest with you, most of the time I am the one doing the breaking. That's part of who I am too."

The part I don't want to share with you.

Alice reached for one of the cardboard boxes atop the piano. Her mother's hand stopped her. "Show me again."

Her mother's voice was shaky but holding together as she spoke.

"You want me to break something else?"

"I want you to prove what you're saying so I can understand."

Alice looked at the broken wrench in her mother's hand and then glanced around the room.

"Mom," she said, focusing on her mother once more, "I was born an etherealist. When I was a child, my difference didn't show. It normally doesn't until the teenage years. Since I was taken away, I have trained to be what is known as a hunter. Meaning I am very, very good in a fight. Here is one of the ways I gain the upper hand."

Slowly Alice called forth her magic until, ever so slightly, it covered her skin. Her body reported the sensation as anything from a tickle to an itch, depending on the location. A second later and Alice bent the light around her body so that she disappeared from view.

She watched her mother's eyes go wide but didn't avoid her mother's hand as it shot out.

"Alice, where are you?"

"Right here. I'm right here, Mom," she said, pulling the magic back and away from her face. Her mother's hand had caught her arm and was squeezing hard, as if she could hold her in place forever. "When I have magic inside me, I can do impossible things. I'm strong and fast, and I can heal from wounds that would kill a normal human. But I also have had almost fifteen full years of training and practice to be a weapon. You can be my mom and you can worry. But what happened to me will never happen again. I need you to know that."

Alice watched as Dede looked at her face from one angle than another. Then looked for the rest of her body that wasn't visible to the naked eye.

"Mom, are you going to say something?"

"No," she said, looking up and down.

"Here," Alice said, pulling the magic back in so only a small amount was used up. "Is that better?" she asked as she was fully in the visual spectrum.

Again her mother didn't answer. She just continued to hold her arm with a viselike grip.

"Mom?"

"I want you to break another of your father's tools. Show me again," Dede said, letting go and opening a bigger drawer of the toolbox. "I want to see it again," she added.

Alice stood with a fresh cup of coffee in hand beside the black upright piano, now back in the living room beside the fireplace. Her mother was sitting on the little black stool, a dust rag forgotten in her lap as her fingers danced over the keys.

"Hey, honey," Dede said as Liam walked in and smiled first at his wife and then at Alice.

"What's going on here? Who decided to bring the piano back inside? And how did you get it in?" Liam asked.

"I'm guilty on both accounts," Alice said, raising her cup.

"What do you think, Liam? Alice asked, and I said it was okay."

"Oh, it's fine by me. You know I love your playing. And what's that bucket on the kitchen table? Is that from the garage?"

"Alice snapped and/or twisted twenty-two of your tools because she isn't a normal human," Dede said as her fingers continued to dance across the keys. "But she still needs to tell us the whole story."

"Is that right? You broke twenty-two of my tools, and you're not a normal human?"

"That is true," Alice said.

"Well, okay. But next time can you break the neighbor's

tools? I would love to see the Humphrees' faces when I give them back," he said as he went over to the bucket to see for himself.

"I'll replace them after our talk. I just thought it would be better to get the conversation out of the way first. Really, I have the money for them," Alice said as her father continued to pull halves of his tools out to inspect each one.

"No, you won't. I asked you to do it. And your father doesn't care. Do you, Liam?"

"Hardly at all. Just don't ask me to fix anything for a day or two. How did you do this, precisely?"

"She did it with her hands. Alice used the magic that is inside her. It can reinforce her muscles and protect her skin," Dede said, drifting her song to the higher notes as she spoke. "She plans to tell us all about it."

"Wife, are you okay?" Liam looked from his wife at the piano to back Alice's way.

"Don't look at me. She started acting like this after I showed her I could strengthen my skin against being stabbed."

"Stabbed?"

"Alice took your screwdriver, a flathead, and then pounded it down into her leg. Only it ripped her jeans, but her leg is fine. And look at the screwdriver. It's all bent."

"Alice?"

"It's true. That's what happened. Though working that sort of magic is difficult. It takes a lot of practice and effort to maintain." She pointed to her right thigh, where the torn hole could easily be seen.

"That's not what I am asking. Are you sure your mother hasn't taken anything? She is acting odd."

"I am not. I just found out my child is a superhero. Now that you are back, please come sit down so she can tell us the rest. I, for one, am tired of not knowing the full story."

"Okay, but I'm still not clear on how she broke my tools."

"She used her hand and snapped them. Honestly, Liam, sometimes I think you don't hear me on purpose."

"You can snap a tool with just your hands?"

"Toss me one of those broken ones, and I'll do it again for you. Yeah, that one in your hand will do. Toss it to me." The half wasn't very large, but it was large enough.

Alice caught the tool and set her cup on top of the piano in the same motion.

"Here, watch," she said, ethereal magic rushing back into her hands and arms.

A push, and once more the handle of a long crescent wrench snapped.

"The trick is to do it fast," she said, holding up both pieces for her father to see.

"Okay, well, that's new. Okay." Her father stuttered the words out but raised his eyebrows in a way that said he might be acting. After the conversation last night, it could be either way.

"Liam, don't make her feel awkward. If the Lord blessed her with a special gift, don't make her feel bad or odd about it. I'll get you some more tools. Now come sit down so we can finally understand what happened that day."

"Okay, first, you should both understand there are many of us out there. Many of us, and we are called etherealists, humans born with a well of ethereal magic inside them. As we grow, so too does our capacity and hopefully our control. But there is another type of being out there who can also use ethereal power. And they are called the We."

Alice took a breath as she looked down at her parents. *Just rip off the bandage.*

"Owen is like me, an etherealist. And about now, he would most likely prefer I tell you that not all the We are bad. That some We can be kind. But the one who came into the church that day was not so kind. His name was Kerogen and he was a level six We. And since the levels of We only go up to seven, that should tell you he was very powerful.

He wanted more power. So what happened in the church was he used magic and influence to force his soul to be bonded with mine, intertwined with mine, to the point where he could have control over me."

Alice held up both her hands to forestall any questions.

"Kerogen knew if he bonded my soul to his, he could use my magic for his purpose. But at the same time, as my well—or the amount of magic I could hold—increased as I grew older, his own well of magic would grow too. In other words, as I grew in power, he also grew in power. Making him very scary."

Alice remembered Kerogen at his full strength, only a few months back, and her body shuddered. He had been a walking monster of nightmare proportions.

"I remember going into the church that day after school. I was to sing a solo for the visiting cardinals. And so, Mom, you took me to Grace Cathedral to practice. Father Patrick met us at the door and let us come in. He wanted to practice at the organ, and we started. I remember the back of the room turning dark and a man standing in the center of the blackness. You turned to look at him, at Kerogen, and he used his influence to force you to sleep. I remember you dropping hard to the floor."

Alice could feel the fear, shame and guilt pulsating within her mother. It was so real and raw that she couldn't look away even as tears formed in the corners of her mom's eyes, then fell down her soft cheeks.

I am so sorry. It wasn't your fault. "There was nothing you could do. I know that with every fiber of my being. Kerogen was an asshole, but he was also a very, very powerful asshole, and there was nothing at all you could have done."

I need you to accept my words.

Alice simply held her thoughts in the air, hoping her mother could and would take them into her body and soul. For far too long, her mother had blamed herself, and the lie needed to end.

"What happened next?" Liam asked.

"Kerogen used his influence to force Father Patrick to keep playing. Only the song was one designed to break the natural order of things. He then forced me to sing with him." Alice gulped air, and for once wished she had something stronger to drink than coffee beside her. The song still haunted her at times. "It takes some time to bond two souls together. And when it was done, Kerogen was exhausted. But I never would have escaped him if it hadn't been for Father Jacob and Father Patrick. The older father had been taking a nap in the back of the church and must have woken up at some point. He distracted Kerogen, and Father Patrick picked me up and rushed me out of the church. The last thing I saw was Kerogen snapping Father Jacob's neck right there at the altar."

Alice listened to the shock that came out of her mother and then a whispered prayer. Her father simply tapped his foot, but his right hand was squeezing his knee to the point his knuckles were white.

"So, by pure luck, as Father Patrick comes running down the steps with me in his arms, the visiting cardinal's car pulls up. And it's seconds before we pull away, and as I look back, all the glass of Grace Cathedral is blown out, and the front doors fly out into the street. The next thing I know, I am on a private plane, and then I'm asleep. I simply couldn't keep my eyes open."

Alice glanced between her parents. She was looking for condemnation and scorn. For anything she might have missed. But neither spoke. Neither moved.

"I don't think I need to give every detail right now. In truth, I don't want to give you half of them." Alice breathed out her frustration and moved away from her perch at the piano.

This was all too much. Too much to share with her parents, and she wasn't half done.

"A secret part of the church trained me, and then I left them. So it was only Father Patrick and I, and together we hunted Kerogen down. We followed him from one country to another. I got close a couple of times, and he almost had me, more than once. Then I lost him, and finally I found he had come back to the United States. So a couple of months ago, Father Patrick and I followed."

"Where?" her father asked.

"What do you mean?" Alice asked.

"When you say you followed, where do you mean?" her father asked.

"I mean just down the road. We double-checked that you were safe, and then I went back on the hunt. I couldn't come in and see you. To Kerogen, you weren't on the map, and I didn't want to put the idea in his head. I had a good lead about an old We in Miami who would know where he was. So I went to Miami and left Father Patrick to keep an eye on you."

"Father Patrick was here? Watching us?" Dede asked.

"He's not a hunter, but he knows what he's doing. I trust him. He's been my North Star through all of this. He could have—should have—left me straight away. His soul wasn't tied, and he's not like me. And yet he stayed. He stayed by my side over and over again."

And I'm not out there hunting for him right now. It wasn't the first time she had the thought, but this time it felt different, and a truth inside shifted forward.

I have been staying here because they needed me to. My mother and my father were in pain, but now they know and can heal. But Father Patrick is in danger and needs me more. He's a good man.

"I wouldn't be here right now without him. Anyway, everything came to a head in Miami at Owen's adoptive mom's bar. There are details here, but we don't need to discuss them today. Just know I was stuck, and Father Patrick ran to the secret sect of the church for help. It didn't help. Kerogen came for me, but you should know he never left, and that's how I was able to come home."

She tried not to look at her mom as she shifted the full

story away from her being a killer, but she looked despite herself. She had to see.

Her mother's head shook from side to side, then she looked up, and her green eyes held Alice's. "What do you mean he never left? Is he dead?"

Alice stood with her feet apart, ready for anything, as her head nodded yes, needing her mother to understand.

"How? Wait, you killed him?"

Alice felt the hit from her heart to the back of her throat, and for a moment she couldn't speak as her mother's face scrunched in denial, and her head shook the word *no*.

I don't want to hurt you. I am so sorry, Mother. Alice was careful not to let her thoughts show. Not now. She could take this. She could own the hit. *I did what I had to. And burn my soul, I would do it again, a million times over.*

"Dede. It's okay. She didn't kill a man; she killed a monster. It was the only way for her to come back to us. Isn't that right?"

"I believe so. There might have been one other way, but it was out of my reach."

"You killed him. You, yourself. You did it."

Alice remembered driving her knife into the back of his head. For good measure, she had twisted the blade as hard as she could as his body fell forward.

"Of course I did. And if someone up there has a problem with it, I would invite them to spend some time down here with us. He was a monster, Mom, and he bonded my soul to his when I was just nine years old. It wasn't murder. I was being hunted."

"I don't know how I feel about this. The Bible tells us that murder is a sin, Alice."

"I know it does, Mom." Her words were as gentle and as soft as she could make them. "But it doesn't talk about the We. And it sure doesn't talk about my kind and our world, where life and death are always on the table. Where those who are weak are taken advantage of. I live by my own book even if it costs me my soul. Mom, it's the only way I know how to live. It was the only way I could come back home."

"I, for one, am very happy the bastard is dead."

"Liam!" Dede scolded.

"No, De, it's true. From everything I have heard, I am overjoyed he's dead and our daughter came home. And now we know what happened. This Kerogen was to blame for all the pain you and I and Alice experienced. I know it's difficult when you and I are not on the same page, but, Dede, I swear if I knew where his grave was, I would sneak out there and piss on it."

"This isn't a joke, Liam. She just confessed to a crime."

"No, I didn't."

Both parents turned back toward her.

"You killed a person. That's a crime, Alice."

"No, it's not. Because I didn't kill a person. There are different rules in the world I live in. In the world I have been living in." Alice looked from her parents to the room she was in. And for the briefest of seconds, it was as if she could look right through the walls and see the shape of the outreaching earth itself. "There is no body, no police report and no criminal justice department in the world that could convict me. Let alone a normal jail that could hold me. And the reason is I don't live in your world. I have just been visiting these last three weeks." Alice shook her body as if waking up from a dream.

Father Patrick needs me, and my parents now know the truth. They can heal.

Owen's words came back. *A lie will stop you in your tracks.* And she pictured his face and eyes and soft lips.

I live in a different world than this. It's time to move.

"Alice, this is where you belong," Liam said, speaking over his wife.

"Dad, it's okay. I had to come home. I had to come home," she repeated. "But this is your life. Mine is more like the Wild West, with a different set of rules than the world you live in. It might have been wrong to tell you the truth. Perhaps I should have lied. Because to ask you to understand how I live . . ." Alice trailed off, and her parents didn't speak.

"They—" She stumbled over what she was feeling, what she needed to say. "Ethereal power is what the magic was called before it came to Earth. They say it's the same power of creation. They say it is how the stars were born. That is the magic I have inside me. I love you both so much. But I have to go back out there. Now that you know I'm alive and safe. I have to go get Father Patrick. I'm sorry if this hurt you today. I want you both to know I love you so much, and it was wonderful to meet Kendra."

Both parents came to their feet, but Alice was already heading toward her room to gather her things.

"Wait a moment, you're not leaving," Dede said, and her father said, "Alice, you can't go."

"It's okay," she said, knowing the words were true. Her mother and father had the truth of what happened. But Father Patrick still needed her. The simple fact she had let someone else take on the responsibility was wrong.

With each step she took, she felt her old self returning.

CHAPTER SEVEN

Owen stood before the Grand Hotel in northern San Francisco, high on ethereal magic. Cars, vans and taxis moved with rapid speed on the streets to his left and right, but the street before the hotel was calm, as if somehow only those vehicles that had business with the hotel were allowed to drive down it.

In his mind, he replayed the conversation he had just had with the others when the call to pick up the invitations had come in.

"I'm fine now. Just a little tired. No reason I have to leave. Come on . . . Let me stay in the city," Max had pleaded.

"Max, we almost lost you," Jessie had said. "It's clear there is something going on in this city that isn't safe for you. You need to get out of here. We can all go."

"No way! Look at me, I am fine now and I'm not leaving San Francisco and never coming back. It's San Francisco! Look, now that I know there's a problem, I'll do what Owen said and keep a lid on my magic. I can do this with my eyes closed." In mockery, Max closed his eyes and smiled.

Clover let out laugh and Jessie shook his head.

"We are fine now," Max went on. "Seems like the rest of the city is fine. Besides, it will take weeks for my well to fill back up to where it was. Less magic means the less it can grab on to me. Right? Clover, fight for me here. We aren't leaving. We just arrived, and since when are we scared of magic? Let's just figure it out, like we always do."

"You're not feeling or seeing anything weird now?" Clover had asked.

"Nothing," Max had said. "I can't see anything but Jessie's big forehead. Come on. Owen said we get to go shopping. Don't let me miss out on shopping."

That had been the deciding factor. Shopping. Not music, not safety but new clothing and gear. That was the deciding factor in why Max was allowed to stay in the city. That and an unspoken understanding between everyone. No one wanted Max too far away from the safety of the group.

"Hello, sir, and welcome to the Grand Hotel."

"Thank you," Owen said as he walked past the doorman and into the Grand Hotel.

Owen took the stairs down to the lobby two at a time and went straight toward the reception desk. Casually, he took in the room filled with polished stone and shiny brass. The large open space was upscale, as if dust didn't have a place within the hotel. Inwardly, Owen smiled. This was the kind of place that had never been built for him and his kind. It was too controlled, with far too many rules, from standing up perfectly straight to controlling one's voice to all the other niceties of social etiquette. And yet Owen couldn't help but slow down and begin to take even, measured steps, rolling his feet so his boots made less noise. And yes, he stood to his full height as he approached the woman behind the desk.

"Welcome to the Grand Hotel. Do you have a reservation?"

Owen followed the woman's eyes behind her smile as she assessed him. "My name is Owen Brown, and I believe you have a package for me."

"Okay, let me take a look," she said.

"The package would have come in no more than thirty minutes ago. I was sent a message from the courier," Owen supplied.

"Oh, I don't see any notes here. But my manager just stepped away, and he was at the front desk. He should be back very soon. If you like, why don't you step into our lounge, and it shouldn't be more than a couple of minutes. Or the bar is open, and I can send him to you there."

Owen looked at the time; it was a few minutes after twelve.

"Five minutes, you think?" Owen asked.

"Yes, about that," she said. "I'll send him right over."

"I'll be at the bar," Owen said.

Moving toward the open door, he spotted a lone man working a long vacant bar. Empty chairs and tables were all around under low lights, despite the hour.

"Hello! Are you here for a drink or to see the ghost piano? If it's the latter, you probably won't see much until later. Our ghost has been playing closer to seven the last couple of nights."

The underglow around the bartender's face told Owen he was a level three We. The way he moved spoke of years behind a bar.

"I'll have a beer, if you don't mind, and I don't believe in ghosts."

"You might if you come back at seven." The bartender smiled, and it was warm and inviting. Owen had given that same smile countless times while standing on the other side.

"What kind of beer can I get you? Light or dark?" the bartender asked.

"As long as the beer is local, I don't care. So it's true? I had heard a rumor, but you actually have a ghost that plays piano?" Owen asked. On the long drive, Max had looked up the Grand Hotel, and the story of the ghost piano had been right there to read about.

"It's true. They say a portion of a musician's soul is stuck inside, and he likes to come out and play. Unless you make him mad, then he sulks in silence for a while." The bartender lifted his eyebrows to say this last part was a joke.

"We read about it on the drive in. A friend was telling me that a TV crew did a whole workup to prove it was a gimmick for the tourists a couple of years ago."

"They did, and they didn't find anything. No machinery or electricity, so I guess they didn't find what they wanted. Just a ghost who likes to show off. Now more than ever, people come from all over to watch and hear him play." The bartender gave a nod toward the piano, which was roped off with brass poles and red rope. "Go ahead and have a look for yourself."

Owen looked at the piano from across the room. Even from this distance, it was easy to see the beauty and craftsmanship layered into the instrument. It was like looking at black smoke caught in a crystal glass. Her lid was up and open, and Owen wanted to see inside.

"Here's your beer. It's roped off right now, but some like to touch it. I look the other way when it's quiet like this. They say sometimes your hair will stand up, but that's just nonsense," the bartender said with another grin.

Owen took his cold beer and moved toward the piano, which shined like glass. He stopped and called back. "Hey, I heard a rumor people used to play with the ghost. Is that true?"

"A long time ago, maybe, but not these days," the bartender said.

"All right, thanks. And this beer isn't bad."

"Anytime," the bartender said.

Owen stepped around tables and chairs until he was a few feet from the roped-off line. There was a call from the piano that he could hear in the air. A demand to be played. It pulled at him. So full of ethereal magic and creation, after weeks of basically only playing in his head, Owen wanted to sit down, open up his mind and simply let it all out.

For a time, he stood there, the red rope touching his thighs as he leaned forward, beer in hand, and just followed the curve of her—the piano. He followed the carvings and the white and black keys. He didn't miss the absence of the name. Typically, it would have been sealed on the front or side. But he couldn't find it, and that was odd. Only a master artist could have produced such a beautiful instrument.

Owen felt the man walking in his direction. With a glance, he noticed a blue pinstriped suit and a gold name pin over the left breast. However, it was the blue underglow around the face that declared the We as a level four. The package he carried filled in the rest of what Owen needed to know.

Owen raised a hand in greeting.

"You are Owen Brown?" the manager asked as he came forward.

"I am. Is that my package?" It was more of a large envelope.

"I believe that it is," the manager said as he double-checked the label and handed it over.

The We was about the same height as Owen, but there was something in his polished demeanor that spoke of age, of longevity. As if he had stood in this space since the beginning. Or, at least, that was the feeling Owen was getting.

"Excuse me for asking, but are you also from Miami?"

"Originally, yes, I am," Owen said.

"Are you, by any chance, *the* Owen Brown? Adoptive son of Mara at the Golden Horn?" The way the We spoke, Owen wasn't sure where this was going.

"That's me. Are you a friend of Mara's?" he asked.

"A long time ago, I was. Damon even more. They used to visit me often. My name is Sebastian. When you see them next, please send them both my warm regards. It's been too long."

"I can do that. Thanks."

"Of course," Sebastian said.

Owen expected the manager to turn and leave, but he didn't.

"Is there something else?" Owen asked.

"Excuse me, it's just that I've followed some of your exploits," Sebastian said. "The rumors say you're quite the musician. An etherealist who comes around once in an age. And that you were given one of our sacred keys—the guitar, in fact—at the very young age of eighteen. With it, you've made numerous successful runs to the gates. Along with a young woman who plays the violin? Is any of that right?"

"Clover is her name, and yes, we might have done some of that," Owen answered, still trying to understand where this was going.

"Is she here? We have a small stage set up from time to time in the corner right over there. It would be an honor, and I could spring for rooms along with meals, drinks and anything else you need. Any tips you gather are yours."

Owen's body relaxed; managers manage, after all. And he was used to his group having a rep inside the world of the We and musicians.

"That's a solid offer, but right now, we're just running some errands for Mara, and I want to see an old friend. Besides, I would hate to anger your ghost," Owen said with a grin.

Sebastian didn't grin in return. He didn't really react at all—he just stood there.

"Have you met our ghost yet?" Sebastian said, pointing toward the piano.

"I can't say that I have. In fact, I had never heard of him until one of my friends told me the story last night. And, being honest, I thought he was making most of it up just to help keep me awake. So the ghost is real?"

"Very real. What did your friend tell you about him?"

"No details, just the basics. You have a ghost that plays piano, that he's not just a gimmick to sell drinks and that apparently he has great skills."

"He does have skills, had them even before he died. The We was an exceptional musician." The manager paused, and it was easy to see he was thinking about another time. He let out a breath.

"It's fine," Owen said. "I know what it's like to get lost in thought. No harm in it."

"Do you like our piano? You should hear her. After all these years, she is still perfect. The ghost sees to that, at least. I haven't even had her tuned or needed to change a part since 1936."

Before Owen could respond, Sebastian moved to the red rope and unclipped one of the shiny brass hooks. With perfect poise, the manager reclipped the rope on the corresponding pole, leaving a four-foot opening beside the piano.

"Come on. I bought her in 1930. She came in from New York by train. It's easy to remember the cigarette smoke in the air, and the low light as the staff and I unveiled her to our regulars. It was three years before the end of Prohibition, not that Prohibition mattered much in our city. Nine years before World War II. If this hotel is my true love, then this piano was my mistress since the day she arrived. That's what Damon said to me once."

"She's beautiful," Owen said as he came closer.

Sebastian made a sound of approval, but he wasn't focused on Owen, and Owen didn't mind. He knew the feeling of being so wrapped up in something that he couldn't give time to anything else.

Regret and heartache pushed forward in Owen's chest as he thought of Alice. He took a sip of beer, and this time, he couldn't taste a thing.

You are too far away from me. I can't keep you safe, I can't reach you.

"You need anything, boss?" the bartender said as he came back into the room, a case of vodka in his hands.

"Two glasses and my special black bottle. Thanks, Bo," Sebastian said. He added in a low voice, "Let's see if we can wake that bastard up."

Owen positioned himself to the side of the piano, careful to keep his beer far from the instrument.

Sebastian moved the dark wood bench and straightened his jacket before sitting. The man's back was perfectly straight. "You should know before I play that I am not a musician. I don't have that call in my heart. It's like I can touch it, but I can't see it. Not like Damon, not like others I know or have known. And yet still here I am, a blind man before his mistress."

Sebastian's fingers moved slowly and softly as he pressed down keys in a gradual rhythm, the small layers of sound overlapping. Owen watched and listened.

Hyped up on ethereal magic, a cool beer in his hand, Owen let the sensation of music vibrate through him. Sebastian had skill, if only through years of practice, and it was enough to show in his song.

So he was surprised that after only a minute of playing, Sebastian started speaking again.

"Everything changes. I just never thought it would be something so pure as this instrument. Did you know most people, ordinary people, don't know there is a harp inside? I find that hilarious and completely disturbing. All the education in the world, the internet, and most don't know that a piano is a harp with keys." Sebastian looked up and smiled.

"People really don't know that? How is that possible?" Owen asked, dumbfounded. He had spent all his life around instruments, and although some were native to different countries, a piano was as basic as they came.

"I don't know, but one of the universities took a poll, and it's true," Sebastian said, shaking his head as his fingers gently danced, filling the room with sound.

"Here you go, boss," Bo, the bartender, said quietly, setting a black bottle of booze and two crystal glasses down on a small side table to the right of the piano.

"Thank you, Bo," Sebastian said. "I first fell for the piano because of its kindness, I think. Most other instruments make you sweat, burn or bleed. Don't even get me started on the sax. Damon forced me to try it once, and he fell off the bar when I did. I was terrible. The worst. But the piano is all about ease, simplicity in the face of overwhelming complexity, so even a blind man like me can do something right." His fingers suddenly stopped, and Owen swayed from the abruptness.

"You're leading me somewhere. I can feel it," Owen said. He looked down at the black bottle and recognized it as one of Damon's private labels. A label that wasn't for sale and hadn't been made in a very long time.

"Maybe I am. Maybe seeing you and thinking of Damon, I miss the old days. When music was the world's greatest entertainment, and people traveled the world to come to San Francisco and hear some of the best musicians play. Some would even come right here in this room, with her," he said, staring at the piano. "And now all my hotel has is this goddamn ghost, who was a bastard before he died."

"Wait, you don't want the ghost?" Owen asked.

The manager of the Grand Hotel let out a breath that was filled with history.

"No. I want him gone, out of my piano, out of my hotel.

I want this charade to be done and over with. I wanted it done years ago, but to break the curse, it requires someone far more talented than I am."

Owen didn't miss Sebastian flexing his hands into fists and forcefully stretching them free.

He's telling me the truth. He hates every part of this, of the ghost in his piano.

Sebastian reached over toward the small black table and took Damon's personal stock of whiskey in his hands. Using his teeth, he bit down over the cork stopper and pulled, the bottle making a popping sound before he poured the amber liquid into each glass.

"That bottle is close to empty," Owen said without thinking twice.

"I have one more."

Owen leaned over the red rope and placed the large envelope and his half-empty beer glass on a neighboring table. It was a stretch, but his arms were long. As he turned back, Sebastian was standing with two glasses in hand.

"Here you go. I think it's time for a toast," the manager said.

"Very well," Owen said, taking the crystal glass.

Sebastian raised his and then nodded for Owen to proceed.

"You want me to make the toast?" Owen asked in surprise.

"Damon was always better at it. And Mara, well, she always had the spotlight no matter what room she walked into. Go ahead."

Owen thought about everything he had heard since the manager approached as he looked at Sebastian and the piano and this room. Then he shook his head and lowered his glass.

Sebastian's eyes narrowed as if he were locking onto a target.

"This has been your show since you identified me,"

Owen said. "You have something on your chest you can't say or have said so many times you think it's pointless to say again. I don't know what happened between you and Damon and Mara, but something did. I can see you are both pissed and deeply sad. I can relate, but it's your pain and sorrow. You make the toast, and I'll drink with you no matter what you say."

Owen could see the layers over the man's heart. He didn't understand them all, but he could feel them in the air like gravity, trying to pull the We down.

"You are so much like them. It's crazy. Not of their blood but of their spirit. What you just did? Both Mara and Damon did it to me a hundred times, and I am a better man for it. They cut down to the quick." Sebastian swallowed the rest of what he was about to say. He raised his glass, and Owen did the same.

"Till death. May our spirits be lighter in death than they are here on Earth."

"Till death," Owen said, tapping his glass. In one smooth pour, he tossed back the refined whiskey. His throat burned, and the heat dropped down lower, the sensation to play music vibrating through his soul.

"You want to give her a try?" Sebastian said, pointing a hand toward the piano.

Owen looked at the manager, then at the piano. The need to play jumped tenfold. With effort, he tore his eyes from her pearly white and black keys and looked around the room. An old grandfather clock in the corner had the time—a little before one.

"I have some time. What do I need to know about the ghost that I don't know now?" Owen asked.

"He hates to be upstaged. I love to see when it happens," Sebastian said as he poured the very last remains of the black bottle between the two glasses. "Go ahead, take the seat."

Owen didn't move at first. Instead, his left hand reached out and touched the side frame of the piano. Some instruments, like his beat-up acoustic guitar, were just bent wood and string. But others, like Betsy, Clover's violin, had so much love poured into them that they seemed on the verge of having a soul. Extra energy when you believed in it was like a rabbit's foot or a lucky shirt. Or a special bat—it gave you juice in the swing.

If what Sebastian said was true, this instrument had been given love by some of the best piano makers of that time. Sure, he hadn't named the piano makers, but everyone knew that a custom piano out of New York during the 1930s could only be one company. And by the look of her—liquid smoke drifting up through the floors—it had to be from S&S piano makers. Then there was the love Sebastian himself had been pouring into her for the last ninety-plus years.

Owen let out his own breath and could feel the pressure in it. A pressure to play, a pressure to let go and fly. He breathed in air through his nose as his left hand moved over the piano's smooth, polished finish. For a moment, he could smell smoke and salt water. He opened his eyes, and he thought he could hear laughter and music as a crowd of people and We from a forgotten time filled this room.

Owen looked over as Sebastian handed him the crystal glass, the amber liquid just over a full shot, and it reminded him of Damon. One of the greatest musicians he had ever known.

"I can have this entire room full of people in thirty minutes, if you want a crowd. I can have them waiting down the block inside an hour and a half."

Owen took the glass. "You have been pushing me this whole time. What do you want?"

"I want the ghost gone. I want my piano free, and this hotel filled with music from the living." Sebastian paused. In a calm voice, but one filled with weight, he added, "I want my friends back."

"I don't know anything about ghosts or getting rid of

them. I can't help you with that. But I'll speak on your behalf to Damon and Mara. Tell them what you told me."

Owen looked down at the contents in the glass, gave it a
small swirl, and brought it a few inches from his nose to
smell. Warmth filled his senses, and the individual flavors
separated.

"I'll play for you and this room, but only as it is right
now. No crowd, no one else."

"My staff might come in," Sebastian said. "Most are
We. Most love music, like me."

"Fine," Owen said, sitting down.

"You'll wake him, the ghost. He might join you at some
point."

"Fine," Owen said again.

"Why don't you want a crowd?"

"A woman unlike any other woman I have ever met
ripped out my heart and stabbed me just the other day, and
she did it for a good reason."

"So you're heartbroken. Good," Sebastian said. "A broken musician is far better than a solid one."

"I mean it. Right now, I like this room empty. I know
you want to hear the living, but . . ."

"Stop. I'm here, and you are there. We toasted death
before, so here's to being alive. In this time."

Owen tapped glasses, but this time, he sipped the contents and turned toward the piano that was as much a work
of art as an instrument.

Sebastian took his glass from his hand, and Owen didn't
waste time.

Despite Sebastian's words about the piano not needing
to be tuned, Owen couldn't help but test the notes. Every
key that Sebastian hadn't touched while he played—and
that was most of the right side—Owen touched one at a
time. It was like walking upstairs with a full load in your
arms. He went slow, needing to be sure of each step.

When it was done, and every black and white key was

accounted for, Owen felt a little zip of pleasure dance up his spine.

"You're right. She is perfect, and I can't feel the age in her. After this long of a life, I thought I'd feel some loose bits. A shading in the keys, maybe, but there's nothing there. It's as if she is fresh off the train you unloaded her from."

Owen didn't close his eyes, didn't fall into his mind. Instead, he leaned forward, and his hands danced over the keys. It was a warmup, a challenge to the cold room and stale air. *Wake up, get out, live in the fresh air*, his fingers and soul said through the harp and keys.

Sebastian made a sound and raised a hand for Bo to come over and speak to him, but Owen didn't care. His well of ethereal magic was overflowing, and here in this space and time was a piano that was pure and loved and full of history, no matter what else they said about it.

Like a cage with a thousand locks, Owen opened his chest and pain poured out faster than he could hold it back.

I know why you couldn't come with me, Alice. I know it. I understand you not wanting to hurt your parents. I know why you had to stay, but you don't know what I know. That time changes everything. Everything changes with time. You can't control it. You can't escape the change.

And I waited my whole life to find you. The miles and miles and trials of my whole life, and then there you were. But you're not here, and I couldn't stay.

Owen let the waves of sound ripple over one another as his fingers spoke from inside. He lingered over his words and shouted across the room until his music spoke to the glass behind the bottles over the bar.

You don't know, you can't know, and I can't have you,
I can't hold you.
In such a short time, a tiny time,
You became my world, and now I am lost,

> *floating through an endless void of space*
> *amongst people who need me.*
> *But what about my need, my heart?*
> *I miss your voice, your skin, your touch.*
> *I miss your soul next to mine,*
> *I miss the burn and the fire, the heat.*
> *Is this my punishment for all that I have done?*
> *For all that I wish to do?*
> *Is this the price of my sins here on Earth?*
> *Could the powers that be not wait until I die to punish me,*
> *or is such a thought far too simple for this world?*

Owen let his hands linger, the melody he was rolling hanging in the air. The taste of Damon's personal whiskey climbed up and bit him in the mouth over his tongue.

Owen flattened out his fingers and pressed all ten down. The piano screeched and shouted as he lifted off, and the sound died.

Owen shook his head and rubbed a tear from his eyes. He wasn't ashamed of his feelings as he noticed his surroundings once again.

There, standing with the red rope in between them, were the two We. Sebastian held Bo's hand up to his chest, and both had tears running down their faces. Sebastian visibly shook, and it was clear he was trying to speak but couldn't.

Bo gave a couple of nods, and Owen looked away.

He closed his eyes, and his head tilted to the side as a raw red pain sliced through his heart. One by one, he closed the clasps in his chest, locking Alice away.

"No one said you could do that," Sebastian said, his voice shaking.

Owen didn't speak, didn't open his eyes, just folded the layers back over Alice even as the image of her face—the short hair, the full lips, those eyes that could see everything—wouldn't wash out of his mind.

"That was truly amazing," Bo said to his back. "Who is the person you wrote that for?"

Owen didn't answer; he just wiped his hand over his face and then shook his head, trying to dislodge her.

"Bo, go get my last bottle of the black," Sebastian said.

"No," Owen said, raising a hand.

"You earned it," Sebastian said. "Besides, it would be an honor to finish it with you."

"I don't think I can. I mean, I don't think I should." Owen shook his head again. And still, she refused to go away, out of his mind. "Whiskey is for doing the impossible, for doing the stupid, the insane. The reckless and the road." Owen stood up. "I think, right now, I am afraid of the fire."

With effort, he pulled ethereal magic back down into his well, because there was a part of him—a large, overwhelming part—that wanted to burn so hot that the fire would consume him. Free him from this world and the pain in his chest.

"Okay," Sebastian said, reaching out a hand to thank him and seal the bond.

Owen shook the manager's hand. The manager's grip was firm and unrelenting, refusing to let go. "You are welcome here anytime. You understand me? Anytime. Night or day. During bad weather or sunny."

"I understand. Thank you for sharing your mistress." Owen smiled a little and Sebastian let out a popping laugh.

Before he could speak, musical notes danced through the air, and Owen turned to see the keys of the piano dropping down as if pressed by two invisible hands.

"Ah, the asshole wakes up and wants to say hello," Sebastian said, still holding Owen's hand in his grip.

But Owen was lost, watching as the keys moved in perfect time, and the song vibrated out through the air.

Smooth, creative, perfect, Owen thought to himself as his mind cataloged and memorized every note, every drop of the keys.

The song went on, and Owen listened and watched, his

appreciation for the ghost growing as the song continued to take his soul on a ride.

At some point, Sebastian let go of his hand, and it dropped down by his side. This close, he was a spectator to the ghost's skills and precision.

The music was loud and moved between the right side of the room and the center of the room, constantly building and dropping, only to pick you back up again right before a fall. It was complicated and complex, but in a way that left you grounded in the heart of the ghost's song.

"He's showing off. This was one of his most popular songs back in the day," Sebastian said from Owen's right.

Owen moved his head, swearing that he could feel a presence in the room as the keys shifted up and down all by themselves.

For a time, no one moved but the music and the keys and the foot pedals beneath the piano. Bo, Sebastian and Owen just watched and listened.

But then Bo must have remembered he had a bar to attend to and that his manager was standing beside him, for he shook himself, picked up the empty bottle and headed around the piano toward the bar.

Owen waited for the song to finish and for the keys and strings to come to a rest before speaking.

"So that's your ghost. He's very good."

"He knows that. Knew it when he was alive too. I think he's intimidated by you, not that he would ever say it."

"I am sure he is. After all, I can still have sex, and he can't."

Laughter spilled out of Sebastian, and the sound of it warmed a cold stone in Owen's gut.

He reached over, grasped the remains of his whiskey and took another sip.

The piano keys started to move again. This time brash and violent like the crashing of a storm over a fishing boat.

The manger gave a small chuckle. "I don't think he liked what you had to say about him."

The music redoubled in gravity and storm, and Owen couldn't help himself. There was something here that was fundamentally wrong. Heaven and Hell, he understood. A soul trapped in a piano for all time just didn't seem right.

"So you killed him, right? And this is his way of paying you back?" Owen asked, turning his focus away from the ghost and the piano and back toward the manager.

"He sort of did this before I killed him." Sebastian stared at Owen. "I kicked out the musician and his followers after a series of bad nights and banned them for life. Somehow, they linked another piano to this one. So when they played that one, this one would play. After three months of refusing to break the link between pianos, I shot him in the head. The next full moon, he was here."

"That's . . . I don't know what to say. That's shitty."

Sebastian made a sound in agreement, but he didn't say more.

"Was he a We or an etherealist? And why haven't you used his name?"

"He was a We and was a great musician, but I don't use his name because he was an asshole and doesn't deserve to be remembered. How did you know he wasn't a normal human?"

"I can feel magic radiating inside the piano while he's playing. Maybe it's time you tell me the whole story."

"I like you. Why don't we save it for another time? Save if for when you have *more* time. Besides, his playing grates on my nerves. I honestly can't stand to hear it anymore."

Owen could see a shift in the man, a crack in his armor. "Fair enough. Thanks for the drinks."

"Thank *you*."

Owen was focused on the look the manager was giving him, sincere and open. And Owen felt the same way. There was kinship between them, perhaps a similar sensation to be free that they could both feel. But Owen was also listening intently to the ghost's current song as it danced and rang throughout the empty bar.

The manager of the Grand Hotel turned away and headed toward the open doors that led back into the reception area of the hotel.

Six steps away, Owen finished his whiskey, then with as much force as he could muster, he threw the crystal glass at the small black table beside the piano. His aim was true, and the glass shattered and spread out ten feet in all directions as the sound punched a hole through the music in the air.

Bo yelled, "Hey, what the hell?"

Owen could feel the manager turn around. "What is going on?" Sebastian asked.

But Owen ignored both as he watched the keys and listened.

They both spoke again, but Owen just held up a hand for them to be quiet. The ghost played on, never missing a stroke or shifting a key.

Till death, fuck you, Owen thought to the ghost.

Moments later, after offering to clean up the mess himself and being denied, Owen answered the manger's question.

"Why did I do that? Everyone keeps calling this a ghost. It's not. It's just a machine, an echo of what someone once was. He can't change his music, he can't adapt, he doesn't have ears outside the piano. He's not alive."

"I could have told you that," the manager said, a little of the whiskey showing in his face.

"You didn't. You said he didn't like what I had to say. But he can't hear what I said. I needed to know it."

"I don't understand."

"Your ghost isn't a soul. It's a mechanism. He's a wheel with pegs that turns to play a song. Not a living, breathing, heart-pumping soul. A real musician would have caught part of the sound, shifted with the shock in the room to either enhance or reduce the feeling."

"So, what's your point?"

"If you want to get rid of him, I would look for the power

source. Someone or something must be feeding him the magic, but whatever or whoever feeds your ghost is strong."

"I know that too. Again, you could have just asked instead of breaking my glass and causing more work for my staff."

"And you could have told me instead of directing me down this path, but you didn't. Since the beginning, you wanted that ghost under my skin. I can feel it."

"Yes, I have been. Yes, I do. But it's not safe."

"Safe for me or safe for you? That's why you aren't telling me the whole story? Why not?"

"Because if I tell you the whole story instead of just this part, and you truly get involved and fail, Mara will kill me."

"What the hell are you talking about? I've been here for an hour," Owen said, feeling like fog was starting to settle into his mind.

"This"—Sebastian pointed toward the piano and its moving keys—"is the end of the story, but the story starts with a young musician staying at the Russian Embassy and thirty or forty of some of the craziest groupies I have ever come across."

"The Russian Embassy?"

"Yes."

"The Russian Embassy?" Owen repeated.

"You know of it?"

"Every musician knows of it." Pieces of a puzzle were floating around in Owen's mind, stories and markers circulating around San Francisco and the Russian Embassy. Owen grabbed on to a few and stuck them together.

"It's not far from here, is it?"

"Ten blocks west, not hard to find; just go straight up the hill. Same side of the street."

Owen's eyes went back and forth, checking for signs of anything in Sebastian's face he might be missing or that would give him another clue.

If I get involved and it goes bad, Mara might kill him?

Damon and Mara used to be friends with Sebastian, but they stopped? There's a ghost of a We in the piano and it's connected to the Russian Embassy? And what or who is supplying the ethereal energy?

"I heard a rumor about four years ago that there is another of what the We call keys in the Russian Embassy, but if you fail to earn it, it slowly drains your magic well and your soul until you die, and your body is tossed into the boiler."

Sebastian didn't say anything.

"Damon and Mara never mentioned you, the Grand Hotel or the Russian Embassy to me. And you're saying this ghost is connected to that place."

Sebastian's eyes went hard, but his lips didn't move.

"Sebastian, did Damon try for the musical key in the Russian Embassy and fail?"

"Yes."

"He didn't do it for the key, but because the piano at the Russian Embassy holds the way to solve your ghost problem? And he was your friend? How did Damon survive?"

"He is my friend. He only survived because Mara stepped in. She unhooked him from the piano there." Sebastian shook his head from side to side in a back-and-forth motion. Pain radiated off him. "I am not going to say more."

Owen knew the rumors about the place. Before today he thought they were just that. Rumors. In total he had heard of six keys out in the world of We and musicians. A key was a special instrument made of ethereal essence made with the will to do the impossible.

Damon tried and failed.

"That's why Mara and Damon stopped coming here. Mara blames you."

The ghost song ended, and Owen glanced over his shoulder at the piano.

"Kill it. Burn the fucker to the ground and let's get you a new piano."

"I tried that. Several times. Almost burned the hotel down. Not a scratch on the thing. You should go. I wasn't thinking about the consequences. If Damon couldn't do it . . ." The manager paused. "The risk is too high, and too many musicians have died trying. You're welcome back anytime, but you should go."

Owen grabbed the We's shoulder and gave a hard squeeze. Sebastian was right that he should go. If Damon and Mara couldn't solve this, it was only arrogance within that said he could do it.

"Sorry about the glass."

"I have more."

They both smiled, and Owen walked away, remembering to take the envelope that was addressed to him.

Ghosts, salt water and pain. Not exactly Miami, but close, Owen thought with whiskey still on his lips.

CHAPTER EIGHT

DAYS UNTIL A+O

"Clover, I said one! Only one!" Owen said. "It's too loud. Turn down the music or get out of the shop. You can't hear me, and I can't hear you."

Almost everything he could hear was very loud rock music and a host of people yelling at one another with Clover's voice mixed in between.

"One?" Clover asked. "One what? I can't hear you, Owen. You have to speak up."

Pulling looks from the people passing him on the sidewalks of San Francisco, Owen spoke louder into the cell phone. "Yes, one. I am trying to tell you there was only one invitation. We came all this way for only one freaking invitation, and I am standing outside the address now."

"What? Owen, I can't hear you in here. Hold on. Hey, can you turn it down?"

Owen stood facing the glowing glass sign of Mystic Mona. Red corded lights were wrapped around pale pink scarves and a sign that said **PALM READER**.

The blaring sound on the other end of his phone dropped in decibel, and Owen shook his head in relief.

"Owen? Are you still there?" Clover asked.

"I'm here. Where are you?"

"We found this awesome vintage shop with these really cool owners, and they are showing us all this old rock and roll stuff. I can't believe it. You should be here right now."

"Next time," he said. "I just wanted you to know that I only have one stop, then I'll find you. Now, how is Max doing?"

"He looks like crap, even with the new glasses he just picked up, which are slamming. He's bruised all over his neck and still a little pale and tired, though he's had about four energy drinks. So far, everything else seems fine. And before you ask, yes, Max has been keeping his well of ethereal magic shut. Hence no healing. What took you so long? We thought you would be done by now."

"Long story. It involves a ghost and a glass of whiskey. Is Max seeing lines of power in the air again?" Owen asked as he looked over the cars zooming down the street.

"Not yet. He's keeping the lid tight, though I don't think there is much energy in there. You know Max is not very impressive. Ouch!"

Owen heard a scuffling and just made out Max's voice on the other side.

"Be nice, Clover," Max said loud enough that it was easy to hear him, even with the ongoing background noise.

"Don't punch me again, Max. You already look like I beat you up, and I'll do it again."

"Sounds like everything is good there." Owen left the underlying question of his words open, but the meaning was clear enough: *How's Jessie?*

"Everything is good, but then again, we *are* shopping. I do miss Daphne. She had excellent taste and normally didn't flirt with the staff like Jessie is doing right now, unless it was a really hot guy, then we'd flip for him. So who is the one invitation for? The queen of California?" Owen understood her meaning.

They had just driven halfway across the country to hand-deliver this single invitation.

"You won't believe me, but she's a palm reader over here on Powell Street. I think. The address is right, but the name is wrong. I'll find out in a minute."

"Wait, you are standing outside a palm reader's shop?" Clover asked. "And one that Mara is personally inviting to her grand opening? She must be the real thing. This is awesome. Wait for us. I'm coming to meet you. Don't you go in there without me!"

"No, Clover, I want this done. Stay there. This whole day started great and has gone downhill ever since we crossed the bridge. I just want to get this over with so I can go see my friend at Whiskey Jack's. Kick back and blow off some steam. You and the others just keep doing what you are doing. I'm hoping this won't take very long."

"Damn it! That's not fair. Hey, no, Jessie, you cannot wear a fedora. We've told you at least ten times. With that forehead, it just doesn't work. Stop trying. Everyone in the room, say goodbye to Owen!"

Owen heard eight different voices all yell "Goodbye" at the same time.

Well, at least my people are having a better time than I am.

He paused, slipping his phone away, and couldn't help but think, *I wish you were here.*

Owen pulled on the handle of the door, and it opened easily. A series of little metal bells rang as he stepped into a waiting area complete with two blue plastic chairs and a sheet of red-and-pink lace and gemstones blocking the path into the next room.

"Hello? Is anyone there?" Owen said as he moved closer to the hanging cloth.

"Yes, come on in. Don't be shy," a woman's voice said, perfectly clear despite an accent he couldn't place.

Owen used his hands to push the draped cloth and intertwined gems out of his way. They jingled and brushed his skin and clothing as he moved deeper into the room.

The room was what he had expected: a round table with a dark cloth cover and a large crystal ball. Incense thickened the air in the room, and the lighting was dramatic with reds and blues. But that was where Owen's expectations stopped.

Before him were three We. All female and grouped together, they carried a crap ton of ethereal magic between them.

Two stood with teacups and saucers in hand, while the third sat at the table, her teacup left untouched beside her. But it was the power of the two standing that had Owen more on guard than anything else. The two We standing were level fives, whereas the woman at the table was only a level two.

"Hello," he said, trusting in his reason for being there. "My name is—"

"Owen Brown," the younger-looking of the level fives said before he could finish. She was pretty in a timeless sort of way, with long red hair. "Yes, we know who you are. And yes, we have been waiting for you. For almost a half hour." She lifted her teacup to her lips and took a little sip.

Owen looked from the woman at the table to the two women standing behind her, and his gaze locked with the older of the level fives. She looked to be around her early sixties but fit, sharp and dangerous, wearing a black-and-white suit that reeked of money and taste.

She's the boss, the leader of the pack.

She didn't move as he studied her, but he could feel her scrutiny of him all the same.

A woman who lives by making life-or-death decisions on a regular basis.

Owen trusted his instincts, had been around this type of We for most of his life. Some part of his soul giggled at the moment. This wasn't right. He was here for Mara, to hand over a piece of paper. Nothing complicated in that. Simple. Easy. But how good would a fight feel right now?

The younger of the level fives spoke again. "My name is Jessica Joyce, and this is my mother, Elain Joyce. Gwen, you can leave us now. Thank you for the tea and company while we waited." Without another word, the level two at the table stood up and walked out of the room with a clear sense of relief.

She was afraid.

"Madam Elain? I believe I have a letter for you," Owen said, holding up the envelope.

Owen's skin itched as he pulled a trickle of ethereal magic into his blood and body.

"Do you know what you are holding?" Madam Elain said in a voice that cut the air cold.

"I believe this is an invitation for a New Year's party. My understanding is Mara would very much like you to attend. You might like to know that this is the only invitation she asked me to personally deliver."

"He thinks it's an honor," Jessica said to her mother.

Elain smiled. "Mara is not a friend of mine, and yet politics will be politics." She sighed before pointing a finger, and Jessica glided over to take the letter.

Owen found himself distracted as Jessica moved closer. There was a polished edge to her personality that had him ready for anything as she took the letter out of his hand.

"Well, it was nice to meet you both. I hope I will see you

at the party anyway," Owen said, turning to go as Jessica handed the letter over to her mother.

"Not yet. I haven't dismissed you," Madam Elain said. "Let's see this letter once and for all. I am tired of having the same dream."

"I'm not trying to be rude. I was just asked to deliver that invitation to you. I was told it was important. I think I should go now."

Madam Elain opened the envelope, but to Owen's surprise, what came out wasn't one of Mara's invitations. Instead, there was a long handwritten letter.

"That fox," Madam Elain said as she started to read the letter to herself.

Jessica pointed her finger at Owen's chest, the motion's intention clear: she didn't want Owen to move, let alone leave. As if this was all casual instead of intense, she took another sip of her tea.

The smell of incense permeated the air as if it came up through the floor, and it crawled into Owen's mind. He did not like anything about this room or these women. There was too much power, too much control and too many rules he did not understand.

The last thing he wanted was to hurt Mara and her plans, but the vibe in the room was growing more and more uncomfortable.

"That crafty man. You won't believe what he said in here," Elain said to Jessica.

"I do not need all the details, Mother. Is he still like you remember?" Jessica asked.

"As if time has yet to change him. Still brash and brazen."

Man? Him?

"We are talking about Damon. Your uncle, I believe."

"Damon?"

"Yes," Elain said, slipping the letter back into the envelope. "He tricked you. Lied to you. It wasn't Mara who sent you but him so that you could deliver this to me."

Damon sent me. He lied to me. How? I would have heard it in his voice. And why?

"Damon has always been clever," Elain said with a deep smile that touched her eyes.

"Mother, please don't share any more," Jessica said.

"I won't, dear. I won't, but the number of nights he didn't let either of us sleep could almost outnumber the stars."

"Mother, I only came here because you promised you wouldn't talk about Damon and the details."

"You are right. I am sorry. It won't happen again."

"Thank you. Now, is it as you saw it in your dream?"

"It is. Damon is claiming I owe him, and he has asked that I assist his nephew. A large request, but I am required to comply," Madam Elain said, indicating Owen.

Jessica didn't respond with words, but Owen thought he saw her eyes sparkle with an internal light that scared the hell out of him. And for a moment, he had to fight down his natural response to pull more ethereal magic out of his well and into the rest of his body.

Palm reader and level five We. And women. And Damon lying to me. This is over my head, but I can't leave. Why? Because I haven't been dismissed yet? How about I go through that wall?

"Relax, Owen Brown," Elain said. "Though I do agree with you. Let's get out of here. This place holds too many ghosts for my liking. To think, I once lived here. Upstairs. But that was a simpler time. We are taking him with us. Quickly. Jessica, I still have meetings, and I have been here for far too long."

Jessica set down her teacup and pointed toward the door. Owen understood and started walking out the way he had come in. Fresh air cleansed his mind as he stepped back out onto the sidewalk.

Do I run?

"And where would you go?" Jessica said, her arm suddenly sliding under his so that they stood locked arm in arm. "My mother meant what she said. Relax." There was power in her words, but Owen's own magic blocked its influence.

"Normally, I go anywhere I want to go. Again, I don't mean to be rude, but I did what I came for."

"You traveled a long way to get here. Don't you want to see the rest? Why your uncle really sent you?"

"Jessica, stop playing with him. Remember his place. We are not trying to start a feud with Mara. The tension between his family and ours is high enough," Elain said as a tall black SUV pulled up next to the sidewalk. "Owen, it's very simple. Get in the SUV. I have something I am supposed to give you." Elain held up the letter.

Owen considered it, looking from Jessica, with her snake-like green eyes and red hair, to Elain, who looked as if she could tear down a tower if she wanted to. *And yet, Damon sent me here. It's for a reason. Only one way to find out.*

"Where are we going?"

"City hall," Elain said, climbing into the SUV as if the conversation were over.

"And why are we going to city hall?" Owen asked, looking to Jessica, but the answer came from inside the SUV.

"You are to marry my daughter."

A cold shock ran down Owen's spine as Jessica whipped around toward Elain and the open door.

"Mother, that's not funny."

Laughter came back. "Sure it is."

"She has been making that same joke since they named her the mayor," Jessica said. "It hasn't been funny, not once. Now, get in before anyone notices and we draw a crowd."

"What?" Owen said, completely taken aback.

"I said my mother is the mayor. Now get your ass in our car. We have appointments."

* * *

Owen had gotten into the SUV, been brought down into an underground parking lot, hustled into an elevator, given a guest badge and now sat in the mayor's waiting area just outside her secretary's office.

"Would you like a coffee or a water?" a nice-looking young man said, leaning down close so as not to be loud. He was human and had no idea he worked for a We. Or what a We was, for that matter.

"No, thank you," Owen said, and the young man in a suit wearing an "Elain for Mayor" pin on his lapel backed away.

What the heck is going on?

Jessica stepped out of a side door, and Owen stood up.

"My mother thinks it's a good idea if I keep you company while you wait. Ever since she has become the mayor, she thinks it's her job to throw me in front of any good-looking prospects. If you can believe that."

"Prospects for marriage? She doesn't know I'm a musician, does she?"

Jessica laughed, and some of the bite melted out of her.

"That's funny. You really didn't know she's the mayor of San Francisco? You know, this is a pretty high-profile position. We make international news from time to time."

"Not my town, not my city. I can tell you the top one hundred songs from Billboard in order for the last ten years, so don't go thinking I'm completely out of touch."

"All one hundred over ten years?" she asked. "Are you sure?"

"What can I say, I'm a breed unto myself."

"You might be," Jessica said, and even more of her earlier bite disappeared.

"So, do you know what I'm doing here? It's a nice building and all, but . . ."

"You are caught in an old mess between Damon and my mom. They were an item, more or less, about forty years ago. They hadn't talked until that letter you delivered. You might like to know that he's claiming you as his nephew and only heir."

"He did that?" Owen was touched and confused. That Damon considered him family was no surprise. That he had told anyone was something else.

"He did. He wants my mother to help you with your problem."

"And what problem is that?"

"Pick one. Or pick all of them for all I care."

A balance of power settled between them, and the conversation went cold as two women walked by.

"How did you know I was going to be there? Or who I am? You were waiting for me, after all."

"Very strong psychic. We both are. We can read auras and palms and tea leaves and even really strong thoughts. But do us a favor and don't tell anyone."

"And why are you telling me?" Owen said on instinct.

"I have a feeling you would have figured it out. If not today, then tomorrow. She's ready to see you now."

There was a pause in the conversation as Owen looked toward the tall doors with brass handles. And then they opened.

"Mr. Brown," the secretary said. "The mayor is ready for you now."

"Okay," Owen said. When Jessica didn't follow, he added, "Are you coming in?"

"No. I have some work to do. But before you go . . . how is your friend Max? Is he okay?"

A chill went down his spine. "How do you know Max? And how do you know something happened?"

"I'm not allowed to tell you, but is he okay?"

Owen stared at her, surrounded by white polished stones. "You're a real psychic, and you know what happened to Max? That means you know what that thing is?

The art installation with weaves of power too small for me to see?"

"Just tell Max not to touch any of them and to take it very slow. His kind get caught if they do not slow down. How did you get him detached?"

"I choked him until he passed out."

"I didn't know that was possible. I'm once more impressed. You need to get in there. She has a busy schedule, and she's already behind because of you. Max seems like a nice guy," Jessica said, giving a shrug and turning away. Owen walked past the secretary's desk and into the mayor's office. It was smaller than he thought it would be yet larger than any other room he had seen so far. There was an American flag and a California flag behind a large desk, with a sitting area off to one side. Elain was there, a set of black-framed glasses perched on her nose as she read something on the computer.

"Owen, can you tell Mara that Jessica and I will be attending her New Year's party, assuming she gets the proper permissions once again? I have little doubt she will be able to, though North and South can be touchy." Elain held up the invitation. "I received this about a week ago, but I hadn't responded. You don't mind letting her know, do you? Good. So here's the thing—Damon and I once dated. During that time, he asked me for my help. I told him I would, but something came up, and I didn't. I am not giving you the details because it's none of your business. But that is why we broke up, and that is why you are here now. Because Damon is calling in the debt, and I owe him. So let's get this over with. What do you want from me?"

"Excuse me?" Owen said. "I didn't come to your city for your help."

"Your uncle just called in a debt. A debt I take very seriously. What is it that you want? What can I help you with?"

Owen put his hands up, waving her off with all ten fingers. "Madam Elain—"

"Mayor Elain or Elain is fine. I haven't gone by Madam Elain in very long time, not since the city needed me to step up. Now, what is it that you want from me?"

"Okay, but, Elain, I didn't come here to ask for anything. I appreciate the situation, but Damon lied to me. He told me—"

"He told you that you were delivering an invitation for Mara. Yes, yes, I already know—" She cut herself off. "Come here. I want this over with."

Elain came around the desk, her right hand waving him closer.

Out of self-preservation, Owen's own hand came up and indicated for her to stop as he took a step back.

"Hey, I'm serious. I don't need anything from you."

"Everyone needs something from me. You're a musician, right? You want me to secure a recording contract with one of the big four? I have contacts with each. You want someone out of jail? I can do that. Maybe you just want to know your future? Just give me your hand so this can be over with. The price has been paid, and I am tired of being in debt to someone."

"There are always strings with the We."

"Not this time. Let's go. I have other people to see and a city to run."

She moved forward again, this time with a strong stride that said she was going to place her hands on him. On instinct, Owen dropped his left hand, the leather bracelet that wasn't a bracelet dropping into his waiting palm, a thin glowing chain of pure ethereal essence. Its power hummed in the air with violence as its end flicked down, leaving a line of light in the air. Elain stopped her approach, and her eyes went wide.

"The rumors about you are true." Her voice was low, and she didn't take her eyes off the humming chain.

"I am sorry, but you were not listening, and this was getting out of hand," Owen said.

"You think I am scared of that? Of *you*?" Elain said, and Owen could feel her own power starting to move inside her.

"No. I didn't come here for a fight." With will, and the connection and essence in his hand, Owen directed the chain back up. Like a snake, it moved over his hand and wrist and once more formed itself into a bracelet.

The room went silent as he stared at her, feeling the waves of ethereal magic coursing over her skin. She was a storm, a fury, contained by only her strength of will. But for how long? Owen watched the fire, and a part of him that had been ice-cold since leaving Alice warmed at seeing it. And that part could remember what fire felt like inside. He moved just a little, a test, a threat. Unable to help himself.

Level fives were not a joke, but then again, neither was he.

Elain's eyes narrowed as her body shifted to match his own movement. They moved like dancers from across the room. Only this wasn't black and white with a whole lot of frills. This held an edge, the kind of edge that could cut both ways if either of them made the wrong move.

"You are playing with me. How strong are you?" Elain said.

Owen didn't change, didn't react. Of course she couldn't tell how strong he was. Long ago, Owen had learned to invert a portion of his ethereal power to hide his strength. Most We considered such practices to be a waste of ethereal magic. But for Owen and his people, the practice was vital.

"Your city has been messing with me and mine all day. Excuse me, it's been too long since I have done something stupid," Owen said, shaking off some of the tension between them.

"Is that supposed to be a joke?" Elain asked.

"No. I have a bit of the itch. I hope you can understand."

Elain took a moment, then settled. He could see the difference in her as the call for violence disappeared.

"Damon used to get the itch. He would talk about it. I could see it on him sometimes. He said . . . he said he liked to save it up sometimes, let it linger and build for a long reckless night."

"Yeah, he's told me the same thing. That's just playing with fire. I don't know what game Damon is playing at now. I didn't ask for his help, and the last time I did? Well, let's just say it got me into some trouble that I'm still not out of."

"Really? That sounds like something I might be able to help with. You need money? Why don't you tell me what trouble you're in? Is someone hunting you? Is there a bounty on your head?"

Owen was already waving her off. "Whatever was between you and my uncle is messy. I can feel it. I think you are still into him, and I don't want to be caught in a web with consequences I don't understand."

"Oh, for God's sake. There will be no strings. My word on it. I owe your uncle. I screwed up when we were together, the kind of screwup you can't say 'I am sorry' for. Now he is asking me to help you, and we'll bury what happened back then forever. That's it."

Owen looked at her.

I have to trust someone. Here goes something stupid.

"Okay, I do have a problem. The Devil has given me what we call a 'coin,' and I don't know what it means or how to get rid of it."

"Uh-oh . . ." she stammered, taking a few steps away from him and looking at him as if he had just grown horns. Her butt hit the front of her desk, seemingly catching her by surprise. "Oh . . . you're screwed. And you didn't think you had a problem you needed help with?"

Then the mayor of San Francisco laughed. Not just a

normal little chuckle, but a full belly laugh that caused her
head to tilt up and her back to arch.

Owen sat on the couch with a glass of ice water in his
hand in the mayor's office in city hall. Elain and Jessica
talked in whispers by the mayor's desk, poring over a tablet
that he couldn't see. Owen replayed the conversation he had
just had while they all waited for a specialist to come in. He
was supposedly on his way.

>*"So, you're telling me the Devil gave you a coin. And
>you need to know about the rules?" Elain said.*
>
>*"Yes."*
>
>*"Very well. I will tell you what I know, but first . . .
>is it a coin you can hold, or a mark like a tattoo?"*
>
>*"Tattoo. It's coming in more and more every day."*
>
>*"Okay, good. That is better than the other option. Just
>a moment." Elain reached over and used the phone on
>her desk. "Hey, Mike, I need Jason to come to the office
>right away. Tell him it's an emergency, and I need him
>to bring all his tools." There was a pause. "No, no . . .
>Yeah, and push my next three appointments. I know, it's
>fine." Pause. "Okay, that's fine too. Thank you, Mike."
>She set down the phone. "Okay, where were we? That's
>right—the Devil has taken a liking to you. Where is the
>coin?"*
>
>*"On my ankle."*
>
>*"Could be worse. I have seen it before on someone's
>forehead. More than one, actually. I think the Devil
>gets insulted sometimes. You must have given her some-
>thing really nice to get a coin. It hasn't happened in a
>long time."*
>
>*"I didn't give anything."*
>
>*"Sure you did. That's how it works."*

"I didn't, unless you count the music it takes to get to the Devil's bridge?" Owen asked, confused.

"You are kidding me. You went all the way to the Devil's bridge?" Elain's face filled with surprise and appreciation.

"Yeah, I would rather not everyone know that."

"Don't worry about it. I keep better secrets than this."

"Like an art installation that is humming with energy that most of us can't even see?"

"That's Jessica's pet project, and yes, secrets like that one. And many, many others. Now tell me, Owen Brown, when you met the Devil . . . was it actually her, or one of her minions? Or did she just show up as a shadow on the ice?"

"Her?" Owen asked.

"Until I see or hear otherwise, that's what I'll say. Besides, who do you think could truly run hell? A man?" She held the word out like a treat for a dog. "Or a woman?" The way her lips wrapped around the word, Elain somehow lifted the weight of the word to a heavenly height.

"Sure," Owen said, not caring to get into a gender conversation entailing the Devil. "I never met or saw the Devil. I got the hell out of there."

"Nice pun," Elain said.

"Thanks."

"You're not telling me the whole story. Did you drop something there? Leave your instrument? A watch? Think about it. A shoe, perhaps? What? It's moving too fast—I can't read what you're thinking."

"A body. I left a body." Owen did not think now was the time to talk about Alice being there. As far as he was aware, the Devil had only marked him, and the less he shared, the better.

"You didn't go alone? You brought someone all that

way and found the Devil's bridge. That's something, Owen. Something special. I might have to hear you play after all. Who was he or she that you brought with you?"

"If I tell you who it was, I could get others in trouble, but let's say they were a he."

"Fine. Was he important or powerful?"

"Both. Enormously powerful." Owen's mind stopped moving as he pictured Kerogen's last moments of life before Alice drove her knife into the back of his skull and rode him down to the ice-covered ground.

"Is that Kerogen?" Elain said with concern.

"You really need to stay out of my head."

"I have the talent, but I'm not in your head, just in the space around your mind."

"Isn't that the same thing?" Owen asked.

"Almost. You brought Kerogen, the dethroned king of France, to the Devil's bridge and then executed him and left his body and power for the Devil? Another way to say that is . . . you took a dethroned king all the way to the Devil's bridge and then sacrificed him there?"

"I didn't do it on purpose."

"A dethroned king, his body and all the power stored inside Kerogen." She leaned back against her desk and let out a whistle. "Rumor has it, the last couple of years, Kerogen had grown in strength due to a bonding with an exceptional ethereal child."

"Does that matter?" Owen asked. He couldn't be sure how much of his aura and thoughts she was picking up, but keeping Alice out of them seemed like a solid idea.

"Not really. Not now, at least."

"Look, I don't know what the coin on my skin means. I haven't infused my music with ethereal magic since it happened. I need to know what it means."

"You are going to want to get rid of it unless you are

insane. And you don't strike me as the type," she said
seriously.

"You can do that?" The image of Clover cutting off
his ankle with a chainsaw came to mind, and Owen
shook himself.

*"No, but Jason can. If anyone can. He'll be here
shortly. You should drink some water. It will help."* She
went toward a cabinet and opened it up to reveal a
small bar and sink.

*"The truth is that it has been a while since I've seen
anyone receive such a thing. And yes, I understand you
want the rules, but I only know some of them. Chaos
follows whoever has a stamp. That's what they used to
say. Not chaos like rioting or anything like that, but a
change of odds. Like you are far more likely to be hit by
lightning than not. That sort of thing."*

"Now look who's not telling me the whole story."
Owen accepted the ice water for the simple reason that
he didn't wish to be rude. He was tired of feeling cold.
The drive through the desert had felt cold. Playing the
piano at the Grand Hotel had felt cold. Leaving Alice
had created ice crystals stabbing into his heart.

*"Okay . . . It's not a deal with the Devil, like they say
in stories and legends. It's more of a pass—or you
might like to think of it as paid entrance. They say you
can go down into the river of souls and back out without paying the price. Like you have been granted entry.
Souls trapped there can't pull you down. And they say
if you go down deep enough, there is ethereal energy
deep under the water. A pool of power just waiting to be
grasped."*

"Why would anyone want to do that?"

*"I don't know, but the ethereal power in the water is
said to be highly addictive."*

Owen shook himself. She was right. The addiction
of going to the Devil's river was a real thing. He had

*seen it eat the souls of some great musicians. As far as
he knew, it hadn't gotten its clutches on him, not yet.*

*"There is one last thing you should be aware of.
That mark, if Jason cannot get it off you, that mark al-
lows the Devil to find you anytime she wants. Day or
night. While you're playing music or fast asleep. That's
one of the reasons I think you should get it off you as
fast as possible."*

The door to the office opened, and the mayor's secretary
walked in with a level four We.

"Jason, so good of you to come. I hope I wasn't inter-
rupting anything," Elain said to the newcomer.

Jason was of medium height with short cropped hair,
wearing a black polo shirt and jeans. He stood with a stiff,
straight back and carried a black briefcase.

"Mayor, you are well? I am worried for you," he said, coming in close to look her over. His right hand reached out to
shake Elain's. Jason didn't let go of her hand as he set the briefcase down on the ground, freeing up his left hand.

"I am fine, no reason to worry. I have someone here I
want you to meet. He needs your help."

Jason's left hand touched her wrist, and his head started
to shake in an up-and-down motion as if he were reading
the paper. Elain didn't brush him off or act as if this were
anything but completely normal.

"That will be all, Mike. If you could shut the door and
see that no one comes in until we are done. Thank you,"
Elain said to her secretary.

"Mom, I'm going to step out, too. I have a lot of work to
do. Hi, Jason, it's good to see you again, but I have work to
do," Jessica repeated, hurrying past.

"You are always in a rush. A wonderful person should
not work so hard," Jason said, turning to follow Jessica with
his eyes as she smiled back, a look of concern covering her
face.

When the door was firmly shut, Jason, Owen and Elain were left alone in the room.

Jason spoke with a voice that held more of a fatherly tone. "Is she still afraid of my needles?" He shook his head. "Such a strong woman, but she needs to drink more water. I can see it in her eyes. And you, Mayor, you are not getting enough sleep each night. I can feel it. You are tired and stressed."

"Everyone is tried and stressed. But that is not why I called. How is your wife? Your mother-in-law? And your children?" she asked with genuine concern. Or so Owen thought.

"My children are wonderful—working hard, but they make time for family. My wife sent some pot stickers for you. She said she saw you on TV, and you're looking too skinny." He let her go and picked up his briefcase. "My mother-in-law is not doing so good. She still has her apartment, but she has bad days. My wife is there most of the time, or I am. Now, who is this strong, good-looking man you have brought me here to meet?"

Owen stood up, setting his glass of ice water down. "Hello, I'm Owen Brown." He walked over, holding out his hand to shake.

"Hello, Owen, my name is Jason, and it is very nice to meet you."

Their hands clasped, and despite the size and good nature of the man across from him, Owen was taken aback by the sheer strength in his hand. Owen was no slouch in the strength department, but Jason beat him, at least in hand strength.

"You are strong, fit and an etherealist—which means you should be in generally good health." Jason let go of his hand.

"Owen has a big problem that we were both hoping you might be able to help him with."

"A big problem, okay," Jason said. "I will try to help, if I can."

"I have the Devil's coin on my skin, and I was hoping you could remove it. I won't let her have my soul," Owen said.

"Your soul." Jason emphasized his words by pushing Owen hard in the chest, then giving it another pat with his hand. "It's *your* soul, no matter how many marks the Devil places on your skin. Are you sure you want me to remove it?"

"Can I keep my foot?" Owen asked in all seriousness.

"Of course you may keep your foot. Show me the mark."

Owen slipped off his shoe and sock and, with Jason's direction, sat back down on the couch, placing his foot on the black coffee table.

Jason made a sound that traveled through his nose as he looked closely. He then looked to Owen and back to Elain.

"Can you remove it?" she asked.

"I can," Jason said, lifting his black briefcase and setting it beside Owen's exposed foot. "The mark has not completely set in."

"How?" Owen asked. When Jason only looked at him, he asked again. "How can you remove the coin, the mark on my ankle? It's not a tattoo?"

"No, no. Not a tattoo. But it is not in harmony with your body. You were not born with this, it is not part of you yet. So I remind the body who you are, and I redirect the balance within. Your body forces this mark away. But you should know, it requires some of your ethereal magic to do the work."

"Okay. So how do we do this?" Owen asked.

As if in answer, Jason pulled out a six-inch needle with a green gem on the back end. A quick look inside the briefcase, and Owen saw a whole line of long needles with small gems.

"Wow. What are you going to do with that?"

"Oh, don't worry, it only goes in a little way," Jason said, pulling out a set of wire cutters. "I clip them off, and we place a patch over the needles."

"Excuse me, how many needles?"

"Not many. It doesn't hurt," Jason said, dabbing alcohol over Owen's ankle.

Owen looked at Elain.

"Oh, he's lying," she said. "It's going to hurt a lot. But Jason always says it never hurts."

"Pain is how you know it's working. Now, hold very still."

"Wait a min—"

But Jason didn't wait. The needle came in, and for the smallest of seconds, Owen thought the pain wasn't going to come. Like a fluke of nature or a disappearing magic trick. But then it did, just as Jason pushed deeper and deeper.

"Bingo?" Jason asked, but Owen couldn't breathe. "Good, just wait." Owen heard a snip and felt the cool metal of the wire cutters against his skin, but he didn't care, because the needle moved, and it felt as if it had been driven into his bone.

"There," Jason said, "that is not so bad. The pain will go away. Now for the second one."

"Hold on. Hold on!" Owen did his best not to shout. "Fuck me. Come on." He looked from Elain to Jason, who gave a sweet and fatherly smile.

"Just relax and sit back. This will not take long." The second needle went in before Owen could reply, and his body lifted up as his hand squeezed the leather of the couch. White-hot pain shot across his vision, and for the smallest of moments, Owen wished he could just pass out. Then the pain subsided, and Jason clipped off the needle.

"You will have to keep these in your skin until they fall out. It should be with the next full moon. The cycle complete. That will be in just three weeks." Owen barley heard what Jason was saying as another needle was driven in. "Now—you want lots of rest and water, but don't pull it out early, or this will not work."

Owen did his best not to scream again, but air did come

out. Elain made a noise, and he looked up and back to see that she was smiling.

"Oh, sorry, these are just so good. You want one? They really are the best pot stickers in the city."

In reply, Owen bit down on his teeth as Jason drove another needle in.

It was easy to see that each needle was being placed around the circle, but right then, the only thing Owen wanted to know was how many needles it would take.

"What was that? I couldn't hear you with all that heavy breathing," Elain said.

"I said . . . I should have let Clover use the chainsaw."

The last word stretched out as Jason pressed another needle deep into his ankle.

CHAPTER NINE

DAYS UNTIL A+O

Owen limped out of the yellow taxi.

Each time he placed weight onto his right foot, his ankle screamed in pain. The needles were still in his skin, sixteen of them, along with a smelling salve and a sticky bandage covering the whole thing up. It hurt. It hurt a lot, and then there was what had happened to his well of ethereal magic as the last needle had been driven into place. What had been overflowing magic was now drained to about half empty. Worse, his ethereal magic wasn't blocking the pain.

Owen breathed hard as he stepped up onto the curb outside another hotel, this one the Crown Hotel.

"You need a hand?" a large man wearing a black suit and tie asked. "You look like you're not doing so well."

"You ever let a kind Chinese man drive needles into your bones?" Owen asked.

"I fell in love with and married a Greek woman. Does that count?" The doorman laughed, and Owen did the same, although he didn't know why, other than that there was something very likable about the doorman.

Owen took the man's offered hand. "I can't say I know anything about that."

"You need an ambulance or something?"

"I need a drink. Or three. Do you know if Abel is here tonight?" Owen asked, referring to his friend, the owner of Whiskey Jack's, the bar at the top of the hotel.

"Could be he's here, could be he's not. Who's asking?"

"It doesn't matter. If he's not here yet, he will be. Thank you," Owen said as the doorman reached for the glass door.

"If you're going to Whiskey Jack's, it's the second bank of elevators on the second floor. Not the first set on the first floor, but up the stairs. Though, looking at you, I recommend taking the first elevator to the second floor and skipping the lobby stairs."

"Appreciate it," Owen said, despite already knowing the way.

"You take care. Whiskey Jack's isn't always the safest club in the city. It often brings in a different type of crowd than the suits and the Botoxed."

"Sounds like my kind of place."

Owen lingered. For no other reason than the doorman was nice to talk to, and he really didn't want to take another step.

"You know, I could get you a discount at the front desk, get you a room if you just want to rest that leg. Might not be the best plan to go up to the bar. What's the old rule—nothing good happens after dark?" The doorman pointed outside, where the streets ran cold with mist and the sun had gone down at least an hour ago.

"Thanks, I'm good."

"You don't look good. You don't look good at all. Last

chance," he said, already moving back toward a silver sports car that pulled up outside.

Oh, this night is just getting started.

Owen shuffled on as the doorman greeted the newcomers outside.

Owen avoided the front desk and went straight for the wide set of long stairs, refusing to walk the extra steps toward the first bank of elevators.

He moved slowly, leaning on the rail, as customers of the hotel passed by and glanced his way.

"You need help." It wasn't a question, and the voice was filled with power and authority.

"Jessica? What are you doing here?" Owen said with surprise.

He hadn't seen her until now.

"My mom didn't tell you? I'm to be your bodyguard and help you get to your friends so that they can keep you safe. After all, a person in your condition is in no position to just be walking around my city. It can be dangerous." She smiled with perfect white teeth. "Wow, that looks like it hurts. Does it hurt? Jason's work, that man is the best in the state. He used to own a restaurant before switching into healing with needles. Do you want a sip of my martini? The bartenders here are very good at what they do. This is my second, and I feel great."

Everything about Jessica said she was enjoying the power play.

"No, I think I can find my own drinks tonight," Owen said.

"I'm not sure you can. The way you scuttled across the lobby, it was just heartbreaking to watch. So strong earlier, and now you are so weak. And maybe a little sad."

"Why are you really here?" Owen asked.

"I told you, my mother ordered me to watch out for you. She pays her debts and holds to her word. It's how she became mayor, after all."

"You know, you might be able to read my thoughts, my aura and God knows what else."

"Tea leaves and hands too. Then there is this whole thing about when a man is naked, but I think everyone can read that part." She smiled again.

Owen had to admit, she was pretty in her black dress and denim coat, if one wanted to dance with a creature that was constantly thinking about devouring you.

"You should know that *I* know when you're not telling me the whole truth. And right now, I am not in the mood for games," he said, taking another painful step up the long line of stairs, the railing very much supporting a portion of his weight. "So instead of playing games, why not just tell me why you are really here, and we can both move on with our night."

He took another step.

Jessica took another sip. "Can't a woman keep her secrets? I might say I am entitled to them."

"Of course. Of course a woman can keep her secrets, as long as she keeps them far away from me and mine," he said, moving up one more step.

"I like you. Yes, my mother did ask me to keep an eye on you. Or, at least, have our people keep an eye out while you're in the city. I volunteered to watch over you personally. That should be a great honor."

Owen just waited.

"Jeez, are you always like this? So serious? I'm in a dress, after all."

Owen didn't answer, still waiting her out.

"Fine. You and your group are intriguing, and I wanted to know more. Plus, from what I can tell, Max seems kind. I don't like hurting kind people. I thought I would check on him. I swear that's it."

"My group is the best, so I get that," he said, then held out a hand for her drink.

She shook her head in amusement as she handed it over.

He took a long, undignified pull of her martini and handed back an empty glass. "Now, are you going to tell me what that art installation is? The one that almost killed my boy Max?"

"No, I can't. It's top secret, and it stays that way."

"Fair enough. I don't think I want to know any more secrets about this damn city anyway. In fact, I'm ready to get the hell out of here, just after I see an old friend."

"Whiskey Jack?" she said with a smile.

"Yeah, though his real name is Abel. People just call him that because of the club."

"I know him—met him a few times at charity events. Oh my Lord, you are taking forever. Come here and let me help you up the stairs. Take this," she said to a random group of men who were walking up the stairs, holding out the empty martini glass.

Jessica's voice was laced with power, and three of the four men moved as one to take the glass. The fourth was the farthest away, and his foot missed a step on the stairs.

"Of course. Thank you," said the man whose hand was closest. Jessica just waved them all away like gnats in the air and slipped an arm under Owen's shoulder.

From this close, he could smell her hair, her perfume and the raw ethereal essence humming in her system. For all her bravado, she was ready for a fight, he realized, as she moved in closer to support some of his weight.

"You should know that my city is the best. It grows on you the longer you're here because it likes to move in ways that no other city in the world can. It has this motion to it—you'll see."

"You mean it grows on me like cancer?" Owen asked.

And to his surprise, she laughed. A pure joy filled the air as her body shook a little.

"No, not like cancer. San Francisco calls to the artist in us all, the freedom to be different than what the script tells you to be. It has its problems and darker streets, but in the heart of my city, it calls to the souls who wish to be free. That makes it special."

"So I should watch what I say about San Francisco?" Owen said as they moved up the steps.

"Say whatever you like, just know there are great people here. And you should look a little closer before running."

"You know you're a level five We, right?" Owen said with some curiosity in his voice.

"What does that mean? That I should leave you to climb the last few stairs on your own? Or carry you like a baby?" Jessica said.

"Funny. No. I just mean most level fives have so much power that they tend to go after more. You don't seem to be focused on that."

Jessica made to speak and then didn't. She stayed quiet for a few more steps as they climbed almost to the second floor.

"Elain and I have been connected for a very long time. I don't remember when we started calling each other mother and daughter, but it fits. She now has this city in the palm of her hand, but that's only because she fights for it. She fights for the people, the businesses and the heart of the city. She's given herself to the cause. If I'm different, it's because she taught me how to be. Now shut up, because you're heavier than you look, and the elevator to the club is at least another forty feet to go." She pointed with her finger as Owen finally reached the top step.

Owen and Jessica came up the elevator and, after finding their names on the VIP list, were shown straight to Whiskey Jack's personal lounge area overlooking the large dance floor, DJ and three fully attended bars. They followed the black steel rail and walkway as it curved around the upper level, passing other VIP tables and moving toward the last booth, blocked off by a set of red ropes and a lone security guard.

"Here you go. Whiskey Jack will be here shortly, I've been told. That's Big John, if you have any problems with anyone. Now, what can I get you both to drink?" a waitress with a black mini skirt and ample cleavage asked in a pleasant voice.

"We're good. We'll wait for Jack," Owen said.

"Are you sure? The drinks are on the house," the waitress said.

"I'm sure, thank you," Owen said, twisting as he sat down on the soft leather couch.

"Okay. Let me know if you change your mind. There is a blue button on the table that goes straight to me." She tapped her earpiece.

The woman left Owen and Jessica alone but for the swirling lights, pounding music and anyone who was looking up.

"That was a little rude. I wouldn't have minded a martini—you drank mine," Jessica said as she stood over him.

"I know. It's just customary for us to wait. Don't worry. There will be plenty of time for drinks tonight."

Owen placed his booted foot, the one with needles still in it, atop the small black coffee table and leaned back. Jessica moved toward the black steel railing and looked out over the dancing crowd and lights.

"How's it looking out there?" Owen asked as he settled deeper into the cushion. "You see any of my people?"

"It looks like fun. I haven't gone dancing in months. The house is full, and I like the music."

"And my people?" he prodded, closing his eyes for a moment as the pain turned down now that he wasn't moving.

"I don't know what they look like. How could I possibly pick them out in this crowd?"

"Haven't you been grabbing thoughts out of my head since I met the two of you?" Owen asked.

"No—you have been sending your thoughts out like radio waves. When the space around you is quiet, it's easy to see things. But there have to be more than a thousand people in this club right now."

"I don't understand how you work, but right now, that's okay. My people will find me. They always do."

"Are you going to sleep?" Jessica asked.

"It's been a long couple of days, and Abel isn't here yet."

"You have got to be kidding me. Aren't you worried that I'll hurt you or something while you're sleeping?"

Owen opened his eyes to see her once more. "No. You're not here for me; you're here for *you*. Wake me when Abel arrives."

And just like that, surrounded by people and We, Owen let sleep take him. The needles had hurt far more than being shot, stabbed or anything else he had ever felt. And the pain wasn't going away, wasn't being blocked by his magic. Add in that his day had been all twisted up, and he was thankful as sleep took his mind on a dark, quiet ride.

Owen heard voices around him, and he did his best to blur them in with the pounding music of Whiskey Jack's as he refused to open his eyes, refused to allow sleep to escape his grasp.

"No, I'm telling you, that jacket is fantastic, and it looks completely authentic. Where did you find it? Was it Harp and Carol over on Twenty-Fourth Street?"

"Yeah! How did you know?" Clover asked.

"Harp and Carol are both friends, and they have the best vintage in the city. I love going in there," Jessica said.

Owen pushed it all aside as the warmth of the couch called for him to go back to the great void of rest.

Lightning arced through his blood as he snapped wide awake with one single realization: *My head is not on a pillow but on someone's shoulder.*

Owen sat upright and turned to see who it was. Expecting Max or even Clover, he was shocked to see Jessica staring back at him.

"Here's our sleepyhead. You okay? Or did you have a bad dream?" Jessica asked.

"Hey, Owen, you slept long enough! Thought you might miss the whole night," Clover said from across the black coffee table as she leaned against the steel rail beside Max.

"Hey, boss. You okay?" Max asked.

"Fine," he said, staring over his shoulder at Jessica. "How long have I been asleep?"

"About two hours, give or take ten minutes?" Jessica said. "I thought your friends would wake you up, but you seemed to double down on sleep when they came in."

He wiped his face with both hands and moved to stand up.

"Whoa, be careful," Jessica said too late.

Owen set his hurt foot down and tried to place weight on it.

"I'm fine." But he wasn't fine. Instinctively, he reached out a hand for Max. But Max, all battered and bruised, seemed confused as to why he would need help. So it was Jessica who caught him, with one strong hand pressing hard on his butt, steadying him so he didn't fall back down onto the couch.

Pain shot up through his bones and drove deep into his mind. Owen swore silently as the fresh waves washed over him.

"What did you do?" Clover asked.

"I took care of that problem I talked to you about," Owen said.

"The Devil's coin?" Max asked.

"You told Max?"

"Yeah. Jessie too. We did a lot of bonding. It's been a fun day," Clover said without any guilt. "So the coin thing is all taken care of? Looks like it hurts. How long before it heals?"

"Three weeks. Right now, I have needles in me. In three weeks, I can take the bandage off and pull out the needles if they don't fall out on their own," Owen said.

"Well, you look like crap, almost as bad as Max, but that's one problem solved," Clover said, raising an espresso martini in a toast.

"Yeah, speaking of Jessie, where is he? And how is he?" Owen asked.

Clover and Max glanced past Owen toward Jessica, who was clearly listening and an outsider.

"She's okay. Tell me," Owen said, waving a hand at Jessica.

"He'll be fine," Clover said with a shrug. "He's downstairs, flirting with some girls who like the tall and handsome type."

"You seem irritated . . ." Owen said.

"No, it's been a great day, and the night is just getting started. I'm ready to party. And I can't wait to meet your friend Abel," Clover said, but there was a tone there that Owen recognized as Clover not being her full upbeat self.

"She thought there would be more cowboys," Max supplied.

"You like cowboys?" Jessica said from the couch. "Me too. Something about a man you can rough up and take on a ride is just sexy."

"Right! Who doesn't like a cowboy? But, no, it's fine. The DJ is really good, and this club is pounding, and did you see we have bottle service? I am good," Clover said.

"Clover, we're in downtown San Francisco, not at a rodeo. Why did you think there would be cowboys?" Owen asked.

"The name is Whiskey Jack's. That's a cowboy place. It's fine."

Owen smiled at Clover's discomfort; it didn't happen very often.

"Back to Jessie," Max said. "I got him to open up, and, Owen, it's not just you sending Daphne home. He mentioned that you don't push him or teach him like you do for Clover. I think he thinks you are going to send him home next."

Owen looked from Max to Clover, his gaze meeting his hers. She shook her head from side to side, and some of the joy she had been feeling was washed away and replaced with sadness. Owen felt it too.

"Do you know why I don't push him the same way?" Owen asked Max, ignoring Jessica completely.

"I think so, but I don't know for sure." Each word Max said was careful and measured.

"What are you talking about?" Jessica asked.

"Band stuff." All three—Max, Clover and Owen—said the words at the same time.

"Right. Well, whatever it is you are talking about, it's killing the fun vibe. And I want to have fun tonight. After all, look at me—I'm all dressed up," Jessica said, reaching over and grabbing the bottle of vodka out of the ice bucket. Owen noticed it was one of three bottles in the oversized tray.

Clover's eyebrows rose as if to say, *You move fast, Owen.*

Owen shook it off, trying to indicate, *She is not with me.*

Owen glanced at Max. Max gave him something like a shrug with only his lips, a quick twitch up and down, but his eyebrows rose as if to say, *Jessica is superhot.*

"Right, so I'm guessing that you all met Jessica while I was asleep," Owen said.

"They did," Jessica said from behind him.

"She's the mayor's daughter, some sort of hyped-up palm reader on top of being a level five. And, Max, you know that art installation that almost killed you? The one with the pretty colors of ethereal magic? Jessica here is the one who put it there and oversees the whole top-secret project."

Owen looked from Jessica back to Max, giving his boy a nod that said, *Go for it, stud. She's all yours.*

Max didn't hesitate. His most charming smile split his face, and his voice deepened. "You are kidding me. You know all about the lines of ethereal magic? Can you see them? They were so beautiful. Like a living tapestry in the sky."

As he spoke, Max moved smoothly past Clover. With grace, he sat on the end of the coffee table so that he could talk face-to-face with Jessica.

"I did, and yes, I can see them. But it's as Owen said: a secret. I'm not supposed to talk about it."

"How can you keep such a thing a secret?" Max asked. "It's right out in the wide-open sky. I assume it's a net, connecting points and people? But what is it all for? I've been racking my mind ever since I was connected to the power and the object. I thought I could hear voices. You have to tell me."

Owen took small steps, moving away from the couch and circling the low table, taking Max's place beside Clover at the rail. He didn't ask Clover to change her position, but Clover matched his body, turning her back on Max and Jessica and looking out across the wide-open dance floor below them.

Owen moved in close—close enough that neither would have to speak loudly to be heard.

"Max moved fast there," Clover said.

"He has a not-so-secret thing for redheads," Owen said.

"Who doesn't? She's hot, Owen, *and* a level five. With good taste," Clover said, touching her new jacket.

"And why did you let me sleep against her?" Owen asked.

"What?" Clover said, turning her head to look at him.

"You let me sleep on her shoulder. How long was I there?"

"I didn't! And I have no idea how long you were there. About forty-five minutes ago, I convinced a security guard to let us up here, and there you two were on the couch. She waved us in and introduced herself. What's the problem? You're all punchy. Is it Jessie?"

"It's everything. It's this damn city." Owen swore.

"Let it out, man. Whatever is bothering you, just let it out. This place is too hopping to be brought down," Clover said with a smile.

He swore again. "First, there is a ghost in a piano at the Grand Hotel. I don't even know what to make of that. Second, there is Jessie. Third, my ankle really hurts, and I can hardly walk. But fourth. *Fourth*," he repeated, "is that my uncle Damon lied to me. Clover, *he* sent us here, not Mara. It turns out he used to shag the mayor. Then something happened between them, and the mayor owes him a favor. So Damon called in the favor by that personal letter that I hand-delivered. It was awkward and it almost went south, but in the end, the mayor facilitated and paid for the needles to be drilled into my bones."

"She used a drill? I assume it was cordless?" Clover asked.

"No, she did not use a drill. This acupuncturist did it by hand. It only *feels* like he used a drill."

Clover studied his face as hundreds—if not a thousand—partygoers danced and jumped and simply moved beneath them.

"Are you going to list Alice on your set of problems? Because I can feel the heartbreak rolling off you," Clover said.

"I don't want to talk about Alice right now."

"Why not?"

"Because she didn't get in my truck." Owen let out his breath as if the stress of the world could pour out of his mouth.

"Owen, you know that's not reasonable."

"I do. So let's not talk about Alice. She isn't here. Let's talk about Damon. Something is wrong. I can't understand why Damon lied. I don't even understand how he did it. You know I can hear a lie, and I didn't hear one when he said that Mara needed my help delivering personal letters."

"Does it really matter? So what if Damon helped you with the Devil's coin? It's not like either of us really had a solution there anyway. The coin was far outside of our normal. He probably understood we needed help, and so this was his way of helping you. And maybe he thought that if he told you it was an old ex of his, you might not take the help. Or maybe Mara has a huge jealousy thing, and Damon was just doing this on the sly?"

"Sure, okay, say that *is* true—and I could buy some of that. I still don't understand how he knew about the coin. I didn't tell him. I didn't tell any of them, and yet he put this whole thing together."

Clover glanced at Jessica and Max, then her gaze wandered back down toward where Owen had spotted Jessie talking to two women.

"Mara and your uncles do things differently than we do. They live by these old rules of theirs, and they are not human," Clover said.

"But a lie? They hate lies. They know lies tear people apart, tear the bonds between people apart. Whereas telling the truth pulls people together, no matter how bad the information is."

"Well, I don't know about all that, but maybe it's like I said, maybe it's a jealousy thing between Mara and Jessica's mom. That could be why Damon didn't tell you."

"Elain. Her name is Elain. Speaking of, she will be at

Mara's grand opening. I am missing something, Clover. I can feel it." Owen paused. "It's like I've been played. Like Damon made a big move, but I can't see it. Like the message is there, but I'm missing it."

"Are you sure?" Clover asked.

"Yes, there is more here. I can feel it," Owen said, looking right at her.

"Okay. Then start over. In fact, start with the ghost," Clover said.

"Right—the ghost," Owen said. He leaned away from the railing and noticed a large shape move fast at him from his left.

Owen's hands came up, and there was just enough time to open them as the big form of a man gave him a huge hug, lifting his feet off the ground.

"Owen Brown is *in my house!*" Abel said with a voice that carried forty feet around them regardless of the loud music. He was Owen's friend and a level three We of medium power.

"Abel!" Owen said, ignoring the pain in his leg and giving the man a squeeze just shy of breaking his ribs.

Owen was tall, clearing six feet, but he had to look up ever so slightly to meet Abel's deep black sunglasses.

"You're here," Abel said. "I can't believe you're here, and you brought your crew this time! That's perfect. Hello, everyone. I'm Abel, though some around here like to call me Whiskey Jack for fun. Oh my, you must be Clover. Everyone says how pretty you are, but they don't give nearly enough details. It's nice to meet you."

Clover shook his hand and said hello, but Abel was already moving toward Max, who was now standing beside Jessica.

"And you're Max, am I right? Owen has told me quite a lot about you. I can't wait to see one of your magic tricks. And then—" Abel shifted as he looked more closely at Jessica.

Owen watched the change in Abel's body as recognition set in, his shoulders pulling back and down, his feet planting. Not ready for a fight but more like standing at attention, waiting for a command. When he spoke again, his voice was low and controlled.

"Jessica Joyce, I apologize if you were waiting long. I meant no offense."

"And none was taken." Jessica moved to him, taking his hand and giving a kiss on each cheek.

"I wasn't aware you were here. If you would you like me to, I can clear this floor so we might talk—or I have a private office in the back?" Abel said, hesitating.

She waved him off. "Nothing of the sort. The mayor didn't send me. Consider this to be simply my night off. You see, I came across your friend Owen, and I guess I wanted to be part of the stories I have always heard rather than simply reading about them the next day."

"Of course. Is there anything I can get you to make your stay with us more enjoyable?"

Jessica was close to Abel, and the look Owen had seen in that palm reader shop slipped over her features and into her eyes once more. It was that of a predator considering her next meal.

Owen made to step in, but Clover's hand pressed against his chest. The motion pulled Jessica's attention, and her eyes met Owen's. He shook Clover off.

For a moment, Jessica simply stared, weighing his command, and the tension inside Owen ratcheted up. Jessica wasn't the type who took an order—yet that was what he had just given.

"Your staff have been wonderful, and I'm enjoying your club," Jessica said finally. "I mean it when I say this is my night off, and I just want to have fun. Do you think it would be possible for me not to be the mayor's daughter tonight and just be one of the many? Part of the crowd?"

"Of course. Anything you wish," Abel said with a small

bow of his head. "But are you sure you want to spend your time with Owen? He tends to get people arrested."

"Excuse me?" Jessica said.

"I do not!" Owen said.

"He does. It's true. Oh, he didn't tell you of our first night drinking together? What music festival was it again, Owen? World of Lights? I don't remember, and it doesn't matter. The point is, I am sure a wonderful person like yourself, Jessica, should not be spending your one night out with this hooligan."

"It was night number three at the festival, not the first night, and we never got arrested," Owen corrected.

"This sounds like fun . . ." Jessica prompted.

"It started out innocently enough. Owen here asked if I had ever gone van surfing. And I said, 'What are you talking about? How do you go van surfing?' And then he goes, 'Come on, I will show you.'" The small impression Abel made of Owen's voice wasn't close, and it wasn't meant to be.

"Let me guess," Clover said. "Was it one of those nights when you just *had* to do something stupid?"

"Yes," Abel said before Owen could speak. "Yes, it was one of those nights. Because the next thing I knew, Owen had me up on top of a van with a bottle of whiskey in hand, on a dirt road, fields of produce to either side, and the driver—neither of us knew who he was—started driving as fast as he could. The pedal was on the floor while we were standing on top!"

"It wasn't so bad! And I knew who the driver was—he was the one who bought us that last set of drinks. And he owned a van." Owen smiled, remembering.

"So apparently . . . apparently, when you are out in the middle of nowhere on private property, standing on top of a van with its headlights on and driving at breakneck speeds, it turns out you can easily draw some attention. The next thing that happened, as I was trying to stay standing and not fall off, was that the local police were after us. There must have been half a dozen of them, at least."

"Like three trucks, and I think they were state troopers," Owen corrected. "You always build it up bigger than it was."

"So there I am, on top of this van that's hitting every pothole and rock on the road. The driver is not slowing down even though the cops are closing in. Instead, he's driving like a crazy man, and I just know it's going to end badly, as we have flashing red and blue lights behind us." Abel couldn't hold back as he reached over and grabbed Owen's arm. "That's when Owen here, the all-knowing, let's-follow-him-to-the-end leader says—"

"—'Get ready to run!'" Both Owen and Abel said the words at the same time.

"What else were we going to do?" Owen said.

"I have bugs and dust in my mouth, the cops are closing in, and I'm barely able to keep my feet. Before I even register what he said, Owen grabs me by the arms and shoves me right off the top of the van. We hit the ground, rolling sideways, knocking down corn or something."

"It was a wheat field. You're an educated guy—you should know the difference between wheat and corn."

"And then I have Owen pulling me up to my feet, yelling at me to run. But does it end there? No—because now we are in a field of whatever, and there's no light, and I'm thinking we are fine because the first of the cop cars follows the van, but then I see headlights turn our way." Abel took a deep breath.

"It wasn't so bad, and you did well at the van surfing part. A natural, I called you," Owen said.

"I get to my feet, and bam, the cop cars are in the field chasing us. I swear, right here, that those cops were trying to run us down. It was only by the grace of the Almighty that we survived and got out of there."

"How did you escape?" Max asked.

Owen spoke before Abel could embellish. "We ran as fast as we could. Our bodies were already filled with ethereal magic, so we were moving through the field pretty fast, and the troopers tried to keep up, but there was a water runoff they couldn't see because of the wheat and the speed they were going."

"That's right—the police truck did a nosedive and went ass over teakettle, but we never saw it land because we were gone," Abel said.

"Owen, you never told us this story!" Clover said.

"Wasn't much to tell," Owen said, but he shared a genuine smile with Abel.

"Sounds wonderful. So what kind of trouble are we going to get into tonight?" Jessica asked.

"I heard something about ghosts?" Abel said. "We could track down the lady in red. I heard she is the real thing, and I've never danced with a ghost. Not even in the pale moonlight."

"She's in New Orleans," Max said

"That's a little far for one night. I've missed you, my friend," Abel said, and Owen understood. Abel was a level three We, with more brains and heart than muscle. Meaning that he cared far less about being a We and worrying about ethereal energy than about having a good time and making connections.

"I've missed you, too. Where's your wife, Michelle, and that little girl of yours?"

"You think I was going to bring either of them around you? Michelle almost didn't let me out of the house when she heard you were here. That's what took me so long—I had to sign several life insurance policies."

Owen could hear the lie and didn't care at all. "I think you're giving me a bad reputation."

"I am hoping to. I need to keep everyone safe." They both laughed, and it felt good. "Have you started drinking without me?" Abel asked, nodding toward the drinks in hand and bottles on ice.

"They have, but I haven't. Wouldn't think of it."

"He took a nap," Clover said.

Abel gave a chuckle that shook his body as he spoke. "You needed a nap, like an old man. That is so adorable."

"Are you goading me?" Owen asked.

"Why in the world would I do that?" Abel asked, signaling to one of his staff who was standing out of the way. "Now, fill me in on everything. What's new?"

"Oh, I know," Clover said. "Owen is heartbroken over a girl he just met. His aunt Mara sent us all the way here to deliver an invitation to her grand reopening New Year's party."

"I received an invitation for that. I don't think I can leave the club, but it sounds wonderful."

"I'm not done," Clover said.

"Oh, my bad," Abel said, putting his hands up in surrender.

"Turns out that we are in the middle of a mystery because Mara didn't send us. Damon did, but he told us it was for Mara."

"I know this part," Jessica said after finishing her drink. "Damon used to be an item with my mother. And the letter was from Damon to her, and in it, he asked Elain to assist Owen with his Devil's coin problem."

"Wait, hold up, you have a Devil's coin? A marking, or a real coin?"

"Marking, that's why I have needles in my ankle that are supposed to suck it out or something over the next couple of weeks, but that's not the mystery or important," Owen said, "because I just figured it out. I missed the first clue. It wasn't mayor Elain and the letter. The first clue Damon gave was the Grand Hotel."

Owen looked from Jessica to Abel and watched as some

of the carefree joy left Abel's face. His amber eyes became serious and weighted, as if his wide shoulders were carrying a heavy load.

"You have to know all about the Grand Hotel, the ghost and the piano," Owen said. "This is your crazy, messed-up city, after all, yet you never mentioned it to me. Nor have you ever mentioned the Russian Embassy or the corresponding piano that's located there."

CHAPTER TEN

ONE DAY UNTIL A+O

Alice pulled her van outside the Golden Horn in downtown Miami and stepped out. She wasn't fully strapped with weapons as she had been the first time she had ever stepped into this club, but that didn't mean she wasn't armed. The sign outside said CLOSED, but she ignored it and pulled open the main door anyway. It might have been her imagination, but for a moment she thought the door wasn't going to open before it swung on its hinges.

"Welcome back, Alice," Jones, a level three We, said from the main bar as he polished a glass. "Is Owen with you? And how are your parents?"

The questions came so smoothly they caught her off guard, and only then did she realize she was looking for a fight. Her blood was pumping hard, and she had pulled ethereal magic into her bloodstream, and her body was pulsing with go-energy. Her neck bent from one side to the other before she answered.

"Thank you, Jones. And no, Owen's not with me." She ignored the question about her parents. "I'm looking for Cornelius. He isn't answering his phone."

"Sorry, I haven't seen him. Can I get you a drink? Or anything else? We have some sandwich things in the back."

"No, I just need Cornelius or one of his people to tell me where he is. Or how I can get ahold of him."

"Mara or Damon might know. You want me to see if I can get one of them?"

"They aren't at the back table playing cards?" Alice asked.

"Not for a couple of weeks. The place has been mostly shut down after you left."

"I thought Mara was going to open up—" Alice wasn't sure how to speak about the room downstairs. It was a private club for We and etherealists alike. She found herself hushing her voice. "The ballroom downstairs?"

"Aye, she is. But first we have to get everything in order. It's best I don't talk about that side of things until after they have already happened. Keeps my job here safe, if you know what I mean."

"I do. No problem, Jones."

"Alice, what in all that is holy are you doing here?" Mara said, moving into the room from the main hall. Mara was tall, strong and thin. Her skin was flawless, and her hair shined black. Mara could have easily been snatched right out of an old-school gangster movie.

"Hello, Mara. It's nice to see you. And I see you're all dressed up." Her slim-cut black dress ran from her shoulders to the floor, and across the chest were gold bees. "I am looking for Cornelius. He's been working to get Father Patrick back to me, but he's no longer answering his phone. And I came here to help. That is some dress."

"Thank you. Now, is Cornelius not answering his phone or not answering your calls?" Mara asked, raising an eyebrow that was just short of hostile.

Alice wasn't sure why she rubbed Mara the wrong way more often than not. Perhaps the reason had to do with their first meeting, when Alice had torn up the club and broken the faces of a number of Mara's friends. Or perhaps it had something to do with Owen. But one thing was for sure: Alice wasn't scared.

"What's up your ass, Mara?"

"Excuse me, child?"

"Don't call me child. I already warned you once, and you don't have me chained to a wall this time."

The room seemed to bubble out as she and Mara stared at each other. Their relationship wasn't perfect, and they both knew it.

"Jones, take the rest of the night off," Mara said.

"Are you sure? I don't mind."

"I'm sure. The place looks great. Thank you for all your help."

"Of course."

Both women waited for Jones to grab his coat and exit.

"He's not here," Mara said as the main door swung shut.

"That's what Jones told me. Any chance you know where Cornelius is or how to get ahold of him?"

"Not for the last nine days, no. He went north, he said, and hasn't come back. And don't bother asking how that could be. Or how I don't know where he is. Cornelius doesn't answer to me. Never has, never will. However, now that I'm staring at you, I think he might have left a message behind the bar."

"What do you mean, might have left a message?" Alice couldn't help but move closer as Mara went around the bar, presumably searching for a letter.

"The letter is titled 'O girlfriend.' We assumed it was one of his lost loves coming around. They do that sometimes. Apparently he's a wild lover in the bedroom department."

O girlfriend? Owen's girlfriend? Alice thought.

"Here is the letter. Now, I need you to leave before my guest shows herself," Mara said, handing over a sealed letter.

Alice accepted, glancing at the words *O girlfriend* written with black ink in a flowing script, and she breathed easier, knowing in her gut this was for her.

It wasn't bravado that had her thinking so. It was understanding how Cornelius worked. He was always coming at things from more than one angle at a time. He had shown such skill in the battle and, more importantly, in how he handled the Kerogen problem.

Crazy-ass man.

"Now, if you need a place to stay, grab a hotel tonight, and you come back tomorrow. But I need you to go."

"Everything okay? Do you need my help?" Alice asked, tapping the letter against her hand.

"Thank you, but no. I believe as long as you're gone before my guest arrives, everything shall go as planned."

"You do look great—and that is one hell of a dress on one hell of a body." Slowly she started to walk back toward the door. She couldn't help but go slowly. There was something about Mara—despite the love she had for Owen—that rubbed her the wrong way. Like the woman was used to being the center of the world all the time. Yes, they'd shared a moment of kindness, but Mara tended to make her skin itch. And yet, for Owen and perhaps a debt, she had to try.

"Thank you, Alice." Mara made a point of using her name. "And I assume when you saw Owen last, he was fine."

"He's fine. Enjoying San Francisco, is my guess. But then you already knew that."

"I didn't know he was in San Francisco."

Alice whipped her head around. "What do you mean you didn't know? You sent him there. You asked him to personally hand out the invitations for the New Year's opening party downstairs."

"I haven't spoken to Owen in two weeks. And last I

heard, he was sitting around waiting for you to be done playing house. I never asked him to hand out personal invitations for me." Mara swore, then pounded her fist on the bar loud enough that Alice was sure the woman would have broken a number of bones if she had been human.

"If you didn't send him, then who did?" Alice asked.

"Who else could have? It was either Cornelius or Damon, the asshole. Toss a coin, but it was one of them. What does your letter say?"

Some of the itch between Mara and her vanished as Alice could see the real concern in the woman. For all Mara's faults, she deeply cared for Owen.

Dear Alice,

I knew you would come looking for me. Well, come looking for your priest, but a man can hope. I wish I had good news for you. If you are reading this, then most likely my attempt to negotiate went poorly, and I am now being held in the bottom of Saint Adam's Church in New York. The catacombs beneath the holy house have been used before to hold my kind. But don't worry about me or Father Patrick. He is fine and will stay in good health while I make my escape. Such possibilities have been well planned for. And my people are circling me even now, I can assure you.

Here is what I need from you: Stay by Mara's side. Keep her safe. It's imperative.

See you soon, and happy hunting.

Sincerely,
Cornelius

Alice finished reading the letter, then scanned over it once more.

"Cornelius has been captured and is being held in a catacomb in New York, but he doesn't want me to worry. It doesn't mention Owen or San Francisco. It just states that I need to protect you while he's tied up."

"Let me read it."

Alice crossed back to the bar and handed over the letter, then waited as Mara read without moving her lips.

"I take it back—he's the asshole. No, they both are . . . I just want to kick them sometimes."

"He wants me to protect you, so it looks like I'm staying."

"Oh, my girl, don't you see? If they took Cornelius and aren't sending him back to Spain on the first plane out, it means they don't believe he killed Kerogen. And if they don't think Cornelius did it, they most likely believe you did. So, no, Cornelius isn't asking you to protect me. He's asking me to protect you."

"What the hell are you talking about?"

"The church knows he didn't kill Kerogen, or he would have already been shipped off and wouldn't be held in New York. Did you think there wouldn't be consequences for killing a dethroned king? His wife, Norah, will want your head on a pike the moment she knows for sure it was you who killed him. Her people are coming for you, and the people Cornelius was negotiating with can't keep this a secret, not from her. So he's asking me to protect you again."

"Hello?" a familiar feminine voice asked as the main door opened.

Both women turned toward the voice.

"Daphne? What are you doing here?" Alice asked.

"Hi, Mara. Hi, Alice. I was hoping I could stay here, just for a little bit. I don't actually play the bass and was hoping you could help me."

"Daphne, you couldn't have picked a worse time to come back," Mara said. "Quickly store your things in the back, then I need you to leave for at least ten hours. Just ten hours, okay? Then I can help you with whatever you need. I'll tell you why you needed to leave when you get back. If you need money, take whatever you want from the cashbox. And take Alice with you," she added.

Her voice was far sweeter than anything Alice had ever heard from her. Well, besides that one time. "Seriously, Mara. Who is coming here? And you have to know I'm not leaving until we talk about Owen, and now Cornelius— who is captured, by the way, and it doesn't seem like you are very concerned. And how is it Kerogen's wife wants me dead? I did my research on her. They haven't seen each other for over a hundred years. Why would she care?"

"They were king and queen just at the end of the Dark Ages. That's before the church backed out of their deal and forced them off the throne. You aren't married to someone for over thirteen hundred years and don't care how they die. Of course she cares. Norah cares very much, and therefore anyone attached to her is going to care. That includes the church. And you should know Norah isn't a forgiving woman. And you killed her husband. Even though you had cause. If the church can give you to her, it will go a long way toward forgiving the time some of their people tried to kill him. So watch out for anyone watching for you. Damn it." Mara looked at her thin gold watch. "We might be too late. Why are you never wearing a suitable dress?"

"A dress? I don't know, I didn't come from church," Alice said, turning her head to the side as if to ask, *What is wrong with you?* "Okay, pissed-off widow, I can deal with that. But if Cornelius did not send Owen to San Francisco, why would Damon do it? And why are you afraid for Owen?"

"We don't know Cornelius didn't send him. We just don't have proof either way."

"What are you two talking about?" Daphne asked.

"Mara never sent Owen and the others to San Francisco.

We think Cornelius or Damon made the phone call and lied to Owen."

"It was Damon," Daphne said.

"What?"

"How do you know that?" Mara asked at the same time.

"I overheard part of the call. I was in the van, and I don't think Owen knew I was there. But I overheard him answer and say hello. It was Damon."

Alice looked from Daphne to Mara. "How sure are you?"

"Very sure," Daphne answered.

"Well, that's the worst-case scenario. Did Owen tell either of you where he was going or who he is supposed to hand the invitations to?"

"No," Daphne said.

"The Grand Hotel," Alice said. "He talked about it with me," she added, reading Mara's expression as both fear and darkening concern. "The invitations were to be delivered to the Grand Hotel by noon for pickup."

"Well that's it, then. Damon sent Owen to solve the puzzle of the two pianos and the ghost of Brando. I am going to rip off his hands so he can never play the saxophone again."

"What are the two pianos, and the ghost of who?" Alice asked.

"It's a trap that's for musicians with ethereal energy. In the form of a contest between a ghost and anyone stupid enough to try and perform with him. Over the years, it's killed untold numbers of musicians with power. I should have been watching for this. Damon has been upset over the contest since I pulled him away from it forty years ago."

CHAPTER ELEVEN

Owen watched Abel. He watched as the man he knew, his friend, shifted into a side he had never experienced before.

Abel took a small step back.

"We talk music and musicians every time we get together, and you never said anything," Owen pressed, a piece of the puzzle in his mind shifting into place.

"Hey, you never asked. Besides, it's none of my business—that place is evil. It's a trap, Owen. You can't beat the ghost, the red piano. No one can. Last place in the world we should go, where *you* should go. The last place I would ever want you to go."

"I am sorry, but what are we talking about? I'm confused," Max said.

"Yeah, I am too," Clover added.

"We are talking about dead musicians. And there's an instrument out there that sucks the magic right out of any musician stupid enough—or desperate enough—to sit down and play her. Of course I never mentioned it to you, Owen. You think I am an asshole, but she kills We and etherealists who are musicians, so I don't tell anyone about it. It's that simple."

Jessica poured herself another drink, then to everyone's surprise, she offered Clover another one.

Owen's foot started tapping, and a trickle of flame danced inside his chest.

The rumors are true. Rumors I have heard since turning eighteen years old, whispered in bars and halls all over the country. I have just never believed.

"What? What are you doing?" Jessica said, eyeing him.

"Damon tried to beat that red piano. He tried to outplay a ghost. The story goes the ghost plays ten songs and you play ten songs, and if you play better in all ten, you win and the key is yours. Damon failed, but he believes I can do it. That's why he lied to me and set this whole thing up. He didn't want Mara to know. He couldn't afford Mara finding out because she would have done her best to keep me from coming here."

The conversation stopped, and the music drifted in as Owen looked from his friend Abel to Jessica. One had his thumb over the pulse of the music scene in this city and beyond, and that included musicians of all levels, be they human, We or etherealist. The other was the mayor's daughter, a level five We who clearly knew this city and everything in it. Both had information, both knew what he had only believed to be rumor.

A tray of tall beers came in and was set down on the table. The waitress, taking note of the stall in conversation and Abel's direction, didn't linger. Abel said a thank-you to her back.

He leaned down and held a beer out to Owen, keeping the other for himself. They clinked glasses, and Owen took a drink. The cold and carbonation settled some of the ap-

prehension in his gut. It had taken too long to understand
Damon's plan.

"I thought we were going to have fun," Jessica said.

"Who says this is not fun?" Clover asked. "Owen, what
is Abel talking about? I don't love that there is an instrument that kills musicians and that you're thinking about
finding it."

"It's called the red piano, and it's in the Russian Embassy," Abel said. "Only it didn't use to be red—if the rumors I was told are true, it used to be white. And a long time
ago, anyone who wanted to come and play the white piano
could. Musicians traveled the world to give her a try and
celebrated the chance. Everyone with skill was welcome.
And it was rumored that the first time you played her, she
would open you up, as if you were ten times the musician."

Owen watched for a signal in Abel's face to see if he was
off track or missing something, but Abel was giving nothing away.

"It *is* red. I've seen it several times." Everyone looked at
Jessica as she spoke, and she smiled. "And I do remember
when it was white. Now—Max, you want to go dance? I
have a feeling we aren't staying very long. And you're cute.
I even like the bruises."

"I would love to dance with you," Max said. "Owen,
you've got this whole evil ghost and red piano thing. Grab
us if you're leaving. Abel, I really like your club, and thanks
for the free drinks." He and Jessica headed across the steel
walkway and down toward the dance floor.

"Does Max know what he's doing with her? I feel like
someone should warn him," Abel said as he watched them
go. "And what happened to his neck?"

"Owen choked him out," Clover said. "But don't worry
about Max. He has a way with people, even very dangerous
people."

Owen couldn't help but notice the change in Clover's
voice, and he gave her a look that she brushed off.

"How about a shot?" Owen said as he stared at her.

"Owen," she said in reprimand.

"What, Clover? You afraid of a shot? Come on. You, me and Abel."

"We didn't order whiskey."

"I see a bottle of tequila—and look at that, it's silver. Abel?"

"Let's do it," he said, a little more comfortable.

Drinks were poured into three shot glasses that had been chilling in their own small bucket of ice.

"I heard a toast that I liked today. The manager of the Grand Hotel toasted to death. So here's to the living and the dead. Let your soul be at rest, or barring that, let your soul be free."

"To the living and to the dead," Clover said.

It was Abel's turn to swear before he dropped the drink into his mouth.

"What was that for?" Clover asked, but Owen already knew, and he reached down and poured another shot.

"Are you two going to fill me in with what you know? Instead of giving it to me in teacups and spoons?" Clover prodded.

Abel and Owen looked at each other, each with a full shot glass in hand. Then both shook their heads and said, "No."

"Assholes."

All three tapped glasses.

Four shots later, Clover tried again. "Owen, come on. I know about the Russian Embassy and the long legacy there, but nothing about this deadly red piano, and I don't understand what it has to do with a ghost piano player at the Grand Hotel."

"The reason why it's confusing is that it has history to it. And I thought it was mostly a myth that I didn't believe to be true. So, let me start at the beginning. As you know, there are a number of keys out there—musical instruments that are made out of pure essence. Each item or instrument was created to give the most gifted and powerful musicians a chance to do impossible things." Owen held a beat, wanting his words to sink in.

"Like your guitar," Clover said.

"Yes, just like my guitar. There are two ways of thinking about the keys. One is that they should be spread out around the world to help musicians with ethereal energy everywhere. The other belief is that when the time is right, all the keys will come together, and the band that holds them will be able to change, well, everything."

"The fourth gate of Heaven," Clover said. "And back. What you've always talked about?"

"No," Abel said without looking up, studying his half-empty beer. "It's far more than that. Music is inside each one of us. It's in everything. Imagine hearing a sound so pure that it could reshape people. Reshape the landscape."

"I don't understand."

"It's a legend or myth, Clover. They, a secret sect of true believers out there, think impossible things are possible if all the keys come together. Like freeing every soul caught in the Devil's water, freeing them from their torment. And just about any other crazy thing you could think of. I have heard such theories as causing plants to grow, making it rain, all the way to breaking the moon. Or bringing people back from heaven."

Owen poured another shot.

"Okay, so . . . what does this have to do with the red piano?" Clover asked.

"Since I've accepted my key, there have always been individuals out there who have whispered to me rumors of what and where some of the other keys are. Including that the white piano at the Russian Embassy is a key," Owen said.

"Only it's not white anymore, and it kills musicians now?" Clover said, trying to understand.

"It's red now, but it was white," Abel said. "A We musician named Brando was fixated with the white piano and took up residency at the Russian Embassy. It's said that he was an amazing musician and had a very large We following. He also made it clear he didn't like anyone else using what he considered to be his."

"But it wasn't his," Owen said.

"No, that part is clear," Abel continued. "You see, when the piano was white, the general thought was that the white piano was just waiting for the right player to come along, and then it would give itself to him or her. But Brando hated that it didn't give itself to him. So he and his followers decided to change the game."

"And get revenge on the Grand Hotel," Owen added, "after they were tossed out and banned from the place for causing too many problems. I just learned this part today."

"Right. No one knows for sure how they did what they did, but whatever they did reforged the white piano into red and connected the piano at the Grand Hotel at the same time."

"So now there is a ghost piano player, presumably part of this Brando's soul, at the Grand Hotel. And the white piano is red?" Clover asked.

"Yes, and now the common thinking is that you must beat Brando, the ghost, in order to break the curse and restore the red piano to white. And in doing so, you might gain the gift of a very strong key," Abel said. "But most of us with common sense see it more as an evil trap that kills musicians, and so we don't talk about it. Or tell anyone. And we never, *ever* go see it."

He raised another shot to his mouth, forgetting to hand out the other two he had poured.

"So that's it," Clover said.

"That's it, only it's been a very long time, and no one has ever beaten the piano," Abel added. "And yet the promise of a key is more than enough to have We musicians and etherealists with musical talent trying and dying. They

show up in the city all confident, and instead, they all die."
Abel looked right into Owen's eyes.

"Damon would have died, but Mara had to save him,"
Owen said.

Abel swore with understanding.

"What?" Clover asked.

"There is only one way to save someone, because the red
piano doesn't kill you in one night. It forms a bond with you
and then sucks out your ethereal magic over about a week
until you die. Depending on how strong you are, that is.
The only way to save someone is to have the red piano bond
with someone else."

"I don't get it," Clover said. "Maybe it's the tequila."

"Mara sacrificed someone—forced someone to play the
red piano," Owen said. "Then she took Damon and went
back to Miami. Neither have been back to San Francisco
since."

"Right, okay . . ." Clover barely spoke the last word. "So
we're not going there, are we?"

"Your DJ is good," Owen said as he looked from Clover
to Abel.

"She is, isn't she?"

"Yeah," Owen said, lifting the shot glass to his lips.

Clover swore, then tipped back her own shot.

"Hey, guys, did we order a limo?" Max said outside on the
street with an arm around Jessica's waist.

"Abel did," Jessie said.

"Okay, but there is still one part of this plan to go see the
evil red piano that I don't understand."

"What's that, Max?" Jessie asked.

"How do we get into a Russian Embassy at two, two
fifteen in the morning? I don't have a passport. I don't even
think I have two forms of ID."

Jessica laughed; Clover did too.

"Oh, Max, if ever we needed proof that you aren't a true musician, it would be that question right there," Clover said.

"What do you mean?" He looked at Jessica, but she just gave another little laugh.

"Come on, Max. San Francisco. Russian Embassy. Music history," Clover said.

"It's okay, Max," Jessie said, putting his arm drunkenly around his friend. "Most people don't know it either, but I will tell you."

"Hold on," Abel said, coming out onto the sidewalk at a jog with two bottles of top-shelf tequila in his hands. "Don't tell him. It will be so much better to show him."

Owen felt Abel's smile, and his own smile matched it. It was good to be with friends, friends who would go anywhere with you.

You must be kidding me. *This* is the Russian Embassy?" Max asked. "This is not an embassy—there are no guards, no security, no flags, no diplomatic immunity. There is nothing Russian about this place. It's . . . it's . . ." Max trailed off as he stood elbow to elbow with Clover and Jessie through the sunroof of the limo and stared at the four-story building that sat on the side of a steep hill.

The building was draped in glass and dripping in true Victorian style.

Owen was the first out of the limo as Max continued to choke on his words. Clover, Max and Jessie all watched him hobble out as he tried his best to keep weight off his right foot.

"Wait! I know this house," Max said, and everyone laughed. "I know this house!"

"You should," Owen said, one hand braced on Abel's arm.

"It's the William Westerfeld House," Abel said. "Also known as the Russian Embassy. Legends have lived and played unbelievably great music here. And then I guess this Brando came with his groupies, and he did his trick with the two pianos, and now this place eats people's souls. I am not sure we should be going in." He paused. "And why are all the lights on at this hour?"

"We are going in because I want to see it," Owen said. "I looked at the ghost and piano at the Grand Hotel earlier today. There was something shameful about it. Now I want to see what's truly behind it all. I want to see its heart."

"Well, I'm with you, but if my wife finds out, I might need a place to hide for a year or two."

"Owen," Clover called out. "Wait a minute." She disentangled herself from the others and stepped out of the limo.

"What's up?" Owen asked.

"Just wait a second," she said, covering the distance so she could talk softly. "Yeah, so, I've been thinking maybe we should have a chat before we go into the supper creepy house armed only with our wits and my good looks."

"About?" His voice was pure sarcasm.

"Hey, I love an adventure, but even you must admit we aren't on our best game right now. It started at the beginning of this trip with Daphne and the Jessie thing, then Alice stabbed you, then Max when we arrived in the city, and then there's the whole ankle and coin thing. And that leads into Damon lying to you, and now two pianos, one with a ghost and another that steals musicians' souls."

"Okay, I hear you. We are not at our best, I can agree with that. But if Damon wants us to solve this problem, we aren't going to just walk away from it. I know he lied to me, but I still trust him. If he believes I can break the curse and set things right, then that's what I am going to do."

"And how much of this has to do with the idea of you getting your hands on another key? Owen, you heard what Abel said. The piano in that house has been draining the life out of musicians. How many innocent people have been murdered trying to solve this?"

"Again, I hear you, and I don't plan on doing anything rash. I just want to look. Then we can go back to Abel's swanky apartment and wake up his wife and drink all his booze."

"I'm good with that plan," Abel said.

"Or my place," Jessica added. "You all should definitely see my place; the views over the city are amazing. I just finished the remodel on it."

Clover continued to whisper. "I'm just saying, you aren't at full strength right now. You haven't slept in more than twenty-four hours. You're heartbroken over Alice; you're upset over Jessie. Come on. It's two o'clock in the morning. Let's go have a slice of pizza, and we can come back tomorrow."

"I hear everything that you're saying. And you are right about all of it except for one thing. I think this guy that did this . . ."

"Brando," Abel provided.

"Thank you. Yes, Brando—and by the way, what kind of name is Brando?" Owen asked to the group.

"I think it's from *Star Wars*," Max said, coming into the conversation.

"No, it's Italian. Just like Marlon Ernest Brando. And before you ask—"

Abel was cut off by both Clover and Owen. "We know who Marlon Brando is."

"Two-time Golden Globe winner," Jessie said.

"Everyone shut up and let me finish," Owen said loudly. "We aren't talking about Marlon Brando, we are talking about this Brando, and, no, I don't think they are related. And this Brando, who again is not from *Star Wars*, was an asshole. And so we are going to go into the spooky house with all its lights on at two in the morning. We aren't going to touch the nameplate and the C key, because that's how the whole thing is supposed to get started. We are just going to look for clues on how to break the curse. Okay?" Owen gave a particularly stern look to Clover.

"Okay, but you should know right now that I'm hoping there are a lot of stairs in that house," Clover said.

"Well, that is just mean," Owen said as Clover moved toward the wrought iron gate that separated the sidewalk from the walkway.

Owen shambled behind her, Abel staying close to help with balance as Owen fought the pain of his ankle.

He looked up at the building and couldn't help but feel a sense of awe filling his chest, his body and his mind as the details and size of the building became clear. The crafts-manship and style pulled his eyes from detail to detail. Everywhere he looked, there was an artist's touch in the building. "Impressive" didn't begin to describe what he was seeing.

Owen put his hand over the gate's handle, and to his surprise, it swung open easily.

They climbed the many stairs in a pack, with Owen leading the way. The door of the house was large, with round glass and old wood. The craftsmanship was exqui-site, and it looked to Owen as if the door and the stairs they had just climbed had been painted recently. Even the edges around the glass were clean and shiny.

"It's late. Do we use the doorbell, or should you knock?" Max asked.

"Max, are you okay?" Jessie asked. "Your voice is sad."

The question drew a few glances.

"I thought we were going to see Russians."

Everyone who wasn't looking turned and did so. Then, to the surprise of everyone, the front door opened on squeaking hinges.

"Oh, hell no," Jessie said as he turned back to look in.

Jessica gave a small giggle, covering her mouth. Abel took such a big step back that he almost fell down the stairs—if not for the banister, he would have.

"Hello, everyone," a voice from inside called out, and it

took Owen a moment to understand the man speaking was standing behind the open door. "I had heard you might be coming, so I kept an eye out for you. Come in, come in. Don't be shy," the man said, coming out from behind the door, where he set a wedge to hold the door open.

Owen looked on in confusion, for the man seemed to be human—not one of the We, and not an etherealist either. And yet it was as if his proportions didn't quite add up correctly. He was large in the chest but skinny in the waist. He wasn't a tall man, nor was he short. He wore a black pinstriped suit with a black tie and red vest. And for the smallest of moments, Owen thought the man could be a bellman; only he didn't carry himself like a bellman.

"Hello, sir. My name is—"

"You are *the* Owen Brown," the man said, lowering his voice. "It's quite all right, I know her first impression can be stunning. She stole my heart when I was just a boy. But yes, you are Owen Brown, and his faithful Clover—though I don't see your violin. You must be Jessie, tall and very handsome. Max, you seem a little worse for wear. I do hope our city hasn't been too cruel to you. And the last requires no introduction, for everyone knows the new and cunning owner of Whiskey Jack's. Though I've said it before, I will say it again: you need to change your name permanently to Jack now that you own that place and are doing so well. I did, and it was the right decision."

"I was thinking about getting the name Jack tattooed on my forearm. My wife says not a chance, but I like the idea. Do you think that will work?" Abel asked from the back of the group.

But the man had locked on to Jessica like a turkey locks on to a wolf.

"Excuse me, Jessica Joyce. Sebastian from the Grand Hotel didn't tell me you would be here. It's nice to see you again."

"It's been a couple of years, Tom," Jessica said. "It's nice to see you and your home. Forgive me, but I am crashing the party because it seemed like a fun idea. And it has been."

"Most of you are drunk. He didn't tell me that part. But I guess it doesn't matter. Come in, come in. My name is Tom Westerfeld, and I own the Westerfeld House. Your timing is perfect."

"Thank you," Owen said, stepping into the receiving area, the others trailing behind.

"I have been asked to grant you access to the red piano, and you will likely want to see my current guests. I believe they are just now wrapping up with their recordings." Tom Westerfeld pointed toward the stairs. "They are upstairs."

"Called it—this place has stairs!" Clover said.

Owen heard different levels of laughter behind him, but he was more focused on the first part of what Tom had said. "Wait a minute, you have guests staying with you, and they are recording?"

"Oh, yes. I try to keep the piano from your kind, but it seems people always find a way. I even locked up the front door and every window one time when I went to visit my uncle over in North Carolina, but I came back to a number of musicians who had set up shop in the main room. It was sad. But this group, the one upstairs now, said they were here to visit the different gardens of the city and asked to rent the fourteen rooms for one week. They lied, as so many do when it comes to the red piano. But at least they pay their bill. I'm thankful every day that I don't have a touch of musical talent. Imagination and love aplenty, but no musical talent."

"You have never played the piano?" Owen asked.

"Oh, sure, many times, but it doesn't want me. I belong to the house, not to the music. Now, before you head up, you should look at some of the details of the house. It's amazing, the craftsmanship—I just love it. I've striven to keep the original works. I wish I could give you a proper tour, but Sebastian said I should show you up right away.

Here you are," he said, walking toward the stairs. "I would make the introductions, but they really don't like me up there, and some of them are rather large."

Abel hadn't followed by Owen's side, so Owen did his best to hide the limp as he moved toward the stairs by himself.

"I can help you," Jessica said, removing one arm from around Max.

"No, we got it. Jessie?" Clover said, and Owen didn't look back as Jessie and his number two moved to either side of him. Together, they climbed the stairs.

"Is this night getting more and more surreal, or is it just me?" Clover asked.

"Owen, if there are musicians up there, they might not want us to interfere," Jessie said. "Some musicians are touchy, and if they are trying for a key and know who you are, we might have a problem."

Owen didn't answer.

"He knows, Jessie," Clover said. "Whoever is up there is playing with death, *and* they are recording it."

"And the owner said they've been here for a week," Owen said.

As a group, they climbed the many stairs, slowly making it to the second floor. They followed the muffled sound of people above until they came to a second set of stairs.

Owen heard Max whisper, "We might end up throwing down when we get up there. You might be safer staying here."

"I was right about you. There is something so refreshing about how kind you are. And I like the way you look at me," Jessica said, loudly enough that everyone could hear her.

Owen, Clover and Jessie stopped and turned from the fourth step to look back down, Abel a second behind them. There, standing on the landing, was Jessica with her arms around Max, and they were in the middle of a deep kiss.

"A superhot level five We redhead with full psychic power, and Max looking as if he just had the crap kicked out of him, yet even so, here he is getting to first base," Clover said quietly, so as not to interrupt.

"That's my boy," Jessie said as they continued climbing the stairs.

"Rock-star status," Owen added.

"Are you jealous?" Clover asked.

Owen shook his head. "Happy for Max. Happy for Jessica."

Clover made a smug noise, and Owen ignored it. He had too much concern for what was happening upstairs. From what he could hear, there were a number of people up there, and nothing about this was right.

Owen pulled on his well of ethereal energy. With a firm direction of will, he forced pure ethereal magic to cover his ankle. The pain dulled, and Owen didn't need to look under his jeans to know the bandage was blanketed in a perfect black glaze of ethereal magic.

Voices became clearer with every step they climbed, and Owen's people remained quiet, taking their cue from him.

"Is everyone almost completely packed up? I want to get the hell out of this place, man. I feel like the walls are moving." The voice Owen heard sounded closer than the others.

"We are getting close. It's always Johnny who takes the most time." Another voice said.

"I don't see anyone volunteering to help me. It's not like all I do is unhook my guitar, take a bump, and say I'm done."

There were a few laughs, and Owen heard a glass bottle break.

"I told you, Johnny, just leave everything for the label guys to clean up. Isn't that right, Markus?"

Owen climbed the last set of stairs without help, ignoring the pain and pouring ethereal magic into his skin, his bones and his blood.

The scene was unfolding in a large round room with black cables crisscrossing the ground, and black speakers, mics and stands. Owen counted ten people all about the room, and in the center was a shiny red piano.

There was more to see, from the long blond hair to the leather jackets to a woman who was currently letting a man snort drugs off her chest.

"I can give you a hand, Johnny," a large level four We said, then turned around and looked at Owen.

The large We was surprised, but he didn't show an ounce of fear.

"Hey, this is private space," he said, drawing the attention of most of the people in the room.

Owen ignored him and let the layers of civility fall away. "What the hell is going on here?" Owen spoke loudly and pulsed out his words. "Now *this* looks like a party. What am I looking at, Clover?"

"Oh, just a bunch of legendary rock stars trying to fly under the radar," she said, leaning up against him. "That one over there is Alex Storm, the one and only bass player for Midnight Madness."

Jessie spoke up next. "I see Rhythm of Steel, Danny Man, and a hot honey having some fun. And is that the legendry drummer *Johnny White* putting away his own drums?"

The only one in the room wearing a suit said, "Hey, I'm sorry, but this is private property, and we aren't doing pictures or signings right now. You're going to have to leave. Bucky, Roman, get them out of here."

"Wow, wow," Alex Storm said.

Followed by Danny Man, the rhythm guitarist, echoing Alex.

"They're cool, Markus. It's all right," said the man with the long blond hair, who hadn't stopped eyeing Owen.

Owen knew who he was—so did every rock fan in the world for the last forty years. Eddie R was a legend. And this was his longtime band, Midnight Madness.

Owen didn't move, with Clover still leaning in and Jessie beside him. The others—Abel, Jessica and Max—stood behind him as they watched who had to be the manager,

Markus, try and fail to have a private conversation with Eddie R.

"It is not all right! No one is supposed to know we're here. No witnesses, no social media. This isn't cool," Markus said when Eddie didn't even look at him.

"Hey, Markus, we're all good. This is Owen Brown and Clover. We met them on the comment tour," Alex said.

"We good, Eddie, or do you need some time with your manager?" Owen called out.

Eddie stood up from the speaker he was seated on. "Get over here, you son of a bitch."

Owen crossed the room with an ice-cold stone in his chest that burned hot as he clapped hands and gave the lead guitarist of Midnight Madness a hard embrace.

Introductions were made as his people came in, including the two security guards and the two women.

"That's Donna, and that's Dana, but you can call them anything you want and they won't mind," Eddie said with a big smile.

"So . . ." Owen said, pointing toward the recording equipment. "If I would have known you were set up here, I would have brought my guitar, and we could have laid down a track."

"Fuck it, let's go right now. We have like seven guitars here, and they can have everything wired back up in a few minutes."

Owen leaned in. "So, why are you all recording here?"

Anyone with ears could hear the change in Eddie's voice. "This place has great bones. Real juice when you need it. You know her history. Man, I used to come here twenty years ago, and she is just the same."

"And this is the famous red piano?" Owen asked.

"That's the fucking one, man," Eddie said.

Owen moved toward the instrument, and every instinct he had was on high alert.

He had expected a deep crimson red, but looking closely, he realized he was wrong. This was a red-hot cherry, the kind muscle cars were once painted. She shined without a blemish or scratch, and Owen's stomach turned at seeing her. She had been a pearl white—representing purity—and now she was this.

"I wouldn't touch her, man. They, um, say she's cursed," Eddie said, then he gave his nose a large sniff.

"Yeah, that's what I hear. Have you never played her?" Owen asked, somehow already knowing the answer.

"Not me. But I, um, have played with others who have."

And what about this time? Who did you sacrifice? Who did you beguile to connect to the red piano? Because everything in this room reeks of guilty.

"Is that right?" Owen asked, looking back at him.

"Eddie," Markus said in warning.

"It's fine. Owen lives for the music. You can smell it on him. Oh, shit, are you here to try for it? Are you going to beat the ghost? Take the key and rock on?"

Markus just shook his head.

"Me?" Owen asked. "I'm a strings-and-steel guy, everyone knows that."

"They also say you can play just about any instrument. You really not making a try for her?"

"Can I confide something in you, Eddie?" Owen said, moving away from the red piano and over to where there was an ice cooler with bottles sticking up from it.

"Sure," Eddie said.

Owen pulled out the only bottle of water, the bottom dripping from the ice and water.

"I can't play the sax to save my life," Owen said.

Eddie laughed, and even Markus let out a small grin.

Owen cracked the lid to the bottle of water and took a small, careful sip. The black cast of ethereal magic over his ankle was eating up his remaining well of magic. If this was going to go south, it needed to happen now.

Owen looked across the room, checking each of his people's positions, seeing that they had spread themselves across every member of the band and party. Owen took a deep breath.

"So, who played the piano?" Owned asked, knowing there was only one way this was going to go. If he included Max, who had an empty well of ethereal energy, and he included Jessica, it placed the numbers on his side—six against their eight, and the two groupies.

As Owen's words circulated the room, all heads turned in his direction.

"Like I said, no one did. That thing is cursed." Eddie R spread his hands wide, knowing everyone in the room could hear the lie.

"Who played the piano?" Owen said again, as if Eddie hadn't spoken.

The room iced over in silence until Danny Man spoke up. "Hey, maybe you all should go. We were just packing up to get out of here, and the owner doesn't like musicians in here anyway."

Owen moved toward the recording equipment and loaded the last saved track. His fingers were about to press play, but Eddie R caught his hand.

"Why?" Owen asked.

"Screw you. You want to go? Let's go. Come on. You think you know anything? You're a baby, and I am Eddie R—"

Whatever he was going to say next was cut off as Owen balled his left hand into a fist, reinforced it with ethereal energy and broke Eddie's jaw.

CHAPTER TWELVE

O wen felt the bones break in the rock star's face as his fist connected. A small, internal part of Owen's soul took flight. Eddie wasn't down, but he wouldn't be back in this fight. Eddie wasn't the fighting kind. That's why the two large bouncers were here. Abel sucker punched one in the back of the head, and the other, Bucky, didn't hesitate as he threw a full-strength haymaker at Owen's head.

Owen ducked and came in behind it, punching with his right fist, hopefully breaking a few of Bucky's ribs. It was just enough to cause the big man to turn his body. Three hard and fast hits to Bucky's face, yet the security guard still didn't go down despite the blood covering Owen's hands. Instead, he smiled as blood poured down from his nose and into his mouth.

"I'm going to hurt you!" Bucky said with a mad glee.

A bottle broke hard over the back of Owen's head, and moving on instinct, Owen tossed a sharp elbow into

Markus's face before he could follow up. Markus stumbled back—a good thing, since Bucky immediately came in on Owen.

Owen ducked and backstepped, slipping to his right, and got smashed by the wrecking ball known as Bucky's left fist. The hit broke several of Owen's ribs, and for a moment, two things happened at once. First was that Owen couldn't breathe. The air went out of his lungs and simply wouldn't come back, so he choked on pain without air. Second was that the amount of pure force in Bucky's left cross had Owen flying up and over a stack of recording equipment and speakers.

He had just enough time to see his people in a full-on fight with the rest of the band.

Owen shook it off as Bucky's large frame hovered over him.

"Well, good on you, Bucky. You *did* hurt me," Owen said with the little breath he was able to take in.

"Get him, Buck. Get him!" Markus called from just out of sight.

Bucky wasn't in the mood for talking.

As Bucky's body dropped hard onto Owen's chest with a huff, Owen timed his fist going for the man's face. Bucky blocked and pushed Owen's arm wide. His smile of teeth and blood was more than enough to signal that Bucky was enjoying the moment—until his eyes changed from joy to panic to pain.

In the half second it had taken the security guard to land and then block Owen's punch, Owen had snaked his ethereal essence around the level four's waist. With a command of will, the essence shaped into a silver whip that burned orange with energy.

Bucky let out a scream, and Owen punched him in the throat before shoving the large man off him and climbing to his feet. Owen, with his whip eating into Bucky's flesh, stood to his full height and surveyed the scene as Clover finished dropping Alex Storm to the ground with two hard hits to the face. The only ones left standing were Markus and Eddie, both tucked up against the wall nearest to Owen.

Owen stopped pouring energy into the whip and commanded it to shorten so that it hung from his hand without hitting the floor. He left Bucky on the ground, writhing in pain, and moved toward the other two.

Markus pulled out a small Beretta handgun, but Owen was faster and saw the move coming, knocking the deadly weapon to the side and out of Markus's hand.

"I asked before, and I will ask again: Who played the piano?" Owen said in a voice that promised death.

"Why don't you go—"

Before Markus could finish his insult, Owen broke his nose, sending the man hard into the wall.

"Eddie? I was talking to you," Owen said, moving in closer.

He spat blood. "You broke my jaw."

"You'll heal. Answer the question."

"Why do you care? He was a nobody. The boy wasn't good enough to play with us, not by half, but he begged us. *Begged us* to let him play. Don't act holier-than-thou, Owen."

"Is he still alive?" Owen asked.

"I don't have to tell you shit! Get out of here. I paid for this place," Eddie said.

"Jessie, Abel, I don't care how you do it, but toss every one of these assholes out the front door."

Johnny White, the drummer, spoke from the floor. "Just give me a minute to grab my things, and we're gone."

"You didn't give a shit about a kid's life, so I don't give a shit about your stuff. Jessie, Abel? *Now.*"

Jessie and Abel weren't alone. Jessica, Clover and Max helped pick up and push each of Eddie's crew toward the stairs. Danny Man got pissy, and Abel shoved him hard, sending the man tumbling down the stairs. All the while,

Owen just held stares with Eddie and kept an eye on Markus, who was still holding his bloody nose.

It was Jessica who ordered Bucky gone, and whatever he saw in her eyes had him moving until the room cleared— all but for Eddie and Markus.

"Are they staying outside?" Owen asked.

"Yeah, the owner told them not to come back. He has a shotgun, Owen, and he looks like he can't wait to use it. Kind of jumpy. 'Eager' might be the right word," Clover said. "What do you want to do with these two?" She pointed toward the manager and the rock legend.

The blood had dried on Markus's face, and a couple of minutes ago, Eddie had reset his jaw with the help of ethereal magic.

Max came up the stairs two at a time. "That's all of them. Jessie, Abel and the owner are watching them out front, but no one is making a move to come back in."

That left Jessica, Clover, Owen and Max in the room with the other two.

Inside Owen's chest, the fire was burning, catching more and more heat with each passing moment of inaction. *You have a responsibility as the leader of the group. You have a responsibility to the musicians who are coming behind you.* Oh, he understood the need to fly and be reckless, but not at the expense of someone else.

"Where is the body?" Owen asked, looking straight at Eddie.

"I am not telling you shit, and when I get out of here, you are done. Get out of my way," Eddie said.

Owen didn't let him pass. Instead, he hit him in the stomach and shoved him hard enough against the wall that Eddie's head bounced.

"You are a piece of shit. Now tell me where the body is," Owen pressed.

"Hey, you can't touch him!" Markus said. "He's protected by the record company. So just back off and let us leave."

Owen spit in his face, then he punched Eddie so hard in the stomach again that the legend doubled over.

"I want the kid's name, and I want the whereabouts of the body!" Owen said again.

Eddie let out a string of curses.

Markus cleaned off his face with his hand. "This is over. We are leaving now," he said, "or the label will place a price on your head. I'll see to it. Do you understand who you are dealing with? He's signed with Mary Cross Records. They will skin you alive if you don't let us out of here. He's protected!"

Owen looked at the manager. "Tell me where the body is, or you aren't leaving this room alive."

"You can't threaten us!" Markus shouted.

But Eddie, who'd finally stopped swearing, said, "He's on the second floor. I don't know what room they put him in."

"Is he still alive?" Owen asked, more with hope than belief.

"He was last night. Now we're leaving."

Owen let Eddie pass and watched him head straight for the stairs. Markus moved off the wall, and for a moment, Owen thought he might take a swing. He didn't.

"No," Owen said as Eddie picked up his guitar case.

"I'm taking my axe, and Markus is right—when the label hears about this, you are all screwed. You will never play on tour or sign a deal. It's lights out for you fuckers."

"Eddie, I said no. You don't have need of a guitar anymore."

The legend, who had given his music to the masses for more years than Owen had been alive, turned angrily. Owen snapped the essence forward, filling the metal with burning heat and reshaping the end.

Eddie tried to move, but it was over before he could. The long black guitar case dropped to the ground with a bang.

And Eddie's right hand dropped beside it.

"You lost your right to play music," Owen said.

Eddie screamed and covered the stump of his wrist.

For a moment, everyone just watched.

Owen couldn't think of a worse punishment. A guitar felt like an extension of his voice. Death was too easy for Eddie's crime, but this would have to do.

"You are all dead," Markus seethed. "I told you that he's protected by the label. That's Eddie R, the rock star! Each and every one of you is going to die, and there is not a place on this Earth where you can hide from them. Do you have any idea what you just did?"

Owen felt Jessica move and knew enough to stay out of the way.

She grabbed Markus under the jaw and, with a hand enhanced with magic, lifted and pinned the manager with enough force that the wall shook.

"I am aware of Mary Cross Records, and more importantly, *they* are aware of *me*." Jessica paused, and Owen could see the monster behind her eyes. He had seen it in the very first meeting and again when she and Abel had met. Jessica wasn't just the mayor's daughter; she was the muscle beside the crown.

"The label will also know that you used my town to kill musicians just so that you could add another record to their label, and I'm guessing you don't quite have their permission to do that?"

Markus tried to move his head to the side to speak, but Jessica's thumb didn't allow for it.

"How many? How many times have you come and sacrificed a musician for a record?" Jessica asked, her voice ice-cold.

Markus tried to speak, tried to turn his head to look at her, at anyone. Jessica didn't give him the chance. She let the struggle play out until he understood it was pointless. Owen didn't even feel a buildup of energy before Jessica pressed harder. With just the one hand against his head, there was crushing of bone as Jessica executed him.

Markus's lifeless form dropped to the ground.

"You *killed* him?" Eddie said in shock, holding his wound.

Jessica, Owen and everyone else in the room turned toward him.

Eddie, holding his bleeding stump, stood just before the stairs leading down, his guitar case still sitting upright a few feet away.

"You know this isn't over," he said, taking a step backward. "And I'm not done with you." He took another step down, and Owen took another step closer.

"You think that because you took my hand, I can't make music. You think I won't see you burn for this, for everything. I am a legend."

Owen took another step, following the asshole.

"Owen," Clover said, caution in her voice.

"You think I shouldn't?" Owen asked quietly as he took another step closer.

"No, I was thinking we should take his balls as well."

Owen let out a laugh that no one in the room really felt.

"What?" Eddie said as Max and Jessie came up from below and stopped him from taking another step.

I can't believe you took both of Eddie R's hands," Clover said. "The man had mad skills. You know, I think Jessie had a poster of him over his bed when he was in high school. I remember him telling me about it." Clover's loud voice carried down to those searching the rooms below on the second floor.

"I heard that, Clover," Jessie called up. "And no, I did not. This room is clear."

Clover shared a look with Owen, and Owen couldn't help but shake his head.

"This room is clear too," Abel called out.

"Mine too. No body, but the room is trashed," Max called with the door open. "And it stinks a little."

Owen pointed to the far door. "Jessie, that one."

"Yeah," Jessie said in a low tone, following his direction.

Jessica moved up beside Owen, her hand still covered in Markus's blood as she set her fingers on the banister.

"Not worried about fingerprints?" Owen said, more of a challenge then a warning.

Jessica spread out her blood-covered hand as if inspecting the polish on her nails. "Consider my bloody prints a calling card."

"I have no doubt. Jessie?" Owen called down toward the open door Jessie had entered.

No reply.

The reason Owen hadn't gone down to search was because of his ankle. The moment Eddie had left the building, Owen had stopped drawing heavily on his well of ethereal energy, and the pain had come back. But now he simply didn't care.

He pushed off the banister and moved toward the stairs. Jessica and Clover moved with him as they all focused on the door Jessie had gone through.

"Max! Max, get in there," Owen called as he watched Abel follow what was happening and head for the room too.

"I'm on it, boss," Max said.

"I got you," Jessica said, slipping an arm around Owen.

Right then, Owen didn't care that she had just killed someone or that her hand was bloody.

Be alive. Come on, just be alive, damn you.

"He's here! Get in here! I need help," Jessie called out desperately.

They moved in a hurry, Jessica, Owen and Clover trailing behind as they made their way down to the second floor.

"Is he alive?" Owen called out.

Again, no one answered.

The room they entered had high ceilings and no windows. It contained a single made-up bed and a dresser with a duffel bag atop it. Max and Abel stood at the door to the bathroom, waving a hand for Owen to come forward.

"Is he alive?" Owen asked again.

"Yeah," Abel said, but there was no celebration in his voice.

"Get in here, Owen. I don't know what to do," Jessie said.

Owen ignored his ankle and moved past the others. Beyond the door was a white Victorian bathroom with large square tiles. Everything inside it was old yet cared for, all but the boy who was naked with steel cuffs around his ankles and wrists, with a leather ball gag strapped to his mouth so that he couldn't yell.

If that had been all, Owen would have taken it for a win, but it was far, far worse. The young man in the claw-foot tub started to open his eyes but closed them again. He was skin and bones, as if his body had eaten him from the inside out. Dark splotches stood out on his skin, which Owen took for bruises.

"He needs magic. I can't tell what level We he is—his face is too messed up and the straps are in the way—but he's empty for sure." Owen was trying to puzzle out the fastest way to give it to him.

"Get that thing off his face," Owen ordered. "Is there a key for the cuffs?"

Jessie removed the leather straps, which came off easily, as if the young man's head had shrunk. With the leather came some of the kid's hair, and Owen filed the repulsive sight away for another time. A time when he could rage about what had happened.

"Oh shit," Abel said. "I don't see any key for the cuffs. You guys out there see a key for the cuffs?"

"Move," Owen said.

"Owen, he isn't taking my magic," Jessica said. "I'm humming and filling the space right in front of his face with ethereal magic, but he's not taking it in. Is he too far gone?"

Owen switched places and set his essence over the cuffs that held the victim's wrists chained to the pipes for hot and cold water. It didn't take long for the set of links to heat up. Judging that it was time, Owen pulled the cuffs apart, careful not to hurt the young man any further.

Only his eyes opening and closing spoke to evidence that the kid was even aware of what was going on.

"We need to give him ethereal magic. I think he's right on the edge," Jessie said.

Owen noticed that the kid's lips were moving. "Hold on a minute, he's trying to say something. Quiet." Carefully, Owen leaned down and placed his ear right next to the kid's mouth.

The thinnest voice Owen had ever heard spoke directly into his ear. "I need to play her."

Owen pulled back and stared. "Fuck it."

Owen reached behind the kid's lower back and placed his hand right at the base of his spine. He could not sense the well, but he knew where it was.

Just as he'd done with Max, Owen directed his will toward the pocket where the magic was supposed to be. This time, though, was different. He wasn't trying to pull magic out, but rather force magic in.

He closed his eyes and concentrated. The bridge between where his magic was stored and where the kid's magic was stored was foggy at best, but he had to try, so he pushed magic in the direction of his hand.

Nothing happened.

"Come on, come on. Take the magic," Owen said as he tried again.

"What's the problem?" Clover called out.

"I can't connect to his well of magic. It's like it doesn't

even exist. Only he's a We, so it has to exist. Come on," Owen said again, closing his eyes.

"Or he's too far gone," Jessica said softly.

"Don't say that. Why can't I connect with . . ." Owen stopped and looked at Jessica, then at Abel. His friend stood in the doorway, sorrow and concern all over his face.

"It's because of the red piano," Owen said with insight. "It works just like that relic Alice had. The piano won't allow him to take in ethereal magic, and it's sucking him dry. You can't save the person connected to the piano."

Owen looked down at the kid on the verge of death, his skin emaciated and bones looking frail.

Mara saved Damon.

Owen stood. "Clover, be ready to give him ethereal magic. Jessie, you too. Then call an ambulance."

"Owen!" Clover said, putting her hands up.

But he ignored the looks, pushing his people out of his way as he moved back into the bedroom.

"Hello, have I missed it?" the owner of the mansion said. "I like to say something comforting before they pass." He held a long, double-barrel shotgun in one hand, and a black body bag in the other. "I can always sense when they are close to death."

"Out of my way," Owen said. "He's not dead yet."

Owen heard the footsteps coming up the stairs behind him, people shouting for him to stop and talk. But talking was over. The kid in the bathtub didn't have any more time for that.

Just above him was the main room, with the red piano front and center. Around the room was knocked-over music equipment, broken bottles and dirty food containers. The right side of the room held a long curving staircase that climbed up toward the domed glass ceiling.

Owen stepped off the stairs and onto the third floor. A hand caught his shoulder, but Owen brushed it off. For the thirty support-free steps between him and the piano, he reached deep inside and embraced the pain in his ankle.

Fire answered his call. Not the fire that consumes wood, not the fire that runs inside engines, but the fire that moves mountains. His internal passion for what was right and wrong burned in his mind and chest and fed on the pain.

Abel tried again, this time trying to pick up Owen by the waist, but Owen felt the move coming and twisted and turned. Abel, being careful not to hurt his friend, tipped forward until he dropped to the floor.

Every step toward the red piano seemed to lengthen in distance. Owen could see the letters printed in gold, S&S, just above the white and black keys.

His hand reached out, and Clover knocked it to the side as she slipped before him and placed both hands on his shoulders.

"Just wait, just hold on!"

Owen couldn't move her. He wanted to, wanted to push her to the side and out of the way, because there was a kid in a bathtub who was dying. But being this close, she might end up falling over the piano, and this wasn't her responsibility.

"Get out of my way and get back to that kid," Owen demanded.

"Owen, you aren't thinking clearly. You're hurt, inside and out, and your well of ethereal energy is low. You're not even hiding it anymore. It's late and . . . and you shouldn't do this."

She leaned in, and her faced begged for his understanding.

"He's not going to die because of me," Owen said. "Besides, I got this."

"You don't, not right now. Let someone else do it," Clover pleaded.

"You think I can't win? You think I can't beat this asshole, this asshole who built a trap that kills musicians? That kills kids?"

"Owen, you are so low on energy and not thinking clearly. Let someone else do it," Clover repeated.

"This is about skill and music. I don't need ethereal energy for this, and I don't need someone else to do it. Now *move*."

Gently but forcefully, Owen took Clover by the shoulders and pushed her aside. He was careful, and she went with his direction.

He turned back, but Jessie stood in his way.

"I think this one is mine, boss," Jessie said, all smooth and in control as he held up his free hand and smiled.

Beneath the fire consuming Owen's heart, he loved the man for standing there.

Owen moved faster. With a full-out lunge, he shoved Jessie. The angle wasn't perfect—Jessie twisted, reaching his hand back to try and touch the letters with his palm, and for a small moment it seemed he might actually make it. Then reality came speeding in, and Jessie hit the side of the piano on his hip, spinning him even more.

Owen watched Jessie hit the ground hard, and he closed his eyes as he pressed his palm to the red piano, right over the letters. Then he reached down and pressed the middle C key.

"Abel, go! Tell the others to save the kid." Owen paused then said it again. "Save the kid!"

"I'm on it," Abel said. For a big man, Abel wasn't a slouch, and Owen heard him jump the staircase in a single leap and land hard.

Owen's face twitched as a hot steel seemed to be pressed into his brain, right behind his left ear.

He understood that was the connection between him and the red piano.

"Why, Owen?" Jessie said from the floor, slowly climbing to his feet. "I'm the piano man in this group. Why did you do it? Why am I not enough?"

"It isn't about you," Owen said, but his words fell short of being the truth.

"You really don't think I'm a good musician, do you? That I am not worthy of your trust or your time."

Owen faced the condemnation in his friend's gaze, flinching as the fire poker in his brain pulsed and then pulsed again.

"Jessie, I think you're one of the best classically trained piano players I have ever heard."

"Don't lie to me."

"I wasn't lying to you," Owen said. "You're so skilled that you should be playing for kings and queens, dignitaries and presidents."

"If you believe that, then why did you just shove me out of the way?" Jessie asked.

The pulse of fire grew in intensity, and Owen understood the connection would continue to grow in pain and speed until he sat down and played.

"This isn't the time. Why don't you both go check on the kid and tell me if he is going to live or not?" Owen said.

"Yeah, we can do that. Come on, Jessie," Clover said.

"No. I want to hear him say it. Come on, Owen. I started taking piano lessons before I could walk. I was traveling the world by the age of eleven, and I went to the most prestigious music school in all of America, but I want to hear you say it. I want to hear you tell me you're a better piano player than I am."

Owen's heart hurt as he looked at his friend.

"Come on, Owen, tell me. Tell me how you're a better piano player than I am because you used to play in a bar. Tell me why you're better."

"Jessie," Clover said.

"No, stop covering for him. You're always covering for him, and I am tired of it all."

"She's not—she's covering for *you*," Owen said, causing both his friends to look at him.

"What?" Jessie shot out.

"I said . . . she is covering for you."

Jessie made to speak, but Owen held up his hand.

"You want the truth, Jessie? No more lies. Here it is. No, I am not better than you are on the piano. If there was a blank room with a piano, and we did a pure skills test, I'd lose every time. I know that. But what you don't know is how I'd beat you every time if we had a room full of people. How I'd kick your ass up and down the street if there was so much as a single other person in the room. What you don't understand is how my music can crawl inside the souls of those listening. And the reason is pretty fucking simple. It's not because I started taking lessons when I was three. It's because the first time I ever touched the keys, I had goals. The same goals I still have in my heart.

"The difference isn't skill, because like I said, you have me beat there. It's all about the living."

"Owen," Clover said in way that called for him to be careful. As if he were a doctor with a scalpel, she wanted him to be mindful.

"What the hell does that mean?" Jessie asked.

"They taught you how to replicate dead men and women. They taught you to take the next expected step. The next block in the chain. But they can't teach you to reshape reality, to hate and love this world so much that you force it to be different. To be better than it was, than it is."

Owen watched as some of the fire cooled in his friend's expression.

"You are a great musician. But being a great musician is not enough for me. It doesn't cross the halfway mark. I want to remake the world, Jessie. I want to grow wings. I want to taste the air in another world and hear the secrets of everyone else in the room because they, too, want to be free. So free that they can touch the stars. Think about that the next time you play a song. Think about how trapped your audience is as they sit across the table from one other and order a drink. Because they didn't come for the drink."

Jessie stared back, and it hurt. It hurt knowing some people needed the lie, needed the lie so badly just so that they could keep their life on track. Jessie might not be able to handle the truth: that there was a vast difference between skill and talent.

Call me a liar, call me conceited—or listen to the truth and grow into something new and free.

The fire in Owen's mind had his eye twitching as it pulsed.

"Do you agree with him?" Jessie asked Clover.

"Not in everything, maybe . . . but yes. Yes, I do. When I was bonded, it changed me in every way. Except my hair. I've always had great hair." Clover smiled, and her voice changed again, becoming soft. "I knew I wanted to be free. To escape this body, this world, and all the pain and injustice of what it meant to be alive. That understanding of freedom cut into me in a way I can't forget. It reforged me, Jessie. Now when I play Betsy, when I play her with my soul, for just a moment, I escape this world. Owen's right— you are the better piano player, Jess, but you don't see that you're caged."

Jessie looked from Clover back to Owen. "And that's the difference between how I play and how you two play?"

"I also have a better smile than you do," Owen said.

"I am sexier than both of you combined," Clover said, just as fast.

"Why haven't you ever told me this? After all this time?" Jessie asked.

"Because you don't need it," Owen said. "Because knowing what we just told you might destroy you. Or send you away from us. And I don't want you to leave. I have never wanted that."

"No one wants you to go back to your old life," Clover said. "Or worse, start a new life away from us. We want you to stay with us. Even if you don't know how to fly."

"Okay," Jessie said, and it was clear to Owen that his friend was trying to process what had been said. But as always, his friend was smooth. "Am I at least a better musician than Max in your eyes?"

"Oh, of course," Clover said.

"Absolutely. You are the better musician when it comes to you and Max," Owen said.

"He's alive," Max said, poking his head up from the stairway. "He's taking in magic slowly, but he's doing it, though he's not talking yet. We found his wallet and clothes. His name is Andrew Myers, and he's from Detroit, Michigan. Abel called an ambulance and—"

Max was cut off by Tom Westerfeld, who had come up the stairs behind him. "I understand that you have a dead body up here and two severed hands that I can get rid of?" With a smile, the owner of the Westerfeld House allowed the black body bag he was holding to unfurl. "I've brought my bag."

Chapter Thirteen

HOURS UNTIL A+O

I s anyone else here surprised that now that Owen is connected to the red piano, his face is looking weirder and weirder?" Jessica asked, taking a pull off one of two tequila bottles being passed around. Her attention was drawn away from Owen for a moment. "Oh, that's convenient," she said as she looked to the wall where Tom had opened up a panel to a wide square opening, just large enough to fit a body.

Owen sat at the red bench before the red piano, the pulsating pain behind his left ear growing with every passing minute. He looked over to what Jessica had seen. To him she was just looking at a square hole in the wall.

"Thank you," said Tom. "Once, this was a dumbwaiter, but I changed it into a body chute. Sort of like a laundry chute, or a trash chute, only a little larger. It goes straight down to the basement, where there is a large furnace that takes care of the bodies."

"Like I said, convenient—and good to know," Jessica added as she watched Abel, Jessie and Max all lift Markus's black-bagged body and shove him headfirst down the chute. The body and bag made a swishing sound, a long pause and then a squishy *thunk*.

"Odd," Tom said. "I thought I remembered to place the wheelbarrow when I was down there last. It hardly matters. It's very late, and you are all welcome to take a room tonight. Ah . . . do you mind if I, um, watch?" Tom pointed toward the red piano and Owen sitting before it.

"It's your house," said Clover, standing closest.

"Yes, it is. Isn't she wonderful? I can't tell you all the little things and artifacts she holds from everyone who ever stayed or visited her. So special." He let out his breath, and Clover moved across the room to sit next to Jessica, who had washed her hands before the ambulance had come to pick up the kid.

I have to get out of this town.

Owen turned to refocus on the piano and looked closer at the lettering of the two S's made of gold paint.

Abel went over and sat down with his back to the piano. Abel was a large man—not fat, but solid from bottom to top, and with arms bigger than most. He had his dark shades back on, and there was stress in the lines of his forehead.

"You okay?" Owen asked.

"One of the groupies jumped on my back. I have scratch marks. I'm healing them, but I just know my wife is going to see." Owen laughed, and Abel did, too, before stilling and adding, "You sure you got this?"

"He's an asshole, this Brando. It's in everything he touched. Without him, Eddie and Markus wouldn't have been able to take advantage of that boy. So, yeah, I got this."

"Then kick ass," Abel said, bumping Owen's fist before moving off.

Owen didn't need anything else. His hands drifted and hung before the keys.

Let's go. Game on.

He was ready, and it was time. He lowered his hands, and just as he made contact, the keys moved, and music rang out through the room. Owen snapped his hands back, careful not to touch anything, not to interfere as the ghost played his first song, the first challenge. Owen followed the notes and the rhythm, memorizing the whole sequence.

"Is that a nursery rhyme?" Max asked.

"Yeah," Clover said. Before anyone could ask, she added, "It's 'The Wheels on the Bus.'"

The song came to an end, and the room was silent as Owen stared at the keys.

Destroy him.

The pulsing in his mind seemed eager as it moved faster and faster.

Owen's hands moved like silk raindrops over the first keys. There could be no doubt who the better musician was, no doubt who was on top. Owen ignored the connection in his mind and started to play a song that had been eating at him all day.

I can't say goodbye. I tried and tried, but I just can't say goodbye.

His fingers moved over the keys, and Owen closed his eyes.

I am lost in this city of fog and forecasts, of earthquakes and artists, and all I can do is think about you. It hurts, but I don't care. I've been smashed and used and lied to, and I don't care. I want you. I need you. Don't ask me to say goodbye.

The words were there in his music, there in his head, taken from his heart.

With his song over, Owen's mouth was dried out, and he had to wet his lips as he opened his eyes. "Well, that's new," Owen said.

"What is?" Abel asked.

Owen was hardly aware of what Abel had said. In his mind, the ball of fire had stopped pulsing and split in two.

"The connection in my mind has split into two points. I can see two balls of fire, and it's almost like they are calling for ethereal magic, or for me to turn them on. Or both. That's what I get the sense of. I know that if I concentrate on them, I could direct my ethereal energy to them."

Owen stopped talking as the piano keys moved once more on their own. The ghost wasn't playing a nursery rhyme this time, but yet again, it wasn't a serious challenge.

The room waited, and Owen thought about his next song.

"Why are you smiling?" Jessica asked.

"I was thinking about when I was just a little kid. There was a song I would do for the crowds." Like unwrapping a gift, he pulled the old song out of memory.

When the ghost finished his song, Owen began.

The rhythm was upbeat, made for dancing on tables and jumping on couches. He heard little giggles and laughter coming from his people, and when he finished, some of the cold he had been feeling was no longer hovering in his chest.

The connection split into three points. Owen had the feeling that if he fed it ethereal energy, something would happen, but he didn't know what, and he didn't want to be distracted.

"Eight more songs to go and this guy is mine," Owen said.

His people clapped and shouted encouragement.

The third song was longer than the first two combined, which meant that the ghost had stopped playing around. His song drifted from side to side as it spoke of a deep sorrow.

"Now it really begins," Abel said. No one else in the room spoke because he was right.

Owen met the next challenges one at a time.

His body had a clean sheen of sweat, and his mind was ablaze with ten points of connection as he completed the ninth challenge.

"The room erupted in applause, all but Jessie, who remained in the corner of the room. He had been stoic, not upset but not joyful either, as each back-and-forth song had ticked by.

"That was amazing," Max said.

"You need a drink?" Abel called over.

"No, I'm good." A tingle in the air had Owen looking up toward the glass dome. A creaking sound had everyone else looking up as it split open on a set of hinges. Owen watched a thick white fog began to billow in from above.

"Look at the walls," Jessie said.

Small lights raced up and down, illuminating the fog as it fell lower and lower, and Owen felt a cool chill down his spine.

But the chill, fog and lights were nothing compared to the fire in Owen's chest—and the knowledge that this musician was an asshole who had created an instrument that killed other musicians. This wasn't a game, and he needed to finish it.

"I guess he wants to put on a show." The words were just out of Abel's mouth as the keys of the piano fell once more.

This was the last song, the last trial to defeat the red piano, and the ghost knew it. Or so Owen sensed.

The music was as complex as it was creepy, sliding over his skin like oil as the room bloomed with light, over and over again. Owen felt the song in his chest as real lighting snapped inside the fog that now ran from one side of the room to the other, and the ghost's song pushed for more. It went on and on. The talent was matched by skill and creativity, but it was missing one brutal detail. Knowing it, seeing and hearing the absence of it, Owen changed his mind on what song he would play next.

The keys finally came to a rest, and Owen had to admit the song and the performance were special. The ghost had put his full weight into the punch. The glass dome above once more creaked shut, and there were scorch marks of black on many points around the room. A small little section of fog remained, trapped as it settled low over the floor.

A minute passed, and no one moved or said anything. Then another and another. Owen was deep in thought, deep in his mind, where the brutality of his soul could blend with the creativity of what he knew.

Of what he understood to be true.

"Owen?" Clover asked. "You good?"

"When was the last time you saw your mom?" Owen asked.

"What?"

"I know you don't like to talk about her, but when this is all over, maybe you should go see her."

"Owen? What the hell?" Clover asked.

"I got this. Sit back."

"Okay," she said.

Owen ignored everything else and thought about Mara—he thought about the fact that she loved him and had helped save him more times that he could count. He thought about his birth mom. A tear fell from his eye as his heart filled with loss.

His fingers found the keys he wanted, the sound he wanted, as he started a letter.

There is no love like your love, there is no heart like your heart. Over and over and over again you gave to me, sheltered me. He let the music sing for him. Let the truth have its voice.

There is no love like a mother's love. You picked me up and held me close. You pulled me tight and tucked me in.

Owen let his words speak through the keys, through the sound under his fingers. It was about them, both his birth mother and Mara. The mother who hadn't survived the fire, and the one who had seen the fire inside him.

When he finished, the room was silent and the fog was gone. Carefully, Owen lowered the heavy wood fallboard back over the keys.

"You did it," Jessica said.

"That was badass," Clover called, and it was clear in both their voices that they had tears in their eyes.

"Beautiful, Owen," Max said.

"I will never understand how you musicians do what you do," Tom said.

Owen watched the red piano, wanting to see if it would change back into the white or if something else might happen.

Owen let out a small scream of pain, turning his head and placing a hand over his left ear. The connections started spinning in his mind as if a steel poker was being pressed into his brain.

Getting ahold of himself, Owen gritted his teeth as the pain continued for a few seconds before abruptly stopping.

"What's going on?" Jessie asked.

Owen didn't answer; he just rubbed the side of his head and looked at the piano.

Come on. Change.

"What's going on?" Jessie said again.

Come on.

"Why isn't the piano changing color?" Max asked.

The connection in Owen's mind slowly stopped hurting, and suddenly he could feel not several small points, but only one small point. As if a church bell went off in his head, that point pulsed once, just as it had the very first time.

Owen swore, bringing his closed fist down hard on the piano.

"What the hell is going on?" Clover demanded. "You

beat him. Anyone with half an ear knows you just beat all ten of his songs. You won."

"The ghost won't let go of it," Owen said as he met the gaze of each person in the room.

"You're still connected?" Clover asked.

"Yes, I am, and I can feel it siphoning off my magic."

"Well, what the hell do we do now?" Max asked.

CHAPTER FOURTEEN

A+O

Bam! Bam!
     A hard knocking on wood sounded over and over again.

Owen thought he'd been asleep, but he wasn't sure. His head was dizzy, his ankle hurt, and his back was on a hardwood floor.

Bam! Bam!

The loud thumping came again.

"Abel, if that's you hitting your head on the bottom of the piano, I am going to tell your wife she married the wrong man," Owen said without opening his eyes.

A violent pain shot through his body as someone kicked his feet.

Owen let out a grunt of protest. He was about to issue a stream of curse words when he slammed his head on the bottom of the piano.

The night had ended with him and Abel looking for any clues underneath the thing.

Owen looked up and found the person who had kicked his boots now standing above him.

Alice Davis.

"What the hell is wrong with your foot?" she asked. "And why are you sleeping under the piano?"

"Alice. I knew you missed me," Owen said as he looked at her.

She wore jeans and a sweatshirt and had a heavy duffel bag strapped to her back, but she might as well have been in her Sunday best. Because right then, she glowed in the morning light coming through the domed glass roof.

"Oh, shut up. Did you . . . did you do it? Did you connect with this thing?" Alice asked with genuine worry in her eyes. "Or were you smart and no one touched it?"

Abel sat up, too, shifting a little farther way, and someone else poked around Alice's silhouette.

"Is that Daphne? Hey, Daphne. It's nice to see you," Owen said warmly.

"Hi, Owen," Daphne said in a voice that indicated she didn't know if she was welcome.

"Daphne, Alice, this is a good friend of mine, Abel. He and I were looking for clues and drinking tequila with everyone else."

"Hi," Daphne said.

"Owen?" Alice prompted.

"Yeah, I'm connected to it. Right now, it's trying to burn a hole in my head, and it won't stop until I play it again." Owen reached up a hand for help.

Alice shook her head and helped him to his feet.

On purpose, Owen moved with her so that his body brushed against hers. For a moment, they were too close, and it reminded them both that they were too far apart.

"You're in danger," Alice said. "Mara told me all about

this thing. It almost killed Damon. And it's killed many others."

"I know. A lot happened yesterday, including that part of the story," Owen said.

"Then why did you do it? Why did you put your hand on it?" Alice asked.

For a moment, Owen thought about telling her about the kid—and everything else that had transpired. But this was Alice. He couldn't lie to her; he was always going to place his hand on the piano.

"It's a trap to kill musicians, all because an asshole twisted its original purpose. The white piano inspired musicians to be better. This thing is an abomination in the face of that."

His words were whispered, just for her, so that she could know the truth, the truth about who he was inside. That a thousand horses tied to his hands wouldn't have stopped him.

"The piano is still red," Alice said, "and you're still connected to it."

"You think I didn't beat the guy who left part of his soul? You think I can't outplay a ghost? Have some faith, Alice."

To his surprise, Alice smiled, and it was like the sun burning away a dark cloud inside his chest.

"How much of this is twisted up in your ego?" Her words might have stung, but Alice had infused her voice with a pure sunlight that edged on laughter.

"When someone only has ego, it's bad. But when you combine years of hard work with real talent and a simple refusal to stop pushing forward, you're a rock star."

"Really. Even here, even now," she said, but her head was already moving to the side as he leaned in.

Their kiss was slow. As in pause-the-world slow. Her soft lips pressed against his, and Owen couldn't help but rejoice in the homecoming.

If there were others in the room, Owen had lost track. It was just her, just Alice and her lips—and her wonderful green eyes and her cheekbones and her body close to his.

"Aw, man. They are doing that again," Daphne said.

The kiss broke, and both Alice and Owen laughed at Daphne's discomfort, their foreheads pressed together.

"I missed you," Alice said.

It was as if his soul had gained wings at the same time his feet had grown roots. In other words, it felt good—*really* good—to hear.

"I missed you too. I wasn't sure I would see you again," he confessed.

Alice leaned in and kissed him again. Chemistry zipped along his spine and down into his toes, and his hands pulled her in closer.

Alice pulled back. "You were always going to see me again. Just before you left, when you wanted me to get in your truck. I knew right then I would find you. You should have a little more faith."

"I wanted you to find me. I am overjoyed you found me." Owen smiled. He shifted his weight, a twinge of pain twisting his face. The ankle was not healing and the pain was not going away.

"Seriously, what did you do, and what happened here last night?" She indicated the room, everything from the broken glass to the leftover food wrappers to the high-end recording equipment. In more than one place, including on the wall, a fair amount of blood had dried.

"Have you met Abel? Most of this is his fault," Owen said.

"Oh, come on," Abel said. "There's no way you are blaming this all on me."

"Alice," Clover said, coming in from a side room. "And Daphne! Jessie! Daphne is here! Hey, Daphne, what are you both doing here? This is a great surprise, though you missed one hell of night," Clover said.

"It looks that way," Alice said.

Jessie came in barefoot behind Clover, still buttoning his pants.

"Daphne, you're here! Hey, Alice," he added as he went over and wrapped his arms around the younger of the two before she could speak.

"Did they just come out of the same room?" Alice asked.

"Yeah . . ." Owen drew out the word, surprised too.

"No, it's not like that. Jessie slept on the floor," Clover said when she caught on to what they were seeing.

"Oh, yeah, we didn't sleep together," Jessie said, still holding on to Daphne. "Clover just fears the house. Like, she's truly scared of this place. Like a little tiny child scared of the big bad wolf. Last night, she wouldn't let me leave her room. She blocked the door until I promised to stay and sleep on the floor. She's worried the walls are going to suck her in, or something like that."

"Hey, this is a weird house. Anything could happen because so much has happened," Clover said, and a few of the people in the room laughed.

"Hey, Alice is here! And Daphne!" Max said, coming out in nothing but a purple towel and sandals. His chest was bare, and his hair was still wet. "I just had to see what was going on. This is great."

The bruises on his neck were mostly gone, and there seemed to be a glow about him.

"And where have you been?" Clover asked.

"More importantly, where is Jessica?" Jessie said.

"Who's Jessica?" Alice asked.

"A level five badass. She's the daughter—and muscle—of the mayor of San Francisco," Owen said.

"And a deadly redhead," Abel said. Several people turned to look at him, and he added, "Just saying."

"So, where is she?" Jessie asked.

"She's still in the shower," Max said with satisfaction.

"Well then . . ." Jessie said, waving him back with his fingers.

"Well, what?" Max said.

"Well . . . shouldn't you be in the shower with her?" Daphne said to his confused face.

"Oh, I was, but then she had enough of me and kicked me out. I still have shampoo in my hair." If this was some sort of admission of defeat, it didn't show in Max's expression.

"Well, now that we are all here . . . What are we going to do about the soul-sucking piano? I vote we set it on fire," Clover said.

At the mention of the piano, the pulsing in Owen's head seemed to intensify. But Owen wasn't a pushover when it came to any type of manipulation, not even from a magical source.

Hide yourself. Hide yourself deep where no one can ever find you, his birth mother had said to him a very long time ago.

And like a moving matrix in his mind, Owen shifted the pulsing into a box, then he wrapped layer over layer until he couldn't see it anymore.

"The sun is up. I was thinking a shower and then some breakfast. I know a place—it's only ten blocks away, and the food is on the house. Everyone in?" Owen didn't wait for a response. "Good. Clover, does that room have a shower?"

"Yeah, go ahead," she said.

Owen started to move toward the room only to find his body arched with pain from his ankle the moment he set his foot down. It was easy to forget until he moved.

"I should get a crutch," he said as Alice placed an arm around him.

"Seriously, what did you do to yourself?"

"I tried acupuncture on the Devil's coin mark. It won't heal for three weeks, and it seems that until then, I'm going to feel like the needles are sawing into my bones."

"You know, there is nothing simple about you, Owen." They were taking steps toward the door Clover and Jessie had spent the night behind. "Thank God or gods for that."

"Um, Owen," Daphne said, coming up behind them.

She moved around so he didn't have to turn back.

"Yeah?"

"I was hoping we could talk. I think there is something I need to say."

Owen looked at her. She was pretty in a young sort of way, but there was a strength in her core that Owen could see as clearly as the fear of being turned away once more.

"I don't see your bass guitar," Owen said.

She shook her head and simply and quietly said, "No."

"Come here." As she moved closer, Owen reached out a hand and pulled her in. He kissed her cheek, and with hard eyes, said, "I'm glad you're back. We can talk later, okay?"

"Okay."

Owen nodded, then he and Alice moved toward the nearest bedroom.

The room was a little on the messy side. The bed was a tangle of white blankets and pillows, and there were rolled-up towels and a pillow on the floor where presumably Jessie had slept.

Owen ignored it all and headed straight for the bathroom, where the promise of a warm shower waited.

"So how did you end up here with Daphne? I thought you couldn't leave your parents' home." There was a touch of vinegar in his words; he couldn't help it.

"I couldn't leave them. That was . . . until my father told me a story I am still not sure how to process, and then I told them the truth about me and the day Kerogen bonded me."

"What did your dad tell you?" Owen could hear the change in her voice, in the vibration between them.

"Not yet, okay? Everything is fine, and he loves me. I just want a little time with it before I share."

"Okay, no problem. How did your parents take the news about Kerogen and his death?" he said as he looked at a white claw-foot bathtub with a rod and curtain around it.

"I think they took it as best they could. In truth, I didn't stick around very long after I told them. Hey. What's wrong? You stopped moving, and now you are just staring at the shower."

"That is not a shower. No one should take showers inside a bathtub."

"Why not? It's fine. The water pours out from up there, and the curtain keeps the rest of the room from getting wet. What's your problem?"

"My problem is that it's inelegant. No one wants to stand in a claw-foot bathtub. Just keep it a bath or build a real shower."

"You're grumpy. Are you sure the ghost didn't kick your ass last night?"

"I beat him, but he cheated—much like calling this a shower. So, you're telling me your parents kicked you out because you killed Kerogen?" Owen turned to look at her, needing her to know that such a thing wasn't right.

"No, they didn't. They were both great. Really great. My mom was a little loopy, but in a great way. She had me break a bunch of my father's tools to prove that I have ethereal energy."

Owen loved hearing the security in her voice, and it calmed him.

Alice set down the duffel bag that had been hanging on her back.

"Well, that doesn't sound so bad," Owen said.

"Not so bad at all. As soon as I told them, I understood that I need to go save Father Patrick. That once they were armed with the truth, he was the one in the greatest danger, and I need to get him back."

"So you went to Mara's, found out about the red piano and . . . what? She set you up on a private flight to San Francisco, and that's why your bag is so heavy?" Owen guessed.

He arched an eyebrow as she grasped his black shirt in one hand and raised it up over his head.

"I did. Also, Cornelius left me a message behind the bar. A real handwritten letter! He has great penmanship."

"Really," Owen said.

Alice went over and started the hot water. Carefully, Owen took off his boots. "What did Cornelius's message say?"

"It turns out the negotiations for Father Patrick might not be going very well, and Cornelius might be in chains inside a catacomb under a church in New York."

"Which one?"

"There's more than one?" Alice asked as she slipped off her sweatshirt.

"Many."

"Cornelius doesn't want me to go after him. He says his people will break him out, and he wanted Mara to look after me. Apparently, I'm in danger from Kerogen's wife, or widow."

"Really? He was married?"

"A very, very long time ago. She's a dethroned queen of France who still has power there. She might want my head now."

"And you say *I'm* complicated."

"I say you're not boring," Alice corrected.

Owen stood naked but for the wrap around his ankle, and Alice took her time looking him over.

With every word Alice had spoken, with every small motion she had taken, the flame had returned, the chemistry between them stoking the fire. Now his skin tingled, and his full attention couldn't be pulled away from her.

Slower than necessary, Alice slipped her pants down, and he could have sworn her eyes shined brighter. The green was a river he could live within, a color his soul could be stolen by.

"Come here," Owen said, not caring anymore about the world. Alice was the only thing that mattered. Not ghosts and pianos, not details and troubles. His skin, his *heart*, was a smoldering fire, because he needed her. Just *needed* her.

"Looks like you're happy to see me," she said.

As Alice tilted her chin to the side and stalked forward, Owen had to admit that she was all woman.

The kiss was as heavy as it was freeing. Freeing from the world, from the body, as his hand pulled her cool skin in closer. Together they slowly spun, and Owen ignored his ankle, far too consumed with Alice.

His naked backside found the cool lip of the tub as the hot water ran freely just behind him. Alice's green eyes climbed as he pulled her in and guided a leg up and over the edge. In just a moment, they broke the space that separated them. Together at last, body to body, skin to skin. Steam, hot and clean, filled the space as Alice slipped a hand low in between them, her fingers wrapping around his shaft. Gently and slowly, with power and promise in her eyes, she guided him into her.

Owen felt her breath and watched her eyes close, and the world simply held still, sound separating into oblivion as his body rejoiced at having her so close.

Chapter Fifteen

A+O

Owen slipped his old shirt, jeans, socks and boots back on, all the while feeling time ticking in the back of his mind. He was running out of it.

I have to figure this out, or I'm dead.

No, you're not, his own voice contradicted him.

I have to figure this out, or one of them will die.

This he understood to be true.

The image of the kid in the bathtub, nothing but skin and bones yet reaching to play the very piano that was responsible for murdering him, was locked in Owen's mind. No. He knew it down to his toes—one, if not all, of his people would take over the connection, knowing it was their death. *Loyalty* was too small a word for the bonds between him and the others. But Owen couldn't allow that to happen. He had only one choice now: to solve the puzzle of the red piano.

But now it felt like he was looking at a lock without a key.

"You ready?" Alice asked.

"Yeah, I'm ready. You could probably leave that bag here. I know at least I'm coming back."

"I'm good, and that wasn't funny," Alice said.

Owen kissed her, letting it sweep his mind clear of worry, then they walked out of the room together.

It was clear he and Alice were the last to arrive. His crew, Abel and Jessica stood waiting for him on the third floor of the Westerfeld House.

The room was trashed with too much blood and too many empty bottles and music cases that belonged to Midnight Madness.

"Excuse me, Owen," called a familiar voice from the stairs leading down to the second level.

Jessie and Abel turned to look down over the railing. Alice helped Owen move over to the rail so he could see too.

There on the second level was Tom Westerfeld with two We dressed in fine black suits. The taller of the two had facial hair around his chin, and the bones around his eyes were detailed, as if his skin were pulled back. He was fit and very large, and he had chosen a stance that said he was ready for a fight. The second man wore designer sunglasses with gold rims, and his shoes shined in the low light. There was a polish to him that his companion simply didn't possess.

"Good morning, Tom. What's going on?" Owen asked.

"Um, these two people are here to speak with you. Can I send them up?" Everything about his voice said he was uncomfortable.

"Please do." Owen watched as the two men moved past Tom and casually climbed the stairs.

Alice squeezed his arm; when he looked, she gave a quick shake of her head.

These men are dangerous, her look said, but Owen

didn't need her assessment. Violence was in the air as the two men moved like wolves.

Owen turned toward Max, and with two fingers, he pointed at Daphne and the nearest side room.

Neither Max nor Daphne put up a protest, but instead they moved quickly and quietly, Max going so far as to not shut the door and give his position away.

Owen had just enough time to take a quick look around the room and understand there was no time to hide any evidence of what had happened the night before. Of course, he had never planned to do so anyway.

"Well, look at this. You all stayed and had a little party. Sure makes it easy to find you," the taller of the two We said as he came up into the room. Somehow, his body seemed to grow larger as it reached the last step.

"We were just about to get some breakfast," Owen said.

Owen drew the attention of both We. From this close, it was easy to see they were both level fours, but the smaller of the two had a well of ethereal energy that was high enough to make the hair on Owen's skin rise up as he focused on it. Clover would say the man was crazy strong.

"Were you? Hungry after a long night of killing managers and cutting off rock star's hands? Creating an appetite, huh? Need to refill some of what you lost?" The big man moved from side to side in a way that said he'd had training as a boxer somewhere down the line.

"That's what I said. Are you hard of hearing? I could write it down for you," Owen said.

Owen watched his eyes bulge, and the We was ready to charge.

Alice took a single step forward and to the side, drawing the big man's attention as easily as the light atop a lighthouse might.

Owen looked at the man who had yet to speak. "Is your show over? Because I don't find it impressive."

"You want impressive? I'll show you impressive," the large man said as he started forward.

But the smaller man was faster, and he held up a hand to stop the larger one. "There's no need for that, Frank. Thank you. Please go down and wait with the others while I have a chat with Mr. Brown."

"But I thought I was here to put the beat on them for what they did to Eddie?"

"You thought wrong. Go down and wait in the car with the others and make sure no one comes up."

Frank looked around the room, then he reluctantly did as he was told.

"Excuse me for the 'show,' as you so elegantly put it. My name is Harvard Blackwater, and you might have already guessed that I work for Mary Cross Records."

"I'm Owen, this is Alice." When Jessica took a step off the wall to stand beside Alice, he added, "And this is Jessica Joyce."

"Hello, Jessica. I had hoped that was you when I received the report. You look radiant."

"Blackwater. I thought you were in Germany or Hell," Jessica said.

Harvard Blackwater smiled with perfect white teeth. "I *was* in Germany, but the world spins, and they moved me again. You killed the manager?"

"I did. Are you going to come for me? Because you better bring a whole lot more than Frank."

Harvard Blackwater took off his gold-rimmed sunglasses. "I wouldn't waste Frank on you. But no. The manager wasn't protected by us, and even if he was, what happened here would have voided his contract. After all, Mary Cross Records doesn't believe in taking advantage of musicians."

"They have you doing their PR now?" Jessica said.

"All part of the show, after all. It's what they pay me for.

Now . . . Owen Brown, do I have it right that you are the one who took not one but *both* of Eddie's hands?"

"I did," Owen said.

Blackwater bent his head to the side and smiled. "Okay. You should know he was protected—*is* protected."

"You know about the kid they forced to play the piano so it would inspire them all to create an album? You know it wasn't the first time Eddie R has done such a thing?"

"We do now," Harvard Blackwater said.

"You're telling me you didn't know about it before?" Owen asked, pressing the point.

Blackwater held up his hands. "I can tell you I knew nothing, but then that's probably why they sent me instead of Midnight Madness's handler." Blackwater's hands came back down. "Now, you might like to know that I stopped by the hospital before coming here, and Andrew Myers is healing nicely now that he is no longer connected to"—he waved a finger at the red piano—"that." He took a step closer into the room. "So, naturally, he signed a solo contract with our label. You should be able to hear his single sometime next year. And of course we are taking care of all his hospital bills, along with a nice signing bonus. He will be taken care of from here on out."

Owen's people all shifted with the information, all besides Alice.

"You're buying him off," Jessie said. "Giving him a recording contract so he won't tell people about Midnight Madness and Eddie R. You're buying his silence."

"Yes. Yes, we are, and I plan to buy your silence as well," Harvard Blackwater said.

"Done," Owen called out.

Everyone looked at him.

Owen went on: "Well, in the way that we won't put what happened here online, and we won't tell the masses. We will tell other musicians, but it will be a slow rumor you can deal with. Also, the kid gets three records, and I don't care if you can't sell a single copy."

"Three records is a heavy price," Blackwater said after taking a moment to think about it.

Owen understood the real meaning behind the words: it would be easier and cheaper to kill the kid.

"Three records, and we want an A-class deal for him, not a C," Owen said. "I'll give you what you came for, and this can be done."

"Wait, what are you talking about?" Jessie asked.

"It's okay, Jessie," Clover said. "It's the only way the kid stays alive."

"What is?" Jessie asked.

If Blackwater cared what was being said, he didn't show it. Instead, he simply watched Owen.

"There were a few votes to do what Eddie wanted, to have you pulled out into the streets and made an example of. It was Mary herself who asked me to settle this another way, but she wants you to never do such a thing again. Her words."

Owen let out a small laugh and looked inward.

"There is not much funny about Mary," Blackwater said coolly.

"You don't know your boss as well as I do. Here." Owen held out a memory stick.

"Three A-class records, and your silence on social media and to the masses. It's a deal," Blackwater said, taking the memory stick from Owen's hand.

"Is that the recording?" Jessie asked. "The recording the kid did with Midnight Madness? You're giving it to him? Owen, that's not right. There's blood on that album."

Blackwater turned to look at Jessie. "It's not the first album made with blood, and it won't be the last. At least this time, the kid you saved will get paid, and I'll see his name is on this. The last record Eddie R ever made." He tapped the memory stick against his palm before slipping it inside his jacket pocket. "Oh, there was one more thing. About Eddie's guitar and all this music equipment . . . I'm going to say that I couldn't find it. And if you or your people ever want to sign with Mary Cross Records, here's my card." He placed it on the post of the railing. "Good luck with that." He pointed toward the red piano and then slipped on his gold-rimmed shades and calmly walked down the stairs.

When it was clear that Blackwater was gone, Jessie was the first to speak. "Owen, that record has blood on it. I don't understand. They basically forced that kid to play against his will, then they left him to die, and now they plan to make millions off the album."

"Record companies always plan to make millions off musicians. At least this time, the kid—Andrew Myers," he corrected. "At least he will get a cut, and that will start him on his way."

"You're okay with this?" Jessie asked.

"Jessie, if we didn't hand it over, they would come for it. And if we proved to the label that we destroyed the copy, then there would be a huge piece of evidence gone."

"I still don't understand," Jessie said.

It was Jessica who spoke next, her voice cool and refined. "With the record gone, there's no money in it for them, just a big mess," Jessica said. "They would kill the kid, they would kill us, and then Eddie has an accident where he dies too. Then there is no evidence of any wrongdoing by the label. They are clean."

"Yeah, what she said," Clover said. "This way the kid—dang it, Andrew Myers—stays alive, and he's under their protection. But I still don't understand why they are letting you get away with cutting off Eddie's hands. And since when have you met Mary?" She directed the last part to Owen.

"Protection only works when you're the strongest one on the playground."

"Are you telling me you're *more* protected than Mary Cross and her label?" Jessica asked.

"In one or two social circles," Owen said, looking over to Alice.

"He's protected now too," Alice said, and before Owen knew what was happening, Alice and Jessica faced each other.

"So . . . you're Alice," Jessica said. "Max says you're a badass and a hunter, of all things?"

"I hear you still work for your mother," Alice said back.

Jessica laughed, but it didn't touch her eyes.

At any moment, they will start circling like lions.

"That's your handiwork?" Alice said, pointing to the dried blood on the wall.

"Oh, that was just a nibble."

Alice nodded her head. "Owen told me . . . he told me you had his back during the fight."

"It's a very nice back," Jessica said

"It is, and now that I'm here, it's covered."

The room stilled, and Owen had no idea if they were going to start fighting or not, but he had the good sense to stay out of it.

"I like you," Jessica said. "No wonder he had his heart broken. Now, are we still getting breakfast? I want some coffee before I go into work."

"That's a good idea," Clover said.

"Yeah, let's go," Owen said. "Max, Daphne, you can come out now. It's time to eat. Abel, where did you get fresh clothes?"

"Oh, you like these? There's a shop over on Franklin Street. I know the owners."

"Alley Cat, right?" Jessica asked. "I love them."

"Yeah, they are great, aren't they?" Abel said.

"Abel, I mean, how did you get fresh clothes *here*?" Owen asked. "You weren't wearing those last night."

"Oh, I brought a bag—along with survival gear and my passport. I'm not dumb. I know what can happen when *you* come around. Also, my wife is tracking my phone just in case, and she gave me a code word."

"Nice," Owen said, and waved everyone else down the stairs.

"Hey, your girl brought a bag! She knows what's up when she's going to be around you," Abel said.

"That I do," Alice agreed.

"So, what did you bring? What's in your bag?"

It was Alice's turn to smile. "Two assault rifles, ammo and small arms explosives."

"I think I'll let you go first," Abel said.

Tom Westerfeld was waiting for them when they made it down to the foyer.

"You're leaving?" Tom asked in confusion.

"We thought we would go get some breakfast and then come back later, if that's all right?" Owen asked. Technically, they weren't even paying guests.

"Uh," Tom said, moving closer to Owen with concern on his face.

"Yes?"

"Well, it's just that . . . you're connected to the piano. Normally, people can't leave here if they are connected. It gets worse."

"I understand. This isn't, shall we say, my first connection, and we aren't going far—just down to the Grand Hotel to grab a bite. I hear it's ten blocks away and downhill. Would you like to join us? We would love to hear any information you have on the red piano and the musician who changed it from white to red."

"Oh, I love the Grand Hotel. They are very kind to me there. Now, Brando . . . That was before I took over ownership. There might be some of his things in the lower storage areas. Wait! We could take the cable car down to the hotel. Oh, this is great. I just finished restoring it a year ago, and I am not supposed to share it, but I'm sure Sebastian wouldn't mind since you are friends with him."

"Um . . ." Abel said. "There isn't a cable car that runs from here to the Grand Hotel."

"Yes, there is," Tom said. "It was used all the time during Prohibition to run guests and supplies from here to the hotel and back again. I'll show you."

Tom moved to the front door and snapped the locks closed, then he waved to the group to follow him down the hall.

Abel swore. Only Max and Daphne didn't turn back, as they had been the first to follow Tom.

"What is it?" Owen asked.

"The cable car has to be underground, and I didn't pack a shovel or a hard hat," said Abel.

"You know, for a big guy, you sure whine a lot," Owen said.

"I haven't had my tea this morning," Abel said as they moved down the hall.

"You drink tea?" Jessica asked, her voice and expression betraying that she didn't think much of the idea.

"Most of the world drinks tea, and it's better for you," Abel shot back.

They moved down a flight of stairs and came to what seemed to be a storage room with two racks of supplies on either side of the door. The room smelled old and dusty.

"Everyone in! I can't open the secret door until that door is shut all the way," Tom called.

Owen's people crammed in together, and Abel shut the door behind him.

"The door is shut," Abel called out.

"Okay, here we go," Tom said in a giddy voice.

Owen couldn't see and didn't really care as the wall in front of them moved and slid to the right.

A set of steel stairs led down six steps, then they were ducking into a large brick tunnel.

"Here it is. I just need to start the cable, and we are ready to go."

Owen was one of the last into the large room, which, sure enough, housed Tom's very own underground cable car.

"Well, you don't see this every day," Jessie said, and Owen had to agree as he looked up at the curving brick ceiling overhead.

"All aboard," Tom called. Just then, his people moved enough so that Owen could see the whole of the cable car.

The top was red, and the brass poles shined. There were lights that looked like lanterns on both the front and the back, and although the car was shorter than one might find out on the streets, it was only by a few inches. It was amazing to see.

His crew felt it too, and even Jessica seemed to be in awe.

It didn't take long for everyone to climb on. Owen couldn't help but wrap his arm around Alice, and she took a moment to look up at him.

"I bet you have never seen anything like this," Owen said.

Her voice was teasing as she said, "You mean . . . a bunch of people taking a one-way trip into Hell?"

"What?" Owen asked.

"Owen, you didn't notice we are on top of giant hill, and now we are going down on this thing? That this guy just rebuilt himself?"

Owen looked around his crew toward the opening of the tunnel they were about to enter and understood that Alice was right—the route was drastically steep.

"Don't let go of me, and you'll be fine," Owen said with more bravado than he felt.

"I'll be fine no matter what, but even odds that the brakes give out, and we all crash at the bottom."

"Sounds like fun," Owen said.

"Sounds like a lot for a cup of coffee," Jessica said, but she leaned over and gave Max a big kiss right in front of everyone. "For luck."

"Here we go! Um, everyone, hold on," Tom said. He rang the bell, and they lurched forward.

The first part of the ride down toward the Grand Hotel, in a tunnel that Owen was sure almost no one knew about, happened fast. But for what must have been the last couple of blocks, the ride leveled out, and everyone relaxed in relief.

"Thanks, Tom, this was fun. A true San Francisco experience if ever there was one," Owen called back to where Tom stood before the controls as the cable car came to a stop.

"I'm glad you like it. Um, you won't tell anyone though, right?" he said a little sheepishly.

"Your secret is safe with us."

Tom moved on ahead of the group to help with the secret door that led into the hotel, and Alice slipped her arm inside Owen's for support as everyone followed.

"Odd man. I can't tell if the mansion fried his brain a little or if it's the oddity inherent in his mind that the house was able to connect to," Alice said.

"What?" Owen asked her.

"I like him, but I can't help that he reminds me a little of Mara—only in a different way."

"He's human. Without ethereal magic, without a well. But I know what you mean. The house is a part of him. He gave himself to it, and perhaps she—the house—is giving something to him in return. I doubt the man ever gets sick anymore."

"And he has perfect skin," Alice added.

Her finger pointed to a thin, shiny line in the wall.

"I see it."

The line was black and had thin silver metal drifting through it, like a gold vein in a mountain. Only this wasn't naturally made. Owen recognized it as the same material that a set of handcuffs and chains had been made out of. The kind of material that interacted with ethereal magic.

"What do you think it's doing here?" Alice asked.

The others had climbed the stairs, and a gap had formed between them.

"I think it's all part of the puzzle, and I'm guessing the line of metal runs straight from the red piano in the Westerfeld House to below the ghost piano in the bar. It has to be how they connected the two."

"That's a long way, and the last time I went up against that metal, I couldn't break it. Does this help us solve the puzzle?"

"It helps us understand, but I still have no idea how I am getting out of this." Owen paused. "That's it. We need waffles."

Alice shook her head, then she said, "I could eat some waffles."

Owen pulled her in tight. He couldn't help himself. She was trusting him to find a way out of this mess, out of this problem that he still had no solution for.

CHAPTER SIXTEEN

A+O

Owen sat at the end of a table loaded with breakfast trays. Potatoes, eggs, bacon, sausage, grits and gravy . . . but most of all, coffee and waffles. Everyone dug in hungrily.

In the distance, Owen could hear the ghost playing the piano over in the bar on the other side of the hotel. As if excited, or as if simply rubbing it in Owen's face that he had failed, the manager of the Grand Hotel, Sebastian, had informed him that the ghost had started up again and had continued to play nonstop since about three in the morning.

Owen looked out over the table of food as his people moved and chatted. He let the world blur as his mind worked through everything that had happened. From the phone call with Damon . . . to Daphne . . . and even to Alice. He replayed it step by step. Clover called his name, but he ignored her, instead walking through his odd conversation with Sebastian, the history of the piano, as well as the fact that Damon had tried to help solve the problem and failed. He walked it all through. Jessica and her mom. The note Damon had gone all that way to deceive Owen over. Jason and his needles that could do the impossible with the Devil's coin—and that even now seemed to be drilling into his bones.

Absently, he drank his coffee. The hot liquid burned as it traveled down his throat.

"I don't understand orange juice," Max was saying, and something about his tone had Owen looking over to where he sat between Daphne and Tom.

"Okay, I'll bite," Jessie said. "What don't you understand about orange juice?"

"They say that if you drink a lot of orange juice, it's bad for you. Or, at least, bad for normal humans. But eating an orange is good for you. It's full of vitamins and all kinds of good stuff, plus it's fruit, and all doctors say you should eat fruit."

"Yeah, so what's the problem?" Clover asked.

"It doesn't make any sense. When I take a bite of an orange, my teeth squeeze the fruit just like the machine that squeezed the orange and made that," Max said, pointing to the pitcher of orange juice. "There is no difference. You can squeeze it by hand, or with a machine, or you can just let your teeth do it, and it's the same thing. But they don't want us to believe it's the same thing!"

"Max, none of this matters. You have ethereal energy in your system. You can't get cancer. You can't get sick. You don't have to worry about blood sugar problems. Though if you were not an etherealist, you definitely would have blood sugar problems with how much candy you eat. And maple syrup," Clover added after looking at his plate of waffles.

"Funny, but it's also not the point," Max said.

"What *is* the point?" Daphne asked.

"The point is, everyone wants you to eat fruit because it's good for you, but they don't want you to drink orange juice. It's crap. First off, orange juice tastes great, and it's one hundred percent from fruit because . . . wait for it . . . that's right, orange juice is fruit."

"We always made it out of a frozen can," Clover said before taking a large bite of her waffle.

"Oranges have a lot more than just the juice. The juice is where all the sugar is. That's the problem," Daphne said in a voice that said she was trying to help.

"Okay, I've heard this before, but just being honest, it's crazy," Max said. "No one eats the outer skin unless they are a farmer or something, so then what are we talking about? All that's left if you remove the outer skin is orange juice and that thin white membrane stuff. The white membrane stuff cannot make all the difference, no way. This is a bill of goods that is being sold to everyone."

"All right, Max. Say you're right, and there is no reason why orange juice is bad for you. Then why do so many people say it is?" Jessie asked.

"Soda companies. Ta-da!" Max said.

"What? No way," Daphne said.

"Yes way. Think about it, Daphne. Soda companies would just hate it if everyone understood that you can drink fruit and get all the sugar without them and their advertising. So instead, they start a rumor and then pay people to go on TV and in classrooms to say orange juice is bad for you. Because they know they can't compete against fresh-squeezed orange juice. So they start the lie that too much of a good thing turns it bad."

"You didn't get enough sleep last night," Clover said. "Because it's fact, not a lie, that too much of a good thing is bad for you. Moderation is the key to being healthy."

Owen stood up as the beginning of a thought occurred. All eyes turned to him.

"It's okay. I'm just going to stretch my legs." He waved Alice off. She still had half a plate of waffles left, and he wasn't all that hungry.

The pain was there as he shambled away from the table, waving away help as he moved toward the open door and headed in the direction of the piano and the ghost that continued to play.

As Owen walked across the hotel to the empty bar, he couldn't help but take in the change a single day had made. He had come here just yesterday to receive a package from Mara. One day, and now look at him.

The front desk still shined, but the feeling of him not belonging was no longer there. The same woman worked at reception, and the same stairs led up to the large glass doors and the street. The room gleamed, clean and polished, as Owen moved toward the open doors of the bar, and the ghost piano continued to fill the hotel with soft music.

Owen recognized the bartender as Bo, the same level two We from before, who was polishing glass and prepping for the later crowd. Bo offered to pour him a beer, but Owen signaled *no*. It wasn't the time for drinking, nor was it the time to be social. If he didn't put the pieces together, someone was going to die. The horrific image of the boy handcuffed to the tub while the life was slowly sucked out of him crept once more into his mind. A reminder of what was to come if he didn't solve this once and for all. Only it wouldn't be a random kid's face; it would Max's or Jessie's or Clover's.

Or maybe some random musician, like Mara must have found to save Damon.

Owen stood over the piano, not directly behind the keys but to the side so that he could see the length of her as he listened.

"Too much of a good thing is bad. Maybe Max is right," Owen thought out loud as he stared.

"I am always right, but what am I right about this time?" Max asked from behind him, biting into his last piece of bacon.

Max had been following, but Owen was so caught up in his thoughts that he hadn't noticed.

"I'm honestly not sure," Owen said as he looked at his friend.

Tall and lanky, Max had the spirit of youth, but Owen understood that there was another side to him. That other side held a deep need to do impossible things, like an itch he couldn't refuse to scratch. In this, he and Max were kindred spirits.

"So, this is the ghost piano," Max said as he watched the keys move of their own accord. "On the trip over, you and I were just talking about whether it's real or a gimmick to sell drinks to tourists, and here it is, playing for us. And you're connected to it. Our world is an upside-down place sometimes."

"It sure is." They stood there watching as the ghost continued.

"You look better. Healthier. I didn't see Jessica at the breakfast table . . ." Owen said casually.

"She, uh, had to get back to city hall. Something about work. She showed me how to block out the lights in the sky so they don't pull me in. I shouldn't be in any danger as long as I don't touch any more of the cold stones. That's what she called the art installations."

"Okay," Owen said. "Did she, by any chance, explain what that whole thing is?"

"Only that it's a matrix for her and her people, one that covers most of San Francisco. They help her keep the place safe, keep the crime down, or so she says."

"Like a web, and she's the spider."

"Yeah, I guess? She said that too. How did you know?" Max asked.

"When I was at city hall, it was clear that the mayor ran her platform on cleaning up the crime in the city. Abel said the city is far safer now than it's ever been."

"You're thinking a physical web to . . . what? Detect when someone is about to commit a crime?"

"Something like that, maybe. This town is something else," Owen said as if it didn't matter.

"How far down the hole are we right now?" Max asked.

"Far enough that I haven't been able to see the light," Owen admitted.

"Who needs the light when you have me?" Clover asked as she stepped up beside the two of them, all three standing in a curve around the front of the piano. Her words may have been light, but the voice was that of his number two, the woman he'd asked to stand in flames beside him. "I liked Jessica. She fit in," Clover added.

"She did," Owen said as the keys of the piano continued to drop down and the music played.

"What are you thinking, boss?" Clover said, quick and to the point.

Owen looked at her, then he turned his head as Alice walked up.

Even here, even now, Alice made his pulse quicken and his mind stop. She was the image of strength, intelligence and beauty, and a single glance at her had him thanking God above.

"What's the plan?" Alice asked.

"I don't know," Owen said honestly. "There are too many things that don't add up."

"Like what?" she asked.

"Like everyone must be lying to us, because none of this makes sense. For starters, Damon is twice the musician I am. Sure, he's more about the sax than the piano, but come on—he's a legend. So why would he send me here after he failed? Only I don't think he *did* fail. I think he kicked the crap out of the ghost just like I did last night. But he didn't say anything about the ghost cheating. And there is no way he was the first to find out that the ghost cheats. Brando isn't as good as he should be, and yet I've never heard a rumor about anyone beating him. Have any of you?"

Max and Clover shook their heads. Alice just looked at him.

"So, it's a secret? A secret that beating the ghost doesn't do anything?" she said.

"Yes. Because it can only be a trap if no one knows it's there. It has to be a secret. However, how can anyone keep this big of a secret? And don't tell me they are all dead. You're telling me that Sebastian, the manager here, doesn't know you can't beat the ghost? You're telling me he doesn't know that there is a line of that magic metal stretching from under his hotel all the way back to the red piano? And he doesn't say anything? Just hints and pushes me to go solve what Damon couldn't? And he was being honest—I could hear it in his voice that he wants this ghost gone, yet he didn't share any of that information. Why not? It doesn't make sense. Instead, he leads me to think that the reason he is being vague is because of Mara and not wanting to upset her, but he had to know. This thing is a part of his life every day, and he's had to know for years that the solution isn't beating the red piano fairly, so why didn't he just tell me? Why didn't he tell me it was a trap? Why didn't Damon? There are too many lies to unravel."

Owen let out his breath, and Jessie and Daphne walked in, joining the group so that they surrounded most of the piano. It reminded Owen of the campfire during the last night they had spent at the barn in Denver.

The space between everyone was silent.

"*And* I have this damn ankle sucking my energy, and now I have the red piano doing the same thing. Clover, I should have had you just cut off my foot. At least then I wouldn't be in so much pain."

No one spoke at first. Finally, Clover raised her hand. "I still can. I just need the chainsaw, and one of those face shields and I guess like . . . what, three big towels?"

Everyone laughed, even Owen, as Clover mimicked

using a chainsaw in the air. "I'm sure I could make a straight line."

"Why did Damon send me here and not tell me everything?" Owen said.

Like a wave rippling across a pond, one by one his people stilled and went silent.

"I don't know. Are you so sure he beat the ghost?" Alice asked.

"Yes," Owen said. "I'm sure. Damon is too skilled, and the ghost just isn't that good. Like I said, I'm sure there have been plenty of musicians that have beaten him long before last night. Long before Damon. Even if most of them died, there should be someone out there like Damon who beat the ghost and lived to tell about it, or their people sure would have spread the word, but we have nothing."

"So the lie is part of the trap," Daphne said. "It's not elaborate. It's simple, like a carnival game. You think you can win because the ghost isn't that good, but you *can't* win, so—bam—your soul is sucked dry until you die."

"Yes, that's right." Suddenly he remembered what Abel had said when they first spoke of the red piano.

You can't win.

"Where's Abel?" Owen asked.

"He stepped outside to call his wife. Should be back soon, I imagine," Jessie said.

"Owen?" Clover asked, sensing the change.

"No, it's okay. I just . . . Damon wouldn't set me up to fail. So why didn't he tell me you can't beat the ghost? The answer must be that he wasn't allowed to. Not that he feared Mara, but that he wasn't allowed to share that information with anyone." Owen said it like he was trying out a new flavor in his mouth. "Maybe that's it," he went on. "Maybe, for some reason, Damon isn't allowed to say anything. Or give help. Maybe whoever knows the truth isn't allowed to give me the answer."

"Like a test?" Daphne asked.

Everyone including Owen looked to her.

"In school, you aren't allowed to help someone when it's a test." She paused. "What? I liked school."

"It's a test," Clover said.

"I think so too," Jessie said.

"So . . . what kind of test?" Owen asked.

But it was Alice who moved to the center of the group. "Who is giving it? Who is enforcing the rules?" she asked. "And why?"

"The white piano," Owen said. "It's a musical key. That's what this is really all about."

"I don't understand," Daphne said.

"There are We out there who believe when all the musical keys come together, the set of them can change the world with sound. In other words, lift their souls back up to Heaven without death. They can go home. But in order for the story to come true, the people wielding the keys must prove themselves. So they made a trial, or a test, and we stepped in it. No—we were *led* into it. Damon led us here."

"So, what do we do now?" Daphne said, concerned. "I don't want to be the first one to freak out, but Owen is looking more and more tired by the hour, and we still don't know how to break the connection."

Owen put his hands on the piano and leaned forward, feeling the solidity of the instrument under his palms.

"What's the one thing I have that Damon doesn't have?" Owen asked.

Again, his people went quiet.

"I am serious. What's the one thing?" This time, when he said it, he couldn't help but feel lighter as he looked from his left to the right, following the line of people by his side.

"Well, you aren't as funny as he is, and sometimes I think you are grumpier?" Clover said, looking around the group for support.

"I'm going to stop everyone before they follow in Clover's footsteps," Owen said. "And let's keep in mind that Clover was worried about the walls sucking her in last night while she was sleeping."

"Hey! That's not fair," she said in protest. "That place is cool but scary."

Owen went on, cutting off what she was about to say next. "I have each of you. That's what I have that Damon didn't back when he went up against this thing. He knew if I came to San Francisco, I wouldn't be coming alone. He had just spent time with each of you, and he knew that if I came here, you would come with me. With your talent and your ethereal energy and your skill. Don't you dare tell me too much of a good thing is bad for me."

Owen was looking at each of them when he snapped his head to Clover.

"What?" she asked.

He looked to Alice instead of answering.

"You're going to lean into the fire again, and you are worried I will have a problem with that. That if you do your thing I won't be by your side?" Alice asked.

"What I am feeling inside, I might burn down this whole town."

"I'll be right here if you do." Her perfect green eyes never wavered as Owen felt his soul cupped in her hands.

"I'm glad you're here."

"Me too," Alice said.

"That's nice and all," Clover interrupted, "but what's the plan?"

"It starts by you, Clover, taking this bandage off my ankle. Someone get her a couple of towels; she can live without the face shield and chainsaw. We probably need a set of good pliers too. The way the needles have been digging into my bones, there is no way they are coming out easy."

"I am on it," Max said.

"Where are we doing this?" Clover asked.

"Right here, right now."

Owen pulled out a chair and placed his booted foot upon it and started undoing laces.

Max went for the bar; it would have towels and some sort of small tool set. Most bartenders knew enough to keep something like that to fix whatever needed fixing.

Owen's boot and sock came off, and he rolled up his pant leg.

"So, what happens when we take these things out?" Clover asked.

"I'm not sure; I'm just going with my gut. The acupuncturist, Jason, he asked me serval times if I was sure I wanted the mark gone. He didn't seem to think the mark on my skin was a horrible thing. He said no matter what, my soul belongs to me. That my soul is mine. So I'm going to trust him."

"I've got the towels and a set of pliers. Do you need a leather belt to bite down on?" Max asked, handing the towels over to Clover.

"Thanks," Clover said, kneeling. "You want me to unwrap it, or should I just try to cut off the bandage?"

"Cut it," Owen said quickly, handing over a knife he had in his jacket pocket.

"Is that my knife?" Alice asked. "You kept my knife."

"Of course I did."

"That's sweet," Alice said, not caring who could hear her.

"I'm a sweet guy. *Ow!* Clover, be careful," Owen said.

"Sorry, the knife is very sharp, and these wrappings are very thin."

"It's fine. Just keep going."

Owen watched what he could as Clover bent over his ankle, cutting the layers of bandage away to either side of where the needles were, leaving a square of the bandage atop the needles.

"Ready?" she asked.

"Do it."

Gently and carefully, Clover tried to pull back one corner of the remaining bandage. The tip of the cloth curled up enough that she had a grip with her thumb and finger, but then nothing happened. The bandaged stayed on.

"That hurts a little," Owen said.

"I didn't do anything yet. This part of the bandage is stuck. Maybe glued?"

"Jason said it would come off on its own in a couple of weeks."

"Here," she said, readjusting, and this time it was clear she was going to put more muscle behind the pull.

Before Owen understood what was happening, his body flooded with pain.

"Hold his leg!" Clover shouted, and Owen felt Alice and Jessie pin his body down.

"Oh my God, what is that smell?" Daphne asked.

Clover made a noise as she continued to pull back on the bandage. Owen smashed his hand on the arm of the chair as he did his best to keep his mouth shut, the pain threatening to roll back his eyes.

"Almost there, almost there, I'm almost there," Clover chanted, pulling.

Owen felt the change in grip as Clover went from one hand pulling back the bandage to two hands.

And then it was over.

"Ew . . ."

Daphne and others all made a similar sound as yellow slime stretched between the wound and the bandage Clover held out away from her.

"Oh, the smell is so bad," Clover said.

Jessie swore, and Max said, "That's not right. That is just not right."

"Some of the needles came out. They are sticking to the bandage. I can see some of the others. I'm just going to try and use my fingers to get them."

"Oh, don't touch that," Daphne said. "I can't watch this."

"This might hurt," Clover said, but she wasn't waiting, and Owen knew she wouldn't.

There was a spike of pain, then another one, then one more, before the pain was finally gone. Instantly, Owen poured ethereal magic into the spot as Clover covered the wound with a fresh towel.

"There! I think that's all of them. And for the record, that was disgusting."

"How do you feel?" Alice asked.

"Better. Max!"

Max turned just in time to catch the keys Owen launched his way. "You know which parking garage my truck is in. Bring it here and park it out front. If the hotel has a problem with it, they can talk with Sebastian. Alice, give him a gun."

"I can go with him and grab the van if you want," Jessie said.

"Nope. Clover—you and Daphne go get the van and meet back here. Jessie, I need you to do something else."

"What's that?"

Owen wanted to be standing for this, but his ankle wasn't healed, and it wouldn't be for at least a little while. "I want you to study the ghost. The one that's playing here. I want you to track everything he does, every song and how he plays it as if you were playing for him. But you can't touch the piano. Not yet, not until I get back. You can bring in your keyboard and practice, but don't touch the piano." Slowly and carefully, Owen asked, "Can you do that?"

"You have a plan?"

"No one likes a copycat. When the time is right, I'm going to have you piss off a ghost. If you can."

"I'm in," Jessie said.

"Good."

Alice said, "Now . . . if they are all doing those things, what are *we* doing?"

As if on cue, Abel walked through the open bar doors.

"Here you guys are. I should have known. Sorry! I was just checking in with my lady. I didn't want her to think I was in the hospital or abducted by aliens. Anything is possible when Owen is in town."

"Your timing is perfect," Owen said, loudly enough that Abel could hear him across the room.

"Oh yeah? Why is that?" Abel said with a friendly smile.

"You still have that limo around?"

"I can have it here in a few minutes. Why? Where are we going now? The zoo?" Abel asked cheerfully.

"City hall. I need to have a hard conversation with the mayor."

Chapter Seventeen

A+O

Alice, Abel and Owen sat in the limousine as it made its way through the streets of San Francisco to city hall.

With every passing block, the silence between them thickened with tension. Alice sat in the black leather seat beside Owen, who had a hand on her leg, while Abel had chosen to sit in the seat farthest from them. He wore dark sunglasses, and it seemed to Alice that there was worry behind those shades, but it was his silently tapping foot that best expressed what was clearly in the air.

"Owen?" Abel asked.

"Yes, Abel?" Owen said coolly, and it was clear to Alice that part of Owen's mind was deep inside itself, puzzling out the pieces.

"What exactly are we doing, going to city hall?" Abel asked.

Alice understood there was a bond of friendship be-

tween the two, but something was off, and it had been off
ever since Owen had started to grasp what was going on.

"I told you—I'm going to have a chat with your mayor,"
Owen repeated.

"I don't think that is a good idea." Abel was having a
hard time getting the words out of his mouth.

Alice understood fear, and right now, it was a living
thing clawing around inside the big man. Owen was off too.
It was like his friend was suddenly on the outside of the
group, and she was taking her direction from him.

"Why is it such a bad idea?" Owen asked.

"Because she's the mayor of San Francisco. This isn't
concerts and festivals, or even rock stars and record labels.
This is the actual mayor of San Francisco, and she's a level
five We on top of it all. You can't understand the power she
has at her fingertips."

"Enlighten me," Owen said.

"She isn't just any mayor. The city was starting to descend into chaos. Crime grew to the point where high-end
shops and homes were broken into in broad daylight. People
were being mugged or just beaten in the middle of the sidewalk on a crowded street. No one could stop it. No one,
until she came in. She and Jessica and their people. Now
everyone is behind her. Do you have any idea how much
power that is? When the whole city is behind her and
more?"

"I don't," Owen said honestly. "But perhaps enough
power to keep people silent about a piano that is killing my
kind. Say, one involving a ghost and the color red and the
whole thing being a sham?"

Abel started shaking his head back and forth, almost as
if he could wash this moment away. His forehead scrunched
up in stress and worry.

"You don't understand," Abel said as the limo came to
a stop outside of city hall. "Don't go in there. Please,
Owen."

Owen opened the door, not waiting for the driver. The sounds of cars and street noise grew in intensity.

Alice thought Owen was going to climb out, but then he stopped.

"I don't understand everything, it's true, but I can see when someone feels like there is a gun to their head. And I know you have a wife and a daughter and a night club. And a lot of good people who work for you. It's okay if you are sitting this one out. But if you could just wait here and keep an eye on Alice's bag? We won't be very long."

"I'm sorry that I can't go in there. She is very strong and very dangerous. Owen . . . Owen, please don't go in there. I'm sorry," Abel said again as Owen climbed out of the limo.

Alice sat for a moment before slipping a handgun out from behind her back, then another one from around her ankle. She took out her knives and laid them atop her duffel bag without saying a word.

"You should stop him," Abel finally said. He had taken off his glasses, and Alice could see the genuine worry in his face. Hell, at this point, it was radiating off him like heated air on a cool night.

"He won't blame you," Alice said in response. "Owen doesn't blame people when they are looking after others, and you should know that it's not my place to stop him from doing anything. Well, besides sleeping with another woman. For that, I can cut off his balls. For this, Owen doesn't know any other way to live."

"He still shouldn't go in there," Abel said, shaking his head. "*You* shouldn't go in there. She could kill you both, and no one would stop her."

"The mayor lied to him. She was at the heart of the red piano this whole time. That's why Jessica was there last night. That's why she didn't stick around this morning. Moreover, Owen thinks the mayor screwed over Damon and left him for dead years ago, all because of a legend about these stupid musical keys."

"What's he going to do?" Abel asked.

"I don't know, but whatever he does, I'll be beside him and have his back. Now, my bag better be right here when we are done. I don't care if she calls in the National Guard. You understand me? My bag doesn't move, and you and this car stay right here." When Abel nodded his head yes, she added, "Good."

Alice stepped out of the limo. The driver stood beside the door. "Thank you," she said as she looked up the white stone stairs. The building was large, with every type of person moving in and out through its pillars.

Owen was waiting just ahead at the top of stairs, his ankle healed enough that he didn't show any sign that it had been hurt.

"Are you okay?" Alice asked as she came up beside him.

"I'll be okay when we are out of this city," Owen said.

"I don't know, it's not so bad. The buildings are pretty." She made a point of looking around.

He laughed. "Anywhere is not so bad when you're by my side."

"Smooth talker." She leaned in and gave him a kiss.

"How about you?" Owen asked. "Are you okay?"

"Oh, sure. I love that my boyfriend is connected to a soul-sucking piano, and now he's asked me to go into a federal building where not one but two level five We are in charge. And I'm not allowed to bring in my weapons. You're still sure about that?"

"I am. There's security and metal detectors everywhere." He paused. "But you have your knife?"

Alice tapped her belt buckle. "I do. Security can examine it over and over, and they *still* won't know what it is."

"Wait for me!" Abel said, coming up the stairs at a run. "I'm coming too."

"No, it's okay," Owen said. "You have a family and a business. I meant what I said. I understand that."

"Kiss my ass, Owen. My wife loves me, and I can always start up a club somewhere else. You know, if we get out of here alive, that is."

A look passed between Abel and Owen, then Owen looked to her.

Watch over him, Owen's eyes seemed to say.

"Let's go, boys," Alice said, and they all headed into city hall.

It took time to move from the front doors deeper into the building, where the mayor's office was located. There were metal detectors and questions about appointments, but Owen simply insisted that the mayor would want to see him.

They continued until they encountered the reception desk, and the familiar secretary blocked the entrance to the mayor's office. After giving Owen's name, they were asked to wait and shown the same set of seats Owen had sat in the day before.

"Yeah, that's it. Right in there is Elain's office. It's nice. Big, with a couch on the right," Owen said to Alice.

Abel was quiet, his eyes continuing to scan the walls and halls as if they were about to be attacked.

"What are the odds she even lets us in to see her?" Alice asked.

"Better than average," Owen said as the secretary rushed over.

"I am supposed to see you in right now. Right away," the man said.

"Was she expecting us?" Alice asked in confusion.

"She didn't say," the secretary said, startled. His hands waved at them to move quickly as he showed them past the desk and into a set of familiar doors.

The doors opened, and both Jessica and Mayor Elain

stood before the desk, their feet planted. It was clear that they were expecting a problem.

"Thank you, Mike. Please don't let anyone disturb us," Mayor Elain said.

"Of course," Mike said, backstepping and shutting the door as he left.

"Owen Brown and company. I didn't expect to see you again. I am shocked you could even leave the Westerfeld House. How is that possible?" Mayor Elain said with a chill in her voice.

"I won't lie," Owen said. "It's painful, but since just after I turned eighteen, I have been connected to the guitar and its strings. The piano uses a similar connection as my guitar, which often wants to have influence over me too. So . . . you could say I have had a lot of practice. A whole lot of practice making sure *I* am in charge and not the other way around." Owen held up his wrist to show the leather bracelet that wasn't a bracelet.

"Still, there must be a cost?"

"I'm being drained of ethereal energy, and quickly." Owen took a step closer to Elain and Jessica. "But, then again, I have more than most."

He nodded in greeting to Jessica and took another step closer so that there were only fifteen feet that separated them.

"Well, I guess that explains how you are here," Elain said. "I was sorry to hear about the boy in the hospital. That was a nice thing you did, saving him. Jessica informed me of who was involved, and we'll make sure they stay out this city, or there will be consequences."

"Is that so?" Owen said, taking another step closer.

"What does that mean?" Elain asked.

"You know, I tell my people not to lie to your kind. Not to lie to the We because you can hear it, feel it. I tell them it's better to tell the truth even if the truth is something as drastic as, for example, 'I have killed your brother.' Oh, sure, I've seen high-level We in positions and companies all over this country, but you were so smooth with me. It was a show. A very, very nice show that you put on in this very room. The way you confused and distracted me at the same time. 'Damon lied to you, we were in a relationship, look at my daughter, look, I am the mayor.' Boom, boom, boom and then, 'What is the problem you have? Whatever it is, I'll solve it. Oh, the Devil's mark. Done! I can fix that! My debt is cleared.'" Owen took another slow step forward, with Alice and Abel right behind him. Ten feet now separated them.

"Does Jessica even know what you did to Damon? She seemed very upset last night, and she doesn't like to lie. I can feel it in her. She's not like you. She loves a good fight face-to-face, in part because it's honest. But you are more of a politician."

"Mother?" Jessica asked.

Elain held up a hand, and the power in her gesture had everyone stopping.

"I think it's best if you turn around and leave. I won't force you out of my city, because I know you're tied to the red piano, and by the look of you, I assume you will be dead in two days, or one of your friends will take your place. But I am banning you from my presence and city hall."

Owen watched as her eyes moved over him, as if she had finished her meal and now wanted something else to eat. He watched as her focus glanced at then bounced off Alice and settled over Abel.

"Are you the head of the secret society known as the Silver Keys? Or did you bow to them after you became mayor?" Owen asked.

"That's insulting. The Silver Keys are made up of zealots and people who think about the past instead of the here and now."

Owen shook his head from side to side, because this time the lie was clear in the mayor's voice.

"Mother," Jessica said with a mix of shame and sadness as she, too, heard the lie.

"It's hard to lie when everyone is watching for it," Owen said. "It's just not natural for your kind. And you were better before, sliding the truth just to the side instead of opposing it as you just did. Now, I'll ask again . . . Are you the head of the secret society known as the Silver Keys, or did you just bow and help them after taking office?"

Power moved inside Elain, rippling beneath her skin, and black ethereal energy like ink spots formed over her hands.

"You think you can talk to me like that? You think you have any idea who I am? You don't know what I can do to you! For Damon and your family, you need to turn around and leave my office before this becomes worse for you and everyone you know."

Owen took another step forward, and this time, he was close enough that Jessica took a single step forward too, placing her body slightly in front of her mother.

He looked from mother to daughter, and it was easy to see that for all the violence and hard depth of Jessica, she was on the verge of crying. Owen understood why. She had heard the lie, and that meant her mother had known the truth all along. You couldn't beat the ghost, but the rumor mill continued to tell everyone that to receive a key, that is all you had to do. It meant her mother was responsible for all those musicians who had died and been fed to the furnace.

"I came here because you have something of Damon's, something you were supposed to give me. I think it's an item, and I want it," Owen said, his voice calm, cool and insistent.

Elain's eyes seemed to flare, and it was clear she was about to threaten him again.

"Enough posturing," he said. "I figured it out. In one day, I figured it out. Stop acting like you're going to do anything against me or mine. You are one of those in the Silver Keys who worships the idea that one day there will be musicians that all come together. I have a key, I have the guitar, and I am not like Damon. You can see it in me, the difference between him and me, and because of that difference, you can't be sure I am not one of the favored you seek. One of the champions foretold to play your keys and change the world." Owen's temper flared, and right then, he didn't give a shit. She was guilty.

She opened her mouth, but once more, Owen spoke first. "Don't lie to me. The lies are over. I know the truth."

"Hey, back off," Jessica said. "I get you're pissed, and she lied about things, but back it down. She is still my mother."

Owen pressed on. "What version did your mother tell you, I wonder?" Owen looked from Jessica back to her mother. "What version of events did you tell yourself after you left my uncle for dead?"

"What are you talking about?" Jessica asked.

"Back in the day, I am sure that Elain was with Damon. I'm guessing in the apartment above the palm reading shop, that's where they were a couple. Damon wouldn't have cared two licks about the red piano, let alone about any key. Not back then, not now. It's not the instrument, it's the soul. He says that all the time, and he believes that. But he was friends with Sebastian at the Grand Hotel, and I'm guessing he had heard the ghost play, so when Sebastian asked for his help, he said sure. He said yes. Did you go with him when he played the red piano?" Owen asked Elain. "Were you there when he connected himself to it, thinking that he just needed to beat the ghost, as he placed his very life on the line for a friend? Not out of greed or want, but because he believed in friendship. He believed in the connection between people."

"Of course I was," Elain confessed.

"And you didn't tell him that the ghost was just a trap? A test made up by your secret society to weed out those who are considered unworthy?"

"No, I didn't. I couldn't. The vows I'd taken wouldn't allow me, and he was wonderful and sweet, and he played so beautifully. I could feel his soul in the air around me. Anyone could."

"And then you left him there to die," Owen said.

"Mother?" Jessica pleaded.

"Don't you understand? I had to. I *had* to leave him. Damon is not what the prophecy is all about. He doesn't even like to play with most musicians. It's just him, his sax and the world. So yes, I left him there. I said my goodbye and left him there the night he beat the ghost. I didn't think I would ever hear from him again. But then . . ." Owen watched Elain force her mouth shut for a moment. "Then I started to have dreams of a letter."

"Who was it? Sebastian? I'm guessing he showed up asking for your help after you left Damon to die. Or was it Mara? Because Damon had a plan. He had given you something special, and he wanted you to bring it to him so that he could be free. You agreed and then didn't go."

"How do you know this?" Jessica asked.

"I had most of the pieces, but it was your mom who slipped. When we first met and we were out on the street, your mom wanted me to get into the car. She said she had something to give me. Not *do* for me, but something to *give* me. Later, she convinced me it was her help, but there were too many lies, and I started looking, going over every word that was said—"

Jessica cut him off. "You put it all together?"

"Enough of the pieces, and they point back to someone who has enough power to reshape the truth into a lie. I have met We, and even one or two etherealists, who are true believers and are in your secret society. They like to give me hints about where the other keys are. But the ghost . . . Hell, turning the white piano into the red piano created a trial, a real test. And I had to ask myself . . . who would want a test?"

"You thought I was part of it?" Jessica asked.

"You *are* part of it. She just didn't tell you that you were helping her," Owen said. "You are her muscle. They cross her, and you're there. Only you didn't know you were working for the secret society."

Jessica turned around to face her mother. "Is all this true?"

"We can talk about this another time," Elain said.

"People died horrible deaths because of that thing. I didn't know the ghost couldn't be beaten." Jessica shook her head. "Mom, you should give them whatever it is that you're holding back so they can get out of here." Jessica moved away, heading toward the bar in the cabinet.

"Jessica?" There was a plea in Elain's voice, a plea for understanding.

"Just give it to them, whatever it is, so they can get out of here."

"I can't," Elain said. "I have sworn oaths that I will not break."

"Yes, you can," Owen said with understanding, and this time he took another step forward and held out a hand. Not for an item, but for a reading.

Elain's eyes opened wide with shock.

"Go ahead. I give you my permission. Just don't tell me anything of what you see. I won't have my free will tampered with."

"Owen," Alice said in warning, but Owen understood, and so he was ready.

"It's okay. Everything will be okay," he said to Alice. "Go ahead, Mayor. Read my soul."

Elain changed before his eyes, the confidence of a predator climbing into her skin. Any signs of weakness were washed away as she stepped forward and placed one hand under his and laid the other over the top and closed her eyes.

Owen twisted his neck and looked back to see Alice right there behind him.

"I love you," he whispered.

Elain made a sound, then another one, both somewhere in the range of a squeal, then her head moved violently left and right in small motions. A wrinkle formed in her forehead, and lines curled at the edges of her eyes, but that was a small detail compared to her skin turning red with heat.

"What are you doing to her?" Jessica called out. "Stop it. Owen, stop!" She dropped her glass and moved toward him and Elain.

"It's not me," Owen said as Jessica tried to pull her mother's hands off Owen's. "She wanted to see who I am."

Elain broke the connection and moved back until she slammed hard into the desk, her hands coming up to protect her face.

"What are you?" she asked in fright.

In a cool voice, Owen spoke: "Mara says I have a storm in me. Damon calls me a true musician, and my friends call me a rock star. But me, I think it's not about labels as much as it is about desire. I desire this world to be different with every breath I breathe. There is no greater force in the world than music, than sound. It connects us in ways that are primal and universal, and it lives inside me."

"There is so much fire in you," Elain said.

"The item," Owen said, not wanting to know what else she saw. "I assume you don't have any more objections to me taking it now?"

"No, no objections," Elain said without meeting his eyes. "It's in the safe."

"I'll get it," Jessica said, moving toward a painting beside the desk. Jessica moved the painting straight up, then she opened the safe with a series of beeps on a keypad.

As the safe door opened, Jessica called out: "Mom?"

"The blue box. At the bottom." The mayor's voice was tired and weary.

"I have it." Jessica closed the safe, lowered the painting and moved around the desk. In her hand was a dark blue jewelry case about a long hand in length.

"Here you go."

Owen didn't thank her; he just gave a little nod and took control of the box. Feeling the weight and judging it not to be empty, he slipped it into his pocket.

"Goodbye, Jessica, Mayor Elain."

Owen had just turned to walk away when Elain's broken voice spoke from behind. "I loved him, you know. I really did. But I made promises."

Owen turned back to look at her. She was older-looking now than when he first came in. The lines around her eyes, the weight over her soul.

"I know. Damon did too," Owen said.

And with nothing more to say, Owen, Alice and a shocked-they-were-alive Abel walked safely out of the mayor's office.

In the limousine, with the door firmly shut, Abel let out a celebratory yell. "We are still alive! How is that possible?" he asked.

Owen and Alice both smiled.

"Well?" Abel said, gesturing to Owen.

"Well, what?" Owen said, pretending he didn't understand.

"The box, the jewelry box in your pocket. He wants to see what's inside," Alice said.

"I don't think he's the only one," Owen said as he shifted to remove the deep-blue jewelry box from his pocket.

"She didn't want to give you that," Alice said. "Whatever it is holds tremendous value. You're damn right I want to know too."

"She didn't want to give it up for two reasons. First—"

"It was a memento of a lost love," Abel said.

"Yes. And second?" Owen looked to Alice to see if she knew.

"I have no idea. This is your puzzle, not mine."

Owen opened the box, and inside, wrapped in soft black velvet, was a single stone with a gold loop and blue cloth tied to form a necklace.

"Oh, it's pretty." As Abel leaned in to get a closer look, he choked on his words. "Is that . . . is that a . . ."

"Yep, it's a key. The whole thing is made of essence. Damon gave it to her as a gift, the kind of gift you give someone you love. He didn't know that choice sealed her opinion of him. Elain believed only the worthy should hold a key. By Damon simply giving it to her, he wasn't worthy. That was the moment she wrote him off as not one of the chosen meant for her secret society."

"That's sad," Alice said. "But I'm still confused. I can feel its power, and I swear I can almost hear its will, but this isn't an instrument like your guitar or like the piano. Is this the whole of it?"

"This is the whole of it, the entire thing," he said as he lifted it from the black cloth and held it out. "Lean forward, Alice."

"What? No, not a chance!" she said as understanding of what he wanted became clear.

"Damon thought someone he loved should have this, if only for a little while," Owen said. "I'm thinking the same thing. Please. For me."

The space inside the car stilled, and Owen couldn't help but be swept away by the woman behind the green eyes.

"That's not really fair," Alice said.

"I never agreed to play fair. Sit forward, please," Owen asked again.

Carefully, he slipped the necklace around her neck and tied the ends with a bow.

"That's a little tight," Alice said as she adjusted the stone.

"It needs to be so that the stone is touching your skin," Owen said.

Abel sat back in his seat. "Ah. It's for a singer."

Chapter Eighteen

A+O

Abel's limousine took them back to the Grand Hotel, and Owen, Abel and Alice stepped out onto the street.

"Is that your truck?" Abel asked, pointing.

"Yeah, that's it," Owen said. "I'll see you inside. I want to change my clothes."

"Okay, I'll see you inside," Abel said as he headed back toward the hotel.

Owen and Alice walked toward his truck. Owen didn't need keys; instead, he called on his ethereal magic, and with a wave, the truck was unlocked.

"You probably should save as much ethereal energy as you can," Alice said behind him.

"Maybe," Owen admitted as he opened the door to the backseat, where his duffel bag of clothing sat. Owen removed a fresh set of black jeans, socks, navy blue boxers and a black T-shirt.

"Owen, I was thinking we should talk about something before we rejoin the others," Alice said.

"Yeah, I know. With everything going on, we haven't had any real time," Owen said, turning to face her around the open rear door. "What's on your mind?"

He slipped his shirt up and over, setting it on the backseat. The cool wind of San Francisco had his skin prickling, and the smell of the ocean filled his nose.

"We need to talk about this necklace," Alice said.

"Okay."

Quickly, Owen untied his laces to his boots while keeping an eye on Alice.

"If you need me to use it to set you free of this mess, then sure, but after this whole thing is done? I can't keep it."

"Okay," Owen said as his boots dropped to the street one after the other.

"Owen, I mean it. I can't keep this. It's not for me. There's so much responsibility, and my life is upside down right now. I have other priorities."

"I gave it to you, so it's yours. Now you can do whatever you want with it." Owen started to unbuckle his jeans.

"Are you getting naked on the street? Owen, this is a city." She started smiling. "You're going to get arrested for indecent exposure."

"The only crime I am committing is not taking you in the back of my truck right this moment. Besides, I can't stand dirty clothes." His pants came off, and his underwear was next.

"You're impossible. You know that? Sometimes you are just impossible."

"Not impossible, just a rock star."

"This necklace is made for someone like you, to do the things your soul calls out for. When this is done, I need you to take it back."

Owen continued to dress, slipping on clean clothes as he

spoke to her. "That necklace is made for whoever is wearing it. If it's uncomfortable on you, if you don't like it, then give it to someone else. But don't get rid of it because you think you have to reshape the world or because you think someone else is more worthy than you are. If Kerogen hadn't done what he did, there's a good chance you would be onstage right now, singing with all your heart and soul. I know it. You know it."

"But Kerogen *did* come, and he *did* bind my soul, and now I'm a mess—for lack of a better word."

"Yes, he did, but now the asshole is dead."

"My God, Owen, how bad do you want to sing with me?" Alice asked.

"Every day since I first met you. Since our first fight and our first shared bottle of whiskey and our first card game. Our first time in the shower too. Alice, I want to play music with you onstage, beside a campfire, behind a dugout, on a boat, even in a submarine—though I am not a big fan of submarines, and I can imagine the acoustics are terrible."

She didn't laugh, but that was okay.

"I hear you sing when you're in the shower. I hear you hum when you practice your fighting routines. I see you work the keys of a piano when you are lost in thought. You might have a broken soul, and one shaped into a hunter, but first you were a singer and a piano player like your mother. And damn it, I want all of you. I want to live this life next to you."

"Owen," she said, touching the necklace that wasn't a necklace.

"Listen, those fanatics out there? The ones who think my guitar and that necklace are religious items? They are just wrong. The way they tie their hopes and dreams to an idea that doesn't exist rather than just making the most of what's here and now. Alice, they don't know shit about you or me or any of our people. They are not musicians. They think that we need a test like this red piano crap to be wor-

thy of something like that. As if we don't live every day
with a trial inside us. The burden of seeing life as it is and
knowing . . . knowing it could be better. That we could all
be better if we just connected more. Cared more. Loved
more. And gave a shit about ourselves less.

"Listen, when I was presented with the guitar, I was in
the Golden Horn, and I remember opening the case on the
bar, and I could feel it. You know. I could feel that hum of
need to go forward and be free. It wasn't even a little bit
religious. The clouds didn't open up, and the hand of God
didn't come down and touch me. It was just . . ." He fum-
bled for the right words. "It was like I understood the souls
that had given up their last will to form this instrument, not
because of a cause but because they just wanted to keep
going. That was their freedom, so I accepted the guitar not
because of some internal mission but because that's what I
want. What I want for everyone else. When I am up on that
stage and letting it all go, that's everything. So if that necklace doesn't hum for you, if it didn't reflect something inside, and you don't want it, that's fine. I'll get you a different
necklace."

The last part he said with a smile as he slipped his fresh
black T-shirt over his head. Owen folded his dirty clothes
and stacked them on the floor of his backseat, then he
opened up the secret compartment and pulled out his guitar
and case.

"You ready?" he asked.

"Ready for what? You haven't really told anyone the plan."

"Are you ready to join the group?" Owen asked.

"What, no formal invitation? No card or candy?" she
asked as he shut the truck door and moved to take her hand.

"We aren't that formal around here," Owen said just before they exchanged a swift kiss.

Together, they looked up at the Grand Hotel, Owen with
his guitar in one hand and Alice's hand in the other.

"I knew you wanted to sing with me." Her voice held spice that had Owen making plans for when this was over.

"Everyone knows I want to sing with you."

"That's because I have an amazing voice. Honestly, you're lucky I'm so talented. And, by the way, I am not calling you 'boss' like the others do."

"I'll call *you* 'boss' if you sing naked for me. I'll call you anything you like," Owen said as he pushed his body just a little closer to hers.

She punched his arm, then she leaned in and their lips met again. There was time in this kiss. Time where the world seemed to right itself, and Owen was lost once more in her green eyes and the pure beauty of her.

Together, hand in hand, they went back into the hotel. There were a few patrons sitting around the bar and at some of the tables, but his people had made it their own around the ghost piano, which had stopped playing.

"Owen's back!" Max said. "Your truck is out front, but I see you have your guitar, so I'm guessing you knew that already."

"Yeah, thanks, Max. I see burgers and fries. Daphne, you get something to eat too?" Owen asked.

"Salad and an ice cream shake," she said.

"What flavor?"

"Avocado-vinegar dressing and strawberry ice cream," Daphne said.

"Good, because you and Alice are going to join us tonight. Jessie, did you see a keyboard up in that equipment Midnight Madness left behind?"

"Yeah, it's a nice one too," Jessie said. "You were right about pissing off the piano. I gave it a try and played his own song right over the top of him. Halfway through, he just went silent."

"All right, that's at least something. Good work, Jessie. Now, here's the plan I have." Owen looked at each of his crew. "The red piano is over in the crazy house, and we know it was changed from the white to red." Owen pointed. "And we also know that there is a rare thread of metal that stretches all the way from the crazy house to under this piano, and that metal is designed to carry ethereal magic. That line of metal connects the two pianos. My plan is to use that connection between the two to overload the system with ethereal magic. In doing so, we burn or change the red piano back into the white piano, and that gets everything the way it was before. If that happens, the threat is gone and the murders stop, and then we get the hell out of this city."

Daphne raised her hand. "How do we change it?"

"I want to melt off whatever is sitting over the white piano. Basically, get rid of the red by flooding the entire system with as much ethereal energy as we can pour into the red piano. So, in every way I can think of, we are all going to pour as much magic as possible when I give the word. That means two groups: all of you and me. While I am doing my thing, I want you to start a run to the first gate so ethereal energy from the other side soaks into both rooms, here and up there."

"Owen? You know I was chained up at Mara's with that same metal. It accepted my ethereal energy, and nothing happened," Alice said.

"Not nothing. It heated up, and you did that all on your own. We aren't doing this on our own, just like those who changed the white piano to the red didn't do it on their own. Now, the big problem is that I need Alice and Daphne ready to play. The other problem is we are going to need to play both here in this bar and over in the Westerfeld House. I believe we can use the connection between the two pianos to help us with coordination, but, Max, I want you to oversee a speaker system and video so we can all play together as if we were in the same room."

"How long do I have?" Max asked.

"We have four to five hours. When the sun goes down,

we are going to start. Now, if anyone has a problem or doesn't want to do this, well that is too damn bad." Owen looked around the room at his people. No one was smiling, but no one wanted to leave—he could see it.

Daphne raised her hand again. "Um, Owen, I don't have a guitar."

"That's okay, we have a number of them, courtesy of Midnight Madness and Eddie R. Take whatever one you want. Hell, take two. If we don't have space for the extra in the van, toss it in the bed of my truck."

"You might have to wash whatever guitar you take and give it a sage bath to cleanse its aura, but I can help you with that," Clover said to Daphne.

"Clover, you are in charge of getting Daphne ready. Jessie, Alice is going to be playing the red piano. She needs to learn to play with you, so get her ready."

"Owen?" Alice asked, but Owen needed to see and feel Jessie's answer.

"Can you do that? Get her ready?" he asked when Jessie didn't answer.

"I can," Jessie said.

"Owen, you want me to play the red piano?" Alice asked.

"It has to be you. What I need to do requires me and my guitar. I need Jessie here backing up Clover. In other words, you are my only musician who has their hands free. Or Max, but that was never going to work."

"This is a lot of pressure," Alice said, one hand touching the necklace around her throat.

"It is. I trust you. You've heard most of my speeches on how a band must work together onstage. Daphne has too, and besides, we have a few hours to practice."

He turned to walk away.

"And where are you going?" Alice asked.

"I'm going up to the house to learn everything I can before tonight. Max, walk with me," Owen said.

"Alice, we can start right now on my keyboard." There was a push in Jessie's voice that told Owen he was taking his responsibility seriously.

He hoped everyone was.

Owen walked out of the room with Max by his side. Not wanting to bother with parking in the busy city, Owen and Max walked the ten blocks up to the mansion. The door wasn't locked anymore. They announced themselves, but if Tom was home, he wasn't in earshot.

Together, they climbed the stairs, and it felt good not to limp up them.

"He cleaned," Owen said as he and Max cleared the second floor and reached the third. "The blood, the leftovers, the broken bottles are all gone. It even smells fresh in here."

"Looks good," Max added as they glanced around.

Where before there had been trash left by Midnight Madness, now there were polished surfaces. Where cables and music equipment had run all across the floor, now there were neat little rolls of cables sitting atop black cases, stacked into a pile. And, as expected, in the middle of the room was the red piano.

"That truly is a horrible color on a piano," Max said as Owen set his guitar case down.

"It is. Max, we have a few minutes before Clover and Daphne show up to pick out a guitar. I need to talk to you."

Owen moved past the piano toward the steel stairs that curved up toward the glass roof.

"Okay, what is it?" Max said from behind as they climbed up two stories of stairs.

"I don't know if this is going to work," Owen said. He tried the small door, but it was locked. With a pull of ethereal energy, the lock released, and Owen opened the door to the roof. "I'm not talking about Daphne and Alice joining us. I trust them. I'm talking about how my band will be split by ten blocks, as well as all those walls and cement. That's a problem. I can mentally connect us before we start, and that's the plan, but we won't be able to see each other, let alone sense each other, the same way as if we were all onstage together."

"I get that," Max said. "And that's why you want audio and video."

Owen looked at his friend. "You saw part of the matrix Jessica placed over this city." He pointed up into the air. "Is there a possibility you could build something like that between this room and the bar? Keep in mind that this room is sort of like the Golden Horn, where the walls have energy, and there is that odd metal connecting this place and that one."

"Absolutely I can. *If* I had a couple years, and Jessica could explain what she did using very, very small words. Then I could do what you're asking."

"Good, then get to work," Owen said, shaking his head.

"Owen, I have no idea how to do what you're asking. None. And I can't imagine trying to mess with what's there. It's just not possible."

"Welcome to the club. Right now, it's like I'm in a game and no one has told me the rules." Owen looked at his friend.

Max shook his head back and forth. "I can't. Not yet. Maybe someday."

"All right. Okay. If the matrix thing isn't possible, go and have a look at the metal line that runs through the tunnel and see if you get a little inspired."

"Inspired to do what?" Max asked.

"A little magic, Max. Give me a little bit of magic," Owen said as his mind opened the space where he had hidden the connection between himself and the red piano. Instantly, his hands started shaking on their own, and his skin felt too tight. His knee bounced, and his lip started pulsing.

"Owen?"

"It's okay, Max. I want to remember this feeling tonight. Go." His words stretched out as his jaw chewed over each syllable. He placed his hands on the edge of the building for support, and he looked over the side.

Carefully, Owen moved back down the stairs and sat before the red piano. Even now, it did its best to dominate his will. When he was ready, his hand hovered over the piano, and the keys moved on their own. The pain stopped as music filled the room.

"Okay, you asshole," Owen whispered to the piano. "You want ethereal energy, you want *my* ethereal energy? Let's see what happens when I give it to you." Through the light in his mind, he sent his will and magic into the connection, needing to see what would happen. To his surprise, a fresh wave of clarity rushed through his mind and sharpened his senses.

"Well, I wasn't expecting that. What else are you hiding?"

Alice sat at the keyboard Jessie had set up. He stood off to the side with Clover and Daphne, watching.

"Now go ahead and start," Jessie said.

"You want me to play a song or something from inside?" Alice asked.

"From inside. Everything is about what's inside," Jessie said.

With a breath, Alice's fingers found the keys, only she didn't press down. Nothing happened as she thought to herself.

"You have to be willing to share," Clover said, her voice soft—kind, even.

"I can share," Alice said. "I was just thinking about my mother. She just, um . . . I just heard her play for the first time in years."

Alice looked down at the keys and took another deep breath. She had felt the music she was going to play just a moment before . . . but nothing happened, as her fingers suddenly couldn't move, and she didn't press the keys. She shook her head in confusion.

"No, you can't. You can't share," Clover said.

"Clover, I got this. Aren't you supposed to be taking Daphne to get her guitar?" Jessie said.

"That's the fun stuff. Why don't you take Daphne and give me and Alice a moment together?" Clover said, getting up out of her chair.

"I can do this," Jessie said.

Alice didn't say a word as she hovered her fingers over the keys. She had loved singing and playing the piano for most of her life. She loved it after Kerogen bonded her, though that had changed her. When she had trained to become a hunter, she and the other kids would sing and play every night. But after the church's betrayal, she would only play with Father Patrick. And over time, it was only at his request.

When was the last time I really played? What the hell am I doing here?

In answer to Jessie, Clover unsnapped her violin case, and with a flourish, she pulled Betsy out.

"It's a girl thing. Jessie, please?" she said, to Alice's surprise. "Just give me fifteen, and then I'll give her right back."

"Sure. Daphne, let's go get your guitar," Jessie said.

"Have you seen them yet?" Daphne said, hopping down from her high stool.

"Nope, but I bet they are all top of the line," Jessie said.

Alice didn't watch them walk away; she was still staring at the black and white keys of the keyboard. She felt more than witnessed Clover move in closer, then the woman started to speak.

"Do you know what a firebomb is?" Clover asked.

"No," Alice said, looking up from the keys.

"It's basically a terrible cinnamon whiskey that you place in a shot glass and light on fire. You drop it into a pint of beer, and then you drink the whole thing in one go. It's supposed to be fun and exciting, and you do it with a group when you really want to have a fun night."

"And you do this?" Alice asked.

"I used to. A lot, in fact. Now I can't stand the smell. So I don't light it on fire anymore."

"Are you saying we should start drinking?"

"Hell yes, I am. Only that won't fix what you're feeling right now. And no matter how cool Owen is being, everyone here, including you, knows the stakes are life and death," Clover said matter-of-factly.

"So, what's my problem? You said I have to be willing to share?" Alice didn't like the sound of her own voice.

"Yeah." Clover tossed her hair back and looked up toward the ceiling, then back down to where Alice sat. "I couldn't play for about six months after Owen found me. For six months, I just stared at Betsy. For six months, I almost left her behind or set her on fire or smashed her into splinters. Again, this was all after Owen saved me from the We who'd bonded my soul, who'd held me with his friends in this shitty little shack in the middle of nowhere. Why aren't we drinking now?"

"I didn't know that. That you couldn't play," Alice clarified.

"No one does but Owen. Have you ever had a belly shot?" Clover pointed to the center of her stomach, then she moved her finger a little lower.

"I can't say that I have."

"Men love them. I used to love them too. You see, the We that had me . . . Adam was his name . . . he and I were partying together for weeks because I thought he was cool and superhot, and I wasn't even eighteen. Anyway, we were drinking as we had been, and then this one night, the next thing I knew, his friends had tied me up, and Adam forcefully bonded my soul to his.

"It was in the days that followed, when Adam thought it

would be fun to keep partying, that he combined the fire-bomb shot and a belly shot." Clover took a breath, and Alice could feel the buildup of emotion behind it. "Adam did this by taking my free will away through the bond he had created, and then he would command me to lie down on a table and hold still. Then he and his cronies would pour the cinnamon whiskey into my belly button and light it on fire. Of course, I didn't have access to ethereal magic, and I couldn't move. As the liquor burned down, they would eventually pour beer over it and drink from here. I don't know how many shots they would do in a night, but it was enough that I can't ever forget what that smell is like. Let's just say I don't do fire shots of any kind now."

"Clover," Alice said, coming to her feet.

Clover waved her away, stepping back. "No, no. It's fine. When I say you must share, I mean you have to share what's really inside of you. If you don't, it will get in the way when we try and do the impossible stuff. Like we are going to try and do tonight. Now listen."

Clover lifted her violin, and not caring about the ghost or the piano or everyone else in the bar, she began to play.

It was soft and haunting, and she pulled back the bow and worked the strings of her violin. Clover's eyes closed as her song dipped lower and sweeter, until there was just a touch of pain in the air, then it rolled off. Washed away by a series of notes that dipped back in.

As Clover played, Alice could feel it. Feel the pain, the trapped woman lying on the table as men played with her like a doll, a doll they could use and laugh at and not care about. With every note, it hurt.

Listening, Alice's tears started to fall, but it was Clover who stole her attention. Clover who stood tall as her violin and bow moved in concert with the music she was playing. The song continued to build an underlying thread that washed away the too-sweet sugar, an underlying thread that reshaped the pain and built the song into another place.

Suddenly, Clover stopped, and the last note drifted out into the air and died.

"It's not that you must play all of what's inside of you all the time, because we are all dynamic people and you don't have to tell the whole story, but you have to be willing to face the truth when it bubbles up. If I let that horrible part of me stay quiet, and I wasn't willing to share, it would be like a cow standing in the middle of the highway just waiting for an accident to happen. Because when we are all up there trying to connect to one another, there can't be voids between us. Do you understand now?"

"I think so," Alice said, giving Clover a small nod. "You're saying I have to accept what happened to me and be willing to share it but also face it, or it will be in the way?"

"If your heart and soul are shut, we can't anticipate each other. If you hide pieces, even if they are horrors, you won't be able to keep up when we run on the path made for angels, when tonight, we make a run for the first gate of Heaven."

Alice swore loud and clear, so her single word bounced off the walls, and several people looked her way. But she didn't look at them; she just looked at the woman before her.

Clover smiled. "That's about it."

Alice sat back down and looked at the keys, then her gaze went back to Clover.

She is just as much of a warrior as I am. Maybe more. Alice closed her eyes and pushed through.

Ding. Ding. The keyboard jingled as she touched two keys at the same time and did it again. It was the start of a dancing tune her mother liked to play for her when she was a child.

Alice let her right hand dance, carrying the upbeat tune. In her mind, she pictured her childhood as she danced around the living room wearing a white dress that had yellow flowers on the hem and a yellow clip in her hair. She was spinning as her fingers continued to create the music her mother had loved to play for her.

"That's good, now shift it into something new, something of you," Clover said.

At first Alice wasn't sure what to do. In her mind, the music danced and mixed with her memories. And then her father's face came into view. He liked to smile and laugh, but in a quiet not-needing-the-spotlight sort of way. She shifted her fingers so that the sound was deeper—still upbeat but in a reassured and timeless way. She sprinkled in some fun but brought it right back to the deeper, heaver side of the keys.

She thought about him drinking his coffee and standing over a barbecue, then she thought about him standing over her grave with the headstone that held her name, which she had yet to see but had been told was there. A ceremony for her father and mother to move on without her.

Alice's fingers stopped, and she couldn't breathe.

"It's okay. It's okay. You just have to let it out," Clover said, coming over and placing a hand on Alice's back.

"I can't . . . I can't do this. How do you do it?" Alice asked in a scratchy voice.

Clover didn't answer at first. Finally, she said, "What's the alternative? Besides, Adam took my free will for a time, and my ethereal magic, and gave me nothing but pain and bad dreams. He can't have music. I'll face him a thousand times in memory if I have to, because my music is mine, and no one gets to take that away from me. And also Owen, Jessie, Max and even Daphne are family. For them, I face my demons and win."

Alice just shook her head as an image played out in her mind—her father standing over her gravestone atop a small rise, a rose in his hand, rain beginning to fall from the sky.

She had never visited her own gravestone, nor had she seen her father there, but she had pictured this before, when word from the investigator had come back to her.

"You won't let him take your music," Alice asked.

"It's mine. It's a part of me that he can't have. Not ever," Clover said.

"Let's try again," Alice said.

Alice started to tap her foot, and then her fingers tapped the keys without pressing them down. "I can't think of anything but the rain."

"Good," Clover said. "I love the rain. It helps wash away the pain. Right now, you and I, let's play the rain. Let's bring it in and let it cover this bar."

Clover raised her violin and started to play. It took a few moments, but gingerly, Alice started to play with her.

CHAPTER NINETEEN

A+O

Owen walked down the steep sidewalk on his own.

Cars, taxis and trucks rolled by as he made his way toward the Grand Hotel. The sun was dipping low behind the buildings and into the Pacific Ocean, but he couldn't see it. Instead, the cool wind pressed at his back, chilled with moisture, as he continued to descend down the street.

Once more, he saw his truck and the entrance to the hotel, and once more, he looked at the building's great height. Behind him, the red piano was primed with as much ethereal energy as he could pull from his body and force into her.

It was time.

He walked into the hotel and was hit with a wave of sound. Not that of the piano but of people. The bar was overflowing with people. Every type, ranging from well-dressed with shiny gold and jewels, all the way down to men wearing sandals and shorts. There were so many people that it was like a sea of floating kelp that spilled in great numbers out into the lobby, where groups stood, talked, drank and laughed.

Owen watched as Sebastian came up beside him.

"You didn't lie about being able to provide a crowd," Owen said to the manager of the Grand Hotel.

"I was told you figured everything out. The test of the worthy musician?"

"You gave me enough hints and pieces. How long have you kept the secret that the ghost cannot be beaten?" Owen asked.

"The first two times I heard of someone beating the ghost, I thought the musicians were lying. Then I watched Damon beat the ghost. After that, I was told if I didn't keep my mouth shut, I would have to leave the city, and if I didn't, my people would be forced to leave too. This is our home. It's as much a part of who we are as our heart and lungs. So I've worked with Tom these years to help keep musicians from the red piano, until I understood that Damon had sent you here. Are you angry with me?"

"Honestly, I just want to play and see that no more musicians die over this." Owen turned to look at him, sensing the shame and pain in the man. "Really, it's fine."

"Well, at least accept this from me." Sebastian held out his last bottle of whiskey made by Damon. The bottle and label were black, with just the indention of the capital letter D visible under the dust that had settled over it.

"That's quite a gift. Hold on to it for me, just in case we succeed tonight. Don't give me that face. It's a party, Sebastian. Come with me," Owen said, turning and not watching to see if the manager followed as he pushed and slid his way into the bar to find his friends.

Thankfully, the ghost was still silent, and it came as a

surprise to find his people weren't gathered around the piano. Instead, they were at the corner of the bar, where Daphne lay flat on the polished surface while Clover poured whiskey into her belly button and placed an orange slice in her mouth. It was Alice who leaned over to take the drink out of Daphne's belly button, while Jessie laughed beside one of the six bartenders who were tending this evening, including Bo.

"What the hell are you guys doing?" Owen asked.

"Oh, I've never had a shot out of belly button," Alice said, her face turning a little red.

"You missed the orange slice," Owen said.

"Oh, come here, Daphne," Alice said, carefully biting into the slice and taking it smoothly out of Daphne's mouth.

Owen just laughed. He couldn't do anything else right then. Because they, his people, were in the middle of a life-and-death situation, and still they wanted to party.

"Boss, we had to loosen up," Clover said. "The pressure was getting to everyone."

"Well, I guess I'm next," he said.

Daphne was sitting up on the bar. Instantly, her face turned bright red, and she looked to Alice. Her thinking was clear enough. She thought Owen was about to drink out of her belly then take the orange slice out of her mouth.

Owen put out his hands to help Daphne off the bar.

She took them and hopped off, and he couldn't help but give her a small hug. "Thanks for coming back," he said, just for her.

Their gazes met, and she nodded her head as if to say, *Yes.*

"You're welcome," Daphne said. "Uh . . . but I still need to talk to you."

"Okay," Owen said. He hopped up on the bar and took off his shirt.

"*All right*, Owen!" Clover said.

"Don't pour it in my eye like you did in Chicago!" Owen said, pointing up to Clover, who stood on the bar and looked down at him with a bottle of whiskey in one hand and Betsy and her bow in the other.

"That wasn't my fault. Jessie pushed me. *I* was aiming for your mouth!" Clover corrected.

"What do you need to talk to me about?" Owen said to Daphne as he took an orange slice from the tray and laid down.

"Um . . ." Daphne said loudly, staring.

"Clover wants her to compete with you up onstage," Alice said for Daphne.

"She wants what?" Owen asked, looking between the three girls.

"She wants me to come after you, to fight you for the lead . . ."

"It's okay, Daphne, he isn't going to be mad," Clover said. "I told you to tell him. We don't keep secrets in this group. Now, stand back, because I like the long pour, and you're in the splash zone!"

"And you think it's a bad thing to challenge me?" Owen sat up before Clover could pour, and his people moved ever so slightly as he did. "Daphne, you think it's a bad idea to have competition between friends, between bandmates?"

"Well . . . can't it tear us apart?" Daphne asked.

"Yeah, it can, but if I don't think—or Clover doesn't think or Jessie doesn't think—that you are giving it your everything, that, too, could tear us apart. Then there is the question of how long you can last in a space where you're not allowed to give it everything. Do you really want to live like that? *Can* you live like that? So, no or yes or whatever. Daphne, come after the lead spot anytime you want. Anywhere. Throw down against me, and I'll only love you more for it. Now, Alice, get over here. If you're doing body shots, you're doing them off me."

Owen laid back, and Clover squatted down and poured whiskey from about a bottle's height above his stomach.

"What's that line you like, Owen?" Alice asked. "Till death?" Then she leaned over and, using her tongue, suctioned the liquid out of his belly button right there in front of everyone. Then she slowly moved up to his mouth to take the orange slice.

Owen was faster, and just as she came in, he freed the orange slice and kissed her. It was clear that she had been expecting something of the sort, and the kiss was hotter for it.

"They are doing it again," Daphne said.

Her kiss turned into a smile.

"Okay, I'm next," Jessie said. Owen sat up to get off the bar, intending to slide in close beside Alice, when Jessie's hand caught his shoulder and forced him back down.

"Oh yeah!" Clover said. "Get it, Jessie!" And before Owen could do much more than shake his head, Clover poured whiskey onto his stomach again.

"Seriously?" Owen laughed. "You guys are all crazy."

"Here's another orange slice," Daphne said as she held it up for him to place in his teeth.

"Not a chance," Owen said.

"Oh, stop moving," Jessie said, then he came in and did the shot.

"Okay, enough of this," Owen said, sitting up and snatching the bottle out of Clover's hands and taking a pull.

Jessie and Daphne both laughed, and Owen didn't mind one bit. It was good to hear the cheer in his people even as the clock ticked away.

"Where are Abel and Max?" Owen asked. "I want to get started."

A round of shots were being poured, and the gathered people were crowding the group a little.

"I think they are in the tunnel. After they ran the record-

ing equipment and speakers from the red piano to right
over by this piano, they headed down with a fireman's axe
and two blowtorches," Jessie said.

"So, there's a fifty-fifty chance someone loses a finger,
or worse," Clover said.

"Well, we can't wait for them. Hand me that napkin,"
Owen said and started to make a series of circles on the
paper. "Alice, look at this. Jessie, too, just in case something like this happens on your end. You see, the connection I have with the red piano separates in my mind into a
number of these little clusters. At first, I thought it was just
to keep track of how many songs I had completed, but it's
not. If you feed it energy, it will do this. Then each cluster
is like a remote. This one here, the first one . . . if you
feed ethereal energy into it, your mind sort of wakes
up, like drinking a couple of energy drinks. I think this is
what Midnight Madness had that kid do so that he could
play his best. But the others, like this one . . ." Owen
pointed to the fourth cluster. "This one puts on a light show
in the room, where the lights are connected to the music
and will strobe and dance on the walls in time with how
you play. And this one opens the glass ceiling, and this one
here requires a lot of ethereal magic, but it powers the platform to rise up."

"What platform?" Jessie asked.

"What do you mean, *rise up*?" Clover asked.

"There is a hexagon shape in the wood floor, under the
piano. If you activate this cluster by pouring ethereal energy into it, the floor and the piano start to climb toward the
ceiling in a corkscrew-like fashion." Owen twirled his finger in the air to show what he meant. "I think it will take
us all the way to the roof if we feed it with enough ethereal
energy."

"So . . . are we going to do that?" Alice asked.

"Not we. *You*," Owen said, meeting her eyes. "As far as
I can tell, everything is connected, and I want to overload

the system. So when I give you the go ahead, I want you to pour ethereal energy into all these clusters. But you won't be alone. Jessie, I think it will flow through your fingers when you play. Clover and Daphne, I hope you are ready to have the whole bar watching you, because you have to be touching the piano in order to connect to it. Sound isn't enough. You need contact with the piano."

"What does that mean?" Daphne asked.

"Take your shoes off and stand on the thing." Owen looked around the room, judging how many We were there. There were a lot. Most who made eye contact seemed friendly, and he imagined Sebastian had placed a whispered word out into the city of what this night was about. "We're going to need this crowd. Now that Max has speakers and mics and video screens here and up there, I want to pull this crowd in early. Jessie, can you do that thing you did in North Carolina?"

Surprise crossed Jessie's face for a moment before he said, "Yeah, I can do that."

"Owen, that's a lot of responsibility," Clover said.

"I will be with you, even if I'm not here. Besides, Sebastian has just offered to anchor you." Owen turned to the manager, who had followed him in, but he was talking to one of the bartenders nearby.

"Isn't that right, Sebastian?" Owen called out.

"Is what right?" Sebastian asked.

"I need you to anchor Clover. She will be in charge here while Alice and I are up in the Westerfeld House."

"You wish for me to anchor her?" Sebastian asked, more than a little hesitation in his tone.

"This is your place, and you want the ghost gone. I think it's the right price to place some of the danger on your shoulders, don't you?"

Sebastian looked at Owen, then he moved his gaze over to Clover, as if he could somehow assess her skill.

"You are Clover, and you play the violin," Sebastian

said. "Your reputation has been climbing for the last couple of years. I agree with Owen—it is the right price. I will anchor you if you are willing."

Clover's hand shook ever so slightly, and Owen didn't miss the way Alice's hand closed around it.

"Temporarily, so there's less chance that everyone here dies," Clover said, as if she had just been asked to jump into shark-infested waters with a T-bone steak tied around her neck.

"Now or never. Jessie, go to the piano and wake this crowd up. I want everyone in earshot sending energy our way. Do you understand me? Pull them in."

"Yes, boss." There was joy and confidence behind his voice. Jessie headed toward the piano.

"I'll go with him," Daphne said, but Owen caught her arm.

"Hold on a second." He nodded to Clover and Sebastian.

"This won't hurt," Sebastian said as he leaned in closer to Clover, whose face had lost all color.

"I know," she said through her teeth.

"Owen, she doesn't want to do this," Alice said, turning toward him.

"Hold up," Owen said, and Sebastian pulled back.

"No, it's fine," Clover said. "I can do this."

"No, Alice is right. You don't want to do this. We can have Jessie do it instead," Owen said, turning to send Daphne to go grab him.

"No, I'm just being silly," Clover said. "This isn't anything like being really bonded. I know the differences. It just reminds me of it."

"Bonding?" Sebastian said. "No, my dear—this goes the other way. If you go too far, or you make a mistake that is too large to come back from, it is *I* who will be in danger from *you*. I am handing over to you a portion of my free will, not the other way around. The fear should be on my side, not yours."

Owen moved over to speak with Clover. "Hey, I meant what I said—you don't have to do this. I wasn't thinking about the details. I'm sorry. Jessie can do this thing."

"No. No, he can't," Clover said, looking him right in the eye.

"He can. We don't give him enough credit, but he has the skill and talent. I trust him."

"He's not ready, not for this. Look around at this room. The amount of ethereal energy you want, the lives on the line, the fire. For God's sake, Owen, you're going to be ten blocks away. You won't be able to save us when shit goes wrong. It has to be me. Sebastian!"

"Yes?"

"Come here," Clover said, reaching out a hand to him.

"Clover, you don't have to do this," Owen reiterated. "I mean it, we can find another way."

"It's fine, Owen. I can do this."

Owen watched as Clover helped guide Sebastian's forehead to touch her own. They looked into each other's eyes. A shiver ran down both their spines, and Owen understood that the temporary bond was in place. The bond would help center Clover in the storm of making a run. When she was in the heart of the path made for angels, Sebastian and his power would be like a lighthouse in the storm.

"That was brave," Sebastian said, but Clover couldn't seem to speak. Owen placed an arm around her shoulder, then handed her the bottle of whiskey. "Here. I know you."

She took the bottle, and Owen turned to Daphne. "Well?"

"Well, what?" Daphne asked in confusion.

"Well, what guitar did you chose? Did you go with Eddie's?"

"No, his smelled bad, and I just didn't connect with it. There were five others, and one of them is this light blue with sparkly flecks, and the bottom is curved to fit me better. I'll show it to you."

"Show away," Owen said, and they all started walking toward Jessie.

There were microphones and amps and black cables on the floor, along with screens and cameras—God only knew where Max got it all from. But then again, that was one of Max's gifts.

The patrons made way, giving room as Owen, Alice, Clover, Daphne and Sebastian made a path into the open ring around the piano.

"Let me see it," Owen said as Daphne opened up a black case and held up her sparkling blue electric guitar.

Owen took hold of it and felt its weight and the curve of the polished wood. He couldn't stop himself from touching the strings. Without the amplifier, they were small tinging sounds, but Owen could feel that sound down to his toes. His will, his want, yearned to take the new guitar for a ride right there in front of a packed house. But that would be rude, and honestly, he didn't feel as if there were time.

"It's wonderful. How about you show us what it can do?" Owen said, handing the guitar back to her.

"Just like that, right now?" she asked.

"You were with us for months. I would say you're due," Owen said.

"Okay," Daphne said.

"Excellent. Alice, help Daphne on top of the piano. Clover, let Sebastian have a pull of that whiskey. He's really not going to like anyone standing atop his mistress. Jessie!"

"Yeah, boss?" Jessie said.

"Daphne wants to show off a little bit." Owen walked toward the open mic. There was a switch. He flipped it, and the little light turned red.

I will never understand why that light is not green.

With the amplifier enhancing his voice for everyone in the room to hear, he said, "Hello, everyone, and welcome to the Grand Hotel! My name is Owen Brown, and we have something special for you tonight. Now, I know some of you know who we are. You might have heard the rumors, the stories . . . hell, even some of the legends. But none of that matters right now. What matters is that you're here with us making new memories and new stories."

Owen spoke to the crowd, but as he did, he listened to his people behind him getting ready to play. Daphne sitting then switching to kneel atop the piano. Alice handing Daphne the cord to the amplifier. Jessie asking her if she needed anything.

Sebastian whispering the words, "Be careful."

While that happened, Owen investigated the faces and hearts of those he could see ahead of him. For tonight, he would need all the help they could give.

"And now, we start," Owen said.

On cue, Daphne's fingers drew across the strings as she pitched down over the neck. She quickly and nimbly attacked the rhythm in a back-and-forth set of chords. She leaned into the music, bringing her hand up the long neck, then back down.

The room went silent but for her song as every head that hadn't been listening was forced to watch, listen and witness.

Owen was in two places at once as he watched and listened. The first place was a huge spot in his chest filled with living pride as Daphne shined. The second place, he was shaping the crowd in his mind and the instant connection they had with Daphne's music.

"Owen, she's great," Alice said, coming up beside him.

"Yeah, she is."

Daphne shifted her tune and started tapping her foot to the rhythm.

"Work it, Daphne," Clover called out like a full-on fangirl.

Owen watched and listened, and in his mind, he assembled his team. Pictured them and held them there.

Owen wasn't a normal human; none of them were. Tonight, they would either shine or be shown that they weren't enough.

Daphne finished her solo, and the crowd rewarded her with cheers and a standing ovation.

"It's time," Owen said in Alice's ear. "Grab whatever you need."

She nodded her acceptance, then she took his hand in hers.

Daphne's face was flush with excitement, and Owen made a point of giving her a thumbs-up and a nod—meaning *well done*—as Jessie spoke into the microphone from his seated position in front of the piano.

"Give it up for Daphne! I think a rock star was born tonight! That's right! That's right!" he said as the room clapped again.

Owen gave Jessie the nod to go ahead while he and Alice headed for the door.

"Now, my name's Jessie, and I'll be duking it out with the ghost tonight for control over this here famous piano! And in just a minute, you'll get to see the woman we call our North Star, Clover, play her famous violin, Betsy. But before we get to all that, before we get to ghosts and challenges and rock stars . . ." Owen heard the change in Jessie's voice and could feel him pulling in the crowd, his tone like honey paper. "Before we get to rock and roll and big party times, I need your help. That's right—I need your help. You see, I was on the road for a very, very long time before I finally came to your fine city. The Golden City by the Bay. And there is one song that I have been wanting to play. But this song, we can't do it on our own. As I said, we need your help." His hands started to play. "So if you could reach into your bag of kindness and join us and sing along . . . I know you know the words, because this song comes from the great band forever known as the Eagles." His hands struck the keys, and Daphne picked it perfectly with her guitar, and the music reached Owen's back as he and Alice left the bar.

"What song is that?" Alice asked.

" 'Hotel California,' " Owen said.

"Right, I hear it now. It's been a while," Alice said.

The air was cold as the glass door opened, and cool wind shot through Alice's and Owen's hair. Owen looked at her, and in that moment, Owen couldn't help himself. He kissed her. Chemistry, hot and fierce, swept the world, and all he could think of was her.

"Owen?"

"I love the way you say my name," he said.

"I love you," Alice said. "Now let's get this done."

They set a brisk pace up the sidewalk, quickly covering the ten blocks, and once more made their way up the front stairs and inside the Westerfeld House.

"Are you ready for this?" Owen asked as Alice sat down at the piano.

"You mean, because I'm taking your place and letting this piano connect with me?"

"Yeah." Owen thought about saying more, promises about not leaving her if this didn't work, but she knew. She knew who he was. He wasn't going anywhere.

"It was odd being home, and I missed you when you left." She placed her hand over the gold letters and was ready to press down the C key that would release Owen from the piano and transfer the connection to herself. "But you should know that I don't think I can sing. Clover thought it best I wait to tell you until after I was bonded to this thing."

"Don't worry about the singing. I understand. We'll get it done without it," Owen said.

"You're not mad?" she asked with some skepticism.

"Not even a little. Singing isn't like playing an instrument. There's no transference. It's just you. All of you standing there being wide open to the world. I'm not worried. You will sing when you are ready."

"And this necklace. I can feel the power inside it reaching for me, but if I don't sing, I'm not sure I can use it."

"If you can use it, if you can feed it into the piano and this house and the line that goes to the other piano, then do it. If not, we will find another way," Owen said.

"You sound different," Alice said as Owen adjusted some of the equipment, including setting an amp under the piano over where he had noticed a plug in the floor.

"It's time, Alice. I can feel it against my skin. I'm so happy you are here with me right now, in this moment."

"Because it's time?" Alice asked.

"Yeah, because it's time. Because it's time for us to create music after all these days of not. It's time for us to fill this space, this world, with our sound, and for a small fraction of time, everything else can sit back and ride the wave we create. It's time, Alice."

Owen picked up his guitar case and set it atop the piano, flicking open both worn brass latches.

"Owen, come here."

"If you insist."

She did insist.

"Have you ever made love on a piano?" Owen asked.

"We're not making love on this one," she said, laughing.

"I don't know." The intruding female voice had both Owen and Alice turning to look at the stairs in shock. "It might be hot to watch. Maybe tag me in, or let me hold a hand."

"What are you doing here, Jessica?" Alice asked.

Owen stood upright, and Alice slipped her hand over the belt buckle that wasn't a belt buckle.

"Relax," Jessica said, coming to the top of the stairs. "My family has a debt, and I thought I might be able to pay down some of it." She wore a long sparkly white dress that came up over one shoulder and accented her long red hair, currently braided down her back.

"And how is that?" Owen asked.

Jessica moved in a straight line toward Alice. "I assumed someone else besides Owen would be playing that thing. I didn't think it would be you." There was a question in her voice, but no one felt like answering.

"Jessica?" Owen said.

"Well, if it's going to be her, I'm here to offer myself as an anchor."

Alice looked to Owen. *Is this okay?* her eyes seemed to ask.

"Done. Let's go," Owen said in response to both women.

Owen turned to the equipment Max had set up and, following a paper note Max had left, turned on the system. The room was suddenly filled with Jessie, Clover and Daphne as they led the full bar in another song: "Sweet Home Alabama" by the infamous Lynyrd Skynyrd. Owen couldn't help but feel the words down to his toes.

He turned back toward Alice and Jessica as the song came to a close just in time to see them touch foreheads and look into each other's eyes. A shiver ran down each of them, and Owen felt calm, knowing Alice had a little more protection. Just a little more safety.

"Everyone ready?" Owen asked, staying away from the microphone that would send his voice into the bar at the Grand Hotel.

"Yeah," Alice said to the side of her microphone. She placed her hand once more over the golden letters as her other hand hovered over the keys.

"Wait." Jessica caught her hand, and she took a big breath that was filled with worry.

"You're fine," Alice said.

"I know . . . Just . . . you should know that we won't be able to break the bond we just formed until you beat this thing, or until someone else comes in and the connection to the piano is transferred."

"Are you saying it will drain your ethereal energy also?" Owen asked.

"That's what Elain told me," Jessica said.

"Good," Owen said. "Alice?"

Without warning, Alice placed a hand over the S&S in gold and pressed the C key.

Owen felt the connection to the red piano in his mind vanish, and his body rocked with its leaving. As if painkillers had been running through his system, it was now clear how low his supply of ethereal magic truly was. Now was the time to change that.

The ghost started to play, and through a small screen that Max had set up, Owen watched as Jessie and the others turned toward the matching screen on their end. The crowd quieted, clearly listening to what was happening in this room.

Owen pushed the ghost's music aside; it didn't matter. It was time.

Slowly, he opened the case. Like a monster under the bed, the hinges squeaked, and there she was. His guitar, the guitar that held so many pieces of others' will that it practically had its own soul.

Owen breathed in the sight and feel of her. It was like staring at a calm lake on a hot summer's day. He was ready to dive in. His breath came slowly, his feet planted, the world so narrow that his fingers tingled with anticipation. The bracelet that was not a bracelet glowed as it unspooled from his wrist and reached for the neck of the guitar.

Everything had built to this moment, this single moment of the guitar finding its way back to his hands. Others might never be able to understand the weight of this instrument, this creation that was far more than wood and strings.

With his left hand, he cradled the neck and lifted the guitar from the worn blue cloth. His right hand found the black strap and slipped it over his head, then he lowered the strap over one shoulder until the weight of the guitar pressed his booted toes into the ground.

A pulse of ethereal will had the guitar case snapping shut. The clasp locked in place, and Owen set the case off to the side.

He looked to Alice, who now shared the piano bench with Jessica.

She was looking at him with her sparkling green eyes, and their love passed back and forth between them. He needed her to know what he was going to do. And part of her was shouting, *I know. Go. Go be free.*

It's going to hurt, it's going to burn, he thought back.

She was spice—the chemistry was there in her eyes, in her face and in her soul. *Burn bright, burn hot. Fuck the rest.*

The ghost's little song finished. Owen took a step back, angling himself, and used the amplifiers like a stepping stool to stand atop the red piano.

"Oh," Jessica said.

But Alice just looked at him, and seeing her there was more than enough to force him forward.

His hands found strings.

To his own surprise, he matched what Daphne had started earlier. There was pulsing as his fingers locked in chords, then released. Then he stopped. Just stopped as the world he knew continued to tick by. The people connected in his mind both here and at the Grand Hotel didn't speak, didn't move, didn't whisper as anticipation built and clawed. His right hand pressed down over the third string as he called it out into the night air, and then he let it out—the rush of sound and speed as his fingers danced like demons. Catching notes, Owen created more, his hand sliding up and down the neck of his guitar, folding sounds into one another. His fingers pressed, pulled and swept the sound free. And then once more, he stilled, and the song died.

"Okay, everyone. It's time," Owen said casually, but the

words were loud enough that the mics could pick up his voice, and Clover and the others knew he was including them. "Are we ready?"

"Yeah," Clover said. "Owen, we can hear and see you loud and clear."

"Who wants to start?" he asked.

CHAPTER TWENTY

A+O

Alice Davis felt the connection of the red piano in her mind, but it was small and inconsequential compared with the pain in her chest. Like a steel cage without gaps or windows, the pain pulsed behind a wall of emotion she didn't realize she had—until Clover had displayed her own.

For so many years, Alice had been trapped, unable to come home until Kerogen was dead. And so she had trained. And trained and trained. Every day. In wind, rain, snow and sunshine. Her skin had broken, her body became bruised, and her mind reached exhaustion, yet still she had pushed so she might have the strength, skills and abilities to beat him the next time they met. In the end, the fight hadn't come, but the years of hard work were still there.

The history of the fight was still inside her.

Alice's fingers found the ivory keys, and her hands moved, the song soft and sad. Her right hand struck a series of keys, adding a shock to the music that pushed the rhythm, the tone and the desire to move. It added a spice that wouldn't hold still. Her hands moved over the keys as her body leaned in. In her mind, she remembered a clear open sky, a small bald hill made of shrubs and hard rocks ahead. She was alone in an empty landscape as she pushed her body to run faster and farther.

Alice's hands moved, and the music pressed in, and then it pulled back as her mind reached the top of the hill and ran down the other side.

Daphne's guitar caught her run. It was easy and fast, like a foot jumping from one broken stone to another, the wind in her face.

The image in her mind faded to a shifting of colors as Jessie matched a series of keys, adding a second layer over her own sound. Owen started tapping his foot on top of the piano, and for a series of moments, nothing changed. They hung there in the world of color and air as each person merged their sound together, allowing the rhythm to take root.

Alice felt Jessica lean in and then back as her body matched the feeling, and for the smallest of moments, she thought she could sense the entire crowd in the Grand Hotel bar move with the motion.

Alice let the notes go as her hands found a new series, then she came back, like a yo-yo on a string, and her head snapped to the screen as Daphne matched her note for note. It was the oddest feeling, and she stared at the eighteen-year-old she had only known for a little while as they moved together in a series neither had ever practiced.

Together, they moved up and over in an arch and settled back into the base that Jessie was laying down.

"Now," Owen whispered. "Open the door now."

Alice opened her well of ethereal energy, softly letting it slip out into her fingers and further so that it laced the sound with magic.

"Perfect. Don't stop, just be you," Owen said as his foot continued to tap out the rhythm ever so softly, and the others played.

It was like she was in two rooms at once. This room with the piano and another one, where each member of the band shined in her mind. And she knew them, knew them in a way that words couldn't describe.

She felt the space around the band inside her mind just begin to open, like a hand on a window where the latch had just switched from locked to unlocked. Owen gave her a nod, and her fingers shifted over the keys to make room as Clover and her violin joined in.

Alice looked up to Owen with a question in her mind. *This is what you do? How do you ever stop?*

Just wait, his smile seemed to say.

A warm wind, one that Alice understood was not native to San Francisco, slowly swept around the room as they created music between them, and with each note, their sound was layered in ethereal power, in the magic of creation.

An image of flame on the walls caught her attention, reflected in the polish of the red piano, as Daphne moved up beside Clover. With their instruments in hand, they leaned against each other and ran a series of notes.

We are in the flames, Alice thought. *We are starting on the path made for angels up toward the first arch.*

This was what Owen's people did so well. They could take everyone in hearing distance on a journey to the other side. "The other side" being the road up toward Heaven and the four gates that stood in the way. Not in physical form, of course, but in spirit—so the flames she saw were real, but not of this plane. But she knew that if she stopped or failed, it was more than likely the flames would burn her to a crisp. And everyone else too.

"You got this," Owen said, leaning down. "Trust in my people, trust in yourself. There is no part of you that we can't accept. There is no part of you that I don't already love."

Her hands relaxed, and her body moved easier as she continued to play with the others.

"Good," Owen said. "Better. Now, when it feels right, start directing ethereal magic into the connection in your mind. When that happens, it will pulse then separate. Continue doing it until the connection looks like the diagram I showed you."

"I can do that," she said, leaning to the side, away from the microphone. "Are you planning on doing more than tapping your foot?"

It was both a challenge and a hope. There was gravity here that she was fighting. Like holding a tray of glassware and just knowing that the longer she went on, the better the chance it would all come crashing down.

"I don't think me joining in would be enough. Like I said, we have to try what no one else has thought of. Something that Damon thinks we can do. That's why he sent us here. Now, listen to them and be free."

Alice gently elbowed Jessica, and the We took the signal with grace, standing up to give Alice the full range of the piano.

Alice found the spotlight in her mind, moving to Jessie, who had been holding back, and keeping steady. It was his time. His head bobbed up then down then up, and she abandoned her sequence and took over his just as he shifted. His music was smooth, like water running down polished stone, but it blended with Clover's violin while at the same time challenging Daphne—to the point where she looked over at him and smiled.

He's flirting.

The thought hit Alice with the shape of true insight, and she laughed at its innocence and bravado. That of all the places, here and now, he would flirt with her.

She looked up and gave Owen the nod he had been waiting for. The connection in her mind had finally separated into the ten points of power.

"Good, let's not wait around. Start with the walls."

Alice understood what he meant. The ten points of power in her mind were each calling for her magic, her own personal supply.

"Screw the lights," she said. "Let's get this thing done once and for all."

Most etherealists understood the depth of their own power. It was a range where most fell on a scale, but she wasn't normal for her kind. From childhood, she had been stronger. Stronger than others, it turned out, and then Kerogen had come in and bonded her soul—and with it, her well of power. Their connection affected both of them, so however strong she'd been originally, she was far stronger now.

The hexagon-shaped wood floor beneath her moved as magic light shot up the walls. The piano started a slow corkscrew spin as the platform beneath her feet climb upward.

"Stay focused, stay with them." Owen's voice was like granite, and it helped as the black cables were pulled tight and two of the microphones were pulled off.

She could see now why Owen had readjusted the amplifier he was using. Even so, even with everything moving, she played. She played as the flames in her mind surrounded her and the others. She played as the music pumped through her lungs and her ears and her soul. She stayed focused as the glass dome above creaked opened to the cold San Francisco night sky and the scent of the ocean immediately drifted in.

The platform rose ten feet, then twelve, lifting off the third floor entirely as the sky opened above them, and still they climbed higher. Owen's last words caught her attention, and she looked to him just as his foot stopped tapping.

CHAPTER TWENTY-ONE

A+O

Owen felt the music in his heart, in his chest and down his spine.

The road to angels contained its own source of ethereal magic, and if they were to overload the red piano, they would need that source. But someone had to have tried that over the years.

It's not enough to go up . . . You have to go down at the same time.

With Clover, Alice and the others climbing the road up to the first gate of Heaven, ethereal magic was already starting to seep into the room, both here and at the other bar. Jessie had given the signal, confirming it when he had winked into the camera.

Owen stopped his foot from tapping. In his mind, he followed the others, his heart racing with their music. He split himself once more, like having a small conversation in a corner while the larger conversation took up the whole room.

Owen felt the others, felt them as deeply as he knew himself. It would be so easy to join them on this run. But again, that wouldn't be enough. It was time to go down, down into the blue waters where souls waited in torment.

"I miss you," he whispered, knowing he spoke about his mother, who had died.

The woman who, for a time, had raised him before her death. His right hand started to shake. In anticipation for what was to come? Or out of fear of the sheer magnitude of what he was about to try? That was anyone's guess. His song shouted out, contrasting to the song that Alice and the others were playing.

The strings of his guitar stuck to the neck, as if a bridge had been tightened down over them, and Owen relaxed back as he started to play. The amplifier and cord glowed with his remaining ethereal energy as he energized his sound.

A few souls out there believed his kind, etherealists, or humans with magic, were part of the master plan from the beginning of time. But most believed it was a karmic accident. That when the We came to Earth and brought ethereal magic, it created a loophole for the human soul to have the same power. Owen didn't care.

It was the ability to create with music, the one substance in the entire world that connected everything, that mattered. And what could matter more for the trapped souls in the river waiting to get into hell?

Can you hear me, Devil? You don't own me, and you can't have me.

His fingers found speed, and somewhere between the two rooms in his head, he could feel the connection as Alice and the others picked up the tempo.

You can't have my soul, my heart, my body or my mind, you son of a bitch.

These were not lyrics he was saying in his mind; this was a promise and a conversation. A continuation of one he had held most of his life.

Blue flames burst from under his booted feet as he entered the river to Hell. The souls of the damned reached their clawed hands for him to come down and join them. His remaining ethereal magic created a thin barrier of protection.

"I think you were played," Owen said with whispered words to the Devil. His hand continued to move faster and faster in opposition to the others' song as they traveled the road made for angels.

This is what it meant to be him, to bask in the fires as the platform and piano beneath his feet climbed higher into the sky and his people played for the angels. Already, he could feel the ethereal magic soaking into the air from the other side, and now it was his turn.

His turn to add another type of flame.

Owen reached inside his mind to the memory he hated the most, the memory he could never forget and never forgive. He'd been about eight years old when he had first found the flame. Eight years old, and he hadn't known what he was doing. The flames he had brought in from the other side had set the walls on fire. Flames that *he* had created as he had infused his music with ethereal energy and played a sound, one he could hear in the space around him. He had been a child, afraid as the flames grew higher. He had stopped playing, but the flames had crossed over from that space into his space.

Owen let go of his restraint as his head peeked above the open glass of the roof and into the night sky, as all of San Francisco opened before him.

Music poured into the night, and blue flames and hands reached up through the red piano, clawing for a hold on his legs and hips, but Owen didn't care. He poured ethereal magic into his song, forcing more and more of the other world into this one while Alice and the others continued down the path made for angels.

Owen breathed in the ethereal magic summoned by Alice and the others and let it fill his bloodstream as he poured more ethereal power into his music, laying down a series of chords as he released the strings.

"I am here, and I won't be denied. I shall use you to the fullest of what's inside."

Owen then did something he never thought he would do. He pulled ethereal magic away from his boots and feet as the blue fire and claws from the deep tried to pull him down.

He spared a glance for Alice, who had her eyes closed, and Owen knew she was watching the others in her mind's eye as she played with them.

He looked down. His leather boots dissolved then flared in the blue flames of Hell water, and yet he wasn't afraid. He felt the greed of the souls as they reached for skin and bone—*his* skin and bone. And Owen shifted his music so that for the smallest of moments, it felt sad. Sad knowing that he had denied the souls one last feeling of real contact.

The mark on his ankle blazed with red light, then pulsed, and like a mouse to a cat, the hands disappeared beneath the flame. A chill went up Owen's spine. His toes grew cold, then his feet, and Owen knew he could pull from the flames right then and there. He could take flames made of ethereal magic and fill up his empty well.

Owen started slow, but there was no slow here, no pure control in the Devil's water. His skin turned ice-cold and the blue flames climbed higher, covering his guitar and hands, licking up toward his chest. Standing inside them was like drinking ice water too fast and not being able to stop, yet still he played. If anything, the shock to his system spurred him to go further and deeper, to let out the storm that was continually hiding within his soul.

His capacity to hold magic hit full and spilled over, and Owen slammed his foot hard down on the red piano. It was as much a sign to Alice that he was ready as it was an attempt to try and physically force ethereal magic into the piano.

After all, that was what they were here for.

* * *

Alice's eyes were closed as she lodged herself deep in her connection to the others, having to force away Owen and his music so she wouldn't be swept up in what he was doing.

The stomp of his foot on the polished red piano moved her, and she opened her eyes to see Owen leaning into his guitar, blue flames covering his body from top to bottom, yet on he played.

It's time, she thought. *Now or never.*

Behind Owen, the moon's shiny crescent hung between the clouds, and a cold, bitter wind blew around them. Alice slowly shifted her keys, suggesting to the others that they turn the ship around. It was the sign they were waiting for. One by one, every member of the band directed ethereal energy into the pianos, both this one and the one Jessie was playing. Alice called on everything she had. Like a hose turned on to full strength, her mind tried to jump, but her iron control held her thoughts still as ethereal magic, black as oil, sprang out of her skin and over her hands. It coated her fingers as she continued to play.

This isn't enough, she thought, not for the first time.

"Owen?" she called.

"I know. Keep going." His voice was strained as he played. "We need to overload the system."

Alice felt the waves of ethereal energy being pumped in by Owen, by everyone, and still, she didn't think it was working.

"I think this whole house is part of the piano," she said, thinking through the problem. "Like another type of anchor?"

"I agree with you. Don't stop."

He already knew, but he didn't say anything. He thinks we can't fail, but the piano isn't changing.

Something burned her right hand, but she shook it off quickly. For a moment, the fire of Heaven flared around her and in the Grand Hotel's bar.

"What was that?" she asked, then noticed that on the edge of the pool of blue flames were small, dazzling white sparks all around Owen.

"Angels and demons. Heaven and Hell. They don't like each other very much," Owen said as he stomped his foot one more time.

He's splashing the flames he created, she thought, still confused.

In her mind, and in the music coming off the amplifiers below her, something happened.

Daphne backed off her roll, and Clover started leading the music back.

"We're turning around," Alice called. "Daphne is almost out of ethereal magic, and Jessie is getting low."

She could see the determination on Owen's face as he continued to play, and the flames rose higher and wider, now cascading over the red piano.

"We need to end this," Owen said. "Give it everything."

This isn't going to work. It's like when I was caged in that room and I tried to burn out the cuffs, but I wasn't strong enough.

Her part of the song quieted, and her hands stilled over the keys. Carefully, she touched the top of the piano, a place where the blue flames had yet to reach. The wood was hot, and she thought the paint was getting sticky, but it wasn't enough—not nearly enough.

She touched the necklace, and the ethereal magic coating her fingers reacted in what could only be described as joy.

Alice leaned over the single mic still remaining, and she started to hum in tune with Jessie and the others. Pain sparked in her chest, and she layered that pain into her voice.

> *I am alone now,*
> *No matter what they say.*
> *I live in the shadows now; it's the only thing I know.*
> *You want me to be simple now when you*
> *get to stay safe and home.*
> *I was whole once but that was so long ago, then I had to go.*
> *Why can't you wait for me? Instead you just let me go,*
> *And I am still here, with tears deep in my soul.*

With every word, she poured everything she had into the piano and the connection in her mind. Sparks flared, and the piano keys grew warm to the touch, and even so, Alice went on.

Alice started to sing as Owen continued his assault into the blue waters. Every moment he was in the water, it was harder and harder not to lose his identity, but then Alice had started to sing.

Her pure and haunting voice cut through the night, the emotion real and raw as it sawed into his heart. For a moment, he wanted nothing more than to wrap her in a thick blanket and hold her tight, shielding her from a world that had been cruel and wrong.

She poured a wave of fresh ethereal energy, and for a moment, he thought it was enough as he stomped his foot. He fanned out the blue flames, looking for a sign that the red paint was falling away and the white underneath would be revealed.

The steel door to the roof banged open, and Max stood there, a red line of blood running into his right eye from a gash on his forehead.

"Owen, Abel and I tried severing the metal connection. We tried and tried, even while it started glowing white, but we couldn't scratch it. The axe . . . the axe exploded. Abel's okay, but he's headed back to the bar. I'm sorry. I don't know what else to do." Max pressed his palm to his forehead and wiped some of the blood away.

"Max!" Jessica said, coming up behind him, a cloth in her hand.

As he played a song from his heart, Owen looked through the blue flames at Max and Jessica. He looked over to Alice, who even now was sacrificing herself for him and his. He could feel Clover, Daphne and Jessie as they gave everything they had to make this work.

Owen didn't stomp on beat this time. Instead, he calmly said, "I love you. It might not be enough for everyone, but I love you. You too, Max."

Owen turned around and looked up toward the moon.

The flames fell to his shoulders, perhaps in anticipation, as his body relaxed. Owen stood to his full height and breathed in the music behind him.

"Owen, what are you doing?" Max said, desperation in his voice.

Owen pushed it aside as he listened to Alice sing. If this was what it took for his people to be free and for other musicians to no longer be in danger of losing their lives, then he could do it. He could take it the last couple steps, no matter the cost.

The crescent moon was framed by low thick white clouds, and he could taste the ocean in the air. His fingers lay over the strings as blue flames covered his hands and ethereal power coursed through his body.

So be it, was Owen's last thought as his hand reached for the strings and a rhythm and sound sprang into his heart.

A saxophone called out through the night air from the top of the building next door, and Owen twisted his neck hard to see who it was. A lone black man wearing a midnight-black suit and tie blew into the sax, his horn ringing out into the city as the moon spotlighted his frame.

"It's Damon. He's playing for us."

A wave of ethereal energy reached across the street and

through the night air, coursing over Owen and moving like a cyclone down into the piano.

Owen looked back at Alice, who continued to play and continued to sing, her eyes still filled with sadness.

Owen lifted his guitar and stamped down hard on the flames by his feet, the ones that were already dimming, and a thought struck him as he listened to Damon's song.

Damon's going to give himself up to this cause, to ending the red piano.

"I won't lose you too," Owen said loudly into the night air.

Owen was about to play when a fresh drumbeat tapped out a rhythm on the roof to Owen's right. Owen looked, but he didn't need to. It was Sco, the drummer he had played with the last time he was Miami. Next to Sco, setting lips to horn, was Zion, whom Owen had also played with.

Lights flared on every rooftop inside four blocks as the musicians of San Francisco started to play. One by one, with amplifiers turned up and wells of ethereal power from We and etherealists alike wide-open and sharing, they came in on Damon and Alice and the rest.

"Don't just stand there, kid. Destroy that thing," Damon called before getting back to his instrument.

Like a four-story wave of fury, ethereal magic poured Owen's way from out of the night sky.

Owen turned and called to Alice, "Your knife."

She didn't hesitate, a quick hand coming across her belt, and the blade made of pure essences was tossed up to him.

The jewel in its hilt felt warm in his hand as he drove the blade down into the red piano.

Any knife of its quality would have driven to the hilt with the force Owen used, but the red piano wasn't made of wood. Still, the point drove in about an inch, and it held in place. Owen placed a foot on the knife and did his best to direct the ethereal energy down into that one singular point as sparks and flames, both from the path of angels and from the waters of hell, burned around them.

And then it happened.

The red paint of the piano started to melt like wax, dripping down and away, leaving a perfect, gleaming white beneath.

"End the run," Owen called as he shut the door to the Devil's river.

Owen heard the music in the sky as he felt Alice and the others getting closer and closer to the end of their small run.

The clouds cleared, and the white of the piano gleamed beneath him as Alice and his people finished. He reached out a hand for Alice to join him, and she took it. They stood on top of the white piano as the musicians of San Francisco played together.

Max and Jessica came over, and Alice gave them a hand to step up and get a better view. From his vantage point, Owen could see the front of the Grand Hotel. A wave of people came outside, flooding the streets as the musicians everywhere played.

"I told you this was a great a city," Jessica said, then she turned to Max and gave him a kiss.

"Alice, is the connection in your mind still there?" Owen asked, wrapping an arm around her.

"No, it's gone, and I can take in ethereal energy again," she said.

"So we did it," Owen said. "It's over. We won."

"Yeah, but I think your uncle wants you to play with him. Look," Alice said, pointing.

Owen looked to Damon, who had stopped playing the saxophone and was waving his hands back and forth.

"I see you, Uncle, and I would love to play with you." Owen readjusted his strap, and Alice gave him room.

But Damon continued to wave and shout in Owen's direction. Because of all the music in the air, it was difficult to hear him, but then a few of his words became clear.

"You are . . . fire!" Damon was calling.

"You know, that's right. My boy is all rock star," Max said. He tried to kiss Jessica again, but she stopped him.

"That's not what he said," Jessica corrected.

Owen swore as a scent drifted up through the floor, and he looked at Alice. "The whole building is on fire. Alice, grab your knife. Max, catch!" Owen disconnected his guitar, slipped it off and tossed it over.

"Run to the far side, it's the nearest building," Alice said, pointing. Jessica was already in motion.

"How long has it been burning?" Max asked.

"Who knows, with all the sparks Owen was making," Alice said.

Owen dropped down from the piano and grabbed the case for his guitar, taking off last after the other three. In a line, they ran to the edge of the remaining roof and jumped.

The next building wasn't nearly as tall as the Westerfeld House, and the structure was built on a lower part of the slope. All four had magic on their side, pumping through their veins and into their muscles and skin, so one by one they landed. Jessica and Max turned back to see the fire as black smoke started to pour out of a few windows and out the top, right where they'd been standing.

"What are you doing? Keep going!" Alice called.

"We should be safe here," Jessica said. "With a little luck, our fire department can contain it. They are some of the best-trained firefighters in the world."

"What is it?" Owen asked as Alice grabbed Max's shoulder and turned him around, pushing him to run on.

"I left my bag in the room we used," Alice said in desperation.

A deep fear rang down Owen's spine.

"Run!" he yelled.

They managed a few steps before an explosion erupted behind them and Owen was tossed from the edge of the building out into open air. Alice was there, too, and it took everything he had to wrap his body around hers as the top of Westerfeld House blew apart.

They hit the ground, along with raining debris, and rolled until finally coming to a stop. The guitar case having fallen out of his hand.

"Ow!" Owen said.

"You going to make it?" Alice asked in a voice that was heavy with adrenaline.

"Sure, why not? What did you have in that bag, and *why*?"

"Small arms explosives," Alice said. "Just in case."

"Might have been overkill for a ghost," Owen said as he pushed up to his feet and offered her a hand.

"Actually, I'm thinking we might have wanted to start with that. Next time, let's try it my way."

Owen laughed and kissed her. "I can't wait to get out of this city. Max!"

"We're fine," Max called. "We made it to the other building. Your guitar too. Your girl sure knows how to throw a party. Never seen such fireworks."

Alice's eyes lit up, and she walked down the alley and picked up the old guitar case.

"Yeah, she's a rock star," Owen said as Alice turned and held out the case. "Well, when you're done playing grab-ass, meet us at the Grand Hotel," Owen shouted up to Max.

"You got it, boss!" Max called from up high.

CHAPTER TWENTY-TWO

A + O

When the dust settled and the fire department declared that no one was hurt in the explosion, a new party started in the Grand Hotel.

One by one, Owen checked in with his people. Abel was fine, healing from the exploded axe head. His wife had shown up, given him a hard slap, wrapped her arms around him and planted a wet kiss on him in front of everyone. Now they danced along with many others.

Damon and Sebastian gave each other a long overdue greeting and hug.

Clover found an urban cowboy, and after kissing him in the corner of the room, she picked up her violin and joined in with the plethora of musicians who were making a go at playing until the sun came up—and then some.

Jessie stayed by the piano—now free of ghosts. Daphne sat beside him, her new guitar right by her feet.

Max and Jessica were dancing, drinking, and exchanging kisses whenever they wanted to.

A couple hours into the celebration of the ghost and red piano being gone, Owen could feel a lasting tension in Alice and understood she wouldn't be able to relax fully until her priest was safe and home. Owen gave Alice a kiss on the cheek, then he made his way over to the corner of the bar where Damon and Sebastian sat and talked quietly.

Owen took out the black bottle of whiskey that Sebastian had given him earlier. Without a word, Owen set the bottle of booze on the bar and looked at his uncle.

"I think I'll give you some room to catch up. Don't leave this hotel without a word, old friend," Sebastian said to Damon.

"I won't."

For a moment, Owen and Damon didn't even look at each other. There was weight in the space between them.

"I'm sorry Elain lied to you," Damon said. "I thought she was past that. Jessica filled me in on everything that happened. It wasn't precisely the plan I started with. I didn't know about the Devil's coin."

"You lied to me, and you didn't give me the information."

"Yes, I did, and no, I did not," Damon said.

"You're not a believer of that silly group, the Silver Keys, so why?" Owen asked.

"I believe in you, and they believe in what they believe. Including that you had to beat their test, their gauntlet, to be worthy." Damon said it like it was poison in his mouth.

"So what?" Owen asked, the irritation alive and well in his voice.

"Damn it, kid, I almost died because I didn't respect what they believe. I almost died for nothing. And whether you believe in their dream or you think it's silly doesn't matter, because it's what they believe. All those We out there. Right now, those We will be watching and helping you."

"I didn't beat their gauntlet, Damon. Alice was connected to the piano, and if anything, I cheated. Hell, we *all* cheated by simply burning it away."

"You think they will see it that way? You brought together a group of musicians, and now the red piano is back to white. Or was, before our girl there blew up half the block." Damon smiled. "Right now, they are saying you are their champion. And if you get yourself in trouble, chances are, more than one of them will be there to help you and yours. Plus, no one else will ever be hurt by that damn thing again."

"And your friend's piano is ghost-free," Owen added.

"That too."

"You know . . . I don't think I could have done it without you. And everyone you brought."

The corners of Damon's mouth turned up in a smile. "Maybe, but I learned long ago where to place my money, and that's right on you, kid. Now . . . have a drink with me and shut up. There is something about this town that rubs me the wrong way."

Owen did shut up, but his teeth showed as he smiled and took a drink.

"What?" Damon asked.

"I was just thinking it's a safe bet to place my money on Mara shooting you when she finds out everything that happened here."

Damon didn't smile, didn't even move until his hand picked up his glass, leaned it over and tapped Owen's, finishing the whole drink in one go. Owen poured as Jessie and the others filled the bar with music, laughter and love.

A couple hours later, Owen and Alice had made their excuses and accepted a key to a top-floor suite.

"Do you want to leave now?" Owen asked as Alice stared at the bed.

"No, in the morning is fine. I know we could both use a good night of rest. No matter how pumped we are, sleep is good. And I don't think it will make the difference."

"A bath might be better?" Owen suggested.

"I could use a bath," Alice said. "Do you think they have bubbles?"

"I'm sure they do," Owen said. "If not, I'll send for some. Now see, *this* is a proper bathtub, where the shower and tub are separate."

"What is that?" Alice asked.

"What?"

"You just thought of something, and it was so strong that your eyes are almost glowing," she said.

"I was just thinking that Max is right. Let's you and I have too much of a good thing."

Owen pulled his black shirt off and moved to her.

EPILOGUE

Jessie wasn't happy with their early departure from the hotel, but he did not complain. Perhaps it was because Daphne was back, or maybe it had something to do with the conversation Owen and he had finally had about music. Max was happy and was looking forward to drawing on ethereal energy the moment they were out of the city. By mutual agreement, the group had decided to leave via the Golden Gate Bridge—which didn't take them in a straight line back to Miami.

No one minded, not even Alice.

Damon, Sco and Zion had decided to stay in the city for a few more days, and they had made plans to catch up back in Miami.

The van, with Jessie driving, came out of the parking lot under the Grand Hotel and fell in behind Owen's truck as they made their way up the street. Everyone looked on in shock and awe at the scattered debris and yellow tape all over the sidewalks as they got closer and closer to the Westerfeld House and the fire and explosion of the night before.

Jessica and Sebastian had assured Owen that everything would be taken care of.

Owen continued to drive up the street, until suddenly, he didn't believe his eyes.

"Oh my Lord," Alice said beside him.

"That can't be," Max said from the backseat.

Owen parked the car on the wrong side of the road, not caring about laws and rules as he stared. He opened up the door and got out to look closer.

There in front him, just as before, was the Westerfeld House. It looked as it always had, without a broken window, scratch or burn mark. The van parked and the others got out.

"You said it blew up," Jessie said.

"I thought this thing was a pile of ash," Clover said.

"We *did* blow it up," Owen said. Alice looked to him, and he completely understood. If the house was back, was the red piano? Was all their effort and work and risk for nothing?

"Can you feel it? The connection?" Owen asked.

She shook her head no.

"Wait, what?" Max asked.

"Max, Clover, go in and check to see if the red piano is there. Don't touch anything," Owen ordered.

"Wait a minute . . ." Max said, but Clover wasn't waiting. "Come on, Max!"

Together, they ran up the stairs, went inside and came back out a few minutes later.

"Everything is just as it was, though the recording equipment is gone. Tom says it won't be coming back."

"The piano?" Owen asked.

"It's white and seems friendly," Clover said. "If a piano can seem friendly."

"Can I just say it?" Daphne asked.

No one responded, but most looked to her.

"Can we get out of this town? It's just too damn weird for me."

There were a lot of looks as, one by one, everyone climbed back in—all except Jessie and Owen.

"You want a shot at her? At the key?" Owen asked, looking from Jessie to the front of the house that was more than a house.

Jessie took his time thinking and then looked to Owen. "Not today."

Owen gave a single knowing nod, and they both got back in their vehicles. As one, they drove across the Golden Gate Bridge and out of San Francisco.

ACKNOWLEDGMENTS

Michelle Greene, for always leading the charge. My mother, Christine Feehan, for your unending support. Michael Greene and Gayle Greene for always having my back, and Heather Wisdom for your creativity. Domini, Chris and Denise for always being there.

My reading group, the League of Awesome (they did not choose the name): Sco, Abel, Rachel, Jo Carol, Peggy, Erin, Judith, Gayle, Manda, Renee, Ann, Diane, Carol, my aunt Denise, and Joyia. You came through for me when I needed you the most, and you told me the truth.

The Starfish Writing Group: Christine, C. L, Sheila, Kathie, Karen, and Susan. Your support is always there for me!

Steven Axelrod at the Axelrod Agency, I will never forget the kind words. Julia Gains and Angela Traficante for editing my work; you both have powerful magic.

I am completely grateful to my editor, Cindy Hwang, and all the fantastic people at Berkley Penguin Random House. Everything you do is a beautiful blend of artistic talent and professional achievement.

This novel is not only mine; it uniquely belongs to every single person along the way who's had a hand, however big or small, in bringing it to life.

Lastly, I'm so grateful to the readers. None of this works without you.

Ready to find
your next great read?

Let us help.

Visit prh.com/nextread

Penguin
Random
House